Praise for

THE ALCHEMIST'S DAUGHTER

"Set during the twilight years of Henry VIII with vibrant characters, a compelling plot, and accurate historical depictions, *The Alchemist's Daughter* brings the darkness and danger of Tudor London vividly to life as it weaves its suspenseful tale. This beautifully written addition to the medieval mystery genre is sure to delight all fans of the period."
—Sandra Worth, author of *Pale Rose of England*

"A smart, scientific sleuth . . . Lawrence uses her enthusiasm for Elizabethan England to create an historical novel within a mystery."
—*Portland Monthly*

"The writing is terrific, with great period details. There are lots of red herrings and a surprising amount of action that will keep readers engaged until the very last page."
—*San Francisco Book Review*

"I absolutely loved *The Alchemist's Daughter*—the characters, the authentic feel of the period, and of course the richly drawn story."
—Dorothy Cannell, author of *Murder at Mullings*

"Lawrence proves herself to be an excellent storyteller with this grim tale of murder, mayhem, and medicine."
—*CentralMaine.com*

Please turn the page for more outstanding praise for Mary Lawrence and her Bianca Goddard mysteries!

Praise for

DEATH OF AN ALCHEMIST

"Lawrence excels at exploring themes—parent-child conflict, dreams of eternal life, and the limitations of medicine—that have period and present-day resonance."

—*Publishers Weekly*

"Another exciting adventure on the backstreets of 16th-century London."

—*RT Book Reviews*

"Mary Lawrence is as sharp as ever . . . this is an exciting and very satisfying historical mystery in Tudor London."

—*Kennebec Journal*

Death at St. Vedast

Books by Mary Lawrence

THE ALCHEMIST'S DAUGHTER

DEATH OF AN ALCHEMIST

DEATH AT ST. VEDAST

Published by Kensington Publishing Corporation

Death at
St. Vedast

MARY LAWRENCE

KENSINGTON BOOKS
www.kensingtonbooks.com

KENSINGTON BOOKS are published by

Kensington Publishing Corp.
119 West 40th Street
New York, NY 10018

All Kensington titles, imprints, and distributed lines are available at special quantity discounts for bulk purchases for sales promotion, premiums, fund-raising, educational, or institutional use.

Special book excerpts or customized printings can also be created to fit specific needs. For details, write or phone the office of the Kensington Sales Manager: Kensington Publishing Corp., 119 West 40th Street, New York, NY 10018. Attn. Sales Department. Phone: 1-800-221-2647.

Kensington and the K logo Reg. U.S. Pat. & TM Off.

eISBN-13: 978-1-61773-715-2
eISBN-10: 1-61773-715-1
First Kensington Electronic Edition: January 2017

ISBN-13: 978-1-61773-714-5
ISBN-10: 1-61773-714-3
First Kensington Trade Paperback Printing: January 2017

10 9 8 7 6 5 4 3 2 1

Printed in the United States of America

For Joe and Kathy

All you that in the Condemn'd-hold do lie,
Prepare you, for to-morrow you shall die.
Watch all and pray, the hour is drawing near,
That you before th' Almighty must appear.

—*The Tyburn Chronicle: Or, The Villainy*
Display'd In All Its Branches (1768) [II,73]

CHAPTER 1

London, December 1543

She would touch the moon.

Her bare feet met the hard earth, and the cold shot through her legs and spine. The shock alone would have startled most to their good sense. Yet she seemed oblivious to her feet turning blue against the ground. The linen smock she wore was of thin service against December's breath—a breath blowing in gusts and catching her hair, twisting it like ribbons. Her neck bent at an unnatural angle and she saw the road slant like milk being poured from a jug. She adapted her steps to this tilted horizon— a toe striking the road, then the flat of her foot, so that she appeared to be dancing to a tune only she could hear.

No one was out at this devilish hour—save for a man burying the corpse of his beloved dog and a drunk cursing the cold as it bit at his face. Most slept huddled beneath layers of wool and fur, their bed curtains pulled tight. Heated stones at the feet of beds grew cold and were irritably kicked to the floor. Tallows guttered in pewter holders, snuffling from a draft through a window.

Though the silence of the night was broken with the occasional lowing wind, only a few heard the loud intrusion of the woman's discordant singing. Her raucous song was mostly nonsense, neither patter nor sea shanty, but instead was an eerie chorus, ranging higher than the screech of a gull and just as shrill. Thinking her drunk, those restless enough to bother shouted from opened windows.

"Stupid trug! Are ye mad with French pox?" yelled one.

"Stop your mouth! It reeks like a common sewer," yelled another. Playwrights grew imaginative when roused from dreams.

But to these insults she gave not a care.

Indeed, she did not seem to give a care about anything.

She dipped and careened, angled toward a front door and curtsied low before it. The door was closed and remained so. This she found comical, and she burst out laughing.

If only her laugh were as pleasant as her song.

She found amusement in her own hilarity and shrieked loud enough to set dogs baying two streets over. But then she tired, ran out of breath, and resumed her macabre dance down the road—toe to heel. Toe to heel.

Turning the corner, she spied the Queen Moon peering down from above. Such ethereal beauty should not be ignored. A shame that man preferred the company of the sun over her sublime charm. Not many chose to keep court with her celestial grace. Think on what they missed!

The woman could not bear to shun her lovely companion. She wished to climb to the heavens and kiss her round face. And why not? Had her mistress moon not kept her company on many a sleepless night?

Her shoulder spasmed, then rose to her ear and stayed there. She continued her dance, and when a dog stepped from the shadows to growl at her, she growled back.

A man, hearing that song, hearing the dogs bark, sought the source of the commotion. He came upon the woman and the dog and stopped. He stood a moment, glanced down at his feet to make sure they had ceased walking, and waited for his body to obey and cease swaying. He knew better than to finish off the dregs of any barrel left behind the Crooked Cork, but it was a cold night and he had no woman to go home to. Indeed, he had no home. His gaze returned to the snarling pair in front of him.

"What is this? A dog on four and one on two? This is not the song of maids," he said, hoping the young woman might desist her gnarring and notice him.

Alas, she did not, and she thrust her jaw forward, trying to out-menace the slobbering cur. With arms outstretched and fingers curved like claws, she redoubled her efforts, growling ever louder.

The man took a tentative step forward. "For whatever bones the two of you must chew, I beg do not subject me to that grisly sight. It is too late for such sport, and you stand between me and my rest." He wobbled where he stood, waiting for the maid to reply.

It appeared that the dog possessed better judgment. The animal probably sensed that this woman was a bizarre creature better left alone. Besides, she produced more saliva, and though she lacked long canines, probably the dog knew humans often possessed longer knives. The dog backed away and at a safe distance turned tail.

The poor sot breathed a sigh of relief. He was just about to speak when she turned her back on him and lurched forward. Down the lane she ambled, her unusual gait making him wonder if she might be a hunchback, the way her spine curved like a fisherman's hook. His curiosity niggled him to follow. He hurried to catch up but trailed a few steps behind in case she decided to suddenly turn and gnarl at him.

Four parish churches abutted Foster Lane, not counting the ones tucked behind yards and chantry chapels. The woman stopped beside St. Vedast and leaned back, running her gaze up its exterior. Near the top, the Queen Moon peeked from behind the steeple.

The woman found the limestone less luminous than her mistress's face, but it was smooth and cool to her touch. She rested against the building. In so doing, she finally noticed the drunk.

She did not voice a thought or start from surprise. Intrigued by his presence, she simply stared.

"Where is your cloak, m'lady?" he asked. "It is not such a balmy night."

She did not answer.

He tried again. "Are you lost? I know well these parts, having slept many a night on the cobbles with stone stoops for my pillow. Tell me from whither you be, to yonder you go, and I shall assist you."

Again he was met with wordless stupefaction. He wasn't sure if she was drunk or just daft. She offered no proof one way or the other. Her eyes held a vacant stare and a lack of comprehension. He gestured at the church. "Ye take some comfort here, I see." Perhaps she was possessed—bewitched. Once he'd seen a woman so strange that it took six men to carry her to a church and hold her down while the priest gibbered Latin and shook a crucifix at her. But that sort usually shrank from the sight of a church. That sort wouldn't lean against its walls, admiring the façade, like this pitiful Bess.

Without prompt, she began moving along its exterior, muttering and caressing the stone. She yammered nonsense, giggling at her jest. He decided she had definitely lost her wit, until she turned and smiled at him—a smile that could melt the ice on the Thames. The wind caught her tangled hair and blew it in front of her face, across her forehead and neck. She fixed him with eyes that beguiled, and she recited a rhyme. The words sounded innocent enough, a verse of childish song and simple meter. It was the first intelligible utterance she had managed.

Unable to stem his interest, he followed when she ducked

around the corner of the church and disappeared in its shadows. Normally he would have gone his separate way and left her to her own fate. But he could not resist knowing what she might do next. Even a bracing slap of December wind did not rouse him from her spell.

A beech tree grew beside the church, its branches arching toward the eaves of the roof. Before his eyes had adjusted to the dark, he heard the sound of scrambling and the snap of a brittle limb.

"Fair maid, what are you about?"

She giggled, then implored, "You are not so far. Let me stroke your face. Have you no one to love?"

The man, thinking as a man, blushed as a man grown hopeful. "It has been a long time, but if you wish . . ."

He was interrupted by an unnerving laugh. His eyes adjusted to the dark in time to see her step onto the roof. Blinking twice, he watched her scale its incline like a monkey.

"Are you raving mad? What are you about? Quit this folly at once!" he cried, and when her foot slipped and she fell forward, he gasped.

She slid down the roof, her fingers clawing for a handhold. Down she slid, the pads of her fingers rubbed raw, her bare feet seeking purchase. To his relief, she grabbed on to a protruding edge. Pausing a second, she then pulled herself to her knees. Stunned, the man could not wrest his eyes from the sight. She knelt, silhouetted against the moon, tenuously clinging to the roof, her hair and night smock buffeted by the wind.

The slurry of ale in his belly made quick his decision (which was not based on better judgment). He scurried toward the tree. He did not want to be party to her lunacy any more than he wanted to set foot next to her, but he believed he could coax her to safety.

He jumped for a limb, and, as he hung there, he gathered his strength and swung a leg over it. He hauled himself up and straddled the branch. With no small measure of grunting and cursing, he climbed the tree to the height of the roof. The dark obscured the distance between his perch and the ground, and for this he was grateful. He shinnied along the limb, feeling it dip from his weight, until he touched the roof of the church. Wrapping his arm around the branch's girth, he reached out to the woman.

"M'lady, take my hand."

She studied his proffered palm as if it were a fascinating device, then shouted her childish rhyme at the top of her lungs. He startled and fought to keep his balance as she serenaded the steeple and the moon behind it. Such a loud, screechy rendition was surprising coming from such a thin-boned maid, but her jubilance spurred her on and she rose to a crouched stand. Fearlessly she scampered up the slope and pranced along the ridgeline.

The man drowned the woman's singing with pleas to stop. He could barely watch as she danced along the peak of the church, her feet slipping, her body tottering, but neither could he drag his eyes away. She was beyond his help. If she fell, he had no way to break her fall.

She paused to croon at the moon, then galloped toward the steeple. The drunk held his breath until she reached the bell tower. He wondered if she had the sense to cling to the structure while he went for help. If he started shouting, perhaps someone might rouse from his bed. But the wind blew in whistling gusts, and even the woman's clamorous song got lost in its howl.

To his wonderment, she did cling to the tower. She spread her arms and flattened herself against it. Her head tilted to spy the moon with one eye.

"Stay you," he cried when the wind calmed. "I shall enlist an army of men to help!"

What would become of her once she was rescued? Would she be tossed in the Clink with other nattering fools? Perhaps a loved one might find her and soothe her wretched soul. If that were true, thought the man, where was her lover now? Perhaps she needed *his* love and once he had delivered her to safe ground she would shower him with affection. The man grew suddenly warm. A woman would give his life purpose. He would right his wrongs for a woman's love. Besides, she was not so fearsome in appearance if he ignored those vacuous eyes.

Again he shouted that he would soon return. He inched his bottom down the limb toward the trunk. When he met the bole of the tree, he paused for a last look at her before his final descent.

Ignoring his plea, she climbed the belfry toward the spire. Her rhyme carried to his ears as she pulled herself onto the tower's ledge. Wrapping her arms around the spire, she began to scale the tapered structure, inching her way to the pinnacle.

The man could not move or shout. Did she wish to touch the moon? At the top, she cooed and spoke to the celestial queen as if she expected a reply. She held tight with one hand, and with the other she reached over her head.

He glanced down, thinking of the dangerous distance between himself and the ground. Where she held reign, it was doubly high. His toes tingled from the fright of it. His false bravado, from guzzled swill, disappeared.

Was she a sylph—a creature of his imagination—a vaporous woman inhabiting the air? He rubbed his eyes to remove the vision. He dug at them as if to pluck them from their sockets. It was a man's noble duty to save a lady fair. And was she not a woman in distress? He blinked hard, then realized he was just a drunk sitting in a tree watching a gibbering madwoman. What spell had she tried to cast on him? He returned his gaze and saw her pull herself onto the peak, as if she meant to stand on its very top. Whether the woman was real or not, he shouted in panic, "Nay, leave it!"

Did his words give her pause? He blamed himself when her grip missed. She swiped in vain at the spire as her weight carried her away from it. Her arms and legs flailed. She was falling.

She hit the roof of St. Vedast, and the man felt the jolt of impact rip through his own body, as if he, too, had fallen and cracked every bone in his spine. She slid down the incline toward the eave. Nothing would break her fall now. Not even the branches where he sat reached that far.

He would remember her eyes, wide with terror as she screamed and tumbled past. Even as witless as she appeared to be, he knew she sensed the approach of her final moment. Her body met the ground with a sickening thud. A sound he would never forget.

And the Queen Moon watched, as was her pleasure, cold and distant.

CHAPTER 2

If there was one benefit to sitting outside the Stone Gate in December, it was that the cold wind carried away the smell of rotting flesh and dispersed it somewhere over the Thames. Bianca gazed up at the display of heads on pikes and watched one miscreant swivel dangerously close to coming loose.

"I should not like it if he lands in my lap." Bianca rearranged a blanket over her knees as she sat on the narrow seat of a dray between her husband, John, and Meddybemps, their streetseller friend.

"It cannot be much longer," said Meddybemps, looking east at the faint, burnished glow on the horizon. He handed over the reins to John and hopped off the wagon to stand at the gate and holler for a guard.

"He seems to think they will answer," said John.

"He is ever hopeful." Bianca turned to tuck in the flapping corner of a blanket covering her wares. When one was moving alembics and the accoutrements of her science, it was best to travel at night, but since that was not an option, they made do with traveling just before dawn.

Meddybemps bellowed into the arched entrance of London Bridge and rattled the iron portcullis, which refused to yield. After a moment, a guard toting a halberd ambled up to the bars. He glared at the streetseller.

"It is day's first light. Can you give us entrance to cross?"

The guard looked past Meddybemps to the dray. "What is your hurry?" he asked suspiciously.

"We want to start across the bridge before the road becomes clogged. Besides, it is not so pleasant waiting in this cold."

"It is no concern of mine if ye haven't the sense to arrive after curfew ends."

"Man, look to the east. The sun is broaching the horizon." Meddybemps tipped his chin in its direction. He stomped his feet to get his humours flowing and blew in his hands.

The guard walked back through the gatehouse, disappeared from sight for a minute (presumably to confirm Meddybemps's claim), and returned. "What's that ye got in your wagon?"

Meddybemps knew there was no use in leading the man astray. He could easily inspect the cart and prevent their passage. Delay would prove only more challenging for them. "We have the stuff of alchemy."

"Do ye, now?" The guard looked past the streetseller and eyed Bianca. "Which one of ye is the alchemist?"

"He is." Meddybemps waved an arm at John. He ignored John's startled look and hoped the lad had enough sense to lie when asked. Not only did the streetseller wish to deflect attention off Bianca, but if he had called her an alchemist, he would have been subjected to another one of her diatribes explaining why she was most assuredly *not* an alchemist. He was not in the mood.

Spending half the night obtaining a horse and dray had left him in a foul temper. Meddybemps was an inexperienced driver, and to entrust him with the means to a man's livelihood required an act of faith. But the threat of ruin from unsavory gossip persuaded Arthur Milbourne to part with his conveyance—at least until noon.

Not only did Meddybemps have to back the horse and cumbersome wagon down the narrow alley where Bianca had her room of Medicinals and Physickes, but he had to help Bianca and John load all of their belongings—including several cages of live rats—into the bed under dark of night. He'd nearly expired from the smell of chicken manure from her neighbor's coop in Gull Hole, and the odor clung stubbornly to his clothes. Then the nonstop howling of Hobs, their cat, in a box behind the seat had rubbed his patience raw.

"So's the dabbler got any gold?" asked the guard, leaning in.

"It's a rare alchemist who can hold on to anything of worth," replied Meddybemps.

"That's a sorry state. Then I guess the alchemist will have to wait a while more. It may be dawn fast upon us, but it will be a while 'til the curfew is lifted."

Meddybemps irritably tromped back to the wagon. "He needs some encouragement. Have you an incentive?"

Bianca and John looked at each other and shrugged.

"Perhaps we should offer him your immortal cat?" he suggested after Hobs voiced a particularly pathetic yowl.

Bianca's eyes flashed. "I think not!" She reached under the blanket and withdrew her purse. She searched through it and pulled out a half crown. "Offer him this."

"That's more than I make in a month," John protested. "You'll have to do a keen business with your salves to make up for it."

"We'll save that much in rent living at Boisvert's. It will even out. Besides, my feet are nearly frozen."

Meddybemps didn't wait for them to come to an agreement but strode back to the guard, holding up the coin.

"Wells," said the man, "that gets me interested." He stuck his arm through the gate, but Meddybemps held the coin beyond his reach.

"Either you are interested enough to give us leave or you are not. We've nothing more to offer."

The guard's mouth turned up in a lopsided grin. He glanced around and, seeing no one to object, agreed. "Close enough." He took the money and pocketed it. "Mind ye keep your counsel. I've a memory for faces."

Meddybemps hastened back to John and Bianca, his errant eye rolling with annoyance. The streetseller had an eye that could best be described as "loose." At rest, its focus veered west, as if perpetually looking at his ear. "He would have had us sit until someone wanted out."

"Then it is coin well spent," said Bianca.

The squeal of chain and pulley broke the morning quiet as the iron bars lifted. Meddybemps urged the mare on. The wagon bumped up the cobbled ramp, and they rode under the Stone Gate.

The three nodded to the guard as they passed, and he watched stoically as they lumbered by.

The road across London Bridge was damnably narrow. If they had left later in the morning, it would have taken hours to reach the other side. There were no turnouts, only areas where two average-sized carts might squeeze past if they were perfectly aligned. Even this was fraught with difficulty, as jutting axle nuts could lock with a passing wagon and stall traffic until the two vehicles were maneuvered or rocked free.

Overhangs and abutting buildings afforded little light to see by as they trundled along. Meddybemps was thankful the mare was unexcitable. He preferred her plodding pace to a more spirited and probably unmanageable animal. At least one part of this endeavor was going smoothly.

"I'm certain you will like living in Boisvert's rent," said John. "Aldersgate is a short walk, and you can collect plants in Smithfield. Or you could walk along the city wall to Morefield." It had been a week since Bianca had agreed, but John still felt the need to convince her that this move was to her benefit.

"My only misgiving is where I shall set up my chemistries." For Bianca, that was a major concern. She had entered into marriage with John eight months before and had nearly lost him to the sweating sickness only a couple of months later. He blamed his illness on the foul airs of her rent in Gull Hole in Southwark.

Bianca was not so sure; the sweat seemed to pick its victims at random. It didn't matter whether one lived in a crowded neighborhood near the Thames or on a country estate.

"Perhaps if you limit your dabbling to a few unobtrusive decoctions until we figure out where you could work."

Bianca didn't reply. "A few unobtrusive decoctions" meant anything that wouldn't offend the French metalsmith's sensibilities—meaning his nose.

John's acquaintance with Boisvert had begun several years ago with a kidney pie. John had lived the life of an orphan, sleeping in a barrel behind the Tern's Tempest, surviving on table scraps from the tavern. One night, he watched from the safety of his dark drum while Boisvert insulted his attackers, then puked on them. The Frenchman was thoroughly trounced for the indiscretion.

Once the Frenchman had been left for dead, John emerged from the cask to search the man's pockets. The battered snail eater surprised John when he opened his eyes and asked the boy to help him home. Always the opportunist, John saw his chance to pinch a few valuables once he helped the swaggering outlander inside his residence.

However, it was not to be. The balding Frenchman had enough of his faculties about him that he declined John's offer to see him to his bed, and once he'd stumbled over the threshold, he ungraciously slammed the door in the boy's face.

Nothing came of the incident except John's growing dislike of all things French, until one day Boisvert sought John on Olde Fish Street Hill. He needed an apprentice, and if the boy could tolerate living in a proper rent, then he could use the help. "Of course, if you prefer a barrel," he had told John, "we could move one into the alley behind the shop."

So John became Boisvert's disciple, confidant, and surrogate family. His apprenticeship was nearing its end, and soon he would be able to set up shop on his own. But that required more money than he and Bianca had. When Boisvert announced he was marrying the wealthy widow Odile Farendon and would be moving into her home, John offered to look after the forge and adjoining rent.

The arrangement made sense to Boisvert. Leaving a silver shop vacant was ill-advised no matter what safeguards were in place. The silversmith agreed on condition that Bianca forgo her chemistries. Boisvert claimed he did not want to incite his neighbors, but, in truth, he could not tolerate the thought of his immaculate rent being turned into a workshop for the dark art. Boisvert had seen Bianca's domestic skills and did not want his walls, painted with murals of Provence, coated with soot and stink.

John knew there was little chance that Bianca would completely abandon her work. He arranged a compromise, convincing Boisvert that not all of Bianca's efforts resulted in smoke and chaos.

Eventually, Bianca relented to John's pleas and pondered how she might skirt Boisvert's restrictions. Her room in Southwark was too far to travel to on a daily basis, especially in the winter. So, with regret, she abandoned the dilapidated rent. But as yet she had not thought of any way she might remain useful on Foster Lane. She envisioned long days of creating only simple infusions and balms. If she could not pursue her passion, how would she relieve her boredom? Her enthusiasm for the move remained subdued, and with every cheery reminder from John of how much she was going to like living there, Bianca grew more sullen.

However, she did agree that the money they would save might be worth the upheaval. Certainly she could make a few decoctions to sell at market. Decoctions that were not offensive smelling, and it might keep her busy over the winter. But the long months of inclement weather were Bianca's most productive. She tried not to dwell on how much she would miss her work.

She reminded herself that marriage was a partnership and there were some advantages. Living alone with a cat and the trappings of what appeared to be an alchemy room looked suspiciously diabolical for a woman. Bianca was well aware that her in-

terest in experimentation and chemistries could be miscon-
strued. Perhaps moving to London with her husband might temper any rumors that might be hop-frogging on the tongues of
wary neighbors and malcontents. For the time being at least, she
would put aside her own interests for the benefit of furthering
John's. However, she would keep an eye out for a discreet va-
cancy where she might be able to work her chemistries incon-
spicuously.

At the other end of the bridge, a steady stream of pedestrians
began to enter through the opened gate. The wagon squeezed
past, and just as it merged onto Thames Street, a rooster announced the new day.

"How do you find Boisvert's betrothed?" asked Bianca, dis-
tracting herself from brooding. The courtship had been brief,
and to John's surprise the wedding announcement had been a
sudden, unexpected outcome.

"Odile Farendon is a generous woman. She is also blessed with
wealth. I can think of no argument against his marrying her."

"I never thought Boisvert would marry anyone. He seemed
content to advise you about love from a safe distance." Bianca
unwound her scarf and draped it over her head to keep her cap
from blowing off. It was difficult to squash her thick waves flat
enough to keep her coif on, even on a calm day.

John sat on his hands to warm them. "I don't expect he will
ever stop advising me. It will be interesting to see how he man-
ages."

"This is his first marriage?"

"It is. For a man who loves his creature comforts, I would have
thought matrimony a necessity for him."

"He only just met her?"

"He has known her since his arrival from France. Odile's first
husband was master warden of the Goldsmiths' Company and
served as an alderman and lord mayor. Boisvert was admitted to
the livery under Farendon's appointment. Granted, Boisvert paid
a healthy redemption for that privilege. He had no choice in the
matter if he wanted to stay and work in London."

"I'm surprised the guild let him join," said Meddybemps.

"They admit a few 'stranger brothers' if they prove worthy. But the Company has its standards and does not readily admit foreigners."

"Worthy in the sense of being able to pay whatever fee they ask?" Meddybemps smirked.

"It probably helped Boisvert that Lionel Farendon's wife was French. I suppose he was more tolerant than most."

"And where is this home he has moved into?"

"Around the corner on Mayden Lane."

"That is convenient for him," said Bianca. "Boisvert will be breathing down our necks. No chance of me sneaking in an experiment without him knowing."

The cart bumped along, turning up Bread Street, and Bianca could not ignore the smell of loaves baking in ovens. She asked Meddybemps to stop and ran inside a shop, returning with a warm loaf for each of them. The three continued on, devouring their bread, until they jagged up Friday Street, where the strong scent of fish clashed with their breakfast.

"Soon it will be broad daylight, and we won't have the dark to hide us," said Bianca. She gestured to the nag, who seemed to be slowing down. "Can you urge her on a little?"

"Pinch its arse," said John.

"I may not know much about horses, but I know more than you. One does not pinch a horse's ass to hurry it." Meddybemps clicked his tongue and jostled the reins. The mare took a few spirited steps, then fell back to her lead-footed plod.

"We shall get there when we do." Bianca resumed munching on her loaf of bread. "At least we are making progress in the right direction."

Either in agreement or, more likely, in discontent, Hobs complained until they crossed Cheapside and turned onto Foster Lane. The sun still clung to the horizon, and the buildings blocked the eastern light, keeping the road cold and fairly dark. Frozen ruts pocked the lane, rattling the dray and nearly spilling its contents and its passengers. Meddybemps did his best to avoid the hazards, but only one side of the wagon could be saved at a time, and the opposite side would drop into the next trench.

They had just gotten the back wheel free from a particularly troublesome rut when Bianca noticed a crowd gathered in the street up ahead. She shook John's arm and pointed.

"So much for getting you moved into Boisvert's unnoticed," he said.

"Meddy, stop. I want down."

"Just as well," said the streetseller. "Perhaps it will lighten the load."

"By about as much as a bird's beak," said John, smiling.

Bianca hopped off the dray and started up the lane to Hobs's yowling objection.

CHAPTER 3

Bianca wasn't the only one sorry about leaving Gull Hole and Southwark. There was another who regretted their move as they rode across the bridge on their way to London. The smell of her, the smell of alchemy—its acrid tang stung his nose, and he looked up to follow the wagon's wheels as they rolled across the drawbridge.

Once an alchemist himself, the Rat Man knew the discipline's allure. The bubbling concoctions, the dance of imperfect metals, the quickening heartbeat of anticipation. But years earlier, his chemistries, his experimentation, had gone wrong. Horribly wrong.

Like all alchemists, he desired to turn base metals into gold. But transmutation required reverence for the dark art *and* perfect technique. It was both a spiritual and a scientific pursuit. To create gold, one must first achieve perfection in attitude and knowledge—a nearly impossible task.

In an alchemist's world, there were only seven metals—gold, silver, iron, lead, tin, copper, and mercury. These metals had in common certain properties. Except for mercury, all could be cast, hammered, and shaped. Because of these common properties, al-chemists believed that the metals must be composed of essen-tially the same ingredients. Ingredients whose proportions could be adjusted. Whether through fire, distillation, or putrefaction, a key existed that would unlock a metal's transmutation. Every al-chemist searched for that perfect combination, that perfect se-quence. The ultimate goal was gold, the father of perfection.

Why was gold desired above all else?

Only gold resisted tarnish and corrosion. No other metal could withstand soil's capacity for decomposition. One could bury a lump of gold, and a hundred years later it would still look as bright as the day of its interment. Gold was wrought from nature underground, and it took untold years to accomplish the task. Al-chemists merely wished to create gold faster than nature did—they strived to bend it to their will.

But to do so required the philosopher's stone—the *lapis philosophorum*.

The "stone" was the requisite agent of change. No one knew from what it was made or exactly how to make it. But if its seed were added to a base metal and the projection were performed correctly, the stone would transmute, would "correct" the metal and change it into gold.

Just as gold was the embodiment of perfection of the tangible, material world, immortality was perfection of the living, spiritual realm. For some alchemists, discovering the elixir of immortality took precedence over transmuting base metals into gold. Of re-cent note, Ferris Stannum, an alchemist of great ability, had en-deavored to create the fabled potion. Stannum had stopped shy of creating the "white stone," the catalyst needed to transmute a metal into silver. Instead, he had created the white elixir—the foundation for the elixir of immortality. Perhaps, thought the Rat Man, he had even succeeded in creating the desired elixir. But Stannum had been murdered soon after his discovery. Such was his reward for his achievement.

Originally, the Rat Man had sought the stone for the transmu-tation of metals. He was a capable alchemist; his methods had gained much interest and envy among his peers. If any man could discover the stone, it was whispered, it would be he. He'd known success was close; he'd felt it in his core—the manifestation of change.

But the change that happened was not what he had expected. . . .

The Black Death raged across the continent and arrived on the king's isle aboard a ship. In a matter of weeks, death held sway across the land. Swellings, the likes of which had never been seen, appeared under armpits, disfigured legs, necks, and groins. The buboes started as red bumps—like cherries ripe for the picking. If their victim had felt fine, the buboes could have been dismissed. But this fruit grew to the size of an apple, darkened to purple, sometimes to black—a fruit plump with rot.

Along with the buboes came delirium, vomiting, and the intense desire to sleep. It was natural for a victim to yield to slumber's escape, but doing so proved fatal. Inevitably, on the morrow, death would take a life.

Havoc and heartbreak descended on London like a suffocating fog. Bills of mortality were posted, carts creaked through the streets collecting the dead, homes were quarantined. Barbers performed their bloodletting and the ditch latrines ran thick with putrid black blood. The alchemist watched healers dispense their futile concoctions: lavender and rose poultices for headaches, mint and wormwood to relieve nausea, vinegar to swab lanced wounds. No remedy proved effective against the cursed malady.

Death claimed too many. The young were not spared, and it was this grievous injustice that the alchemist could not abide. He turned away from his covetous pursuit of gold and instead sought the elixir of life.

Like Ferris Stannum, the alchemist had gone through the gates of projection, each stage building upon the successful completion of the previous one. He created the ambered glass wolf, ground it into a flour most fine. With kerotakis he had repeatedly sublimed the solution until one day he created a splendorous elixir. It did not glow like Ferris Stannum's concoction—its allure was more subtle.

A smell of roses so enticing lured the alchemist to believe he had found the sweetness of love, the essence of God and his angels. To the Moors, the scent of rose represented the sanctity of souls. He believed he had created the elixir of immortality.

The final proof of an experiment is testing its effectiveness. As the smoke of purging fires smoldered outside his door and the echoes of the parish death knells rang, the alchemist crossed himself and drank down this potion, this gift from God.

He dropped to his knees.

The fluid ran down his throat like a river of fire, melting his flesh with the searing pain of a blacksmith's glowing rod. Boiling blood filled his mouth, the dissolved debris of his inner flesh. He tried spewing the vile philter into a bucket, but with it he expelled the viscous lining of his throat. Indeed, the elixir had turned his organs to liquid.

His life began to ebb away. This potion was not the manna from heaven he had expected. His teeth liquefied; he coughed up his heart; his vision was of torment. A chorus of demons surrounded him, grinning as they stripped his skin from his muscle. They placed a hook under his clavicle, then drew out his bones like a thread being teased from cloth.

His punishment for manipulating the natural order of life was that he would forever be denied resolution of his own. He would forever be reminded of what he could not achieve. His was a perpetual purgatory.

And as his screams rattled God's ottoman, he was pitied from above but refused intervention. Into his open mouth poured the anguished cries of plague victims who had died before him. His transformation, indeed, his transmutation, was to become an empty vessel holding the cries and discarded souls of the loved and the forgotten, the victims of an unkind death from plague and the torment of unfulfilled potential.

And so the wraith of the Thames existed between the living

and the dead, dwelling in the dark corners of dreams and the imagination, doomed to ply the waters of his beloved city for . . . eternity?

For centuries the Rat Man observed his city. He watched fires level neighborhoods, plagues wax and wane, people suffer from disease and endure the policies of brutal kings. He navigated the river, hunting for rats, dispensing with vermin, cracking their spines, and gnawing their bones. But what he longed for was redemption. He longed for a resolution to his grim existence.

Until Ferris Stannum, no one had come close to creating the elixir of life. It wasn't that the Rat Man wanted immortality—this limbo where he found himself was essentially never ending. Nay, what the Rat Man wanted was an end to his torment.

Passing overhead was his greatest hope for ending that suffering. He'd watched Bianca Goddard since she was a young girl gathering plants at the river's edge. He'd seen her give her tattered boots to a girl more desperate than she. Observing from his skiff, unbeknownst to anyone, he had grown to know her and to have faith in her. He glanced down at the kerotakis rolling in the hull of his wherry. A book of alchemy retrieved from the water's depths—coughed up by the river as if ridding itself of something unpalatable—sat atop his pile of dead rats. The air felt different when Bianca moved through it. And here he stood, watching the wheels roll overhead as they carried his last hope away from him.

CHAPTER 4

As the pale light of morning squeezed between the buildings on Foster Lane, Bianca squeezed between the gathered onlookers next to St. Vedast Church. As slight as a coal tit, she slipped through the oglers without their noticing.

In the shadow beside the church lay a woman—gray in pallor—a pool of blood for a pillow. Her head lay flat against the cobbles, almost as if a hole had been dug to cradle the back of her skull. On closer inspection, Bianca could see that her skull had been thoroughly crushed. Her bare feet, cold and still, resembled those of a carved effigy on a sepulcher. A thin smock ruffled in the wind, the only sign of movement. As yet, no constable or coroner had arrived, so Bianca took the opportunity to examine the body before the meddlesome officials intruded.

Plenty speculated how the woman had met her end. However, no witness came forward to correct the conjectures, and no one recalled ever having seen her before. She was unknown and unremembered.

Bianca knelt beside the body and studied the victim's final expression. The woman's eyes were wide and staring, perhaps a sign of bewilderment, perhaps regret or surprise. The woman had realized she was going to die.

Had she tried to flee an assailant? If she had been forcefully bludgeoned from behind, thought Bianca, she might have landed on her face. Or perhaps she would have fallen in a crumpled heap. But this woman had landed on her back.

The right leg crossed the left, causing a slight twist of her torso. If one were hit from behind, one would not land on one's back with a leg overlapping the other. Bianca looked up. A beech tree grew beside the church, its upper branches stretching toward the roof, some brushing against it. The roof edge had no lip. There was no ledge—just a straight, smooth slope. If the woman had fallen from there, her body lay where one might expect it to land. If she had fallen from the tree, her body would have been closer to the trunk, not beyond the spread of its branches. Her smock would have been torn or ripped—which it was not.

Assuming the woman had fallen, her body could have twisted— a natural reflex. In those last seconds she would have wanted to return to the safety of where she had been. Bianca gently turned the woman's body onto her back, ignoring the protests about touching a corpse—especially if it was self-murder. With the victim's front fully exposed, the crowd took a collective suck of breath. The woman was with child.

"What mother would take the life of her child?" said a woman. The mention of it set off another round of signing the cross. "She is damned. Her soul is unclean."

"It may not have been self-murder," said Bianca, looking round, then standing. "It appears that she fell from a great height. But it is also possible she did not willingly end her own life and that of her child. She may have been pushed." There was a gasp from the crowd.

"But why take her to a roof and push her off? There are easier ways to finish someone." The woman who suggested this drew several leery stares. She met their dubious looks and put a hand on her hip. "Wells, climbin' to a roof is a dangerous undertakin' for both parties."

"Maybe they didn't climb," said Bianca, standing. "Maybe they were in the bell tower to start."

The sea of faces turned to gaze up at the massive structure.

"Give way. Give us way." The back of the crowd parted to allow a constable to elbow his way to the front. A coroner followed at his heels. When they were within a few feet of the body, the coroner moved ahead, his face taut with professional efficiency. The constable took one look at the victim, then faced the crowd and ordered them back.

Bianca was relieved the constable was not Patch—an irksome lawman she had been unable to avoid of late. This constable possessed a capable air, and Bianca dared to hope he might actually handle the situation with some intelligence.

The coroner examined the body, which amounted to crouching beside it and turning the victim's head to look at the wound. He wiped his hands on the victim's shift, then lifted the hem to peek at her round belly. His eyebrows jumped in recognition as he dropped the gown.

He stood and addressed the crowd. "Is this woman's name known? Has anyone seen her before?"

No one volunteered a word.

The constable rocked on his toes and projected his voice. "Who discovered the body?"

The faint clop of a horse sounded; then a calm voice answered. "It was I." The crowd moved aside to let a man forward.

One might assume his opinions would be as narrow as his shoulders—as thin as a blade of grass. Men without chests seemed doomed to bend in the wind of others. "I am Henry Lodge of the Worshipful Company of Goldsmiths and churchwarden of St. Vedast." His dress spoke of a man of station. His composed demeanor confirmed it.

"Good sir," said the coroner. "Kindly tell us how you came upon the body."

The churchwarden spoke in the measured tones of a man comfortable presenting his opinion. "It is a matter of duty that I visit St. Vedast in the early hours. I take inventory, unlock the belfry, check the candles. This morning it was quite cold. I wished to finish my duties early so that I could repair to the Goldsmiths' Hall, where it is more comfortable."

"Comfortable?" inquired the constable.

Lodge turned an indulgent eye on the lawman. "The guild office is never so cold as St. Vedast. I prefer not to spend my day blowing in my hands to warm them."

The constable gave a slight nod.

"This morning as I neared St. Vedast, a man exited the side yard of the church. It is unusual to see anyone at that hour after such a cold night. But to see a man with an expression of panic on his face is particularly noticeable. My first inclination was that he was being chased. He ran into the lane and at the sight of me fled in the opposite direction."

"Did you see evidence of blood on his person?" asked the constable.

"I did not. I expected a pursuer, but none emerged. I moved to the opposite side of the lane in case there was a lurker in wait. As I neared the side yard, it was clear someone was sprawled on the cobbles."

"Was the woman dead when you found her?" asked the coroner.

"Quite."

The crowd murmured—as much from the succinct reply as from the cold manner in which it was delivered.

"I left her where she lay," said Henry Lodge. "There was nothing to be done but call for a ward. I sent the sexton to summon you."

The crowd rustled, allowing a second figure through. A priest, bundled against the cold in a heavy gown overcoat over his cassock, clutched a prayer book against his chest. At the sight of the body, his lips moved in silent utterance as he quickly crossed himself.

He knelt beside her and began his prayers. His susurrations were sometimes drowned by the whistling wind or a nervous cough. One onlooker shouted that it was self-murder. The priest paused but then continued. "*Réquiem aetérnam . . .*"

Once finished, he got to his feet. "If you have conducted your inquiry, I shall see to the body," he said to the coroner, then sent a boy to find the sexton. "Have him toll the death knell and prepare to remove the body."

"Father," said the constable, "this may be a self-murder. Unless we find evidence to the contrary, or we are able to find and question this fleeing witness, I will treat it as such. We can wait for a relation to come forward, but I doubt anyone will claim her. You may call a collector to dispose of the body."

"This woman died on St. Vedast's grounds. If none shall claim her, then I shall see to her."

The constable, surprised at the priest's dismissal of church doctrine, spoke. "There is no seeing to her. She has committed a crime against God. I suggest we drag the body through the streets facedown."

"I will not have it," said the priest firmly. His words hung in the air, before a gust of wind blew them apart.

"But she is a criminal," argued the constable. "She has committed murder. I would not want her body to corrupt *my* graveyard. At the least, I hope your sexton buries her with her feet to the south. Let the flames of hell lick her toes."

"Sir, you are quick to conclude that this is self-murder when you do not know for a fact that it is," said the priest. "St. Vedast's graveyard is not yours. Nor is it mine. It is God's. Let Him sit in judgment of her soul. We know not the bounds of His love and forgiveness."

In spite of the bitter cold, people lingered, eavesdropping and contributing their sometimes wild speculations regarding the death. Bianca remained near the officials, listening to their conversation. Unfortunately, she learned nothing more. She thought she might ask the churchwarden for a description of the fleeing witness; then she noticed, from the corner of her eye, a man slipping the priest a coin.

She heard him address Father Nelson and heard the word "mass" before the crowd drowned his murmur. The dark fur of his collar lifted in the wind, obscuring his jawline and nose in profile. He wore the ubiquitous black and russet brown common to merchants—there was nothing to distinguish this man from others of his kind. Not even his cap set him apart. Bianca barely got a glance before he turned and folded into the crowd. Her instinct told her to follow. She edged through the onlookers, but her height was her disadvantage. She lost sight of him.

Bianca knew that by leaving Southwark she would be mixing with more "citizens" and men of money. She now realized Foster Lane was rife with men of station.

An extra mass is not common unless a priest is prompted to say one. Praying for a self-murderer was not done, but the coin provided motivation enough. Father Nelson encouraged the spectators to accompany him inside. "This is an unfortunate event for our parish. We must pray for God's protection."

Bianca returned to where the maid lay just as the sexton caught up with the priest. The soiled threads he wore for his unsavory chores stank of clay. "I have not been able to sound the death knell," he informed the priest. "The belfry is locked." Father Nelson looked to Henry Lodge, the churchwarden.

"I unlocked the bell tower." Lodge was adamant.

"Nay, sir," said the sexton. "It is secured."

There began an argument. The churchwarden openly doubted the sexton.

"Lodge, go with him and see," said Father Nelson, putting an end to their quarrel. With a weary sigh, the priest made his way through the spectators, disappearing into the church.

Reluctantly, the crowd dispersed, some following Father Nelson inside for the impromptu mass, others returning to their shops or homes. Bianca caught up to the churchwarden.

"Sir," she introduced herself. "You said you unlocked the bell tower. Perchance, could you have locked it, thinking otherwise?"

"All was as it should be."

"There was no sign of intrusion?"

"There was not," said the churchwarden. He quickened his step to be rid of her, but Bianca stuck to his side like a barbed seed.

"I wonder if you might describe the man who ran from the side yard?"

At first Henry Lodge did not answer. His disregard for her was palpable. But Bianca was not cowed by his superior attitude. He took a few more steps, then stopped, realizing there would be no getting rid of her until he answered.

"He was of no import," he said.

"Do you recall how he was dressed?"

Lodge's eyes flicked down at Bianca's brown kirtle, homespun, with a patch sewn hastily of a different color fabric. A look of distaste spread across his face. Bianca expected his disdain. He did not have to respond to a woman so obviously beneath him. But he surprised her and answered.

"He was a man like most."

"A commoner, sir?"

Henry Lodge's mouth pinched. "Perhaps a man of desperation—why else would he be out at such an hour and not asleep in his bed?"

"You remember no unique qualities? Perhaps a particular hat, a limp, or a trait that struck you?"

The churchwarden looked past her, conjuring the man from memory. "Nay, nothing memorable."

Bianca waited a moment, then thanked him.

"Ah, there *was* something that struck me about the man," Lodge said as Bianca turned to leave. "He looked guilty."

CHAPTER 5

John and Meddybemps's progress up Foster Lane had been slowed by the ruts in the road, and Bianca found the streetseller outside of Boisvert's, emptying the wagon, hurriedly removing the alembics and cages of rats to get them out of sight. He tried to appear nonchalant, but the mere presence of a dray outside of a silversmith's shop was difficult for neighbors to ignore. Gone was the hoped-for stealth of an early morning move.

As Bianca neared, Hobs burst out the door with John in heated pursuit. Ears pulled back and fur on end, the feline streaked past, a blur of black tiger stripes. A jar smashed on the cobbles inches from his hind legs.

"What ho! We've only just got here!" Bianca seized John's arm and put herself in front of him.

"That cat is the bane of me. 'Tis a shame he's immortal, for I'll never be rid of the beast." John scowled at Bianca. "And do not remind me that I must either leave or die first."

"There is some truth in that."

"Would you like to see what your cat has done?"

"Are you giving me a choice?"

John took Bianca's hand and pulled her through the shop, up the back stairs to the living quarters. Equipment from her room of Medicinals and Physickes tottered haphazardly in front of her. Other than the room being empty of Boisvert's fine belongings, his tapestries, his silver tureens, Bianca saw nothing worrisome.

Then she caught a whiff of it.

"Bollocks!" exclaimed Bianca.

"Exactly his problem," said John.

The field of lavender of Boisvert's cherished wall mural of Provence had been watered.

John pointed a finger at Bianca's nose. "You have never witnessed Boisvert's anger or had your ears filled with his French fury." He stared at the mural and shook his head. "Bianca, you do not want to be the recipient of his displeasure." He glared at her. "He is your cat, so this is your problem."

Bianca did not disagree. Hobs had been the cat of her mentor, Ferris Stannum, and she felt responsible for his care. Stannum had met an unfortunate end, but his legacy lived on in Hobs. The esteemed alchemist had discovered the elixir of life—the purported potion of immortality. And he had fed it to Hobs. Whether the feline was immortal Bianca did not know. But so far, the cat had skirted disaster, and she did not care to test his privileged status—she had grown too fond of him.

Without a word, Bianca descended the stairs and passed Meddybemps carrying a crate. The streetseller had witnessed John's chase and Bianca's response and said nothing, preferring to let the two hash out their problems on their own. Their ongoing relationship provided him with an endless source of entertainment.

Outside, Bianca searched through the jars in the wagon. After a moment she found a bottle, uncorked it, and ran it under her nose.

Satisfied, she met an irritable John on the stairs. He had grown annoyed that she had just turned and left without an explanation. "What is that?" he said, eyeing the bottle.

"Ascerbis. It will subdue Hobs's . . . contribution." She sidled past, and John followed on her heels.

Meddybemps had just set down the crates and was squinting at the mural. He looked over when they walked in. "I'd rather spend the night on the hard brick forge than try to sleep in here," he said.

"Meddy, would you like a cat? I promise he could make you money. Strangle him over and over again and he will spring back to life. People would never tire of watching. You could make your fortune!"

Without a word, Bianca uncorked the bottle and splashed it on the field of Provence.

"What are you doing?" said John, screwing up his face at the smell of vinegar. "What if it eats through the paint?"

"It isn't strong enough." Bianca found a ewer of water and dribbled it down the wall. She looked about for a rag to mop up the puddle.

"If this fails," warned John, "we'll be banned from this rent and we will have to sleep on the shop floor. We might have to resort to living in barrels behind the Tern's Tempest."

"We could move back to Southwark." Bianca finished cleaning Hobs's critique of the wall mural. She threw the rag in the forge to be burned later, while John and Meddybemps returned to unloading the dray. With a doleful look at her new surroundings, she occupied herself with emptying the wagon rather than stare at the stacked boxes and crates whose contents could not be used.

Meddybemps wished to be done unloading the wagon so that he could return it to Arthur Milbourne. As it was, he would be late to market, and his preferred spot near a popular tavern would be taken. He dreaded having to sell his amulets and Bianca's salves next to a butcher. What with stray dogs being chased away by a knife-wielding meat seller, it never made for a good day of sales. Besides, the silence growing between Bianca and John made him uncomfortable. "You've not mentioned why a crowd was gathered outside of St. Vedast," he said, hoping to distract the two.

"A woman was discovered in the side yard this morning. The back of her head was crushed. I want to finish here and return to St. Vedast. A mass is being said."

"You didn't know her," said John irritably. "Why should you go?"

"I am curious."

"Curious about what?" said John, spoiling for an argument.

Bianca didn't answer. She loaded her arms with clothing and disappeared inside.

"John," said Meddybemps, pulling him aside. "Why do you goad her so? Remember, she is practiced in poisons and such."

"I am not goading her. She should not become involved in matters that are not her concern."

"My boy, I am not a married man. And there is a reason for that. I prefer not to give up my independence. I will not be told by a woman what I should do. Bianca has some of that about her. Although she is a woman, she does not want to be told what to do. You should be grateful that she agreed to leave Southwark. For now, do not ask more of her. She is of a curious mind. Let that be."

John grumbled and hoisted another crate of Bianca's wares.

"Besides," said Meddybemps, "she has already agreed to abandon her chemistries for the time being. What more would you have her do? Sit in front of the hearth with a distaff and spin thread all winter?"

"I could use a new smock; this one is becoming worn at the elbows."

Part of John's petulance stemmed from his awareness that Bianca had not embraced moving to Foster Lane. He had asked her to give up the one thing she loved perhaps even more than him—though he was loath to admit it. She had agreed to give up her chemistries and move because she had wanted to please him, and she knew she would know no peace from his constant badgering until she said yes. He'd used his recent illness with the sweating sickness as leverage, and he didn't like Meddybemps's reminding him that he was playing on Bianca's guilt.

Bianca passed John on the stairs without speaking.

"We are nearly done," she said to Meddybemps. She gathered an armload of blankets. "I suppose you need to return this wagon and can't come with me to St. Vedast."

"Not my choice of revelry, my prodigy. I'm afraid I might be smote dead within steps of the altar."

"Then perhaps keep an ear open and let me know if you learn anything useful."

John arrived and looked at them quizzically. "Have I missed something?" he asked.

Bianca brushed past and went inside.

"John, I will advise you true. Do not oppose her. She wants to go to St. Vedast, and you are antagonizing her unnecessarily."

John removed the last crate. "Anon, Meddybemps. It was kind of you to help us move. But do not scold me in matters of marriage."

St. Vedast stood as a relic of what it once was. The colorful biblical scenes that had graced the walls were now faded with grime; some had been washed with lime to subdue their brilliance and influence. Gone were the gold chalice and ciborium, replaced with humble pewter. The Virgin Mary and St. John no longer flanked the great crucifix, the rood, suspended from the crossbeam. Statues of saints that had once graced the interior had been removed, the candles extinguished, their pedestals empty, cobwebs stretching to the walls. The neglected church attracted a similarly forgotten clientele. Rather than be concerned with a woman's self-murder or even the preservation of their own souls, the gathered saw an opportunity to gather at close quarters and gossip.

Bianca stood in the rear of the nave. She could barely hear Father Nelson's words, only their soft echo bouncing around the cavernous interior.

Word spread quickly through the parish, and even John sauntered in, lured there by the number of people descending upon the church. Boisvert, the silversmith, attended, as did Odile Farendon, his betrothed. They nodded to Bianca and John before making their way toward the chancel. Odile impressed Bianca with her gracious acknowledgment when Boisvert pointed her out. A woman of higher station did not have to show interest in a woman of lower.

From where she stood, Bianca studied the congregation and made assumptions about her new neighborhood. Generally, the parishioners were simple folk. For a parish harboring several guilds, not least of which was the Goldsmiths' Company, there were surprisingly few merchants or professionals in attendance. Those who did attend were obvious in their fine attire. Perhaps not all the guilds had heard of the young woman's demise, but news of a dramatic death moves faster than a rat from light. The desire to milk scandal from the act should have attracted plenty— there being no social bounds for what was, essentially, human nature.

As Bianca leaned against a pillar, a cutpurse caught her eye. She, too, had been a thief in her youth, and she watched the boy deftly clip the strings of a lady's pouch and sneak away with it.

Perhaps the wealthy preferred not to attend the decrepit church. Why should they stand in St. Vedast, with its cracked and missing windows through which the December wind blew? Bianca ran her eyes upward to the clerestory and saw a window replaced with a dingy oiled cloth tacked across. Few citizens of any wealth would want to worship in such a dreary place, and without their endowments the church's upkeep was impossible. Such was a spiral that was difficult to overcome.

The priest finished his liturgy, and Bianca and John moved to the side as the congregation began to leave. Boisvert approached, and, though his face bore a somber expression, the solicitous manner in which he presented Odile Farendon showed his keen regard for her.

Odile and Bianca were of equal height and similar build. "My dear, I hope you shall grow fond of Foster Lane and enjoy living here. I understand that this move was a difficult decision for you."

Bianca glanced at John, wondering what he had discussed with Boisvert.

Odile added, "We all make sacrifices in love, but in time, what first may have been difficult becomes acceptable. There is always the chance to learn from change."

"My lady, your words are comforting as well as wise." Bianca bowed her head. "I wish you every happiness in your upcoming marriage."

"You and John will attend of course."

Before Bianca could answer, Henry Lodge, the churchwarden, appeared opposite Lady Farendon. He ignored Boisvert and John, glanced at Bianca with apathy, then addressed Odile. "My lady, Oro Tand has asked that you not leave until he has spoken with you."

Bianca followed Odile's eyes to where Oro Tand, master warden of the Worshipful Company of Goldsmiths, was engaged in conversation. Tufts of white hair showed from under his black silk coif, on top of which he wore a murrey velvet flat cap. Lofty in manner but not so in height, Tand embodied the spirit of the metal that was his livelihood. His fingers were weighted with it. Around his neck hung a chain of office touting his high position and the considerable skill needed to create the intricate filigree of the medallion.

Odile acknowledged Lodge, who quickly turned on his heel. She continued her conversation with Bianca. "I have a velvet kirtle of carmine that would complement your pale complexion. I have not worn it in years, and it would please me if you wore it to our wedding."

"You are kind," said Bianca. She looked over at John, and her inclination to decline the offer was quashed by the wide grin on his face. Apparently he hoped she would accept. She had never worn the fine fabrics of a citizen. To do so was to overstep her bounds according to sumptuary law and could result in harsh fines. Loss of property, even loss of one's life, could be the punishment for a merchant attempting to encroach on the privileges reserved for nobility. The same held true for those of lower birth.

However, for this occasion and since John aspired to the profession, Bianca understood she had been invited to make an exception. In all honesty, she did wonder what it might be like to wear such a gown and pretend to be a citizen. She decided to make it an experiment. Not one with flasks belching plumes of smoke, but one where she would test how others might receive her.

"Come after the morrow, after your morning devotions."

Bianca stiffened. She was about to inform Madame Farendon of her morning routine—which did not include morning devotions—when John accepted for her.

"Boisvert and Madame," said a new arrival, insinuating himself into their group. "I wish you every happiness in your upcoming marriage."

The man gave the impression of efficiency. His manner of speech was quick and direct, with little patience for pointless prattle. His forehead was a broad, pale landscape—more wide than tall, so that his square jaw made his head resemble a block sitting on his shoulders.

Boisvert made the introductions. James Croft, master of the Brown Bakers' Guild, bowed. Though his guild was of lesser rank than the brotherhood of goldsmiths, the bakers' influence could not be underestimated. Combined with the White Bakers, their numbers were greater than the Gold Guild's. After all, bread was the stuff of life, while (it could be argued) gold was not.

"So grievously shortsighted," said he. "If one chooses to commit one's soul to hell, one should pick a church that can absorb the scrutiny. St. Vedast already struggles. Such a sinister act will certainly be the end of our parish."

Odile spoke. "Master Croft, I share your concern for the continuing decline of St. Vedast. However, today we must turn our prayers to a young woman and her child. It is not certain that this was self-murder. And if it was, what great sorrow hounded her that she would act with such finality? It is a question we should think on."

"What is there to ponder? A young woman was distraught to be with child. The shame of that was not worth the misery that her life would surely become. The circumstance is not one that can be remedied. Her self-murder is regrettable. But she could have chosen a different parish church to leap from."

Bianca was momentarily stunned by the man's callous remark. She could not remain politely silent. "Sir, have you never faced a difficult choice? Her act was one of desperation. If, indeed, it was her act. We do not know, sir, that she was not pushed or thrown from the belfry. In either event, we should be sympathetic."

Croft cocked his head like a crow and studied Bianca. "We all face difficult choices in life. But I have worked hard to ensure that I may never face vexing decisions. It is a privilege that I have earned through planning and forethought."

The discomfort of her toe being squashed beneath John's foot momentarily distracted her. Bianca would have liked to have said more, but Oro Tand appeared beside Odile and spoke.

"Forgive my interruption. I believe we have some items to discuss regarding the wedding reception," he said to her. "I merely wish to confirm our appointment for the day after the morrow."

"Certainly," said Odile. "There are only a few details left to arrange."

Oro Tand addressed Boisvert. "Will you be accompanying the lady?"

"*Mais non.* I have other matters to attend."

Bianca noticed a strained formality between the two men. They barely looked at each other. She also noticed Henry Lodge staring at Odile with a look of blatant disapproval.

"Very well," replied the master goldsmith. He paused, then added, "I know how fond you are of this church. I regret it is the scene of an unfortunate incident. St. Vedast can ill afford more difficulty. I hope this does not cast a pall over your happy occasion."

Odile tucked her chin in agreement. "Unfortunately one cannot control where and when tragedies occur. It is my hope that the wedding shall go on as planned and that St. Vedast can be preserved. It was once a fine structure and I am partial to its French roots. It is the only church in London named after a French saint. A few of us would like to see it endure." She squeezed Boisvert's arm and the silversmith patted her hand.

Oro Tand's eyes slid over to Boisvert and returned to Odile. "Indeed."

CHAPTER 6

The moon glowed through the diamond-pane window, casting a beam of blue light across the bed. It was the first time Bianca had slept in a room in the winter where she could see the moon. As a girl in her parents' rent, she had slept against a wall near the back of their living quarters. In Southwark, she had kept out winter's cold with a wool blanket nailed over the single window. She thought the silvery orb beautiful, but her mind could not rest. A new home, no chemistries to think about, a young woman's death, all conspired to keep her awake.

John blew soft snores at her pillow. She nuzzled close to him, but even his rhythmic breathing did not lull her to sleep. Hobs slept curled in a tight ball near her feet. She eased out of bed, careful not to rouse either of them.

After the mass at St. Vedast, she and John had spent the day arranging crates from her room of Medicinals and Physickes. They had stacked them in a corner away from the door, into a leaning tower filled with crockery, retorts, and jars. Bianca was not used to such a large living space and found its emptiness disconcerting. Her room in Southwark had been a jumble. John said the disarray mirrored her mind. It was true; she found some comfort in chaos. She thrived on the energy of confusion.

By comparison, the silence and orderliness of her new home felt lonely. She missed falling asleep to the burp of some liquid simmering in a water bath. She missed the fusty smell of herbs hanging from the rafters.

With toes stinging from the chill floorboards, Bianca went to the window to look out over her new neighborhood and view the moon. She retrieved her stockings from near the hearth and pulled them on beneath her smock. The layer helped, but she needed more. She dropped her kirtle over her head. Soon she was dressed and wide-awake. She threw a wool cape over her shoulders and headed out the door.

Quiet reigned in the hour past midnight. The scurry of a rat along the lane drew her eyes, and somewhere down the road, a shutter slammed. What was ignored by day was noticed at night.

Her new neighborhood was composed of small shops, with a few residences wedged between. A handsome change from the derelict area of Gull Hole in Southwark. For such an agreeable street, the road itself was in serious disrepair. Loose and missing cobbles turned her ankle when she failed to take care where she walked.

Standing opposite St. Vedast was a second church, St. Leonard. The two were of comparable height and architecture. Was there a reason the woman had died specifically at St. Vedast? Bianca gave the bread master's complaint a moment's thought. Had the choice even been a consideration?

Bianca stood in front of St. Vedast, running her eyes along the angled roofline up to its tower. Had someone thrown her from the belfry? Or had the woman purposely taken her life? Perhaps her ghost might inform. Bianca didn't fear the wandering of a restless soul, so long as she didn't beckon her from the crypt of hell.

The churchwarden had claimed he had unlocked the belfry

passage. In his distraction, had he forgotten to unlock the door, or had the door been unlocked and in his preoccupation he mistakenly turned the wards to secure it?

A gust of wind blew her cape open, and Bianca pulled it closed. The woman must not have been in her right mind to be out on such a night wearing a thin smock. Either that or she was forced against her will. Had someone else been involved? Had someone chased her?

No one knew who the woman was or from where she had come. Perhaps in time Meddybemps might hear of a maid who had gone missing. Someone searching for a lost daughter or lover.

Bianca went into the side yard where the body had been. A stain of blood still darkened the cobbles where the woman had lain. She looked up again at the tower and the roof.

There in the sharp shadows of moonlight, a window faced the peak. Perhaps the woman had climbed out the belfry and dropped onto the roof. Bianca followed the ridgeline, then lowered her eyes to the beech tree beside the building. Or could the woman have climbed the tree?

The first branch was just out of reach. Curious to see if it could be done, Bianca jumped and grabbed on to the limb. She dangled, trying to swing a leg up to hook her foot on the limb, but dropped off.

"How could a pregnant woman manage this?"

Brushing off her hands, she focused on the limb. On her second try, she dug her heel into the bark for purchase. Just as she started to hug the branch and pull herself up, hands gripped her waist.

"Leave off!" she protested. Her arms and legs being occupied, she had no recourse but to curse whoever had grabbed her. "You cankered maltworm. You'll wish you never laid hands on me. . . ." But she was pulled off the branch.

Unprepared for her squirming weight, her captor tumbled backward. Bianca landed on top of a foul-smelling tosspot who struck the frozen ground with a lung-jolting thud.

She rolled and got to her feet. She would have run well away if the man had looked to do her harm. Instead, he lay flat on his back, blinking up at her.

"What do you want?" she demanded, straightening her twisted bodice and pulling her cape closed.

The man answered in a wheezy voice. "You looked to be climbing the tree."

"I was!"

He lay there a moment before struggling to one knee. He placed his hands on his thigh and, with considerable difficulty, pushed himself to standing. "St. Vedast is cursed," he said as he found his cap and put it on.

"Why, say you?"

He shook his head. "Have you not heard what happened here last night?"

"Nay," lied Bianca. "Tell me." The drunk may have been informed only by gossip, but Bianca wondered why he was out at this hour. How had he noticed her climbing the tree? It was dark in the side yard, and if one were walking by on the road, she would not have been noticed—unless she was heard. Or unless she was being watched.

"It hasn't been a day since a woman took her life here—a woman with child."

"Probably hearsay."

"Nay. It is not."

"Why? Did you see her?"

The man looked away and did not answer.

"Say you, did she take her own life?"

"She fell."

"From the roof?"

"From the steeple."

"How did she get to the steeple?"

"She climbed the tree."

The thought of a pregnant woman accomplishing the feat seemed incredible. "And did she leap?"

The man shook his head. "Nay, I told ye. She fell."

"Was she pushed?" Bianca watched his face carefully.

"Nay."

"But how could a woman in her condition climb the roof to the tower?"

"You know not how it vexes me," he said, hitting his palms against his forehead. "The sight of her haunts me. She will never leave."

Bianca stepped closer and lowered her voice. "What haunts you? What did you see?"

The spiffled beggar dropped his arms to his sides and blew out his breath. "I have never seen such strangeness in a woman. I came upon her near Friday Street, growling at a dog. Mind you, ale from the Crooked Cork can affect people that way. The two were baying at each other. Such gnarling I've never seen. I stopped to watch. The cur took a fright. It ran off, tail between its legs.

"I called to her and she turned to look on me. Her hair was all about her face, quite like yours, but she was a beauty in spite of her wildness. She were only wearing a thin night smock. And her feet were bare. It was terrible cold and I thought maybe she needed someone to help her home. But she would not talk to me. She . . . danced up the street, like it were a lovely summer eve. All the while she was screeching like a hawk. She had a funny step about her, a stiffness. She didna' even notice her feet were blue."

"Then she was a stranger to you?"

"I'd never seen her before last night." The sot sniffled from the cold and wiped his nose on his sleeve. "I tried to reason with her. Granted, me gut sloshed with a few pottle pots, but I wouldna' let a woman freeze. She ran ahead and disappeared down this side yard." The man looked around and then back at Bianca. "I followed her, wondering what she was about. Then I heard her scramblin' up the tree." His expression mirrored his distress at the memory. "I called after her to come down. She just laughed and kept singing."

"She was singing?"

He nodded. "A song of nonsense."

"Was she daft?"

"She was not right. I wondered if she were possessed—lured by the devil or some demon. I could not see that she had any sense. She was peculiar as ever I have seen. I went after her. I climbed the tree, tryin' to get her to come to me. 'Give me your hand!' I keeps sayin'. But she just laughed. She leapt onto the roof. 'Goosey, goosey, gander,' she says. 'Where shall I wander?' Over 'n' over. 'Goosey, goosey, gander . . .'" The man clapped his hands to his ears. "I canna' stop hearing it!"

"Did you follow her onto the roof?"

A look of shame fell over his face. "I have no stomach for heights. 'Tis a long way down from the roof to the ground."

Bianca nodded. "Go on. Tell me everything you saw that night."

"I watched her. She had no fear, running like a squirrel, scampering up the roof, running along its peak. I couldna' hardly watch." He glanced at the ground and shook his head. "But neither could I drag my eyes away. She went for the tower with no thought and started climbing it. I don't know what she grabbed on to. She hugged it, shinnied up as far as it was tall. Then with the moon shining silver all around, she reached over her head. Stretching her arm like she was tryin' to touch it. She tried inching up the steeple, almost to the tip." The man closed his eyes and shook his head.

Bianca pulled the neck of her cape under her chin. She stared at the stain of blood on the cobbles, visible in the shifting light of the moon.

CHAPTER 7

Odile Farendon remembered her mother saying, *"La culpabilité punit devant Dieu ne."* Guilt punishes before God does. The sentiment wormed through her conscience until she could no longer ignore it.

Rather than be escorted, Odile walked to St. Vedast alone. The road was overly pocked, but it was not far; even in the worst cold she could manage it without discomfort. Besides, she had not slept well. Her agitation ran with thoughts of the young woman with child. The walk would give her time to think. She donned her fox-lined cape and hat and found her betrothed eating porridge and quail eggs.

"Odile, *permettez-moi de vous accompagner?*" Boisvert asked, watching her pull on her gloves.

"My love, I wish to go alone. I need to clear my head." She bent and kissed the top of his balding crown, then patted her spaniel, who was shamelessly begging for food next to Boisvert. "I shall return after I have seen Father Nelson."

Only a few were out on Foster Lane when she turned down it, walking toward St. Vedast Church. She passed the Goldsmiths'

Hall, looming silent and dark—a bitter reminder of her dead husband and the power he'd once had.

An attendant of Lady Anne Boleyn, she had met Lionel Farendon at court. Odile had come from France, and she became a favorite of Anne's—a friend and confidant. Anne did not trust easily, but Odile managed to serve and protect her lady while remaining neutral in court politics and gossip. Still, Odile saw the treachery there and secretly wished to be done with keeping secrets and dupery. When offered the chance to wed, Odile seized the opportunity, and Anne regretfully gave her blessing. But the two remained in contact.

Lionel Farendon was two decades Odile's senior. Perhaps it amused him to parade a woman on his arm who was younger than the rest of the guild wardens' wives. Like the king, he hoped his virility and allure were understood. A wife who had died while pregnant and another two dying in childbirth had left the master goldsmith without an heir. As a result, Lionel had no beneficiary. No other living soul could claim a familial connection to the man—not even a distant cousin or illegitimate issue. It was his great hope that Odile would change his misfortune. But a man suffering from the consequences of a lascivious youth should not hope that maturity would heal his disease-riddled pipe.

As he grew older, his inability to father a child became his embarrassment, and then it became his vexation. He blamed Odile. He told others she was barren. "She does not please me in bed," she'd overheard him say to a fellow goldsmith. Odile suffered in silence, but she was wise enough to know this was a blessing. She was saved from the danger of childbirth. And she was saved from mothering a child that was of his blood.

If his denunciations were all she had had to endure, she would not have despised him so. A daily diet of humiliation was not what she had hoped for in life. She had escaped Queen Anne's unpredictable behavior for her husband's more abusive one. The missing tooth and purple eye were more difficult to conceal than her bruised pride.

Why did she submit? In England, only the king divorced.

Solace came in two ways. The relief of seeing her husband grow infirm was one. Peace in prayer was the other. Eventually Lionel Farendon died, releasing Odile from their unhappy marriage, but her spiritual suffering had not ended. She sought Father Nelson for help with her guilt.

Stopping in front of the double oak doors of St. Vedast, Odile read the inscription etched in its pediment above. *"Qui enim ingressus est in requiem corde"*—peace be to those who enter with a pure heart. "And if your heart is not pure?" she asked aloud. She glanced around to see if anyone had overheard, then crossed herself before hauling open the door.

Odile preferred St. Vedast to St. Leonard and St. John Zachary, also on Foster Lane. As Odile had mentioned to Oro Tand, she took some comfort in the church being named in the memory of a French saint and the connection to her homeland. When King Henry made himself the supreme head of the Church of England, St. Vedast's image was removed and his lamp extinguished. A saint, particularly a French one, had no privilege under Henry's reforms.

The stripped interior stood in stark contrast to Odile's memory of St. Vedast from even six years before. In spite of its shabby appearance, Odile would not forsake her beloved church. Nor would she forsake her belief that the pope was God's appointed representative on Earth. But such opinions she kept to herself. Only Father Nelson and Boisvert could be trusted to keep that secret.

Her footsteps echoed through the sanctuary as she neared the chancel screen. Odile could see her breath in the cold air. The rood still hung high above on the candle beam, though St. John and the Virgin Mary had been removed. Their impressions were still visible against the surrounding darker wood. She knelt for a moment of prayer.

When she finished, she was startled to see Henry Lodge watching from the rear of the nave. *"Bonjour, Henri,"* she said, walking toward him.

The expression on Lodge's face was as cold as the air inside the church. No sign of acknowledgment or even civility was forthcoming. When she got within a few feet of him, he turned and walked away.

Odile sighed. She wished him peace. Sixteen years is too long for any man to resent a woman.

She found Father Nelson sitting at his desk, reading. He looked up on hearing her light rap upon his doorjamb.

"Will you hear my confession, Father?"

Father Nelson closed his book. "Of course. I shall be but a minute."

Odile crossed the nave to the confessional booth, removed her fur hat, and knelt before the screen. She heard the steps of another and assumed them to belong to Henry Lodge performing his duty as churchwarden. She made no attempt to call to him a second time. Presently, Father Nelson arrived.

"Forgive me, Father, for I have sinned. It has been a year since my last confession." Odile hesitated before going on. "My husband, Lionel, died thirteen years ago. I feel no grief for his death. I never have." Odile crossed herself, then continued. "Father, I ardently wished for his demise. If heartfelt thoughts are the stuff of prayer, then I fervently prayed for his death."

"Did you resist these selfish thoughts?"

"Alas, I did not. I chided myself for feeling grateful when he died. But as his chest grew still and his final breath escaped his lips, my heart became light. Is it a sin to feel relief from my burden?"

"And you regarded your marriage a burden?"

"*Oui*, I did."

"It is a sin to take comfort in the demise of another. If you wished him dead, if you held hatred in your heart, you are as culpable as if you had murdered him."

Odile sucked in her breath. "I do not wish to die without absolution."

"Of course you don't," said Father Nelson.

"I fear I shall never know peace. My soul is doomed to be tormented in purgatory for all of eternity. Is there nothing I can do?"

"My child, repent your sins with sincerity. But you must not repent for fear of a prolonged purgatory. God sees your intent."

"So I shall suffer the pain of purgatory?"

"Assuredly." Father Nelson paused. "However, there are ways to shorten your soul's torment."

"Father, what must I do to hasten my soul's journey?"

"Ask for God's mercy in prayer. Pray ten Paternosters and ten Hail Marys. Pray that your soul's passage is made easy and straight. Fast today and return here tomorrow. But you must also do good works. Without restitution, you cannot return to God's grace."

"*Oui, oui*, Father. *Certainement.*"

"God looks favorably on those with a charitable heart. If one is blessed with wealth, that gift has come to you through God. For it is written, 'Sell your possessions and give to the poor.'"

"Oui, Father."

"One must support and sustain one's church. Without a fold of wealthy Samaritans, St. Vedast will not survive." Father Nelson leaned close to the screen and lowered his voice. "The king seeks to intercept those monies for his own use. He glories in the preparation for war against France. He has forgotten what matters to God. It is not war."

"Father, I should not like to see St. Vedast fail. My wealth is more than I shall ever need. Your good works must not be undone."

"I will intercede on your behalf, but for a place on the bede roll, you must bequeath a gift."

"*Oui*, Father. I shall make it be. Is there more I can do?"

Father Nelson did not hesitate. "If you wish, a mortuary mass may be said on the day of your farewell. The day of your burial can be marked with a mass. Or the day after your burial and seven days later could be commemorated. Even a mass of intercession can be scheduled a month or two months later." Like a lapidary laying out his assorted gems, the priest was not content with showing just a few. "Perhaps more to your liking—an intercession upon the anniversary of your decease?" He paused a second; then, not waiting for even a grunt of reply, he rambled off several more choices . . . surely something might appeal to the woman. "I can do this for as many years as you have money."

Odile listened intently.

"Ultimately, the best assurance to hasten your soul's disposition is to endow a chantry." By the time Father Nelson had absolved Odile of her sins, she would leave absolved of all her money.

The priest walked Odile Farendon past Henry Lodge, who was speaking with James Croft, master of the Brown Bakers' Guild. The two men stopped talking at the sight of Odile and Father Nelson. Croft nodded respectfully, whereas Lodge stiffened at the sight of Odile.

"I shall see my solicitor, and he can take care of the matter," she told the priest as he saw her out the door. "Now is the time to make these arrangements. Not after I have married."

CHAPTER 8

Father Nelson was startled from his contemplation when Henry Lodge approached his door. It could only be the churchwarden, as no one else had such a weighty step—surprising, given the man was as thin as a blade of grass.

"Enter," he called when Lodge inquired.

"Father, I have a matter that requires your approval."

Henry Lodge was a goldsmith and careful record keeper. In fact, the priest had never seen a more conscientious churchwarden. With Lodge keeping the books, no royal commissioner would dare question their accounts. But it was precisely his findings and attention to detail that worried the priest. He could no longer pretend there were enough funds to keep St. Vedast viable. Father Nelson laid a feather on the page of his prayer book and closed it.

"I have completed the accounts for the week. All is in order. Or as ordered as we may hope." The churchwarden handed the papers to Father Nelson, who began to look them over. "However, sir, it has come to my attention that the tower bells need greasing."

Father Nelson's eyebrows rose, and he looked up at the warden. "The necessity of which is what?"

"The bells creak. Their axles are becoming brittle, and there is a crack. We can ill afford if one should break."

"Another unfortunate repair that we haven't the funds for. There is plenty of upkeep that we should address. You must add it to the list of others. As it is, we can barely keep candles lit on the altar. If you can think of a way we can lessen our expenditures, I welcome hearing it."

Henry Lodge nodded. "As you wish. I shall be on my way, then." He turned for the door, but Father Nelson called him back.

"Lodge," said the priest. "What was James Croft speaking with you about?"

"He asked about the hosts. He wanted to know if we were receiving them gratis. I told him that we were. I told him such gifts are appreciated."

"He took issue with this?"

"He demanded to know the name of our sanctioned bakery. I did not care for his accusatory tone, so I refused to tell him."

"I would think he would appreciate our savings."

"Croft is the newly appointed master of the Brown Bakers' Guild. He is a strict adherent to precedent. I suppose he wants a record of such gifts for accounting purposes."

"In order to wield another one of his guild's penalties? I see their officers creeping about town toting their bread scales. It seems parish churches as well as guilds are feeling the pain of the king's policies. Or shall I say the king's preparations for war. I can scarce imagine who or what else might be left to garnish. The king taxes the guilds. The guilds tax their liverymen. The liverymen pass their cost on to the rest of us." Father Nelson glanced at Lodge and sniffed.

Henry Lodge did not disagree.

"Still, he is a member of the parish and a wealthy one at that.

Perhaps I should pay him a visit and smooth over the misunderstanding. Enlist his sympathy for our cause."

The churchwarden listened. He'd already voiced his opinion of the man.

"Has Buxton buried that woman's body yet?" asked the priest.

"I believe he is still digging the grave. The ground is frozen; it has been difficult. This will likely be the last burial he'll be able to manage until spring."

"Buxton knows she must lie north to south? I do not wish to provoke God's disfavor."

"I have ensured that his compass is true," said the churchwarden.

Father Nelson felt the urge to explain himself. "I know some may disagree with her burial here. But I cannot in good conscience doom her to hell." Father Nelson laid the papers in front of him and absently tapped his prayer book. "Her soul is for God to judge—not me."

"I understand." Lodge had heard the priest's sentiment before but declined to remind him.

"These are dangerous times for a priest," continued Father Nelson. "The king's mind changes as often as he changes wives. So many clergy have been offered pensions and have taken them. There are no monasteries left," he said, sitting up in his chair. The news still left him dismayed. "Every town and village in all of England has been affected."

"You are fortunate to still have your parish."

"Am I?" Father Nelson sounded doubtful. "I am not certain the burden of continuing is worth this effort."

"As you said, Father, it is a difficult time. St. Vedast is not the only church in London that struggles with the taxes and changes. You might invoke your faith," he said, then regretted being obvious. He quickly added, "Cromwell and his men carved Henry's future, not God."

Father Nelson could not soften his voice. He had to speak his mind, and Lodge was an obliging audience. "This instability, this disrespect for the old ways—it affects the parishioners. There is no reverence during mass. Their insolent chatter drowns my words." The priest's eyes became hard with resentment. "They complain that I dawdle and keep them from their breakfast."

The churchwarden had seen it too.

"Why should they complain so?" continued Father Nelson. "Half of them leave after elevation anyway." The corner of his mouth lifted, thinking of the sad reality. "If it weren't for the occasional wedding and mortuarial fee, I would have starved by now."

"But there are those who remain faithful to St. Vedast in spite of the changes."

Father Nelson sat back in his chair. He closed his eyes and rubbed them, thinking of Odile Farendon. "Aye, that." Besides her, there were few parishioners who secretly doubted the rumors of corruption Thomas Cromwell and others had instigated more than five years before.

Those with money and a concern for their afterlife made sure their souls were prayed for as soon as they died. It was not enough to repent on one's deathbed. One must show through charitable works and penance their love for God.

If one were not charitable enough, then one was not penitent enough and one's soul would suffer appropriate cleansing in a cruel purgatory. The vision of God and the bliss of heaven were reserved for those who truly loved Him. Heaven was for those who rejected their sins for God's love—not for the fear of landing in hell.

Father Nelson leaned forward in his chair. "We have been dealt a mortal blow, Lodge. Henry's campaign to denigrate purgatory has been our ruination." His grave eyes flashed. "Men have always feared the pain of purgatory more than hell—as well they should." As a priest, it was his duty to remind sinners that their transgressions would be matched by a suitable punishment there. And the church had profited from this fear.

"It is true, chantries and obiits are not what they once were."

"The king disparages the practice but forgets his pockets bulge from their dismantling. It is only a matter of time before he forbids them altogether."

"But Odile Farendon . . ." prompted the churchwarden. It was difficult for him to utter her name, but his curiosity sat on his shoulder and whispered in his ear. Propriety prevented him from directly asking after her business. Propriety kept the priest from divulging it.

Father Nelson inclined his head, inquisitively.

Awkwardness kicked Henry Lodge in the throat.

"Odile is a soul in pain," said Father Nelson. "She suffers no less than the rest of us." He didn't ask what Lodge's interest was in the matter. His steady gaze inquired for him.

The churchwarden had overstepped his bounds. He had indulged the priest in spilling his heart when he should have covered his ears. They both knew it. They both knew they held each other's honor by a thread. Who would snip first?

Father Nelson watched the churchwarden retire into the hall. He listened to the man's heavy footfall as it faded, then picked up the papers to study the accounts. The numbers, the letters, jumbled and he grew more dispirited the longer he looked at them.

If he could not convince the few parishioners with money to give charitably to St. Vedast, then what other means of raising money were left to him? There were no relics in the church's vault. St. Vedast was not buried beneath the flagstones. And even if either were true, he would not have been able to benefit from them. Not since Henry forbade the worship of relics and saints.

He could hope for a spate of marriages, baptisms, or mortuares. With winter came more deaths. Funerals always outnumbered marriages anyway. The only means to raise funds besides menial tithes, donations, and earned fees . . . was obiits.

So, while he was able, Father Nelson would . . . encourage . . . Odile Farendon's guilty conscience for the good of her beloved church of St. Vedast.

And here Father Nelson sat, in a parish surrounded by guilds with more wealth than he could imagine. The Haberdashers', Goldsmiths', and Bakers' Companies all had addresses in the direct vicinity of Foster Lane. Their lack of interest in the struggling church dismayed him. Surely, St. Vedast was not so undesirable that they would let it fall into ruin to blight their wealthy neighborhood. Father Nelson expelled a heavy breath. Apparently, indifference was the diet of the day.

Of course he did not wish death on anyone, but Odile Farendon's guilty conscience presented him with an opportunity.

After all these years, she was still tortured by a troubled conscience. Well, thought Father Nelson, if she was filled with guilt, he could help unburden her soul.

CHAPTER 9

At Cheapside market, Bianca glimpsed Constable Patch and quickly paid for her head of cabbage, hoping to put some distance between herself and the skulking lawman. She had been giving thought to the nonsense rhyme spoken by the victim at St. Vedast.

"Goosey, goosey, gander, where shall I wander?" The last month of a woman's pregnancy is her month of confinement—her gander month. Usually a woman stayed home to avoid flaunting her sexuality—her grotesque appearance—in public. Her husband often looked elsewhere for "gratification" and so "wandered" to find it. Was the woman distraught that her lover had betrayed her?

Bianca hurried past St. Mary-le-Bow, determined to slip behind Eleanor Cross. The monument was ignored by most and considered an inconvenient stone enormity standing in the way of carts and commerce. For Bianca, however, it would shield her from unwelcome notice.

She had just passed Bread Street, with Friday Street in her sights, when Patch appeared, having outmaneuvered her.

"Bianca Goddard," he said, cutting across her path. Winded but obviously pleased with himself, he held his side and caught his breath. "When on some distant shore, old friends shall meet once more."

"Friends?" said Bianca. "I would not go so far."

"Nay?" Patch smiled, which looked more like a snivel. "Then acquaintances?"

"As you wish."

Constable Patch puffed out his chest like an overblown rooster and tugged on his popingay blue doublet, with recently polished brass buttons to call attention to it, Bianca thought. She refrained from commenting.

It had been a few months since last she'd dealt with the beef-witted lawman. The time had passed too quickly now that she was face-to-face with him again. They had reached some level of respect, or perhaps at least understanding, but Bianca would always view the opportunistic ward with a healthy dose of caution.

Patch glanced down at the cabbage in her hand. "Ye do seem to favor cooking with smelly agents." He pulled his scraggly chin hair. "Still dealing in potions and such?"

"Sirrah, I do not deal in potions." She formed each word carefully so that he could not mistake her. "I create medicinals and physickes for the sick and ailing."

"So ye say." Constable Patch was not one to ignore a chance to be annoying. "Ye are a long way from Southwark. Are there no cabbages left in the borough?"

"I happen to be in this neighborhood," said Bianca. More truly spoken than Patch realized.

Bianca was scheming how to be rid of Patch when shouts came from down the road, interrupting their chance meeting. "What ho!" she exclaimed, forgetting her wish to leave. "Is that a horse dragging a piece of fence?"

"Aye, a wattle with a baker perched on top," said Constable Patch.

They stood aside as the horse and rider passed, parading a disgraced baker on a hurdle, his thighs lashed so that he could not escape his public humiliation. A loaf of bread hung from his neck, along with a placard that read, "Here sits Tom Pate, baker caught for adding weight." He hollered and cursed, to the sport of onlookers, who threw rotten food and mocked him as he rode past.

"He'll not bake sand into his loaves again," said Patch, finding a rock, which he eagerly contributed. The rain of rotting vegetables was topped with a spoiled pompion splatting on the man's crown.

"I shouldn't think he'd ever want to bake again," said Bianca.

Patch eyed the cabbage in Bianca's hand. He looked as though he wanted to throw it, too. "So, ye is taking a cabbage to yer husband?"

"Constable Patch, it is cold and I would like to be on my way."

"Ah, be on yer way. So's it seems. And which direction is that—on yer way?"

Ignoring his question, Bianca started walking. She hoped Patch would leave off, but like a wart, he would not go away until he was ready. He trailed after, then caught up to her, his strides lengthening with self-importance.

"Ye must know of the unfortunate death on Foster Lane. Yer husband is a journeyman for Boisvert."

"I have heard of it." Bianca quickened her pace.

Patch gave Bianca a sidelong glance, then got in front of her, forcing her to stop. "They thinks it is self-murder; is that what ye think?"

"I do not think anything." Bianca sidestepped him and continued on.

Constable Patch called after. "It is unlike you not to think anything, Bianca Goddard."

She could have ignored him, but Bianca was, by nature, unable to resist asking a question when one crossed her mind. She turned to him. "I should like to know what you think first."

A tricky smile flicked across the constable's face. "Wells," said Patch, catching up to her, "I been wonderin' why a pretty lass would takes her life. A woman doesn't become ripe with child on her own."

Bianca tipped her head. "I hope you have more to offer than the obvious."

"What I am saying is that there is a party to this story. A party to her conniption."

"A party to her *condition?*"

Patch stared without a response. He seemed unaware that she was correcting his English.

"One might well assume that," said Bianca.

"So's I'm sayin', we find the man, we find the murderer."

"Constable Patch, there is no proof that the *party* committed the murder. True, there is more to this story than a body on the ground next to St. Vedast. But no one knows who she is."

"I knows a piece ye might be interested in."

"And that piece is?"

Patch glanced around, then leaned in. "She had a mark on her."

Bianca shrugged. "She fell from a great height. How could she escape unscathed?"

"Naws," said Constable Patch, exasperated. He calmed himself, then added, "She possessed a mark like that of a claw."

"Constable Patch, I saw the woman. I looked at her. She had no mark of an animal on her."

"Not true, not true!" said Patch.

"Did you see it with your own eyes? Because I have learned, and so should you, that rumors are not worth the breath it takes to utter them. Besides, I don't recall you were anywhere near the incident."

"I happened into the ward office when the coroner filed his report." Constable Patch looked so pleased with himself, Bianca thought he might burst.

"And where did the coroner see this mark of a claw?"

"It was on her stomach—her womb."

Bianca thought back to the coroner and constable attending the body. She remembered the coroner lifting the woman's smock and peering under it, something she would not have done in the presence of a crowd that had been aghast at her for simply turning the woman onto her back.

"He made no comment at the time," said Bianca.

"Do ye think him a fool? If he had said a word of such a mark, he would have incited a commotion. Such findings are better kept quiet."

"What are you insinuating, Patch?"

"Insinuating? Nay, I do not insinuate. I assume." Patch said this with wholehearted belief. "I think there is more to this death than is clear. Is it the mark of a devil? Is it a warning that she should die beside a church? Ye should think more on this one, Bianca Goddard."

Sleet lashed Henry Lodge's face, the ice stinging like crewel needles being hurled from the sky. The goldsmith trudged against the elements, bound for home and his shop on Watling Street. He had just come from the Goldsmiths' Hall, and this "lashing" only heightened his downcast state. His day had been a disappointing one, a string of aggravations. . . .

Undertaking the duties of churchwarden at St. Vedast had become a more discouraging endeavor with every passing day. With no funds to make necessary repairs—the most worrisome being in the belfry—his ability to effect change and improvement was snuffed, the life blown out of his efforts. Father Nelson did not seem to understand the import, or perhaps he simply did not care. Lodge's frustration with the priest sat like an unwelcome guest at a table: One had to endure the meal with civility and patience until it was over.

If it were not enough to be chided for asking for repairs, there was the master of the Brown Bakers' Guild, James Croft, taking exception to their saving money by accepting hosts at no cost. Lodge's feet stomped heavily as he made his way home, and he envisioned Croft's insipid face under every step. The man was a parishioner of St. Vedast. Could he not see the dire state the church was in?

At his shop, Henry Lodge withdrew a key and let himself into his well-equipped environs. His workshop did not lack for vessels, cruets, or molds. Before his furnace, his working stool and anvil were at the ready, a row of tools neatly hung on the wall. A fire must be laid in the furnace, but first he lit a lamp.

As the goldsmith laid a pile of twigs and wood, then tipped a hod of coal over it, he thought about Odile Farendon praying in the sanctuary. Age had only softened her features, not lessened her handsome appeal. He had thought taking the position as St. Vedast's churchwarden might enamor her to him. With his wife now deceased and his daughter married, he was a man with only his industry and avocation to keep him occupied. He saw no reason why he should not pursue a lost dream.

Lodge struck a flint and held it to the kindling, nursing a shy, smoldering twig to flame. He stood back, then gently pumped the bellows. It was not enough that Odile Farendon was to remarry, but now he had been commissioned to create an ouche for her.

"No one can set stone in filigree as beautifully as you," Oro Tand told him.

The compliment about his skill should have swelled him with pride. Instead, it filled his veins with black bile.

"Make one of those lovely filigree brooches—an ouche," Tand had directed. The master goldsmith's eyes caught his, and Lodge saw the man's mouth work to conceal a vulpine smile. "Then set a stone in a center bevel." The master went to a shelf and pushed his finger through a box of gems; the dull chatter of stones, their excess making them of frivolous worth.

He picked out a peridot, pinching it between two fingers so the light from a candle could play off its glassy surface. "This should do," said Master Tand, handing over the stone. "The lady's eyes are of similar quality, are they not?"

The greenish yellow gem was of exceptional clarity and flawless.

"I do not recall the lady's eyes," he replied, hearing his voice tighten and resenting Tand for conjuring his distress. Peridot bequeathed prosperity and happiness to its bearer, and Lodge wondered if Oro Tand

reveled in that irony. He dropped the stone into a velvet purse for safe-keeping, feeling Tand's eyes watching him.

The gold master returned the box to the shelf. "I admit I was surprised by Odile's betrothal to our stranger brother, Boisvert." He pretended casual conversation. "She had been a widow so long, I assumed she must prefer it. Either that or she had exacting standards of a caliber no one could meet." He tilted his head, pausing for a response. Getting none, he continued, "I suppose those of similar . . . ilk . . . take comfort in that familiarity. Such fellowship is difficult for a Briton to imitate."

Henry Lodge had never stood on even ground with Oro Tand. The elder smith had always assumed a more senior role in their acquaintance. That is not to say that the younger smith lacked in anything—except a few years of age. His talent and skill in all things metallurgy well exceeded those of his brother goldsmith. But in matters of administration, in matters of governance, Tand eclipsed Lodge.

However, Henry Lodge believed himself the more principled of the two. This conscientious adherence to probity was a quality he expected of others, and when someone disappointed, he cut them from his life as easily as butter from a churn.

He deferred to Oro Tand only because he had to. The man sat in position. If Lodge wanted to continue his livelihood, then he had better sheathe that knife. Even if it required swallowing Tand's veiled remarks.

Yet there was one other who, when he put his blade against her warm neck, could turn his mettle to brittle ice.

He tossed the purse containing the peridot on the table. Well, it is done, thought Lodge, fetching his store of beeswax and pulling off a chunk. He would cast a mold for the brooch and he would create a piece that would rouse the praise of the bride and the envy of her silversmith groom.

But as he sat warming the wax in his hand, Tand's voice wormed into his thoughts. . . .

"Do you wonder why I have asked you to create a piece for Odile when others might have sufficed?" Tand had ventured.

"You just commented that I excel in filigree."

"Oh, you do, Henry."

"Then that is where my curiosity ends." He had turned away, not wishing to continue the line of inquiry.

"It is important that the guild show Odile no lingering resentment."

Lodge's palms had become damp at the mention of the past and *"lingering resentment."* He wished Tand would not tread that ground. But he understood the insinuation and knew that the gold master wanted him to acknowledge his meaning. *"Master Tand, I shall make an ouche that shall erase all trace of bitterness."* He refused to declare that his own remaining rancor would be appeased by the creation and presentation of a piece of jewelry.

Tand watched him a moment. *"I realize I have not given you much time to design and finish the piece,"* he said. *"But I should like it delivered as soon as we can manage."* He cast his keen eyes on Henry Lodge. *"You understand me?"*

"Quite."

"We must do all we can to make the occasion memorable."

Henry Lodge squeezed the wax in his hand. "I shall cast a piece that will leave everyone in awe."

That night, James Croft, master baker, found that kneading bread quieted his mind. He slapped the mound of dough, sending puffs of flour into the air that caught in his abundant brows. The day had been a trying one. Being master of the Brown Bakers' Guild came with responsibilities. He had coveted the position for years. The election took place the Monday after St. Clement's Day (St. Clement being the patron saint of bakers), and he had been confirmed by a resounding majority (no one else wanted the position). Only two weeks into his appointment, he was already residing over the Court of Halimote, dispensing punishments to a handful of bakers impudent enough to fob guild standards.

He had ordered Terman Buckle's oven pulled down for his

third offense, this time shorting loaves in Dowgate Ward. Croft frowned at the dough and folded it over, pounding it with his fist.

He wondered if the punishment for a second offense should instead be the punishment for the first. Setting a man in a pillory was easier than having him dragged through the streets on a hurdle with a loaf of bread hung from his neck. For that, one had to secure a horse and rider, then attach the wattle to the rear of the saddle. If it wasn't set the correct distance, the horse shat on the man's head. Croft tsked. Once around town should teach anyone a lesson.

He hoped Tom Pate had learned his.

Never had Croft heard such squawking from a grown man. He wanted to ban the baker from ever selling another loaf after he saw the public spectacle he made of himself. Not a favorable showing, as his petulance reflected poorly on the Brown Bakers' Guild. The guild could ill afford embarrassment of any kind, but standards must be upheld. And the public should respect that the Brown Bakers' Guild was doing its part to ensure the quality of their food.

A baker should accept his punishment in silence, retaining as much dignity as possible. Unfortunately, bakers were, by nature, a robust lot. Hefting five-stone bags of flour and working in front of hot ovens made them physically strong, and they were not afraid to speak their minds. Such was the case with Tom Pate, yowling and cursing all the way.

Croft plopped the dough on a set of scales near his oven. He knew the weight of unbaked dough that would bake into a perfect standard loaf. Rather than weigh the bread after baking, he preferred this method.

After the punishments had been dispensed, there was more discussion regarding the sorry state of the guild's treasury, caused by the increased demand for white bread. . . .

"Physicians tout refined flour as being more healthful," said Under Warden Morys—a man with a straw cornucopia for an ear. He'd lost

the real one snooping where he should not. "*The merchants and nobility cry for more manchets.*"

"*Manchets? One must eat twenty to sate an appetite. What is the sense in that?*" *the second warden asked.*

"*Think they the little loaves look dainty on their tables,*" *responded Morys.*

Croft dug his fingers into the dough and ripped off a piece to adjust its weight on the scale.

"*What more shall I do?*" *he had asked.* "*I've sent an army of officers to enforce the standards. The fines they've collected have helped cover the king's latest taxes. It has helped to a point. . . .*"

No one disputed that the real problem lay in the dwindling demand for brown bread. Croft stared at the scale, then snatched the dough off and began rigorously working it again.

William Pents. Master of the White Bakers' Guild and, in James Croft's mind, a traitor. Croft took the wad of dough by one end and smacked it on the board.

The discussion at Halimote had centered on the white bread bakers' efforts to ruin the brown bread bakers. When Third Warden Jones had reported that the White Bakers' Guild was giving their boulted (the finely sifted flour) to sanctioned bakeries, no one believed him.

"*One cannot make money giving away flour!*" *Croft argued.*

"*Nay,*" *said Jones.* "*The White Bakers' Guild will win the favor of sanctioned bakeries all over London. They give away their flour, and when the bakeries are accustomed and glad to work with it, they will begin to collect their cost. At first they will collect a little less for their flour than we would collect. Then, over time . . .*"

"*Over time, when we are gone—having been put out of our livelihood by them . . .*"

"*They will raise their price. A clever, wheedlesome plan.*"

Croft rounded the loaf and put it aside to rise. He dunked a cloth in a bowl of water left for his dog and laid it on top of the dough. A cup of Spanish sack was his reward.

Peeved that his own parish church might have been lured into this despicable scheme, he had visited St. Vedast to find out if they had been deceived by Pents's plan. Churchwarden Lodge had been uncooperative.

"Fool," he said aloud. "How dare they indulge Pents and the white bakers?" He guzzled down his drink and wiped his lips on the back of his hand, getting a mouthful of flour. Croft wiped his hands on his apron.

The churchwarden had declined to tell him who baked their hosts, as if it were a badge of honor to keep it a secret. "Well, you only made it slightly less convenient for me," said Croft, pouring himself more sack.

It was his good fortune that, as he was leaving church, a delivery boy from the sanctioned bakery had been arriving. When asked from where he hailed, the lad had no qualms telling him. He smiled, wondering if Lodge realized his secret had been discovered.

"Lodge, you are a clay-brained fustilarian," said Croft to his cup. "Goldsmiths are a pompous group of thieves."

Croft cleaned his board of excess flour, sweeping it into a bowl to be used later. His frustration with the tight-lipped Henry Lodge had been further aggravated when Father Nelson arrived at the guild to try to smooth over bruised feelings on the matter.

Croft had not gone so far as to insult the priest to his face, but he'd explained to the man the consequences of accepting hosts made from boulted flour. "You think you are sparing St. Vedast an expense by accepting your hosts gratis," he had told Father Nelson. "But you indulge the white bakers' plan to ruin us—our brother bakers! Once we are gone, they are free to set a price to whatever they want."

At first, Father Nelson had been dismissive of his dire prediction. "The king will not allow it. There shall always be a need for brown bakers. Not everyone can afford the luxury of white bread. You have no cause to worry." But after Croft threatened to leave the parish and take his support elsewhere, Father Nelson and he had come to terms. He had convinced Father Nelson of his cause.

* * *

Croft checked the dough and was pleased with its rise. Its surface yielded to his finger poke. Baking bread soothed his ragged nerves. It had been a difficult day defending the best interests of the Brown Bakers' Guild. He tucked the corners of the cloth over the lump of dough as he would tuck a babe in a crib.

CHAPTER 10

A dog yapped inside Odile Farendon's residence on Mayden Lane. In a moment, the door yawned open, revealing Boisvert holding a squirmy spaniel against his chest. *"Bonjour,* Bianca. *Entrez."* He stepped aside, allowing her to pass, and shushed the creature into behaving.

"Odile is expecting you." He led her to an elegant chamber where the heiress sat near a brazier, embroidering. Colorful tapestries of greyhounds and hunters hung on one wall beside leaded-glass windows coated with frost. Because the room faced north, candlelight lacquered the walls in a warm, golden glow.

"Bianca," she said, looking up at their entrance. She laid down her stitching. "Come in, my dear. I've a gown for you. I am certain you will find it to your liking." She reached for Bianca's hand and led her to a walnut armoire carved in relief with a fleur-de-lis pattern. Bianca knew Odile meant well but found it presumptuous that she would assume to know Bianca's taste. It was not that any particular fashion pleased Bianca more than another, but more that she never thought about gowns and French hoods, velvet or taffeta, pearl beads, pinked sleeves, and stuffing. Such apparel was above her station and she did not bother to dream of entering that world.

Odile threw open the armoire door and riffled through several gowns, producing a carmine one of velvet with oversleeves in amber brocade. The center foreskirt was of the same contrasting material. A bodice of solid carmine velvet was worked with pearl beads into a delicate floral pattern. White coney fur trimmed the squared neckline.

Bianca had never laid eyes on such an elaborate gown.

"This is too fine for me," she said, unable to take her eyes off it.

"It is not," responded Odile. "You have youth on your side, my dear. Why not indulge when you are given the opportunity?"

"It is not my place to dress above myself."

"This is a gift to you. What harm could possibly come from dressing well? I have invited you to our wedding, and I expect you to be presentable." Odile held out the sleeve and put it next to Bianca's face. "*Oui*," she said. "It complements your pale complexion. If your skin were pink, it would not suit you." Odile smiled. "*Mais ces yeux . . .*" her voice trailed off. "You will accept this." She thrust the gown into Bianca's arms, then turned, dismissing any argument that sat on Bianca's tongue.

It was simpler to just accept Odile Farendon's gift. "I shall try to prove myself worthy."

"There is nothing to prove," said Odile with an air of finality. "Come, I want you to accompany me. Oro Tand is expecting me."

It was a short stroll to the Goldsmiths' Hall, home to the fraternity of both gold and silver artisans. The two women entered the building, a magnificent stone structure built in the style of a Roman temple. A liveryman took them up a lengthy staircase to await Master Tand's arrival.

Bianca sat in a heavily carved, cushioned chair near a hearth. She studied the surroundings, another richly appointed chamber, similar to Odile's, but on a grander scale. Odile settled next to her and folded her hands in her lap.

"Bianca, dear, you are quiet, but your eyes tell me you have much to say."

"Madame Farendon, I am simply not accustomed to these environs."

"If John becomes a liveryman, this will no longer be a novelty."

"Truth be told, I had not given it much thought."

"I sense a slight hesitation in your voice."

Bianca did not want to respond. Cavorting with men of wealth and their wives was nothing she had ever aspired to. She supposed that they were not unlike commoners in that they loved and laughed, endured life's disappointments and joys. But she supposed they did not concern themselves with matters that she found important. How many silversmiths' wives would know what an alembic was, much less know what to do with one?

Odile Farendon gave Bianca a knowing sidelong glance. "I understand you have an interest in the noble art."

Bianca flared at the term and could not keep quiet. "When one says 'the noble art,' one is referring to alchemy. Alchemy is not my interest."

"*Non?*" said Odile, unaware that she had veered into dangerous waters. "John tells me you make potions."

Bianca clamped her mouth tight and waited until the innocent barb had lost its prick. "I do not call them potions, my lady."

"Well, what you call them is of no importance to me," Odile said curtly. "We all have our little amusements."

The door swung open, and Oro Tand crossed the room without so much as a glance at either of them. "Madame Farendon," he said, bowing, finally making eye contact with the widow. He settled in his chair, his rings and the gold chain of office around his neck glittering in the firelight. He looked suspiciously at Bianca through hazel eyes beneath half-lowered lids.

"Master Tand," said Odile. "This is Bianca. Her husband is an apprentice to Boisvert. I have asked her to accompany me today."

His gaze stuttered over Bianca's common kirtle, and there was no mistaking what he thought of it and, by association, Bianca.

Without acknowledging Odile's way of introduction, he turned back to the widow. "We will be able to seat one hundred guests," he said. "Some of the food preparations have already begun. If you would like to see the hall, it is being prepared for the celebration."

Bianca noted Tand's terse, almost forced manner. She thought he must not like Odile Farendon, or perhaps he did not like something about the impending event. Odile took no notice. Or perhaps she did not care. The heiress explained how she wanted the courses presented and when. It was almost as if she expected a legion of Frenchmen to come and take over the preparation and serving. Oro Tand listened without comment, and when Madame Farendon stopped to breathe, he broke in.

"Most assuredly, the details will be attended to. Now," he said, rising from his chair, "you may visit the dining hall and take up matters with the steward, but I am unable to escort you." He gestured toward the door, and Odile and Bianca stood. Again Oro Tand nodded to Madame Farendon and ignored Bianca.

Once the door clicked shut behind them, Odile straightened her cape at the neck. "We are left on our own."

The two descended the great stair, passing portraits of former masters of the Company. Odile stopped, at eye level with a painting of one in particular. The silk sash of red and white draped across the master's chest and his proud posture told more about the man than the engraved plaque hanging beside him. The widow lifted her chin. "My dead husband," she said, still gazing at his portrait. She offered no more comment.

At the bottom of the stairs, Odile crossed the open entry hall toward a set of tall walnut doors. Bianca scurried ahead of her and opened them for the widow to enter. It was a high-ceilinged room with long tables rimming the perimeter. The rows of silver plates and goblets reflected a rare cloud break as sunlight entered from expansive arched windows. On the head table sat a silver urn filled with evergreen and holly, from which hung delicate silver cast icicles. Tiered holders awaited their candles, and Bianca could imagine the magical bounce of light off the polished silver surfaces. Odile ran her fingers lightly over the place settings as she strolled toward the head table. A few feet away she stopped to admire it.

"What say you?" she said, her eyes fixed on the table.

"I think I shall never see a more beautiful celebration."

"It is lovely, is it not?" Odile turned to Bianca, and the two of them gazed at the room with quiet awe. "I've spent my entire life hoping for the day when I would feel true happiness." Odile smiled ruefully. "I did not expect my life to be nearly over before finding it."

"My lady, you have many happy years ahead of you," said Bianca. "You and Boisvert have much to look forward to."

Odile looked up at the sun streaming through the windows, at the dust motes dancing in the light. "I suppose it is all in order. I see no fault with their preparations. Shall we leave?"

As the pair made their way toward the entrance, they heard Oro Tand in loud discussion. They did not have to guess what the conversation was about. Two men in luxurious dress stood by; their taste in fabric and colors bespoke men well traveled and with an eye for fashion. Haberdashers. No other men dressed in cloth so richly dyed as to veer toward imperial purple—His Majesty's right alone. Their gowns were lined in imported fur the likes of which Bianca had never seen.

These men were about appearance—and flaunting it.

"Sir, the lane is not solely our concern," said the one with a perfectly trimmed beard and a doublet of leather elaborately constructed and stitched. "It is the responsibility of all who ply their trade upon it. We are three of the highest-ranked guilds, and as such we should uphold the standards for our trades as well as keep our address desirable. I challenge you to name a more riddled road in all of London."

"There is St. Peter's Hill," said Tand without hesitation.

The leather-clad haberdasher tilted his head. "Besides that."

"It does you no benefit to press me, gentlemen. Our guild hasn't the funds to contribute."

The second haberdasher, dressed in an indigo gown furred

with marten, looked incredulous. "I find that difficult to imagine," said he, gazing around the fine interior of the guildhall. His eyes dropped to the Turkey carpet on which they stood, and he took a step back, spreading his arms to present his proof. "Here lies some wealth. Sell a few rugs and you will not miss the cushion beneath your feet. A small sacrifice so that the king does not regard your guild unfavorably."

"It is not for me to make that decision."

"Bring it forward for discussion," ordered the first haberdasher. Loath was he to treat the Gold Guild with more respect.

The second visitor did not wait for Master Tand to reply. "The king will process down Foster Lane near the end of the month, the fifth day of Christmas. If the carrier should stumble into a rut and His Majesty tumbles out, shall I inform him the Gold Guild did not see fit to invest in repairing the road for him?"

"And if that should happen when the king is in a black humor?" prodded the haberdasher with the impeccably trimmed beard. "Sir, I should not want to be you."

Odile and Bianca kept a respectful distance to allow the men to finish. Oro Tand noticed them and grew more wooden. "Gentlemen, I shall bring the matter forward at our next council. Perhaps someone may have a suggestion for raising adequate funds." He left the haberdashers gaping after him and stalked past Bianca and Odile as if they were not there.

"Madame Farendon," said the haberdasher in the exotical furred gown. "My congratulations on your upcoming marriage."

His companion bowed respectfully. "Like your late husband, your betrothed has excellent taste in women."

"Lionel never would have shirked the guild's responsibility for the common good," said the first. "The Goldsmiths' Company was in better hands when he was master."

Odile listened graciously, a thin smile tacked on her face.

Back at the Mayden Lane residence, Boisvert was juggling a flurry of deliveries. While he was allowing in two men hefting a crate of French wine between them, Odile's wedding cloak arrived. Nico, her spaniel, was in a frenzy, yapping at the man who delivered it and nipping at the fox-fur lining.

At the sight of Odile, Boisvert swiped the frantic canine off the floor and deposited him in her arms. "Do something with this creature," he said, "before I go mad." He took the cloak and started down the hall, calling for a servant, but Odile called him back after answering another knock at the door. "*Il est de la guilde d'or.*"

A young apprentice from the Goldsmiths' Company presented Odile with a beautifully carved box. "On behalf of the brotherhood," he said, bowing solicitously.

The two deliverymen, having deposited the wine, sidled past while Odile handed Nico to Boisvert, which pleased neither dog nor man. The spaniel squirmed free and started another round of hysterical barking.

Not wishing to be underfoot, Bianca made overtures to leave.

"Bianca, you mustn't leave without your gown," said Odile, reaching for her arm and summoning a maid in French.

The young man from the Gold Guild accepted Odile's compliments on the intricate design and elaborately cast clasp with inlaid garnets. She had opened the box and was admonishing Nico when her maid arrived carrying Bianca's gown. Odile looked up. "*Donnez-le lui,*" she said, tipping her head toward Bianca. The servant passed the gown over to Bianca in front of Odile just as she reached into the box. "*Mon Dieu! Je me suis piqué!*" She withdrew her pricked finger and put it in her mouth. "It is lovely but dangerous." She held open the box for Boisvert, who withdrew a gold filigree ouche with a center stone of cut peridot.

"To match your lively green eyes, my lady," said the apprentice.

Boisvert's brows danced as he examined the piece with a keen eye, then returned it to the box. "Shall you wear it at our wedding?"

Bianca stretched her neck to look at the brooch. The question was barely out of Boisvert's mouth when another knock came at the door. Another delivery of wine was ushered in. Behind these carters stood a young boy.

"Madame Farendon," said the lad, bowing. He held up a pax loaf wrapped in fine cloth. "Partake of this until you are wed, keeping the Heavenly Father in your heart and prayers."

Odile accepted the gift and crossed herself. "Thank Father Nelson for his concern."

"He has asked that I remind you of your appointment."

"*Oui*, of course," said Odile. She covered the bread with the cloth. "I shall be there."

Bianca folded the dress twice over in order to keep it from dragging on the ground. "Odile, I shall see you anon. The next time we speak you shall be Odile Boisvert."

For a second Odile seemed astonished at the realization of it. "*C'est vrai.* I have been widowed so long that it will be strange."

Boisvert returned the brooch to the box. He took Odile's finger from her mouth and pressed it to his lips to kiss. "Our marriage is a change of mutual choice, *mon ami*. This happiness would not have happened by chance."

Bianca observed Boisvert's display of affection. She was momentarily surprised by the Frenchman's overt adoration for his bride. She had never doubted the silversmith's regard for John or, for that matter, herself, but he never spoke of his affection—it was simply understood. Boisvert saved his emotions for complaining about "*les rosbiffs*," as he tartly preferred to call his British peers.

As Bianca bid them well, yet another man appeared at the door to deliver a beaded headpiece. It was time for Bianca to wander home and run her cheek against the soft fur collar of her dress—while no one was looking.

CHAPTER 11

In the area of Middle Temple, there was a not-so-important building that stood in the majestic shadow of its esteemed counterpart. And in the less important building sat a less important solicitor. Try as he might, Benjamin Cornish would never garner the respect given a barrister. He had given up sitting for entrance to the Inns of Court. He would never be admitted into that exclusive club of erudite thinkers.

He could have accepted his lesser title and done a respectable business preparing briefs and property transfers, drafting wills . . . if respect was all that he wanted, but the man had just enough intelligence to realize what he was missing.

Benjamin Cornish, solicitor and snout-fair swigman of writs, sat in his heavily paneled office. Before him was the wealthy widow Odile Durand Farendon and her fat Frenchman fiancé, Boisvert. An embering hearth warmed the widow's delicately lined face so that her skin looked dewy in its ambient glow. However, the light did not favor Boisvert's sallow skin, and he looked jaundiced at best.

Cornish sat back in his finely upholstered chair, which was

stuffed with horsehair to cradle his perfectly formed buttocks. A lawyer spent much of his day on his arse, and the importance of a comfortable chair could not be emphasized enough. This chair, however, had seen its master sit through countless interviews, contracts, and letters, so that now a hole had been worn in the tapestry, and a nail—which should have been bent over, then padded—poked out, reminding him that he must get it repaired before his tender man parts were effectively skewered.

"Madame Farendon," Cornish began. "Thirteen years ago, you contested your late husband's will. The king decided in your favor and you've enjoyed a sizable estate for the maintenance of your person."

"Monsieur Cornish, I am not here to discuss what was decided years ago. I wish to make out my last will and testament."

"It is usually not done until one's imminent demise."

"And what if I should die before I expect to? I wish to leave St. Vedast an endowment upon my death, and I want to be sure that nothing will prevent it."

"I am certain your betrothed would see to the matter if that should happen. He must be of an agreeable mind, or else you would not marry him?" Cornish shot Boisvert a look—though a skeptical one.

Odile's face grew pink. "I am capable of handling my own affairs. I have successfully done so for twelve years. My former husband took care of his soul and did not care what happened to me once he quit this world. St. Botolph received a significant sum to say his obiits. The chancel priest has been happily praying for him for twelve years with those funds, and I expect he'll ring the bell for another twenty. Certainly that is plenty of time for a decision to be made regarding his soul."

"We cannot assume to know God's timetable," replied Cornish.

"Every anniversary of my late husband's death I am reminded of the bastard by the dissonant clang of his chantry bells. I see no peace from the man for as long as I shall live."

Benjamin Cornish's chin dropped. "Madame Farendon, your vitriol is unbecoming of a woman of your position. If you fear for your soul, such vocal disparagement is ill-advised."

"And does our Lord care what I say about a man who loved me not? Is it not better to say what I think? We are told that God prefers an honest heart over a deceptive one. After all, He does know all. He knows my mind, and even yours."

"For cert He is all-seeing and all-knowing."

"Clip your tongue if you like. Lawyers are practiced in the art of that, but I am not so inclined."

Disquieted by Odile's candor, Boisvert intervened. "Monsieur Cornish, this subject is *très difficile* for Odile. You'll excuse her state *émotionnel*." He took Odile's hand in his. "*Mais* you must understand that she wishes for her soul the same treatment that her husband secured for his."

"Certainly," said Benjamin Cornish, leaning forward in his chair and flinching a little at doing so. To his knowledge, most funds for obiits had been seized by the king and his Court of Augmentations—but a few wealthy patrons, mostly slow to embrace the king's religious supremacy, still wanted their souls spared the unpleasant tortures of a prolonged purgatory. And who was he to deny them? Obiits were quickly becoming a charming vestige of an earlier time, and loath was he to inform or even remind them of their futility. Who doesn't want to save their soul? He expected the funds would end in the king's coffers, but if Odile Farendon did not mention it, he certainly was not going to. Besides, the fee he'd collect for recording her will would go a long way toward reupholstering his favorite chair.

"I shall write your will and testament and file it with the Commissary Court, Madame Farendon." Cornish dipped a quill into a pot of ink, poised to begin. "Now, if you will inform me of your wishes."

Odile made allowances for the care and feeding of her soul. A substantial sum would go to St. Vedast, her beloved parish church.

She also stipulated an inheritance for Boisvert in the event she should predecease him. The balance of her effects would go to the poor.

"You have made no mention of the Worshipful Company of Goldsmiths." Cornish thought he should mention it. Her late husband was once master, and certainly Boisvert was a member of the esteemed guild. The concession would go a long way in smoothing over past grievances between them.

"*Non.* I shall not give money to a group of men who would use it to replenish their supply of Bordeaux."

"Your late husband was a respected leader of the guild. Your wealth is in some part due to his association with them."

"You are speaking once again of a matter that was settled years ago. If it was not in the guild's heart to care for me, a member's widow, then why should it be in mine to leave them a farthing? I had no choice but to contest my late husband's will, or I would have been left destitute."

They locked eyes like two circling cats.

Odile was not finished. "I understand, Monsieur Cornish, that you might yet represent some members of the guild, but I will remind you that I am here as your client, and it is your duty to serve my interest. You know my history. You know my connections. Do not assume that time has diminished those contacts. I could have gone elsewhere, but I chose you because of your familiarity with my situation."

Boisvert slid Cornish's fee across the table.

The lawyer resisted pouncing on the offered coins. He would have accepted half the fee now and half upon the delivery of the signed papers to the Commissary Court. But his clients were foreigners, and Frenchmen at that. They were trusting and naïve in a country of men blessed with superior wit. "I shall draw up the papers tonight, and you can pay me the other half when you sign them tomorrow."

"We've paid you your fee, trusting you'll take care of this," said Odile.

"Oh." The lawyer laughed—unconvincingly. "I see you have paid me in full."

Odile and Boisvert stared until the smile disappeared from his face.

"Well, Monsieur Cornish," said Odile, "I am grateful for your time. My conscience is at peace." She placed her grip on the chair's armrests, and as she rose her left hand clenched like the end of a shepherd's hook. She cried out in pain from the unexpected spasm.

Boisvert sprang to his feet. "*Ma chérie!*"

Odile's shoulder met her ear. Her body began to tremble, and she looked down in horror at her hand as it tightened like an eagle's claw.

Benjamin Cornish watched Odile Farendon's pleasing features twist into a harpy's. Nay, not a harpy, thought he; her countenance looked more diabolical. An evil look splayed across her face, and her eyes were glazed and vacant.

Boisvert gripped his beloved's arm as her body continued to shake. She was rattling in a half stance. With effort, he managed to ease her back into the chair.

Cornish hurried to a cabinet and poured a cup of wine. He glanced at the widow, drank it down, then poured another for Odile. Boisvert put the vessel against her lips and tipped the cup against her mouth. Perhaps a bit trickled down her throat, but her jaw was clenched and a large portion of the wine soaked her neckline.

"Is the lady prone to these episodes?" Cornish asked. He had once seen something similar. A woman brought to court for casting evil on the owner of the Dew Drop Inn began trembling so violently that she fell to the ground. She wallowed about, frothing at the mouth. He wondered if Odile Farendon suffered from the same malady. But her tremors were not so severe. Odile remained seated, and she did not drool like the accused woman had.

Then, as suddenly as the spasms began, they ceased. Odile Farendon calmed. Her contorted face smoothed, and now she merely looked confused.

"I have never seen this," said Boisvert. "I have known her for some time."

"Methinks your betrothed has not told you all of her secrets."

Boisvert straightened and faced the solicitor. "*Monsieur,* I have pledged my love to Odile. I will not renege on my promise to marry her."

Benjamin Cornish pitied the fool the way one might look upon a dog with three legs. What sort of life would the man have if he had to worry about his wife behaving thus? His advice, if the proud toad were to ask for it, would be to postpone their nuptials, indefinitely if need be. How difficult was it for a man to fall out of love with a woman? Not for all the money in the king's coffers would he, Benjamin Cornish, expose himself to such unpredictable public humiliation. But, of course, he was not Boisvert. Nor did he know the mind of any Frenchman—thank providence for small favors.

However, the lawyer was now faced with a bit of a conundrum. Was Odile of sound mind? Her testament could be called into question. Cornish tipped the bottle of wine to his lips and had another drink. For now, he would take the fee and write the will.

But Cornish could not erase the sardonic smile on his face as he watched Boisvert speak soothingly to his beloved. The French could call you a greasy quat-sucking rascal in their flouncy tongue, and you would smile, thinking it a compliment.

Eventually, Odile regained her strong carriage. She blinked out of her stupor and had no memory of her peculiar outburst. "Stop fretting over me," she admonished Boisvert, pulling her hand out of his grip.

Baffled by her quick recovery, the silversmith posed no further argument. His face flushed with embarrassment as Odile got to her feet as if nothing happened.

"I believe our business here is *fini*. Come, *mon prince*," said she.

Benjamin Cornish followed the couple to his office door, discussing their return to sign the will and testament the next morning. "God keep you, Madame Farendon." He nodded to Boisvert, marshaling what little respect he could for the man.

Outside the door, they acknowledged Oro Tand, who was waiting on a bench.

Cornish watched until they were far enough away not to hear, then motioned the master goldsmith into his office. "A marriage made in haste is seldom proof of love."

Oro Tand smiled. "I most certainly agree, my friend."

CHAPTER 12

Flaked and faded lettering made it difficult to determine if this was Foley's bakery. James Croft's nose grazed the sign as he squinted at the remaining letters. After a moment he decided he had arrived at the sanctioned bakery that made St. Vedast's hosts. With him was Third Warden Austin Jones. Over Jones's shoulder hung a set of scales, clanging wildly, a cumbersome burden.

According to the guild records, Foley had been inspected the month before. But Master Croft wanted to dissuade the baker from using white flour. And if Foley refused, Croft had the threat of inspection to help persuade him. He could easily find an infraction and impose some sort of penalty. These hypocrites must be scotched, and he had to start somewhere. Victory was best gotten by vigilance. And vigilance was best achieved when there was an element of surprise.

They did not rap on the door and politely wait for Foley or his apprentice to open. Much can be hidden in the time it takes to answer a knock. Instead, Croft directed his third warden to try the door, and they entered unannounced. It was their right as inspectors to interrupt a shop's business whenever they wanted to, for the purpose of ensuring the quality of a product that bore the guild's coveted stamp.

No one came round to greet them. A few loaves of standard brown bread lined the top shelves. They caught a fading whiff of resting dough. But there was no one to startle. No one to register a look of panic that accompanied the realization that the bakery was going to be inspected without warning.

Disappointed, Master Croft called out. In a moment, the baker appeared from the back carrying a tray of perfectly baked manchets. He glanced at Master Croft and Third Warden Jones before sliding the contraband into a grooved rack to cool.

"How now, Master Croft, Jones?"

Croft, irked at the sight of Foley's perky little buns, could barely contain his disdain. "I shall say 'how' after we conduct our inspection."

"It has not been a month since last we were scrutinized. Your officer found no evidence of misconduct." Foley folded his brawny arms across his chest.

"We are redoubling our efforts," said Croft petulantly. "Take me to your kitchen."

Foley stared back at the master of his guild. "Very well," he said after a moment. His arms stayed crossed as he led Croft and the third warden to his back kitchen.

The room was a spacious workplace, with several windows allowing for light and the escape of heat. An oven with a large capacity made even Croft's tightly clenched jaw loosen in awe. Neat piles of flour waited to be swept away by the apprentice's broom, and the tables had been wiped down. A few loaves cooled nearby on a tray. It was these Master Croft directed his companion to weigh.

Jones set the scales on the most level area of a workbench and removed his weights, lining them up on the board.

Croft watched irritably as the warden weighed one of the loaves. "I see you are baking manchets," he said to Foley.

"Obviously I am. They are in great demand. I cannot make enough."

"So it is a profitable venture."

"That it is!" said Foley.

"It is standard," announced Jones. He removed the loaf from the scales and got another.

James Croft eyed the loaves, looking for one that might be underweight. "Weigh this one," he said, grabbing a loaf and thrusting it at the warden. "And where do you buy your flour?" Croft glanced at Foley but keenly watched his warden balance the weights. There was no room for error here.

"Some I purchase through a miller north of town. The boulted flour I do not buy. It is gifted."

"Gifted," said Croft, seizing the word. "And how long shall you receive this flour?"

The baker shrugged, unconcerned. "For now I am baking wafers. If I have leftover flour, I bake manchets. They sell well."

"No miller can benefit from this."

"It is not the miller who gives me the flour."

"Ah! Then it is Pents?" said Croft, unable to control a rise in his voice.

"It is standard," said Jones, removing the loaf. He wrote down the weight.

Croft ran his eyes around the kitchen. "Where are your books?" he demanded.

Foley answered in a weary voice. "Master Croft, they are out front."

"Well, get them!"

The baker sighed. He strolled off, and Croft stalked toward the bins of flour, lifting a lid to peer inside one. "Weigh every loaf. I want a thorough accounting of Foley's business."

The master looked into the bin of wheaten flour, a mixture of boulted wheat and, from the looks and texture of it, barley. In a sense, one canceled the other. The sifted wheat was so fine as to be considered "white" by comparison. Barley and rye were for peasants and other inconsequential sorts. Over the years, "brown flour" had grown coarser, and many bakers added ground acorns, dried peas, even sand, to extend a bushel. The practice offset the

increased cost of flour caused by the growing demand for the
"white" ingredient. Croft took a pinch of flour and let it dissolve
on his tongue. Any sand or grit would remain.

Foley returned, toting two hefty logbooks.

"Here, Master Croft." He dropped them on the table next to
the scales, purposely jarring the instrument and disrupting the
perfect line of weights. Jones steadied the scales, then chased
after the rolling weights.

Croft slammed down the lid on the bin and crossed the room.
He threw open the cover of the top logbook, rustling through the
pages. Finding the accounting of the past week, he ran a finger
down a page to the latest entry.

"It says you received one bushel of white flour from Barrett. I
happen to know Barrett is a grain dealer who sometimes works
with Pents, master of the White Bakers' Guild."

Foley neither confirmed nor denied Croft's claim.

"My question to you, Foley—where is your allegiance?"

"Why should a man refuse a gift when it is offered? To do so is
throwing good coin in the river."

"Because you harm the greater good. By accepting flour from
Pents, you turn your back on the brotherhood."

"So you believe. But you cannot deny the increasing demand
for boulted flour. Even physicians believe it is more healthful. If
that is so, and I have heard many most wondrous claims proving
that it is, then all of these inspections that you conjure to punish
us are useless in stopping bakers from pleasing the people. It is
only a matter of time, Master Croft. The Brown Bakers will be
swallowed by the White."

James Croft could scarce believe the man's insolence. For a
second he was at a loss for words. How dare he speak with such
unbridled disdain to the master of his guild? He could have
baker Foley put in the pillory. He had Jones as a witness. Croft
looked over at the third warden, who was intently weighing and
recording the available loaves, oblivious. Had he even heard this
man's impertinent blathering?

"Foley, remember to whom you speak."

"I know well what I say and to whom I am saying it."

The man stood a full head taller and weighed at least three stone more than Croft. Unable to intimidate by size or rank, Croft impatiently waited for Jones to record the findings. He fervently wished for an underweight loaf so he could drag the man before Halimote. That would put an end to the baker's self-righteous opinion of himself.

"Master Croft," said the third warden. "I am done with these loaves. They meet the standard assize." He brought the ledger over for his master to examine.

James Croft barely glanced at the findings. He tugged on his doublet beneath his gown and put on his cap. "Next time, see that your scale is properly calibrated." He stormed out the door, leaving Jones to collect his scale and weights.

Henry Lodge stared at the bell of St. Vedast. Finished with calling the parishioners to mass, the sexton disappeared down the ladder of the belfry, leaving the churchwarden alone in the tower. Lodge had asked the sexton to gingercoddle the rope and leave off his customary vigor when pulling it. But once the bell began clanging, the servant's enthusiasm grew and he ignored the churchwarden's shouts to stop. The vibrations from the massive bell still hummed in Lodge's ears as he walked around the platform inspecting the rigging. To his eye, the crack remained about the same; in a word—worrisome.

Other churches had scrapped their chimes to pay the king's taxes. What once was used to call men to prayer was recast into cannons that maimed and killed. Lodge did not want to see St. Vedast's bell suffer a similar fate. Still, with no money to repair the bell's axle, the fissure would continue to grow.

Father Nelson placed his faith in God, as should any servant of the Lord. But to ignore the obvious, to ignore Lodge's warning, showed a distressing lack of concern for the well-being of his church and its parishioners. What if the bell broke loose and crashed through the nave during mass? Such an incident would end Father Nelson's tenure. It might even end his life. Lodge gazed down at the floor, dizzyingly far below. Perhaps he should insist that Father Nelson accompany him to the tower so he could show him the troublesome crack.

Lodge pulled his fur-lined gown closed to the chill of the tower and went to the embrasure overlooking the roof. He leaned out to see the ground in the side yard and thought of the woman found with her head crushed, and he crossed himself.

The wind blew through the tower; a crisp beech leaf rode its swirling tempest to the structure's pinnacle, then floated down to the platform to rest by his feet. With the toe of his boot, he ground the dried leaf into a floor plank.

Henry Lodge climbed down the belfry ladder and descended to the ground floor, his steps tapping in the hollow stone stairwell. He stood in the back of the nave, listening to Father Nelson's liturgy. A man and woman standing at the rear of the congregation slipped behind a column, and the woman slipped her hand down the man's hose.

Perhaps they sought a silent ecstasy beyond the word of God. Lodge watched, wondering if anyone else noticed them. No one did. Or rather, no one seemed to care.

He abandoned Father Nelson to his congregation of sinners and decided to work on the inventory. Working without the priest to interrupt suited the churchwarden. He wished to avoid another conversation like the last.

Lodge removed his gown and laid it aside, retrieved the church ledger, and opened the garderobe of vestments. He counted the robes, remembering Father Nelson's attire, and recorded his findings. Altar sticks and candles were also counted, reminding him that resources should be directed to Master Nimble for additional tapers. The wafers had been recently delivered, and he moved them to storage, placing them next to the wine.

He was thumbing through the altar cloths and linen, when the sound of rustling material distracted him.

"Good day, Henry," said Odile Farendon when he turned. She stood in the door dressed in a fur cloak and a hat of ermine that softened the edge of her face. The cold had rouged her cheeks, so that for a second he saw her as she had been in her youth. His breath caught in his throat.

"I am here to see Father Nelson." She took a tentative step toward him, then, as if remembering the day before, stopped. She watched him as if he were a skittish squirrel. One sudden move and he might run.

Lodge could not bear to be treated so. He lifted his chin, managing the bare minimum of cordiality. "You may wait for him," he said, gesturing to a bench. "Mass will be over soon."

Odile hesitated, then crossed the room to sit. As she did, Lodge noticed a limp in her gait. She settled and met his stare. "Why do you look on me so?"

The churchwarden flushed but did not let it stop him from asking, "Have you hurt your foot?"

It was Odile's turn to warm with awkwardness. "I have some stiffness of late. Perhaps I am not so young as I once was."

The memories of a time when she attended Anne Boleyn came flooding back. "Indeed, as we both once were," said Henry Lodge. He silently cursed himself. He'd spent too many years trying to forget Odile Durand to indulge his memories about a past that was wasted and a future that would never be. When she had accepted Lionel Farendon's marriage proposal, Lodge had realized that the depth of his love had never been matched by that of hers. She'd married for money. She'd married for prestige. She'd married for safety.

Odile smiled. "I am told you created the ouche from the Goldsmiths' Company. I've never seen a more beautiful piece."

Lodge did not respond, though he was pleased she recognized his exceptional skill.

Her eyes held him with a familiarity that pained his heart. Her smile flickered uncertainly. "Years glide away and are lost forever."

He resisted telling her that he cared not a mote that she would end her life marrying a stranger brother. She was making a mistake marrying the French silversmith, a man who would always be less than an Englishman.

"Time steals our youth and our joys," he said. His bitterness bled like rust in water. "And leaves us with age and dirt."

Their eyes met in silent understanding. Odile said, "I regret that time has not smoothed the rift between us."

"It has not, Odile Durand."

With a curt bow, Henry Lodge left the widow sitting on the bench. His duty done, he wished to occupy himself with matters having nothing to do with St. Vedast or Odile Farendon.

CHAPTER 13

"The great whore wore yellow and black to her wedding also. It was a double celebration with Catherine of Aragon's death, was it not?" said Oro Tand, eyeing the bride as she and Boisvert appeared at the back of the church.

"That is true," answered Henry Lodge.

"How appropriate."

Tand's words and priggish smile were not lost on Bianca, who was standing directly behind the two goldsmiths. She exchanged looks with John.

"The French do have a flair for the dramatic," added Tand. "And their women have no taste in men."

Lodge stood a little taller. "I heartily agree. Odile has chosen particularly poorly . . . again."

Odile looked resplendent in a yellow velvet gown with oversleeves of black brocade. A gold necklace shimmered at her throat. The ouche she'd received from the Gold Guild was pinned on her bodice. Her proud bearing, her relaxed face, contrasted with a hitch in her step as she and her betrothed walked toward the altar, her hand resting easily on top of Boisvert's.

The silversmith wore a black velvet doublet with black satin pinking and a gown trimmed in gray otter. But more noticeable than his handsome garb was the unpersuasive grin on his face. Perhaps he was uncertain of his decision. The commitment to marry was more responsibility than he had ever undertaken before.

With the excitement of Boisvert's wedding, Bianca put aside her thoughts of the unfortunate death only three days before and focused on the celebration at hand. She and John were nearly unrecognizable in their elegant garb. A French hood perched on Bianca's head, adorned with beaded biliments to match the brocade of the forepart of her gown. Her wavy locks bulged under the silk veil, as she did not have the skill or patience to successfully plait her hair to flatten it, nor did she have enough pins to keep the hood firmly in place. John wore a borrowed doublet of russet brown, simple, but acceptable to the occasion. It fit him well enough so that one might actually think it belonged to him—except the sleeves were too short.

Arriving at the front of the nave, the widow Odile Farendon and silversmith Boisvert were greeted by Father Nelson, and their ceremony began. It didn't take long for Bianca to grow bored. She soon relaxed in her new attire to almost look as though she belonged there. As the youngest attendees, John and Bianca drew the curious stares of more than a few.

The bride and groom stated their consent, but the ritual of matrimony was a tedious affair. John tugged impatiently at his doublet sleeves, which ended just above his wrists, exposing a graceless expanse of white smock beneath. Folding back the cuff of the smock exaggerated the poor fit, and in frustration John decided there was nothing he could do to remedy the fashion misstep. He might have gone on fiddling with his sleeves and cuffs if a noise hadn't disturbed his preoccupation.

"*Mon Dieu!*" exclaimed Boisvert.

The gathered began to whisper.

"The ring will not go on her finger," murmured Henry Lodge.

"Shameful," huffed Oro Tand. "What silversmith cannot properly size a woman's finger?"

Bianca stood on her toes and saw that Odile's fingers had curled so that her hand took on the shape of a bird's claw. She was unable to straighten her ring finger, and in distress Boisvert tried to shove the ring over the curved appendage. Both he and Odile were speaking rapid French. No one could mistake the sound of frustration in their voices.

Father Nelson reassured the couple, then barreled ahead with the ceremony. The murmuring died down as the priest continued.

The final blessing bestowed, the newlyweds turned to face the congregation. Bianca stared in disbelief.

Odile's teeth were clenched in a spurious smile; her usually welcoming eyes looked glazed and unblinking. Dismayed by the transformation, the guests grew so quiet that Bianca could hear the priest take a gulp of wine.

No one uttered a word as the couple made their way down the aisle toward the rear of the church. Odile's limp was more pronounced. In addition to her peculiar expression, she rested her frozen hand on top of Boisvert's as if nothing were wrong. Their attempt to appear nonchalant looked anything but.

"Apparently marriage does not suit the lady," quipped Oro Tand after the couple passed. "It usually takes years for a wife to become a gorgon, and longer for a husband to realize it. She's saved Boisvert the honeymoon."

Henry Lodge nodded. "Forsooth, Master Tand, I do agree."

"My lord," said Bianca, overhearing the two of them and directing her comment to the master of the Gold Guild. "I see cruelty comes easier to you than kindness. Perhaps you shall be rewarded some day for your quick tongue—in hell."

Bianca made for the back of the church, leaving John to make amends. She did not trust herself to listen to Tand's reply and remain cordial.

She was nearly to the font when John caught her arm. "Why must you set me at odds with Master Tand? Return and ask his forgiveness."

"I shall not abide such a spiteful remark. He should not be indulged."

"He's the master of the Worshipful Company of Goldsmiths!"

"All the more reason to shame him into decency."

"I shall someday go before him to become a guild member."

"Then you should think on the company you want to keep." Bianca stopped and looked for Boisvert and Odile. "Have they left?"

"Do not avoid this. I have worked years to finish my apprenticeship, and your galling remark shows a staggering lack of concern for me."

"Think you on which remark was more galling."

Silence. Just piercing stares.

John softened first—a sign of what he held most dear. "I doubt Odile and Boisvert want to greet their guests at the moment."

Bianca glanced around, giving their contention a rest. "Where might they go? Is there a chamber where they may have gone?"

"They left, my lady," piped a young lad standing near. "A carriage drove them away."

The moment Oro Tand arrived at the Goldsmiths' Hall, the head cook and entire kitchen staff surrounded him. Word about the wedding ceremony—more specifically, Odile's sudden affliction—traveled quicker than he could walk it there. What to do about the dinner, what to do about the food, can we go home?

"Carry on," ordered Tand. "The food will not keep and the guests will not wait to return another day. I regret that we have no couple to honor, but such are the circumstances."

The kitchen staff groused and shuffled back to their ovens and custards, disappointed their larders would not benefit from an unexpected windfall. Tand, however, was relieved he did not have to feign hospitality to the witless couple. He'd had enough of Odile Farendon's scrutinizing every detail of the dinner. No wonder her former husband, Lionel, never recovered from his last illness. Death was probably the only peace the man enjoyed in all the years they had been wed.

Tand stopped at the portrait of Odile's deceased husband, moved to a prominent position next to the dining hall. "Sir Lionel, you would not have approved, my good friend. It is a sorry state when two Gallic thieves conspire to purloin an Englishman's fortune."

Presently, members of the Company and their wives began arriving from St. Vedast. Far be it from goldsmiths to forgo a sumptuous feast, even if their hosts are not present. The hall buzzed with conjecture and exclamations of shock and dismay about the wedding ceremony and the bride's strange showing. Many attributed her behavior to the peculiarities of being French. Some thought she had a guilty heart and was being punished by God. "Evil spills over when it fills the heart," one astute goldsmith reminded them.

When it looked as though the hall was full, Oro Tand raised his hand for quiet.

"Good e'en, gathered brethren and ladies. We are here to celebrate the union of our brother and his bride in holy matrimony. Unfortunately, they are absent, but I am certain that it would be Odile and Boisvert's most ardent wish that we not postpone the merriment because of their delay. Instead, let us celebrate the couple and be all the merrier!" A blare of assents erupted from the menfolk. "Our pleasure making is done in their honor," Tand continued. "And it is my . . . ahem . . . it is *our* fervent wish that the lady recover in rapid measure. So let us gather in the dining hall, where we shall enjoy our *poisson* and the wine shall flow like their Seine!"

As Tand watched the couples repair to the dining hall, Henry Lodge appeared at his side.

"The evening has taken an unexpected turn," said Lodge.

"Indeed. But we shall endeavor to celebrate anyway. I learned long ago that puzzling over unforeseen mishaps does not benefit my health. Incidents transpire whether I ardently wish them to or not." Tand glimpsed the sardonic grin on Lodge's face and lowered his voice. "And what think you of this unexpected development, Master Lodge?"

Henry Lodge snapped to, as if he'd been caught. "Tand, I was only commenting that the incident was unusual."

"As you wish," said the master, remembering a young apprentice who was once wildly enamored with the lady. "You might consider yourself fortunate. It is likely that Boisvert did not expect wedded bliss would be thus." He watched Lodge stalk away, the man trying to control his cheeks from coloring several shades of lady blush.

With a snort, Tand proceeded to the dining hall, where guests began finding their places and settled in. The master goldsmith poured himself a glass of French burgundy. There was much to celebrate tonight.

Father Nelson had never presided over such a disquieting wedding ceremony. From the moment he saw Odile hobbling down the aisle leaning against Boisvert, and the groom wearing a plastered grin on his face, Father Nelson knew he must ignore his misgivings and proceed as if nothing were amiss. He managed the liturgy and communion well enough, in spite of Odile's slight trembling and difficulty with stating her consent. It was acceptable for a bride to show some emotion at the prospect of marriage, and he continued on, hurrying a little in order to be done. However, when it came time for them to exchange their rings, he could not conceal his horror at seeing Odile's hand stiffen like a falcon's talon and Boisvert jamming the ring onto her bent appendage. There was no hiding the difficulty, not with them carrying on, spewing foreign oaths. Eventually the ceremony drew to a close and Odile's odd smile settled into a hideous expression.

Now he was expected to give a blessing at the Goldsmiths' Hall. What would he find on arrival? Would Odile have recovered or would Boisvert force her to sit through the dinner looking as strange as a bird with fur? Though the wind blew through his thickest gown, causing him to shiver, he could not bring himself to walk any faster.

At the entrance to the great hall, he followed a young couple who also seemed to be laggards to the activities. The young man held the door for him, and Father Nelson noticed the ill fit of his sleeves, as if the fellow had outgrown his doublet. Still, it reassured him to see a well-mannered young couple. They even accompanied him to the dining hall, making niceties along the way.

None of them mentioned the wedding couple. He sensed that they, too, hoped to find the newlyweds more themselves at the wedding dinner. St. Vedast had been the recipient of a surge of misfortune, and he didn't want to add Boisvert and Odile's ceremony to the list. He hoped to end the evening on a peaceful note and retire to his quarters for a dram of burned wine and a good night's rest.

Father Nelson sighed, pondering the difficulty he'd experienced of late. The priesthood had provided him with an education and, at one time, a good source of income. Now he barely collected enough tithes and fees to subsist. But how else could he earn a living? Join the legion of pensioned clergy—and live on what? He did not think they were any better off. Instead, he watched, disheartened, as St. Vedast and his parish crumbled from within. Crumbling, too, was his desire to remain a priest.

It had been a cold walk up to Mayden Lane after the wedding ceremony. John's and Bianca's teeth chattered as they stood outside Odile's residence. An aged servant had answered the door, leaving them outside while she fetched her master. They were just about to abandon their wait, thinking she had forgotten them, when Boisvert pushed his face through the slightly open door.

"Odile is recovered," he said. "We will be at the dinner." Without further comment, he curtly closed the door.

They arrived late and were surprised to see the priest from St. Vedast walking up the road toward the Goldsmiths' Hall, also delayed. At the entrance, the priest reluctantly mounted the steps, as if a weight had been shackled to each ankle. The pair pretended nothing was amiss, though they could see that Father Nelson's face remained strained despite their attempts to put him at ease.

They entered the guildhall together, then parted ways as Father Nelson went to find Master Tand.

"Boisvert wants us to sit at their table," said John as they stepped into the dining hall.

"I'd rather sit a distance away," said Bianca. "Then I can watch the guests, unnoticed." She straightened her French hood, which wobbled disconcertingly every time she turned her head.

"I won't abandon my master," said John. "He has requested that we be near at hand."

"In spite of Boisvert's assurance, I don't know how Odile will be recovered enough to attend."

"You may be right, but Boisvert needs us. You can see the guests well enough from the head table. Probably it is a better seat for you to watch others."

Bianca heard the concern in John's voice. It would not do to argue the point. She followed him to the head table, and they sat near the end, facing the room of guests.

Most of the attendees were already seated, helping themselves to the bottles of wine amply provided. John reached for a burgundy and poured himself a hefty amount. He drank it down and poured himself another before offering to serve Bianca.

Around them, the room hummed with good cheer. Faces glowed in the candlelight; the silver candleholders and place settings glinted; the delicate icicles hanging from the holly with crimson berries sparkled. To Bianca, the room did appear magical. It was a shame Odile was not present to bask in its beauty.

While Bianca sipped her wine and looked out at the guests, John leaned back to talk with a goldsmith two seats away. She spied Oro Tand speaking with Father Nelson, and when the master goldsmith began sidling past tables, resting his hand on men's shoulders, bending to speak, then genially greeting others, Bianca tensed with irritation at seeing him head their way.

Father Nelson followed the master goldsmith to the head table, stopping where the married couple would have sat. Unfortunately for Bianca, Oro Tand moved past the empty chairs of honor and settled himself on the other side of John. She reached for the burgundy and emptied the bottle into her goblet.

"Good even, John Grunt," Tand said. His eyes glanced off Bianca, who was drinking her wine as if it were ale. "Your mentor is still missing. I trust you are as sorry as I that we have no guests of honor. What say you about his absence?"

"He will be here anon. Bianca and I just paid a visit to Mayden Lane. Odile is improved."

"Ah! A relief to hear. 'Twould be a pity for them to miss such merriment." Tand leaned close to John. "I see your wife is not waiting to celebrate." He guffawed loudly and slapped John on the back.

Bianca felt a jab from John's elbow and received a scowl when she looked over. She set down her goblet. "Master Tand," she said.

"Mistress Grunt." Tand relished saying her presumed surname, emphasizing its crude meaning.

"Sir, I am not a Grunt. I retain my maiden name."

"You did not join your husband and his worthy clan?"

"I joined my husband, but I chose the name by which I am known."

"A bold move for one of the fairer sex. Such a spirited wife can prove a challenge to a young liveryman. You must have a taste for danger, John."

John smiled thinly, unable to think what to say. Agreeing with the master goldsmith or defending his wife—it was sure to end badly either way. Instead, Bianca answered for him.

"John is not easily cowed by challenges, Master Tand. Not all men can find their way out of a barrel into the apprenticeship of a silversmith."

Oro Tand appeared puzzled. "A barrel, my lady? I follow you not."

"You are unaware that John spent his youth living behind the Tern's Tempest? It is a modest beginning, but one he had the wits to rise above." Bianca took another sip of wine and smiled sweetly at the two of them.

"Is this spoken in truth, John Grunt?"

A flush found John's cheeks. There was no use in denying his low birth. He tugged self-consciously at the cropped sleeves of his doublet and moved his arms under the table to hide the poor fit. But if John had learned anything surviving as a gamin, it was being adept at changing the focus from himself. "Look there; I believe Father Nelson is preparing to speak."

The priest had his hand raised, trying to quiet the guests, but his attempts went mostly ignored. He stood too long before speaking, expecting the reverence and quiet of a church mass.

Oro Tand spoke. "It looks as though I must save a priest." He rose from the table, and just his doing so immediately garnered the attention of the entire dining hall.

"Gentle ladies and brethren, a blessing for this special occasion."

Father Nelson cleared his throat and opened his small prayer book, flipping through the pages. He bowed his head and, after a moment of silence pierced by nervous coughs from the guests, began his invocation. Halfway through, the crowd began to stir.

Thinking the attendees were losing patience, he sped his delivery. However, nothing a priest could say would pry the attention of a guildhall full of goldsmiths away from the sight at the back of the room.

Standing in the doorway were the French silversmith, Boisvert, and his bride, Odile.

No one said a word. No one offered a word of welcome. No one approached them in greeting or ushered them to their table. The collected merrymakers stared with their mouths agape.

Odile lifted her chin and looked round at her guests. Her earlier strangeness was gone, and her regal manner had returned. She hooked arms with her husband, and Boisvert escorted her down the center toward their place at the head table, Odile's gait as smooth as the surface of a pond. The couple claimed their seats, untroubled by the silence and stares.

Father Nelson clamped his slack jaw, offered an "Amen," and crossed himself.

"Father Nelson," said Odile, acknowledging the priest.

"Madame." Father Nelson's eyes remained as round as King Harry's belly.

Boisvert pulled out the chair for his bride.

They could have said nothing, just let the guild men and women squirm until someone dared speak. Perhaps it would have delighted the couple to see their peers agonize over what to do. But Boisvert reached for a bottle of wine, poured himself a glass, and swirled it under his nose. Finding the vintage acceptable, he poured a glass for Odile, then raised his goblet in toast.

"To the men and women of the guild . . . Odile and I wish you prosperity and good health. Let the celebration begin in earnest." He polished off his wine and poured himself more.

Stunned by their wondrous entry, Oro Tand shook off his astonishment and followed with a toast of his own. He intoned the usual sentiments of good wishes and good health, and the guild members offered "Hear, hears" and "well mets," until everyone settled in good ease. Jollity resumed; the gibes and laughter became louder than before.

John leaned over to Bianca. "What say you of Odile's sudden recovery? They act as if nothing happened."

Bianca tore apart a manchet and buttered it with John's knife. "It is unusual for a limp and spasms to disappear so quickly with no lingering effect. I wonder if she has the falling-down sickness."

"If that is true, we had better never mention it."

Bianca stuffed the bread into her mouth. "I'll say nothing unless they ask." She leaned forward and caught Odile's eye, lifting her goblet to her hostess.

She sat back and took a sip of wine. "Let us hope her good health continues."

Speculations were laid to rest as servants brought forth a course of roasted pig and stuffed sturgeon. The fish had been poached in vinegar and sprinkled with parsley and minced ginger. A fig sauce accompanied the pig, and each round of food was applauded and enthusiastically praised.

The bottles of wine kept coming; no one should suffer running out of grape juice at a French wedding. Bianca enjoyed herself in spite of Oro Tand sitting next to John. She amused herself with eating and watching the members of the guild stuff themselves, leaving her husband to rectify the goldsmith's opinion of them.

Even Father Nelson imbibed. He sat on the other side of Boisvert and matched the groom goblet for goblet as only a priest can keep pace with a Frenchman.

As the dinner wore on, couples rose from their places and came forward to visit with the honored couple. Oro Tand intoned loudly how handsome the couple looked and expressed his delight that Odile wore the ouche from the guild. Even Henry Lodge bid the couple well, bowing low over the table to take Odile's hand and kiss it. He nearly toppled Odile's wine, but he was able to right the goblet before it spilled. His gesture surprised Bianca, as she had witnessed his and Oro Tand's insults at the ceremony. Watching Lodge during dinner, she thought him a miserable man. His brief conversations with his tablemates looked strained, and he spent a good deal of time stonily watching Odile and her new husband.

However, Bianca found this parade of people flouncing to their table entertaining. She studied their mannerisms and silently speculated about their attributes—as well as their foibles.

If one removed their sumptuous fashions and wealth, these citizens were no better than she. They, too, loved and lied. Their fashions were lovely, but Bianca had little interest in such conceits. A woman might embellish her hood with biliments of pearls and beading, she might color her lips with crushed berries, but all of this decorating was done to flatter her person and flaunt her wealth. Bianca was not impressed.

Here was evidence of Henry's sumptuary laws, designed to keep the rising merchants in their place. Men must not live like noblemen unless they were born to it or granted the title by the king. The goldsmiths and their wives seemed bent on testing their boundaries.

Thinking about Harry's rules for dress made Bianca acutely aware of her own low birth. She wondered how long it would be before someone other than Oro Tand reminded her of it. She took a bite of John's abandoned custard just as a clatter came from down the table.

Bianca leaned forward but could not see past Oro Tand and John, who were blocking her view. She stood and noticed a red splotch spreading across the tablecloth and Boisvert righting a spilled bottle of wine. In a hysterical voice, Odile apologized to a woman whose dress was accidentally stained. The bride was not content with just expressing her remorse. She insisted the woman come to Mayden Lane right away. "You will have the pick of any gown in my wardrobe."

"My dear Odile, it is not necessary. Your offer is generous, but this was not done on purpose. I can endure the evening. And I know a capable launder woman."

Again the dining hall fell into silence. All eyes were trained on the incident at the head table.

"*Non*, I insist," repeated Odile. She looked as if she would come around the table.

"My love," said Boisvert, patting his wife's arm, "this is not so important that it cannot wait until tomorrow. Please, let us continue our dinner."

"*Non!*" shrieked Odile, jerking her arm away. "I have just stained the most beautiful gown I have ever laid eyes on! Why should I enjoy my evening when I have ruined hers?"

Odile's insistence would have been cause enough for alarm, but then her face ticked with a spasm. A twitch of the eye spread to the muscles of her cheeks and mouth.

"My lady," said the woman, her own voice rising as she desperately tried to reassure her hostess. "You have not ruined my evening. Please do not upset yourself. It is a matter of no consequence."

Odile's jaw clenched. "Come," she said, struggling to speak through her gritted teeth. "Let us solve this immediately." The bride moved to escort the woman to Mayden Lane, but with her first step, she stopped, and her eyes glazed with the vacant stare she had worn earlier.

Boisvert took her hand. "Odile," he whispered in her ear. "Look at me." When she did not move, he shook her by the shoulders. "Odile! *Arrête ça.*" He offered a sip of wine, tipped it against her lips. "*S'il te plaît, bois! Bois!*" But the wine dribbled down her neck.

Odile stood motionless, while her face continued its strange spasms. She was unresponsive to her husband's pleas and appeared unable to control the muscles in her face, so there was nothing to do but hope for the seizure to pass.

"We must get her out of here," said Boisvert, turning to John.

"I see no way but to carry her," he replied as he sidled past Oro Tand.

A line of perspiration dampened Boisvert's upper lip. He glanced around at the gawping guests. "So be it. We must do what we must."

The two of them moved the chairs away from Odile and prepared to lift her. They had just tipped her like a block of stone when she blinked out of her daze. The tremors stopped. She looked round at the dining hall, saw the puzzlement on her guests' faces, and matched their bewildered expressions with one of her own. When she found Boisvert's surprised face, she smiled and touched her hand to his cheek.

"*Mon ami,*" she said, smiling. Her relaxed gesture vanquished her lover's fear. Boisvert's breath caught in the hope that his love had returned to him.

But his respite was short-lived. Odile's neck suddenly wrenched at an awkward angle. Her eyes rolled up in her head, and she collapsed.

CHAPTER 14

Bring a lump of ore into a room of goldsmiths, and they'll run for their touchstones, their crucibles, their aqua regia and smother you with assistance. But if a fellow brother is in need, they will blink uncertainly, shrug, and wait for someone else to make the first move. Bianca wondered if their hesitation was because of surprise, because of their haughty opinion of themselves, or because Boisvert and Odile were French. Being a stranger brother had never been easy for the silversmith, and never was it more evident than now.

Bianca hurried to Boisvert's side, where the Frenchman knelt over his beloved, shaking her and crying, "*Aidez-moi, aidez-moi!*" Odile did not respond. Neither did anyone else in the hall. Odile's eyes bore the empty look of a more permanent kind.

"Boisvert," said Bianca, shaking her head. She held his arm. "No."

The Frenchman looked up in disbelief. "You say no. How can you say no? She was breathing this same air just a moment ago. This cannot be."

"She's dead, Boisvert," said Oro Tand, standing over them. He looked ten feet tall as he gazed down his nose at them. There was no expression of emotion in his words. They fell as flat as the floor.

The master of the Goldsmiths' Company took the matter into his hands. He sent for the authorities, assuaged distressed goldsmiths and their distraught wives. The kitchen ceased operations. When the ward constable and coroner arrived, Tand escorted the men into the dining hall.

Bianca was relieved that her nemesis, Constable Patch, had not been summoned. It was the same men who had investigated the death at St. Vedast a few days before.

The two men eyed Boisvert, who was sitting near his deceased bride, looking as stunned and bereft as any lover would be, especially given so brief a marriage.

Without prompt, Oro Tand described the evening, starting with the wedding ceremony. The master of the Goldsmiths' Company spoke about Odile's odd behavior, how it had disappeared when they arrived for dinner, then returned when Odile knocked over a bottle of wine. The woman whose dress had sparked Odile's agitation stood quietly while her husband explained her part in the incident. Finally, Boisvert was asked to tell his version of the events, but the silversmith could not speak for all of his distress.

"Sir," said Bianca, crouching beside the coroner as he knelt to examine the body. "Do you think this sounds as if she may have had the falling-down sickness?"

"The crank? It is possible. However, I have never heard of limping or contortion of the limbs to be associated with that condition." The coroner took a breath as if to discuss his thoughts, then stopped. "My lady, you must return to your seat; this is not your concern."

"Odile was a friend to me. It *is* my concern."

"All the more reason why I must ask that you allow me to do what I must, unhindered."

"Sir, I have an interest in conditions that affect one's health."

"You may have an interest, but you have no expertise. You may be curious, but your opinion is of no significance to me."

Bianca sighed. Being dressed like a goldsmith's wife did little to inspire the coroner to confer with her. She could not explain to the man that she was not actually as she appeared. She could not tell him that she sold medicinals and studied death and disease on a daily basis. Instead, Bianca politely remained by his side. She would watch—whether he found her presence irritating or not.

"I need more light," he said, glowering at her. "I am being crowded and cannot see."

Bianca ignored his remark and took the proffered candle, holding it at a perfect angle so the coroner could see. Only an ass with no desire to help himself would have complained.

The coroner grumbled as he checked Odile's exposed arms, lifting each in turn. "My lady, you are as stubborn as a fly and about as helpful."

"My husband would agree," said Bianca, undeterred. "Please continue . . . with your examination, sir."

He bent over Odile's face, opening an eyelid to check the white of her eye. "Move the light a little to my right."

The coroner opened Odile's mouth, moving his head for a better look. Naturally, Bianca's curiosity could not allow her to sit patiently by. She leaned over to see, her French hood bumping the coroner's forehead. He clamped shut Odile's mouth and glared at Bianca.

Bianca met his stare. "I didn't see any inflammation of the mouth; did you?" she asked.

"Nay, I did not!"

"Go on, sir. I shall not interrupt."

Sniffing with indignation, the coroner simply wanted to be finished with his examination and return home. He quickly noted Odile's bent neck, took hold of her chin, and straightened her head from its torqued position.

"Before she died, her neck twisted in a most unnatural way.

Her shoulder rose to her cheek." Bianca thought the contortion would be of interest to him.

"A spasm," replied the coroner.

"Do you know of any condition besides the crank that might cause such a spasm?"

"Mayhap a tumor pressing against the skull." The coroner lifted Odile's head and felt its bone structure. His brow furrowed in thought and he laid her head back on the floor.

If the coroner would not share his findings, then she would draw her own conclusions. Bianca handed the candle to John, then lifted Odile's head and palpated the skull.

The coroner stopped his examination. "Are you going to hold the light for me, or are you going to mimic me like a monkey?"

Bianca gently laid her friend's head on the floor and took the candle, positioning it for the coroner. She had not felt any unusual bumps.

Saliva dampened Odile's lips, and the coroner felt its texture. He sniffed his fingers, finally wiping them down Odile's front. His fingers lingered on the ouche pinned to her bodice. With a grunt of effort, he braced himself against the table and got to his feet. He looked around for the constable. "I believe she was poisoned."

"What?" exclaimed Bianca. She nearly caught his sleeve on fire with the candle as she stood. "I never saw her vomit; nor did she complain of chills or stomach cramps."

"Sir," said the constable to Boisvert. "Did your wife exhibit any of those symptoms?"

Boisvert blinked. "*Non,* she did not."

Bianca wielded the lit candle like a weapon, stepping close to the coroner. She looked at him over the flickering flame. "You said you found no redness of the mouth. Why do you believe she was poisoned?"

"A person may be poisoned and not exhibit inflammation of the mouth. There are other ways."

"Say then, what do you suspect?" said Bianca.

The coroner wasn't the only man annoyed with Bianca's persistence. The constable seized her wrist and removed the candle, blowing it out. "My lady, this is not a matter that concerns you. But your insistence makes me wonder. Why are you so invested?"

"I said before, Odile was my friend. My husband's master is Boisvert, and he has just lost the only woman he has ever loved. I want to be sure the coroner's findings are accurate. Or, at the least, I believe they should make sense." Bianca straightened her headpiece.

"And is that your determination? I do not see your involvement as anything but an intrusion."

Bianca ignored the constable and turned back to the coroner. "Could the falling-down sickness result in death?" She was not going to let the possibility go.

"I have only observed such finality if they hit their head or swallow their tongue. But there is no evidence of the falling sickness. This is likely a result of poison."

Both the constable and the coroner turned their gaze on Boisvert. Their stares were enough for the silversmith to feel the heat of their accusation. "Why do you look on me that way? I would never do anything to hurt my beautiful Odile." Boisvert stood and threw out his chest. "I'd rather die than be accused of murdering my wife!"

The constable raised an eyebrow. "We never said a word."

"You do not have to say a word. I know by your eyes what it is that you are thinking."

"Is this your wife's goblet?" The constable pointed to the silver chalice sitting at Odile's place. He picked it up and sniffed the contents.

"What are you saying?" said Boisvert, indignant. "Say what you mean. I do not understand these insinuations."

The constable handed the goblet to the coroner, who took it by the stem and ran it under his nose. He shook his head, uncertain.

"Give me it!" Boisvert grabbed the wine from the coroner and drank it down without stopping. "There!" he said, shoving the goblet back at the constable. He showed great restraint by not throwing it at him. "We shall see if I poisoned my wife."

"Master, calm yourself," said John, placing his hand on the silversmith's chest. He then spoke loud enough so the constable and coroner could hear. "Anyone who knows your love for Odile would never question it."

"Perhaps you should consider other possibilities," said Bianca. "There are plenty of them here." She looked round at the goldsmiths and their wives, who were glaring back at her. She had not won herself any friends. "If Odile was poisoned, as you believe, Coroner, then, Constable, you must find someone with a reason for poisoning her. I do not believe Boisvert can fake his love for Odile."

"The one who loves the most can also harbor the greatest hatreds. I have seen it before," said the constable.

"You may have seen it before, but that is not true of my husband's master," said Bianca.

The constable resented being challenged—especially by a woman who could not properly secure her headpiece. "Who *are* you?"

"I am my husband's wife." She refrained from mentioning her name or her husband's. Neither surname garnered much respect.

"She is Bianca Goddard," offered Oro Tand, smiling. He was only trying to be helpful.

"Goddard? Where have I heard that name?" The constable squinted at Bianca.

"Her father is the alchemist once accused of poisoning the king." Tand appeared quite pleased with himself. Apparently, he had done some inquiring.

"Ah!" said the constable. "I do know of him. In not so flattering terms. And you are his daughter?"

Bianca did not respond—so Master Tand answered for her. "She is indeed."

The constable considered her a moment. He did not question her regarding her father's unseemly misadventure, and for that she was grateful.

"If I may have a word with you, Constable?" Master Tand gestured toward a quiet corner.

"We will be here until tomorrow," groused John, watching the two men huddle. "This constable is too determined. His kind is better suited to lawyering."

Bianca watched the pair carefully as they spoke. At last they seemed to come to some sort of agreement. If the constable's broad smile was any indication, they had come to an agreement that pleased him verily.

"It seems I do have a room of possibilities," he said, addressing the guests and acknowledging Bianca. "However, it is late and I do not see the use in retaining the guests and questioning them into the small hours of the morning. We are all better served to go on about our ways. Master Tand will provide me with a list of attendees and from there I can decide how best to proceed." He glanced at the master goldsmith, who gave a satisfied nod. "Good men and good ladies, I ask your pardon for this unfortunate interruption in your celebration. Death does happen." The constable offered this last comment as if it were a revelation that had never occurred to anyone. "We shall have the body removed forthwith and you may continue your merriment."

"Codso," swore Bianca.

"He seems suddenly cheery," said John.

"If you had gotten a silver angel to leave, you would be cheery too," said Bianca.

The constable wasted no time removing himself from the dining hall, leaving without so much as a glance at his peer, the coroner.

"How typical," muttered the coroner, watching the official exit. "So like the thoughtless cove to abandon me to deal with the body. I should leave these silly goldsmiths to remove it."

Oro Tand responded to the disgruntled look on the coroner's face. "Sir, do not distress yourself any further. We shall send for St. Vedast's sexton to remove the body. I pray you, enjoy the rest of your evening."

Bianca watched the master of the Gold Guild drape his arm over the coroner's shoulders and escort him toward the door. "Far be it from Master Tand to let a possible murder delay a good dinner."

John gave her a sharp look. "I would thank you to keep your comments to yourself. Have you forgotten these are our people?"

"They are not *my* people." She looked around at the guests, the majority of whom had returned to their dinners. "Are they yours, John?"

John's face colored, complementing her carmine gown. "It is a matter of survival, Bianca. You would do well to remember that."

"False friendship is more about vanity than it is a requirement for a smithing license. You say it is a matter of survival. Well, it is not a matter of survival for me."

"What would you have me do?" said John, struggling to keep his voice low. "Shall I go back to picking pockets and scrounging through rubbish for our meals?"

"You should stay your course. If becoming a liveryman is your desire, then you should not let me stop you." Bianca straightened her French hood, suppressing the urge to fling it off. "I only ask that you give me leave to pursue mine." She had no inclination to continue arguing in the presence of John's "people." A few sallied closer as they spoke, and Bianca did not wish to provide them with fodder for gossip. With a brief curtsy, she left her husband glaring after her and went to Boisvert.

"*Monsieur*," she said, "you must need rest. Will you let us see you home?"

The silversmith shook his head. "*Non.* I cannot leave Odile." Boisvert dabbed his eyes with his sleeve, muffling a loud snuffle.

"Father Nelson, will you summon your sexton from St. Vedast?" said Tand upon his return from seeing the coroner out the door.

The priest rose from the table where he had been sitting and trying to disappear into the background. He had given Odile her last rites and had retreated, as much from personal pain as from wishing to remove himself from further involvement. "Of course. I shall go for him myself."

"I want her embalmed," said Boisvert.

Father Nelson nodded. "I shall solicit an apothecary." The

priest paused, waiting for another request, but none came. No one had asked for his comfort or his prayers. Not even Boisvert wanted his support. Why should goldsmiths worry about their consciences today when they could buy their way through purgatory tomorrow? Father Nelson quickly left the dining hall, glad for a reason to quit the place.

As for the mood of the banquet, Odile's death had put a damper on the occasion. Many thought it awkward to continue celebrating a marriage that had ended so abruptly. These were the few who still retained a speck of decency. They filed past Boisvert and Bianca and offered their condolences, whether sincerely felt or not. Eventually even the last revelers grew too chastened by the lack of interest to keep eating and drinking. They filtered out, casting sheepish glances in the direction of their stranger brother, but they avoided speaking to him, lest his sullen disposition further deflate theirs.

Instead of consoling his distraught comrade, Oro Tand busied himself instructing staff to remove the food and begin cleaning up the dining hall. He bid departing couples a good night and apologized for the unfortunate end to the celebration. John avoided speaking to Bianca but asked his mentor what he could do to serve him. Boisvert just shook his head, staring alternately at his hands and then Odile.

As the dining hall emptied, Bianca finally attempted to engage her husband's mentor. "Can you think of anyone who might have wanted to harm Odile?"

"She was beautiful and generous. Who would want to hurt her?"

"I ask because the coroner believes she was poisoned. But we do not know for sure how she died. However, it is strange that her death came on so quickly. If it is not the falling-down sickness, then we must consider other possibilities."

"He does not need to think of these things just now," said John. "He needs rest and a chance to recover."

"*Non*, John," said Boisvert. "Perhaps talking to Bianca will help my grief." He turned back to her. "*S'il vous plaît, continuez*."

Bianca ignored John's irritated look and focused on Boisvert.

"Do you recall anyone unfamiliar who might have attended the wedding or who might have come uninvited to the dinner?"

The silversmith shook his head. "I only had eyes for Odile. I was not concerned with anyone else."

"John, you know the guests better than I do. Did you notice anyone unfamiliar?"

John shrugged. "I am an apprentice. I don't know the members of the guild like Boisvert does. Only on rare occasions do I meet other smiths."

"Mayhap someone lingered at the table?" asked Bianca of Boisvert. "Was there an incident that might have caught in your mind while guests chatted with you or Odile?"

Boisvert shook his head. "*Non.* No one stayed long." He thought a minute, then looked up at Bianca. "Lodge nearly upset her goblet of wine, but he kept it from spilling."

Bianca had seen it too. From the far end of the dining hall they heard Oro Tand's voice outside the door. Bianca hoped he would remain occupied long enough for her to get some answers. "Boisvert, has anything strange happened in the past few days?"

"*Oui,*" said Boisvert. "This strange behavior of hers. Tonight was not the first of it. When Odile and I visited her solicitor, she had an episode there. Her hand suddenly clinched and her eyes— they became as glazed as a dead doe's. One minute she was instructing Benjamin Cornish of her last wishes, and the next, she began shaking."

"He was recording her last will and testament?"

"*Oui.*"

"Have you any knowledge of other occurrences?" said Bianca.

"*Non.* She never spoke to me of them. It is strange. Afterward, she had no memory of the episode. Except for a limp, she had no lingering effects."

"What did she attribute the limp to? She must have noticed."

"Her age. We are not so young."

Bianca nodded. "Often such episodes are brief. The afflicted learn to live with the symptoms and, except for a momentary lapse of memory, may not realize they suffer the falling-down sickness. Did anything else strike you as unusual in the past few days?"

Boisvert nodded. "Outside of the lawyer's office, Oro Tand was sitting. I thought how queer a coincidence that we had the same solicitor. But then I thought, how queer is this, that his appointment followed ours."

CHAPTER 15

It had been a late night, and John opted to stay with Boisvert at Mayden Lane. An elderly maid, a cook, and various other servants were in residence there, but John didn't trust that they would bother themselves with his master's comfort. Boisvert had lived there only a week, not enough time to have earned the affection or trust of Odile's staff.

It was just as well, thought Bianca when Hobs nudged her awake the next morning. No doubt John was still rankled with her, and at least this way she'd had a decent night's sleep, without staying up half the night explaining herself. Besides, she did not feel she was in the wrong. She was merely stating fact. Dressing and mingling with liverymen and their wives made her uncomfortable. She had little in common with them, nor did she imagine that she ever would. What this difference in opinion meant for her and John's future together she did not know, but for now she concerned herself with Odile's inexplicable death.

Bianca fixed herself a porridge and, once fortified with a bellyful of warm oats, headed out the door. It was midmorning and she moved easily down the street dressed in her woolen kirtle and cloak, glad to be wearing her familiar garb. She could not have hopped over holes in the road if she had been wearing the voluminous farthingale of a merchant's wife—another inconvenience of becoming a proper "citizen."

She almost expected to run into John coming home from Mayden Lane, but she did not. He would have asked her why she was returning to the Goldsmiths' Hall, and she didn't want to be told she had no business there. She might be told that anyway, but she preferred hearing it from someone other than John.

Bianca pushed open the massive door and stepped inside. Compared to the bustle of the night before, the silence here today was, she thought, unnerving. On her mind was the thought that Odile's food might have been tampered with. In truth it seemed unlikely given that last night was not the first time Odile had suffered from her symptoms. The incident of Henry Lodge nearly tipping over the glass of wine also troubled her. But if he had slipped poison into her goblet, Boisvert would have succumbed, too, since he had boldly downed what was left in her cup. Bianca crossed the hall, every step clattering on the tiles like a set of keys being dropped in a cathedral. It wasn't long before someone poked his head around a corner.

"Do you work in the kitchen?" Bianca asked.

Wearing an apron, a lad stepped out toweling off a platter. "Aye. On what business do you come?"

"I'm here to see Master Tand if he is in."

"He's in his office. It's been a long night."

"It was a long night for so sad an end to it," said Bianca.

The boy looked at her skeptically.

"I attended the dinner, but I wasn't wearing this." She looked past him. "Might I have a word with the kitchen staff?"

"I thought ye was here for Master Tand."

"I am. But perhaps you might show me where the stuffed sturgeon was made."

"We's busy. We just want to go home. Haven't slept in over a day."

"I won't delay you." Bianca tipped her chin at his towel. "I'll help you dry if you like."

"We don't allow members' wives entrance to the kitchen without an escort."

"I'm not a member's wife."

"That so? Then what were ye here for last night?" The corner of his mouth turned up as if he had found her out and would not be fooled.

"My husband and I were guests." Bianca ignored his arched eyebrow. "If you do not allow wives into the kitchen, do you allow the guild members to enter?"

"They may come and go as they like, but if we is preparin' for an occasion, such as we was last night, then it is not allowed."

"And are those rules obeyed?"

"Generally they is."

"Were they followed for this occasion?"

"No one came back except Master Tand. But it is his right."

"It is my right as master of this company," said a voice from the top of the stairs. Oro Tand looked over the banisters. "What brings you back to the guildhall, Bianca . . . Goddard?"

"I wish to speak with you, sir."

"In regards to what?"

"In regards to last night."

"I believe you were there. Nothing has transpired since. Odile's body has been moved to the apothecary's." He waited for his words to stop echoing off the marble walls. "Did you leave behind a bauble?"

"Nay, I did not." Tand seemed rooted to the railing, and if she did not go to him, she doubted he would descend the stairs to her. "May I come up?"

"I fail to see why I should bother to accommodate you."

"I won't be long." Bianca skirted an apology.

Oro Tand sighed. "Be you quick."

Bianca climbed the long staircase, ignoring Tand's derisive look as she neared. She stopped in front of the portrait of Odile's deceased husband, which had been returned to its place on the wall. "Lionel Farendon must have been a respected master of the guild. I heard he was an alderman for the ward."

"For Aldersgate, until he became too ill to serve. Lionel was appointed lord mayor for one year, and he devoted many years of service to the worshipful company."

"And were you fond of him?"

"He was a friend and confidant. He was my mentor. I owe my current position to him." Tand did not invite her into his office. "Come now, why are you here? It isn't for idle chatter."

Bianca realized the man would never warm to her and could barely abide her. It was disingenuous for either of them to pretend. So she asked him directly, keen to read his face, "Is Benjamin Cornish your solicitor?"

For a brief second, the goldsmith's cocksure manner lapsed. He quickly tugged on his shirt cuffs, fussing over them. "He is my lawyer." He brushed a nonexistent speck of lint from one sleeve.

"Boisvert mentioned you were waiting outside Cornish's office when they left their appointment with him."

"I don't recall." Now he found that his fingernails needed examining.

"Boisvert was not mistaken. He would not forget such a coincidence."

Oro Tand inclined his head, scowling, thinking. "Ah, now I remember. I do believe I saw the two of them leave. My mind was elsewhere. You'll forgive me, I've had a lot on my mind."

"How long have you used Master Cornish's services?"

"God's mercy, I do not recall how many years. And I do not see why that should matter. What is the purpose behind these questions? Eh?" He looked at her suspiciously. "People or, shall I say, citizens often consult lawyers. We tend to seek advice from men versed in the good king's law. We are not like commoners." His eyes dismissively rode down her person, emphasizing his point. "Our disputes are rarely settled with knives in dark alleys. We are a civil lot."

"Consulting a lawyer hardly makes one more civil. Fine dress and money should not be the only criteria in making one a good subject."

The strident creak of the front door opening drew their attention away from each other to the front entrance. In stepped the pair of haberdashers, chattering loudly. They did not immediately see the master of the goldsmith company peering down at them, and even if they had, Bianca doubted they would have softened their voices. Intimidation did not affect them.

After all, thought Bianca, their talents were as necessary as those of any other ranked liveryman. One could not dress in a suit of gold. Bianca started down the stairs, realizing her time with Oro Tand was over. The haberdashers looked up.

"Master Tand," chimed the haberdashers, sweeping off their exceptional caps and dipping low in exceptional bows. "We are here to learn the results of your meeting. We trust you presented our request to your officers?"

The master goldsmith could not hide the irritation in his voice. "We have had an unfortunate incident, and our meeting has been postponed."

"No meeting? That *is* unfortunate," said the one in the leather doublet with the impeccably trimmed beard. "You are not putting us off?"

"You have not heard that Odile Farendon died at her wedding dinner last night?"

"Here in the guildhall?" he said, aghast.

Bianca reached the bottom of the stairs. She was in no rush to leave. Hearing livery snipe at one another was a rare treat.

"Poor Odile," said the other haberdasher. "She was a lovely lady. Had she been ill?"

"It was sudden," said Bianca, nearing them.

"What happened?" they both chimed. "She seemed well when last we saw her."

Bianca informed them about the wedding ceremony and then the reception dinner.

Master Tand could have easily retreated to his office, but he grew annoyed that the haberdashers were receiving their news from Bianca instead of him. He clomped down the stairs. "Gentlemen, if you wish to continue this conversation, I shall see you out. You may finish it on the street."

"Master Tand," said the one in the indigo gown. "Our purpose is to secure funds to repair Foster Lane for the king's progress later this month. We need to make improvements soon and we need your company's help. Why should you benefit when you have not contributed?"

"I have told you before. The guild hasn't the funds to spare. The king shall have to make do with the road as it is."

"Oh ho!" said the haberdashers in unison.

"Wait until His Highness hears this," said the bearded one.

With that, Bianca saw herself out the door.

Most citizens—or, rather, most men and women of social standing—kept their wills secreted away with their solicitors, tucked away in a locked cabinet preferably constructed of thick wood that would take a while to burn if it caught on fire. However, a copy of the will was given to the register of the commissary as a matter of public record.

Rather than seek Odile's lawyer, Benjamin Cornish, at his offices near Middle Temple, Bianca decided to try the register, a shorter walk in the cold. Reviewing Odile's last wishes might reveal something of a motive for her death—if it was indeed a murder.

In a dank room on the north side of St. Paul's Cathedral, Bianca followed the clerk up spiraling stairs of warped stone treads, mindful not to accidentally step on the hem of the man's vestment. A request to view a citizen's will was infrequent enough that John Wemmesley did not mind the lengthy climb to the far reaches of the cathedral, and from the sound of his whistling, thought Bianca, perhaps he even enjoyed it. Once the clerk unlocked the shackled hasp and stepped inside, it was easy for Bianca to see why.

Windows on each side of the tower revealed a sweeping view of London unlike any she had ever seen. From there, the bucolic grounds of Smithfield and Morefield stretched beyond the city walls to the north. A cart moved along Aldersgate Street, loaded with crates headed for market. The archery fields lay vacant, their targets little dots waiting to be speared with arrows on a clear spring day. To the south, the pewter gray Thames curled between London and Southwark, spanned by the bridge, its three stories peering down at her twenty starlings sitting in a broth of foaming surf. Just a glimpse from such a height would thrill even the most dolorous of men.

Bianca was so taken by the landscape and with trying to spot Lambeth Hill, where her mother lived, that she neglected to study the room's interior and momentarily forgot her reason for being there. Even the clerk was more keen to ogle the view than with assisting her in finding Odile's will.

"I never tire of coming here," he said, gazing east toward the White Tower. "It is one of the more pleasant duties that is required of me. There was a time when all of London was contained within the Roman walls. Now lights blink from cottages beyond Cripplegate, which was once only inhabited by sheep and cows." The two admired the bustling town before them, until Wemmesley spoke.

"And the name on the will?" he asked, stepping away from a window and turning his attention to the stacks of loose paper on a table.

"Odile Farendon Boisvert."

"Farendon?" asked the cleric. "He was once lord mayor, was he not?"

"Aye. He was."

"So his widow remarried?"

"Aye."

"When did she remarry?"

"Yesterday. It was also the day she died."

"An unfortunate and highly unusual situation. Is the will being contested?"

"Not that I am aware of. She wrote her testament a few days ago. I am curious to know how her estate is being divided. She died under strange circumstances, and I worry that her death came by someone else's hand."

"Someone eager to inherit money?" He studied her a moment. "And what is your interest in this?"

"My husband is Boisvert's apprentice, and Odile was very kind to me."

"So you want to see if she has left you her gowns," he assumed.

"Nay, I care not a spot about acquiring fine silks. I want to know how she worded her final bequeath. And exactly who might benefit."

The clerk turned to the wills received in the last month. They were piled on the table, held in place by a nail on which each sheet was skewered. "If I have received a copy, it will be here." He pointed to the documents. "These have not yet been filed."

He removed half of the wills and started to hand them to her, then stopped. "Can you read?" he asked.

"My father taught me."

"An enlightened stance for a father. He was an educated man?"

"Nay, sir, he was practical. He taught me in order to make his life easier." She took the papers and began thumbing through them, hoping the clerk would leave it at that.

"Farendon, Farendon," mused the clerk, scanning the shelves of bound folios. "I believe he was lord mayor more than a decade ago. When did he die?"

"It is my understanding that Odile has been a widow for nearly thirteen years."

"Forgive me, I have many testaments to archive and often I have help if it becomes overwhelming. I cannot always depend on my assistant to be careful with his filing. He seems to enjoy his wine and the view more than his required task. If I recall correctly, Odile Farendon contested her husband's will." He went to a particular section of the shelves. "We should have a copy of the original before it was contested." He removed a leather folio and cleared a space on the table. Untying the cord that held the folder together, the clerk turned over the cover and read the name on the first testament. "Not Farendon." He flipped over the page and read the next. "Not Farendon."

Bianca finished the stack of papers and reached for the remaining testaments from the nail. "And if Odile's will is not here?"

"If Odile's will is not in your stack, it simply means it has not yet been received."

"If it was witnessed before her death, then it should be the document of record, should it not?"

"It should. It is the solicitor's duty to file it."

"What if he shirks his duty?"

"It is required of his office. It may be delayed, but eventually it shall be found here."

Bianca went to a window for better light to read through the pages. The testaments had been received during the past two months and had not been ordered chronologically. She went through every single paper to be sure Odile's will was not there.

"Lionel Farendon," said the clerk at last. "I knew it would be here." He began to read . . . " 'In the name of God, amen. I, Lionel Farendon, Goldsmith of London, residing in the parish of Aldersgate, sick in body and expecting hourly my dissolution out of this world into life everlasting . . .' "

He handed the document to Bianca. She read on in silence, then, coming to the part of his bequeaths, read aloud, " '. . . and gift my wife, Odile Durand Farendon, her gowns and personal effects. The residence of Mayden Lane with all gardens and backsides shall be sold.' " Bianca looked over at John Wemmesley, whose eyes widened.

She continued reading. "The usual list of disbursements follows. That his creditors shall be paid; he makes an arrangement for obiits to be said on the anniversary of his death for the next twenty years. All net assets, land, and buildings shall be left in an endowment to benefit the Worshipful Company of Goldsmiths and their charities." She scanned the text to the end. "Odile would have gotten nothing."

"As his wife, she is entitled to the chattels and one-third of his estate."

"There is no mention of that provision. Perhaps he sought to circumvent it."

"It is a protection under the law."

"Then there are problems with the way this will was written." Bianca returned to the first page. "Odile was neither the executor, nor was she a beneficiary. I understand now why she contested it."

"If she was not named the executor, who was?"

Bianca flipped through the pages and confirmed the signature at the end. "Oro Tand."

She handed the testament back to Wemmesley. "Perhaps, sir, there is a reason you have not received Odile's will."

CHAPTER 16

"My master's wife dies on her wedding day, I spend the entire night consoling the man, I've had no sleep, and I come home to find my wife gone."

If Bianca had known she'd return to a bleary-eyed and irritable husband, she might have skirted the place and at least gone to market. "I didn't expect you back for a while. I thought it would be a long night for you. Why aren't you sleeping?"

"Boisvert has been taken to Newgate Prison."

"For questioning?"

"There is no questioning. The constable hauled him away."

"From Mayden Lane?"

"Aye, from Mayden Lane!"

"I thought Master Tand was going to provide the constable with a list of guests from the dinner and from there he would decide how to proceed."

"It wasn't much of a list if Boisvert was the only name on it."

Bianca picked up Hobs and scratched the back of his neck. "Do we know why he was arrested?"

"Odile's will is being contested. The solicitor claims Odile was of unsound mind."

"Paa! She knew well what she was doing."

"The constable believes the will incriminates Boisvert. I told you I had an uneasy feeling about this constable. Boisvert is being charged with murder."

Hobs leapt out of Bianca's arms, spying a mouse scampering along the wall.

John started up the stairs ahead of Bianca. He spoke to her over his shoulder. "Odile must have listed Boisvert as a beneficiary. Why else would he be under suspicion?"

"Constables are a dull and indolent lot. I am not surprised he came to that conclusion," said Bianca. "Seize on what appears simple . . . but the truth is never so obvious." They reached the landing, and Bianca searched through a box of gathered herb sprigs. "It is an insult to Boisvert's intelligence." She hated that her herbs were jumbled together; she would have to hang them from the rafters whether Boisvert approved or not. As it was, Boisvert wouldn't be around to complain. "I went to see Oro Tand this morning." Finding what she wanted, Bianca crumbled mint leaves into a small pot.

"Why must you trouble him? Can you not inquire elsewhere?" John irritably tended the fire, scraping aside the ashes. "I'm sure Tand was overjoyed to see you."

"I wanted to ask him why he was sitting outside of Odile's solicitor's office when they had their appointment."

"And his answer?"

"He pretended he did not remember. He was lying, as sure as the day comes. Finally he admitted seeing them there, claiming he doesn't recall everyone he chances to meet in a day." Bianca ladled water on top of the crushed leaves and hung the pot to boil. "As I was leaving, the officers from the Haberdashers' Company arrived. They are determined to gain some funding from the goldsmiths to help with road repairs for the king's progress."

"How does that have any bearing on Boisvert's predicament?"

"Master Tand claims the guild has no money to spare."

"I should think the Gold Guild has plenty of funds," said John. "Tand probably doesn't want to give any money to the haberdashers."

"Then he appears miserly withholding it. How does that make the Goldsmiths' Company look, if the king journeys down Foster Lane and learns that they did not act to repair the road for him?" Bianca found a small cup and a square of linen. "I should think they would not chance displeasing the king."

A pitiful squeak rose from a corner, and Hobs reappeared, triumphant, bearing dinner for his people. Bianca chased him down the stairs and shooed him out the door.

"If the guild *is* low on funds, that would be news better left quiet," said John when she returned.

"It might be useful to know. In fact, it might have some relevance. After Tand, I went to the register of the Commissary Court to find out the contents of Odile's last will and testament. Wills are public record there."

"Ah! So creditors can settle disputes and make one last attempt to collect their dues?"

"And so estranged relatives might make a claim on the estate." Bianca checked the water and poured it over the linen into the cup. "The clerk was quite helpful. The records are kept in the tower at St. Paul's. It was worth going there just for the view."

"Well and good. But what did you learn?"

"Odile's last will and testament was not there. We went through the stack of papers needing to be filed and it had not been received."

"Mayhap the solicitor has not gotten around to submitting it. Or maybe the will goes elsewhere since it is being contested."

"At some point the will should be filed there. But I got to read Lionel Farendon's last wishes." Even from upstairs they could hear Hobs scratching the door. "Would you let him in? Make sure he isn't sneaking in a half-dead mouse in his mouth."

John trudged down the stairs, the door creaked open, and in a moment Hobs appeared at the top of the stairs. He ran across the room to the table and landed within an inch of Bianca's cup.

"I discovered that all of Lionel Farendon's assets, apart from the obiits to be said on the anniversary of his death for the next twenty years, were bequeathed to the Gold Guild once his debts were paid."

"But Odile got Mayden Lane."

"Nay. She did not. It was to be sold. If she had not contested the will, she might have been cast from their home with nothing but her chattels."

John added more wood to the fire and layered some coal on top of it. "Why would he leave his wife with nothing?"

"Punishment, hatred . . . perhaps he had been coerced." Bianca blew on her cup of mint water. "I wonder if she told Boisvert anything about it." She closed her eyes and inhaled the steam, felt it tickle her nose. "Also, you might be interested that Oro Tand was the executor of Lionel Farendon's will."

"Oro Tand? Usually it is the wife's responsibility." John took an iron poke and prodded the fire. "Lionel must not have liked his wife much."

Bianca took a sip. "I did find it odd that Lionel Farendon's portrait was so prominently displayed on the way to the dining hall last night." She held the cup before her lips. "Why would the Goldsmiths' Company do that if not to prove a point?"

"I think it was disrespectful. Perhaps the intention was to intimidate Boisvert and Odile."

"Methinks there is some history between Oro Tand and Odile." Bianca set the cup down. "So the will is being contested, and Boisvert sits in gaol accused of murder. How convenient."

Hobs flopped over, exposing his belly for a rub. Bianca obliged and he stretched out like a long sausage. "I wonder if the lawyer truly believes Odile was of unsound mind. Or did someone encourage him to contest the will?"

John hung the fire poke and straddled the bench. "You mean nudged with an incentive? Unfortunately lawyers are more swayed by money and threats than virtue. It is hard to say, having never met the man."

"Another thought has occurred to me," said Bianca. "Most people do not make out their wills until they are on their deathbed. It is a person's final conscious statement of his intentions before he dies. I wonder if Odile sensed she was not well."

"Perhaps Odile sensed someone wanted her dead."

"I'd like to know the contents of that will." Bianca tapped a finger on the table and Hobs laid his paw on top. "Someone stands to benefit from contesting it."

Because Boisvert was being held in the most disreputable of London's prisons, John knew he would have to pave the way with coin in order to see his master. He filched several pennies from the cache of coins in the forge, reminding himself that he was only borrowing them; then he and Bianca parted ways, stepping out in opposite directions, sucking in brisk winter air that swirled with snowflakes the size of cobnuts.

Newgate was not so very far from Foster Lane. Once John was past the stalls of market and Christ Church, the stone façade was in sight. Its five stories made a horseshoe, and, entering the "Whit," one passed under the portcullis, above which stood a statue of Richard Whittington and his beloved cat. It was through his generosity that the current building had been erected, ensuring London's miscreants more spacious quarters—the luxury of which was negated by the addition of even more criminals.

After nearly emptying his purse into a turnkey's palm, John was led down a dim corridor to a set of narrow stone stairs. The sounds of human suffering and smell of filth were visceral enough to stun him into somber silence. At the end of the hall, he was handed off to another guard, who laboriously stumped up the treads to a second and then third floor, where the screams were less frequent and the smells marginally less offensive. With each successive level, he was lifted above the rank perfume of the Condemned Hold—the most foul of cells, where men and women, together, awaited their execution. Arriving on the top floor, John passed door after door where debtors and men of higher birth served their time, waited for their trials to be heard, and, in some unfortunate cases, waited for their own execution.

The guard stopped outside a door and peered through the iron lattice. "Owt, horse eater," he called through its woven grating, "ye've got a visitor come about ye. Wake up, fool; no sense sleeping away the little life ye got left."

John's stomach turned; he wondered how he would find his master.

The guard nudged John with his elbow and smirked, thinking John surely enjoyed his gibe. He slipped a cumbrous ring of keys off his forearm and searched for the right one. Pinching a key between his grubby fingers, he pushed it into the lock. With an echoing click, the pins turned and the door creaked open. John took a step, but an arm fell in front of him. With the other, the guard held out his hand.

"I have nothing left," complained John. "Ask the turnkey below. I gave it all to him."

The guard grabbed hold of the door and began closing it.

"Wait!" John dug into his pocket and found a farthing. "It's all I have. I swear by God's blood, it is this or nothing."

The guard's gaze went from the measly coin to John's face. He snatched it away and pushed open the door. "Ye only have the time of one turn," he said, holding up a bulky hourglass that hung from a chain around his neck. He flipped it over. "No more."

John crossed himself and tentatively entered the cell. To his surprise, it was slightly more spacious than he had expected. Boisvert's social standing had served him, if only for the small comfort of a private and more roomy cell.

"Master," John called, squinting into the dim hold. No candle burned from a sconce. Only the light from a narrow window worked against the dark. At first, John did not see his mentor, but as his eyes adjusted, he saw his master curled on a pallet made of rough-hewn wood laid with straw.

Boisvert pushed himself to sitting. "John." His voice had lost the bravado that had once steeled him in a "land of barbarians," as he called his adopted country.

John waited for him to say more, partly because he hoped he was wrong thinking his mentor demoralized.

"It lacks a certain warmth, *n'est-ce pas?*" Boisvert's voice was hoarse. He swept his eyes around the room, their whites barely glinting. "I do not care for *la couleur* of gristle. It does not favor my complexion."

"Boisvert," said John, rushing forward.

Boisvert waved him back. "You will catch the itch of fleas and other unpleasantness." Retrieving his cap from the straw, he brushed it off and struck it against his knees, sending mites to ride the particles of dust to the floor. He smoothed his sparse hair from his face and placed his hat on his scalp, tilted in Gaulish fashion. The Frenchman's dignity may have suffered, but his sense of style had not.

"They make certain concessions for those with money," he said cynically. "I only spent one night in the Hold of the Condemned." He pulled on the collar of his gown and sniffed it. "I still wear the perfume of its open sewer."

"Bianca is seeking Odile's solicitor to learn why you are being held."

Boisvert snorted. "Ha. He will not cooperate. He is the man who benefits from this."

"Why say you?"

"Because he knows Odile's wishes. He knows what happened in his chamber. No one can contradict his version, his words, his exaggeration. His fee, it is made, and he is content. Odile is gone, and now I am gone."

"You are not gone! Bianca and I shall see to this. You have suffered a most grievous loss, and now you are being unfairly accused. Someone stands to benefit from having the will contested, and we shall find out who."

A howl pierced the quiet, traveling through stone, causing John to shudder at its unearthly sound. If he did not have to spend an extra minute lingering, he would not. "Boisvert, what were Odile's wishes? Who would benefit from her death?"

Boisvert stared fixedly at the wall opposite. "I would benefit from her death."

"She bequeathed everything to you?"

"*Non, non.*" Boisvert shook his head. "Her soul, she took care of. St. Vedast has been left an endowment, a chantry for her soul. On the anniversary of her death, requiem masses and recitations would be made on her behalf. She does not wish to spend perpetuity suffering the pains of purgatory." Boisvert dug viciously at an itch through his netherhose. "She wished St. Vedast to be restored to its former beauty and she left money for me. So you see, John, it is me who is suspect, because a church cannot be thrown in gaol."

Boisvert fell into silence, and John waited patiently for him to continue. The room might have been better than most, but it lacked heat, and the cold gnawed to the bone. John was thankful that Boisvert's fur-lined gown had not been taken and wished that his own wool coat were as warm.

Another disquieting scream spurred John to continue. "Bianca visited the Commissary Court. Odile's will has not been received."

"That does not surprise me. Likely it sits on Benjamin Cornish's desk."

"Bianca found Lionel Farendon's will."

"He died so many years ago. It is still filed?"

"Lionel made provisions for a chantry at St. Botolph. He also requested that his entire estate, including the residence at Mayden Lane, be sold. Once his debtors were paid, the balance was to go to the Gold Guild. Odile was to get nothing."

"Ah! The Gold Guild?" Boisvert nodded as if a great mystery had been revealed. "I knew she had contested the will. Ultimately, she said it was decided by the king."

"The king had import?"

"What king does not? Odile was an attendant of Anne Boleyn. And Anne—she was very fond of Odile. Henry was still enam-

ored of Anne's charms when Lionel died. There was nothing he
would not do to win her affections." Boisvert smiled knowingly.
"The queen was a strong ally to have—once." Boisvert scratched
under his doublet. "*Mais non*, I did not know this about the guild.
I thought St. Botolph was the only beneficiary."

"You should know that the executor of Lionel Farendon's will
was Oro Tand."

Boisvert looked at John, surprised, then smiled sardonically.
"Well, Lionel and Oro Tand were like brothers. Perhaps the
guild wishes to settle a score."

John agreed. "The list of suspects has grown by two."

"No, my friend. It has grown by two buildings—the Goldsmiths' Hall and St. Vedast. Alas, they cannot hang a building."

"Nay. I am certain Oro Tand has had a hand in contesting
Odile's will and casting suspicion on you. He oversees the guild's
coffers, does he not?" It also occurred to John that Father Nelson
stood to benefit from Odile's endowment. However, the thought
of a priest murdering for money ran counter to what he wanted to
believe.

A door slammed down the corridor.

"John," said Boisvert, rousing his apprentice from his rumina-
tion. "You must see to Odile's funeral. Alas, I cannot. She de-
serves all of the respect we can buy. I do not trust there are others
who feel genuine love for her. Hire mourners, start the dirges at
dawn, give alms to the poor, have the great window of St. Vedast
replaced with colorful seraphs."

The guard cracked open the door and stuck his face in the
gap. "Be done with your business." He held up his hourglass—
which was short of sand, because John had not been there long.
"I can't be timing out visits all day."

"John, you must take care of these arrangements for me."

Tucking his chin in respect, John took a step backward to
leave.

"John!" said Boisvert. "And take Nico, Odile's spaniel."

"We have a cat who thinks he is king. Hobs will terrorize the
creature."

"Then all the better. Nico needs to learn the manners."

John hated the thought of taking care of an excitable small dog that yipped every time a moth fluttered by. But he could not add weight to Boisvert's brooding. "Very well," he said, caving to Boisvert's request. "But you must take him back when this is over."

"When this is over," said Boisvert, incredulous. "My friend, this may end very badly for me."

Chapter 17

Finished with another difficult morning listening to haberdashers argue for filling the ruts in the road, dealing with legal matters, hearing cases, and dispensing punishments at Halimote, James Croft braved the cold and walked down Foster Lane to St. Vedast. The road *was* in deplorable repair, but the funding was not entirely up to him. A little solace and quiet prayer would go a long way toward soothing his mind. He entered the nave, hoping to find it empty, and was annoyed to hear Father Nelson finishing a mass. The master of the Brown Bakers' Guild stood at the back of the congregation, close enough to hear but not so close as to participate.

The usual covey of parish lowlifes were in attendance. The fornicators and the sinners pretended pious attention to ceremony, as if God would judge them on outward appearance only and not see through their hides into their dark, despicable hearts.

Croft leaned against a column with his arms crossed, running his eyes over the pitiful state of the church's interior. The priest's words ricocheted off the vaulted ceiling, echoed between stark, cracked walls, merged into a muddle, lulling the congregation into complacency. Then, like a mischief-maker who'd gotten into the sulfur and saltpeter, Father Nelson startled the nearly comatose with an impassioned boom of words.

As Croft listened, he noticed Henry Lodge skulking into the nave. He must have taken a break from his duties to soak in a little piety, Croft thought. The master baker glowered at the churchwarden, daring the man to look his way. He still took offense at the churchwarden's tacit refusal to tell him where the church was getting its wafers. Perhaps he should tell Henry Lodge that his secrecy had been for naught—that he had discovered the church's sanctioned bakery anyway.

A mean chuckle rumbled in his throat.

The large wafer was held aloft and the sorry sinners shuffled forward to stick out their tongues at Father Nelson.

Croft sighed, remembering the priest who had been at St. Vedast before Father Nelson. The man's name was Fortin, translated from Firteau. Like other descendants through whose veins coursed alien blood and who distanced themselves from their parents, the man had held his birthright like a closely guarded secret.

Croft was watching the parishioners smack their lips on Christ's body when he heard a clatter from the chancel. The young altar server had dropped the plate of hosts and was crawling around collecting them.

God's nails, thought Croft, a French priest in a church named for a French saint is a more honest fit than a bumbling Anglo-Saxon who can't even dispense communion properly.

He spied Henry Lodge leaving the nave. The bread master's churlish disposition had not softened, and he pottered after the churchwarden, following him into a room where the records were kept.

Lodge looked up in surprise at the bread master's arrival. "Master Croft," he said, both acknowledging and questioning his entry.

Croft strolled around the periphery of the room, scanning the shelves of theological books and bound records as if he were inspecting them.

"Is there some matter I might help you with?" asked Lodge.

"Matter? Matter. Well . . ." said Croft, stopping for a closer look at the spine of a book. "Are you still receiving wafers pro gratis?"

Lodge blinked at Croft and tilted his head. "Croft, I ask that you not start beating that drum again. We must cut our expenditures in any way possible. Our choice is not an indictment against brown grain; it is simply a compromise because of our struggling finances. Surely you can understand that."

"The choice is a violation of tradition."

"And is it tradition to let St. Vedast fall into shambles?" Henry Lodge's voice was tight with emotion.

Perhaps the man did care for the parish church in his own warped way, thought the master bread baker. Still, it was no excuse to toss away hundreds of years of tradition to save a few pennies.

"Master Croft, please excuse me. It has been a long night." The churchwarden returned a book to a shelf and remained with his back to Croft.

Croft was so accustomed to the bluster of bakers that a crack in this liveryman's exterior began to thaw his own cold crust. He studied the floor near his feet.

"We lost a church member last night," said Lodge softly.

"I am . . ." Croft searched for a word. ". . . Sorry?" he finally offered, though, he thought, one less sinner at St. Vedast was a good thing. He saw the churchwarden give a slight nod. Perhaps he should leave the man to his grief.

"Odile Farendon."

"Odile Farendon . . . died?" Croft wondered why Lodge was so shaken. "She was to be wed, was she not?"

"She *was* wed," answered Lodge. "She died at her wedding dinner."

"Oh," said Croft. "But the lady lived a good life. She did not want for anything." He thought it important to remind the church-warden. "Not like some poor wretches we see around here," he added jovially, expecting Lodge to cast off his gloom and vehemently agree.

Instead, the churchwarden withdrew a handkerchief and blew his nose.

When one digs a hole for oneself, the prudent choice is to stop digging. However, James Croft lacked that kind of sensitivity and pulled out a bigger shovel. "Well, death does not care whether one is happy or not." Croft waited for a reply, but none came. The poor soul couldn't speak without crumbling to pieces. Nothing made Croft more uncomfortable than seeing a man show his feelings. "Courage, sir! You must bolster those bollocks!" He said this in all earnestness, believing it good advice.

The churchwarden faced the master baker. His upper lip lifted. "I take no comfort in your words, Master Croft. Obviously you care little for the members of this parish. I cannot condone your attitude, nor does it prompt me to resume purchasing hosts from sanctioned bakeries associated with the Brown Bakers' Guild. If you worry that your guild is suffering from the success of its competition, you might look upon yourself to find the answer as to why. God save you, sir." With a curt bow, Henry Lodge exited the chamber, leaving James Croft buried in bewilderment.

Clean white snow coated the streets and buildings. It stuck to the frozen ground, making the walk a slippery one. John hurried up the steps to St. Vedast and went inside. Unfortunately, the interior was no warmer than outside. John stamped the snow from his shoes and brushed off his jerkin and cap.

Father Nelson was giving mass, so John watched for a few minutes, then decided to wait for the priest outside the vestry. He left the nave, and halfway down the hall he heard voices coming from a room. John slunk along the wall, inching close enough to listen without being observed. Two men were having a duel of wits, and at the mention of Odile Farendon's name, John's interest was piqued. He cautiously peeped around the open door and saw the churchwarden and bread master.

The bread master looked a buffoon, speaking irreverently about the wealthy widow—that there were others one should be more sorry for. The churchwarden abruptly ended their exchange and started for the door.

John feigned disinterest when the churchwarden stalked past with a face as red as smelted ore. A few steps down the hall, Lodge whipped out a kerchief and blew his nose. In a moment, James Croft sheepishly emerged, startling at seeing John loitering within earshot. Without a word, he hurried off in the opposite direction.

John stood a moment, looking after the men, then walked to the vestry and peered inside. Father Nelson had not returned from the chancel. He leaned against the wall, thinking.

It was the bread master whom Bianca had taken issue with the first day they arrived on Foster Lane. She had objected to the man's insensitive remark about the young woman who fell from the church's roof. Perhaps the man simply disliked women. John shrugged. He was not the first to malign the fair sex.

But the look on Henry Lodge's face told a different story. It was as if Lodge had been shaken by Odile's death. On the one hand, Lodge seemed imposing—indifferent to people and their predicaments. During the wedding, he had been party to the gold master's heedless mocking of the bride. So why the sudden strained emotions? Did he feel remorse for his boorish behavior given Odile's unexpected death? But Lodge's expression wasn't one of shame. It was one of torment.

John grew impatient waiting. He wandered back to the nave, where the last of the congregation was leaving. Father Nelson had seen the last of the parishioners out the door and was returning to the chancel. John was following after, when halfway there he heard a disquieting creak overhead. He stopped and peered up at the opening in the ceiling where the bottom of St. Vedast's massive bell appeared.

Father Nelson heard it too. "God save you, son," he called. "How may I serve you?"

"I heard a noise," said John with his head tipped back. "A worrisome sound, coming from the belfry."

The priest walked back to John and led him toward a stone column. "It is all in order. There is no need for concern."

John glanced uneasily at the priest.

"I understand your master has been taken to Newgate," he said gently.

"Unfortunately, that is true. I have just come from there. He is managing to maintain his humor."

"I don't see how," said Father Nelson. "Such a heinous act is not one that should be made light of."

"He has asked me to tend to matters concerning Odile's funeral."

"Her body is with the apothecary and he shall see to the embalming. Has Boisvert further wishes?"

"He wants mourners, a proper burial in St. Vedast's cemetery. . . ."

"I believe the ground is too frozen to accommodate that request. Perhaps a crypt, a carved sepulcher, would be the more prudent choice?" Father Nelson watched John's face for an answer. "Think on it." He hesitated. "Will there be a feast?"

The idea of a funeral feast on the heels of a disastrous wedding dinner seemed inappropriate, unthinkable, to John. Besides, Boisvert might not be able to attend. "I think not, sir. In regards to arrangements, I am not sure what to say."

Father Nelson nodded. "There is time to consider the options. I shall contact you when Odile's body is returned to us."

John had turned to leave when the priest broached one final topic.

"There are fees," he said. "Mourners must be hired; there is a charge for the mortuare. . . ."

"It can be deducted from Odile's estate."

"Perhaps you know who is handling the probate?" The priest inclined his head.

John had no idea where the will was or where it was to be proven, or even if it had been submitted for probate. His indecision prompted the priest.

"Then perhaps the name of the executor?"

John blinked uncertainly. "I should think it is Boisvert."

Father Nelson offered a doubtful smile and waited.

The complications were becoming clear. How could Boisvert direct disbursement from Newgate? For that matter, how could Boisvert, or anyone, have access to Odile's wishes if the will was being contested?

John said, "Mayhap, sir, you would do better to contact Benjamin Cornish, their solicitor."

CHAPTER 18

Bianca found Benjamin Cornish in his office next to Middle Temple. The New Inn housed offices and accommodations for students and solicitors of more prosaic purpose. The lawyer's thin pate showed from behind a stack of books, his head down and his spectacles barely clinging to the end of his nose.

"Put the missives on the table. I shall get to them when I will."

"Master Cornish?"

The solicitor startled from his work and squinted up at her. "You aren't Bendish."

"Nay, sir. I'm Bianca Goddard. I carry no missives."

"How did you get in?"

"I knocked, and, getting no answer, I tried the door."

"That's bold. Doors are closed for a reason. It means *do not enter*."

"Forgive me, sir. But I have a matter of importance I would like to discuss with you."

"Doesn't everyone?" The solicitor removed his spectacles and waved them about to prove his point. "Cornish, can you get my tenant to pay his past due? Cornish, write this disposition. Prepare papers for a writ of sale. . . ." The solicitor leaned back in his chair and winced. "And what matter of importance is so dire that it requires you to interrupt my work?"

Bianca took a breath to speak, but the solicitor held up a hand to stop her. "Before you answer that," he said, "consider whether I shall be helpful. After all, you imposed yourself on me, uninvited."

"I do not suppose you should be helpful in the least. I do not expect your welcome. But I have a few questions about Odile Farendon." Bianca was growing weary trying to convince men of station to spare her a moment of their nonexistent time.

"I do not discuss my clients. And certainly I do not discuss their business with strangers. It is a code of ethics I follow."

"We must lean on lawyers to uphold the moral standard."

Cornish hesitated, regarding her through narrowed eyes.

"Instead of voicing your answer, you might nod or shake your head," suggested Bianca.

The solicitor was unmoved.

"I know that Odile Farendon and Boisvert came here to write her last will and testament."

Bianca took the lawyer's silence as his tacit agreement.

"I know because Boisvert told me. My husband is his apprentice."

The solicitor was not going to make it easy for her.

"Why are you contesting Odile's will?"

A long sigh sang from Cornish's lips. "Odile was of unsound mind."

"Odile had a seizure. The condition does not permanently impair one's judgment or one's mental capacity."

"That is debatable."

"And who shall debate it? I do not trust that lawyers will come to an informed decision."

"I will overlook your insult. However, there is no alternative for debate except a legal one."

"I ask to see the will."

Cornish gave a derisive snort. "You can read?"

"Sir, you'd be surprised of what I am capable."

Cornish stopped. "You may not see the will."

"It is public record."

"It is not yet filed."

"The Commissary Court requires it."

"Are you here to remind me? It shall be there in due time."

"Boisvert is your client, yet you seem unconcerned that he sits in gaol, wrongly accused. If it were you sitting in Newgate, would you accept your lawyer's indifference?"

"I do not have time for your insinuations. Kindly take your leave. You arrived uninvited, and I find your meddling tiresome and unsubstantiated." Cornish rose from his desk and came around to escort Bianca to the door. He took hold of her arm.

"Were you bribed to contest Odile Farendon's will?" Bianca asked, yanking her arm from his grasp.

Cornish glared. "A strict code of conduct prevents me from a lapse of integrity of the kind you are accusing me of. Now, I shall ask for you to take your grievance elsewhere. I should hate to have to call for help in seeing you thrown out."

When hunger pangs pleaded their case, instead of thinking about the priest's questions or the churchwarden's inexplicable grief, John turned his thoughts to his next meal. Was it too much to fancy Bianca preparing a succulent goose while he'd been gone? More likely, she was trudging around London, irritating solicitors and master goldsmiths with her questions. He hoped she had left Oro Tand alone. His acceptance into the guild might one day depend on Tand's support.

He had drawn the collar up on his jerkin and prepared himself to face winter's breath when the door to St. Vedast burst open.

First through was a man John recognized as a local cobbler. He wore no hat, and his jerkin was wet with fallen snow. Wet clay coated his hose, and he tracked mud onto the flagstone floor. "Where is Father Nelson?" he demanded.

"In his office, I presume."

The cobbler stalked across the nave, and John wondered what could be so important, when the door opened a second time, admitting a woman and two men. Between them they carried a lad, delirious and gray from the cold, who looked to be of ten years. They argued where to put him, whether to carry him through the church to Father Nelson.

"It is warmer near the chancel," suggested John, pointing toward the altar. "You might put him there."

John was watching after them when the door swung open and more people arrived, creating a milieu of fraught nerves and commotion. From what he gathered, the boy was senseless, taken by a raving madness. His hunger pangs forgotten, John followed them into the nave.

"He's not right," said one of the men, removing his gown and placing it over the boy lying on the steps. "Yesterday he complained of the cold and started shivering. My brother sat him by the hearth and put a wool blanket about his shoulders. But he kept shivering. Every blanket in the house was piled on him. Finally the chills stopped and his shaking passed. They stopped as fast as closing a door."

"He complained about his stomach," said the mother. "I thought maybe it was something he ate. He slept through the night, and we thought he had recovered. But after breakfast he wanted to lie down. I put him back to bed. He seemed comfortable and I went back to my chores. Not long after, I heard a clunk and found him on the floor."

She pressed her chest as if steadying her heart. "Foaming at the mouth he was. His eyes rolling into the back of his head."

"I never seen such a sight. Just his whites showing," added the brother.

"And his face twisted," said the mother. "He didn't look like . . ." She covered her face.

"Fiendish. He looked like a devil," said the brother.

"All of a sudden," said the mother, dropping her hands, "he jumps up and runs out the door. There was no stopping or calling after. He ran all the way to the river before we caught him. And there he was, up to his knees in muck and water, shrieking to leave him be." She dropped her gaze to her son, who lay motionless before them.

"It took three of us to wrestle him out of the mud and bring him here," said the brother. "He's a whip of a lad, but he suddenly got the strength of a bull. Halfway here, he went limp."

John knelt and pressed his fingers against the boy's throat, feeling his pulse. He was stunned by the boy's cold skin. "His heart still beats, but not strongly. Should you seek a doctor?"

"Nay," said the second man who'd helped carry him. "Something's not right in his head. He's been entered."

"This is not my nephew," said the brother.

A door creaked open from behind the chancel, and Father Nelson appeared, dressed in a surplice of white and a purple cowl. He walked to the rood screen clutching his prayer book against his chest and held a crucifix before him. The boy's father followed, and trailing behind, a boy carried a crucifix and holy water.

Father Nelson signed the cross. He dipped his hand in the pot and sprinkled holy water over everyone present. When the water struck the boy's face, it sizzled, and steam rose like it had touched hot coals. The boy was as cold as death.

The priest began his prayers, and when they slipped into Latin, the boy's eyelids flew open. It was as the uncle had said; only the whites of his eyes showed.

John stepped back, bumping into Henry Lodge, whose judgmental stare centered on the priest and boy.

At one point, Father Nelson touched the crucifix to the lad's chest over his heart. The boy lurched forward to sit and screamed. Taking hold of the rood, he threw it off with a vicious oath. It clattered across the floor.

"Hold him," said the priest. "Hold him down."

In a collective effort, the men leaned their weight on the boy, pushing him back. His strength was as his uncle had said. He writhed against them. His legs kicked, bruising one onlooker and knocking the wind out of another. John seized the boy's ankles to prevent his thrashing and felt his arms yanked in their sockets. Despite the boy's rage, the priest continued his ritual. He sprinkled holy water and intoned in a voice louder than the boy's screams. His hand upon the victim's head, he commanded the unclean spirit to depart.

The boy's eyes rolled. His mouth foamed like that of a tired horse.

The young assistant handed the crucifix to Father Nelson, and when it was touched to the victim's chest, this time it was not thrown off. Holding him fast, the priest made the sign of the cross over the boy's brow, his lips, and his chest. He looked down at his prayer book and continued to read.

More parishioners arrived as word spread through the neighborhood. They watched from the rear of the nave. The mother's weeping drowned the priest's words and the boy's unearthly shrieks.

At last the boy quieted. His thrashing ceased; his struggle ended. Father Nelson made the sign of the cross and removed the crucifix from the boy's chest.

John looked up and saw Henry Lodge walk away.

The boy was at peace. The boy was dead.

CHAPTER 19

Outside, the silver sky of day had turned into the murky haze of twilight as the sun sank behind Christ Church and the city wall to the west. John returned home. His hoped-for dinner of roast goose, of roast anything, was not to be. Bianca presented him with a loaf of bread and cheese for dinner.

"So the parents believed the boy was taken over by a demon?" Bianca sat opposite John at the board.

"I asked them why they did not seek a doctor, and they said that it wasn't like any illness they had ever known."

"So have they seen possession by unclean spirits?"

"I do not know. However, they believed Father Nelson could expel the entity causing their son's strange behavior."

"And now they blame Father Nelson for his death?"

"There was grousing to that effect. The family did not say it to his face, but they asked what he did to their boy."

"So the implication is there."

"An implication that sows seeds of doubt." John cut his bread lengthwise and neatly arranged the sliced pieces of cheese to cover it.

"Tell me his symptoms again?" Bianca propped her chin in her hand.

"I told you everything."

"Did the boy chatter? Did he speak nonsense that you know of?"

John took a bite and chewed. "Aye, he did. I remember the uncle telling me. He certainly shrieked while we were holding him down." He washed down his dry meal with a sip of ale.

"That was a symptom of the woman whose body was found beside St. Vedast the day we moved in."

"How do you know?"

"I spoke to someone who saw her fall."

"When?"

"The first night we were here. I couldn't sleep. I went for a walk."

"In the middle of night? Without telling me?"

"You were asleep."

John stared at Bianca.

"No harm," she said.

"No harm, but there could have been." John tore off another piece of bread and shoved it in his mouth. "There might still be," he grumbled. "Have you told the constable?"

Bianca shook her head. "It makes no difference now. Say you the boy had the sudden strength of a bull?"

"Aye. It took several of us to hold him down while Father Nelson performed the ritual."

"But before that, the boy ran to the river and was practically swimming in it?"

John nodded.

"The woman who fell off the roof was oblivious to the cold too. I'm beginning to see a pattern."

"Does it include Odile?"

"Boisvert didn't say she suddenly became as strong as an ox, did he? She didn't seem to suffer that symptom." Bianca wound a strand of hair around her finger, lost in thought. "And the boy finally died?"

John cut himself more cheese and nodded.

"How were the men holding him down?"

"I had his ankles, the uncle leaned on his thighs, and the father draped himself across the boy's chest."

"Do you think he compressed his son's chest to the point where he could not breathe?"

"God's truth, I could not see past the uncle. They were large men. The father was nearly on top of him."

"Do you think the father could have wanted the boy dead? Could he have suffocated him?"

"And stage such a performance in order to do it? I did not sense that the family was anything but sincere. In truth, Bianca, your preoccupation with death and motivations for murder has made you distrustful. I sometimes wonder whether you even trust me. Does anyone escape your suspicion?"

"I don't look at people in the same way as I did when we first met. Distrust is a consequence of growing older, John. I've learned people act in complicated ways."

Hobs jumped up on the table and padded past, stopping to tickle John's nose with the tip of his striped tail. John pushed him on. "If this is a murder, whether planned or accidental, I do not care to become involved. Perhaps that is heartless of me, but we have enough to ponder with Boisvert and Odile."

"I am not saying we should involve ourselves here," said Bianca. "While I'm sorry a boy died, perhaps the consequences of his death are more important. Think on how Father Nelson is being perceived."

"He looks inept, weak." John dawdled with his bread and cheese. "But what an elaborate theater to show him thus."

"Don't think about whether it was theater or not. Think on the consequences and bear them in mind."

"Something else happened that gave me pause." John took a drink of ale. "Originally I sought Father Nelson to convey Boisvert's instructions about Odile's funeral. I overheard a strange conversation between the churchwarden and the master of the Brown Bakers' Guild. Lodge sounded quite terse, and the bread master sounded like a clumperton in response. The churchwarden stalked from the room, and I believe he was snuffling."

"Snuffling?"

"He was fraught with emotion. Then Croft sheepishly appeared, saw me, flushed an impressive shade of scarlet, and skulked away."

"What had they discussed?"

"I don't know exactly. It seemed to me Croft was angry, and the churchwarden turned the table and directed his anger at the bread master. I heard Odile's name."

"And Henry Lodge was upset?" Bianca thought a moment. "He's a tight-lipped, cautious cuffin. At the dinner I saw him glaring at her. I was surprised when he approached the table and spoke kindly to them."

"I didn't notice."

"He nearly upset Odile's goblet of wine."

Hobs made another pass in front of John's nose, stopping in front of the cheese to sniff. John moved him on again. "So what are you thinking?"

Bianca shrugged. "That is curious about Henry Lodge." She stared at John absently, lost in thought.

"And did you find Benjamin Cornish?"

Bianca's eyes lost their distant focus and pinned him. "I sought the solicitor at his chamber near Middle Temple. He almost threw me out when I suggested he may have been bribed to contest Odile's will."

"A sure sign that he was nudged." John got up to pour himself more ale. "I don't expect you learned anything useful from him?"

"Only that he is typical. But now I know where to find him. And did you find Boisvert?"

John's body rattled with an involuntary shudder. "Aye that. As grim a place as ever. He told me Odile's intent. She left some money for him, but the rest was to go to St. Vedast."

"To restore the church to its former dignity?"

"In a sense. She left money for the care and feeding of her soul."

"A chantry?"

"A chantry and obiits."

"I would have thought she would have made concessions for almsgiving."

John shrugged. "Perhaps she did. She seemed more concerned to hastily quit purgatory."

"So Father Nelson would have benefited."

"Aye. But what are you saying?"

"Even priests can offend God," said Bianca.

John shook his head. "You may consider him suspect, but I will not."

The corner of Bianca's mouth turned up. It was better to let the subject alone. John never ceased to baffle her with his cobbled opinions. His reasoning was usually founded on equal parts gut feeling, accepted convention, and falsehoods.

"I've forgotten to tell you," he said after a moment. "Boisvert has asked that we take care of Odile's dog."

"It can't stay at Mayden Lane?"

"Boisvert doesn't trust it will be properly taken care of by the servants."

"He thinks we can do better?"

"I'll go get him."

"Hobs will not approve."

"Well, if it comes down to a fight, it is not Hobs I'm worried about."

After a night of listening to the shrill barking of a confused spaniel, the intermittent crash of falling objects, and Hobs's hissing, John and Bianca slept in. Each of them had taken turns tossing Hobs outside, only to have him wiggle through a missing pane in the leaded window, and then the whole commotion would start again. Each time they argued over whose turn it was to make sure the house wasn't being ruined. Shutting doors didn't work, and tying Nico outside woke the neighborhood.

"I'm not sure I can survive many nights like that," said John, reluctantly crawling out of bed to take Nico out to water the dormant roses. "I'd rather empty all the jordans at the Dim Dragon

Inn than spend the rest of my life separating those two. We need to get Boisvert out of Newgate as soon as possible."

Bianca watched John pull on his netherhose and search for his shoes. "Perhaps you left them by the door."

John grumbled and shrugged on his jerkin, clumping down the stairs, while Hobs followed, keeping an active paw in further aggravating the two. Bianca rolled out of bed to stoke the fire.

Was it a coincidence that three deaths had occurred at St. Vedast in the course of so few days, or was it simply an unfortunate spate of bad luck? Bianca dropped her kirtle over her head and pulled on her wool socks. The boy and unknown woman had both shown impressive strength and a disturbing lack of common sense. Neither had been affected by the cold, although the boy had had a bout of shivering before he lost his wits. Odile showed no sign of excessive strength but had in common with the first woman an unusual contortion of her extremities.

The door slammed, and she heard John in conversation with Meddybemps in the shop below. She had just finished lacing her kirtle when Nico came bounding up the stairs, followed by John and Meddybemps.

"Bianca, my dove," said Meddybemps, interrupting John's animated telling of the exorcism. "St. Vedast seems to be as cursed a parish church as ever I've heard of."

"Perhaps it sits under a troubled star," said Bianca.

Meddybemps looked around at the interior of their new quarters. "Take heed; you are not so very far away."

"As good a reason as any why we should return to Gull Hole."

"We haven't been here a week," protested John, throwing more wood on the already stoked fire. "You haven't given Foster Lane a chance."

Meddybemps glanced at Bianca and led them out of another spat. "I heard Odile died at her dinner and Boisvert sits at Newgate waiting to dance the Tyburn jig. Now John tells me about this boy." Meddybemps went to stand by the hearth and warmed his hands. "Finish your story, John."

Resuming his tale, John embellished it to greater glory. The streetseller removed his red cap and turned it before the fire, concentrating on drying the wool in the most efficient manner while lending half an ear to John's exaggerations.

Meddybemps dug a finger into his ear. "And so now the priest of St. Vedast is defending the church and his ministry against those who accuse him of being unable to protect it from evil."

"There was some criticism afterward," said John. "The room was fraught with emotion. Likely, the family was looking for someone to blame."

"One man against many," mused Bianca, hanging a pot of water and dumping oats into it.

"One man of God against many," said John.

"By troth, unless this priest has special privileges, he is still just a man." Meddybemps watched Bianca chop prunes and drop them in the porridge. Perhaps he could delay long enough to have a bowl. Though he had never tasted Bianca's cooking, and he did wonder if she could create anything that didn't smell strange or taste like a salve. "I don't recall ever seeing you cook something other than a physicke, Bianca. How do you find cooking food?" Meddybemps's eye quivered.

"I find it mindless. But it's as close as I can get to fire these days." She stabbed a spoon into the pot and stirred, ignoring John's frown.

Meddybemps continued the conversation about the priest at St. Vedast. "His is not a position I envy. Three deaths in a week and two under his watch."

"It's unfortunate that these deaths have all been connected to his church. I'm sure other priests have experienced a bout of parishioners dying," said Bianca. But still she wondered if there was a connection between the priest and the mysterious deaths.

"It might be of some interest that I heard of similar antic behavior occurring in a small village beyond Aldersgate, north of London. The unseemliness happened about a month ago."

"How did you hear of this?" asked Bianca.

"At Cheapside. A woman was admiring one of my amulets that I made from a pigeon skull. It *was* rather winsome, with two per-

fectly round pebbles that fit in its eye sockets. I painted them up
to look like yours truly." Meddybemps batted his lashes and one
eye twirled independently. "She hailed from village Dinmow,
and she needed a charm to ward off the evilness that had over-
taken the village. Always keen for a laudable tale, I asked her
what sort of evilness. 'People acting peculiar, running about all
hours of the night, going for swims in the millpond when frost covers the fields,' said she. I asked if she'd heard about the woman
who had fallen from St. Vedast. She said she had not, and I told her
they couldn't be sure if she wasn't daft, drunk, or taken with an
evil entity. Her eyes got round as a pod's peas. 'Forsooth, 'tis the
same in Dinmow,' she exclaimed. 'Half a dozen acting as witless
as the king's fifth wife.'" Meddybemps smiled tartly. "Remember Catherine Howard? The rose of many thorns and even more
pricks." The streetseller found inspiration in this and erupted in
patter—

> "A pretty man did come to court
>   And wooed a pretty queen.
> He plumped her pillows and smoothed her sheets
>   And laid himself between.
> She was a saucy doxy—
>   He was a jackanape—
> Instead of dancing the pavane
>   He hangs from Traitors' Gate."

"What else did the wench say?" asked John impatiently.

"I'll buy it!" said Meddybemps.

"Nay, that is not what I meant. Did the afflicted die or act as
strange as if they'd lost their sense?"

"I told you they did," said the streetseller.

"I think we should visit this village." Bianca ladled a bowl for
each of them.

Meddybemps sat down with his serving and ran his narrow
nose through the steam. "I believe this is edible," he said, looking for confirmation.

"Horses and Scots think so," said John, tentatively dipping his spoon into his bowl.

"I want to know more about this outbreak in Dinmow." Bianca sat down and stared meditatively into her bowl of oats. "I wonder if they are victim to a disease. One that has never been seen before."

"This isle suffers no dearth of witless fools. Distinguishing between disease and idiocy is a thankless endeavor," said Meddybemps. Nico settled next to him and gazed up at the streetseller beseechingly. "What do you call this groking cur?"

"Nico. It was Odile's and now it is ours," said John.

"Until we get Boisvert out of Newgate," said Bianca.

Nico put his paws up on the bench next to Meddybemps. "He wants my oats."

"Even dogs can be fools," said John.

Meddybemps took another bite, then, unable to ignore the creature, glared at it, his eyeball rolling crazily. Nico yelped like he'd been slapped and hid under the bed. "This is favorably good," the streetseller said, scraping out the last bit of porridge and licking his spoon. He set the bowl down and grinned. "I shall be on my way now. The market beckons."

"How far is Dinmow?" asked Bianca.

"A day's journey, I believe. Faster if you ride." Meddybemps rose from the table and stood by the fire, warming himself as if he could store it up before returning outside. He watched Bianca finish eating. "What shall I do when I run out of your medicinals?" It was a question that needed to be asked. He regretted that John was there and did not look forward to his surly input on the matter.

"I hope to find a room to practice in before long." Bianca glanced at John. "If you hear of any discreet, out-of-the-way vacancies nearby, let me know."

Bianca and Meddybemps waited for John to speak. To their surprise, he did not.

CHAPTER 20

It was August when last Bianca had visited the area off Ivy Lane, where her mentor, Ferris Stannum, had once lived. She had known Stannum only briefly, yet his influence on her work and life had been important. Walking through the run-down neighborhood, she felt a pang of regret remembering the alchemist and the man who had murdered him. It was a murder wrought from love. A love that, unfortunately, found its greatest passion in the murder of a brilliant alchemist.

The crooked stoop outside of Ferris Stannum's rent had not been leveled, and she ran her eyes up to the second floor, where a shutter creaked open. Without so much as a glance down, a young woman dumped the contents of a bowl out the window. The slop of sour milk and vegetable peelings splattered in the lane below. The shutter swung shut.

Even when Bianca had visited during the intense light of summer, the street retained a dreary, bleak feel. The neighborhood was situated in such a way that it never benefited from the sun. The buildings were perpetually gray and furred with mildew. It was no different in winter's stingy light. The lane was forever doomed to feeling like a cellar. Only centipedes and mushrooms thrived here.

But Bianca wasn't here to see what had become of her mentor's rent. She was here to find Ferris Stannum's neighbor.

She didn't expect the boy to be outside in the cold and slush of melting snow. He preferred the street to his mother's rent, which only made Bianca wonder what its interior must be like. But the waif was a bright lad, savvy on how to make a coin. He was a keen observer. It was this final quality that interested her.

Bianca stood on the stoop listening to children cry and the mother shouting. No wonder Fisk liked being outside. Bianca rapped on the door and waited, but no one could possibly hear her knock over the noise. She pounded the door like an irate landlord. The commotion instantly quieted.

"I'm looking for Fisk," she called. There was another moment of silence, then the whimper of a small child. The door cracked open and Fisk peered out. At the sight of her, he smiled a big-toothed grin.

"Master Fisk," said Bianca. "It has been a few months."

"Aye that, Mistress Bianca." The boy opened the door and gestured her in.

"Who is it?" called a voice, and then Fisk's mother entered holding a babe, while a toddler clung to her leg like daub on wattle.

"I'm Bianca Goddard. Fisk helped me a few months back."

"Did he now?" Her tone and expression trumpeted disapproval. "I hadna' heard."

Fisk remained quiet. Apparently he had kept the coin to himself, along with how he had earned it.

"He's a generous and helpful boy," said Bianca. "A keen observer. He helped bring a murderer to justice."

"Now, that is rich." The mother appeared doubtful. "A right secretive boy, he is."

"I'm sure he didn't want to boast." Bianca smiled fondly at Fisk. Unable to think how she might enlist his help without his mother knowing, Bianca simply voiced her request. "I need Fisk to work as an altar server at St. Vedast. He shall earn a little from it."

"St. Vedast!" said the mother. "Its priest is a bumbling dolt. The church is being overrun with demons and he can't keep them out."

"I don't believe that is entirely true, Goodwife. I want Fisk there to tell me what he sees."

"To spy?" She pretended shock. "What business is it of yours?"

"I lost a friend, and another is in gaol wrongly accused." Bianca refrained from mentioning he was a silversmith for fear the mother would expect more payment than she could afford.

"That's not a worriment a lass like you should bother with. Leave it alone."

"It affects me when people I know are in trouble. I cannot look away."

"Lass, I shall tell you. The secret to a long life is knowing when to look away." The mother shifted her baby to the opposite arm. "Besides, who will listen to you? It will likely end badly."

"Like I said, I am prepared to pay for your son's help."

Having dispensed with her motherly advice, Fisk's mother was, above all else, an opportunist. "How much?"

Bianca could hardly afford to pay her a groat, but they came to terms, Bianca rationalizing that the mother had probably earned her share by raising a son as cagey as she.

An hour later there was a rap at Bianca's door. After a moment it swung open.

"Oh," said Fisk, taking a step backward, confused. He checked the exterior of the rent and scratched his head. "I'm looking for . . ."

"Bianca?" The woman hustled him inside. She put her hands on her hips. "Where've ye been? I've been waitin' for ye."

Fisk stared hard. "Bianca?"

"Aye that. You are looking at her." With some ably applied smudges and suet varnish painted on her teeth, Bianca had transformed herself into a harried mother at wit's end. "What say you? Do I look presentable?"

Fisk smiled. "Nay, not presentable—believable. But me mother would have done it if you'd paid her."

"I can't afford her prices."

Hobs wandered into the room to inspect his new courtier and spat at Nico, who was bounding past. The spaniel yapped at Fisk until Bianca picked him up. "This is Nico. There is nothing subtle about him." She opened the door again and let Hobs outside, hoping to avoid another battle of the species. "I need for you to keep your ears and eyes open at St. Vedast. See what you can learn. Don't trust anyone."

"I haven't been to church in a whiles."

"Then all the better. Shall we go?"

The two sauntered down Foster Lane, and within yards of St. Vedast, Bianca grabbed Fisk by the ear and pulled him along. "Come on, ye ungrateful nidget," she said, dragging him up the steps to the church. There was no pretending on his part. Fisk yowled expertly.

Bianca pushed him through the door and proceeded to berate the boy for his thievery and rascally ways. "I've had me fill of ye, boy! If yer father were alive, he'd beat some sense into ye. But maybe if ye learned the ways of God, ye might learn rights from wrongs. I've tried me best with ye."

Father Nelson peeked from behind the chantry screen, and Bianca booted the boy in his direction, hailing the priest for help. Unfortunately for Father Nelson, there would be no sneaking away. Irked that he'd been unable to avoid notice, he stepped into the nave and pressed his palms together. "Goodwife, what is your worry?"

"My worry?" said Bianca in a wretched voice. "'E's my worry. He'll roast in hell if he doesn't change his ways. He'll twist at the gallows someday, I just knows it. I want to see 'e gets right with God." She smacked him on the back of the head.

"I may do confession if he allows it," said the priest.

"'E needs more 'an that. 'E's a long way off, Father. Ye needs to takes him into your good graces and teach him the ways of piety."

"My good woman, I have no means to take him in. I cannot possibly be his guardian."

"Is I askin' ye to be his guardian?" sniped Bianca. "Nay, ye take him as an acolyte. 'E isn't so daft as he can't learn."

"But I have no need for another server." Father Nelson tried to appear pleasant.

"Ye have no need for a soul in trouble?" Bianca took a step forward, getting squarely into his face. "I heard the rumors 'bout you," she said, squinting into his eyes. "They's sayin' ye is weak. They's sayin' that maybe the deaths at St. Vedast is because ye don't have the faith to protect your parish."

"Surely you have a mind of your own and do not rely on fiction."

"I do have a mind of me own," said Bianca, nodding. She looked at Fisk and seized him by his arm, pulling him in front of her. "And me thinks ye will take 'im in and set him right. I wouldn't want to believe what they says about ye. I don't have reason to think it is true . . . at least not yet."

Father Nelson looked from Bianca to the boy and back again. "What is his name?"

"Fisk."

"Very well, Fisk." He laid a hand on the boy's shoulder. "I shall do my best for your son," he said to Bianca.

Bianca grinned a black-toothed smile. "Bless ye, Father."

"If he should give me cause, I shall send him home."

"Aw, he won't, Father. Fisk wouldn't dare." She pinned Fisk with a stern look. "He wouldn't dare."

"Nico has to go back to Mayden Lane. We can't take him with us," said Bianca as she washed the suet off her face. The black tooth varnish took more effort. She dunked a rag into acid and rubbed her teeth. She grinned at John, who cringed.

"He shall be fine there for a day." Bianca dipped a clean end into the solvent and tried again.

"If he were immortal like Hobs, we wouldn't have to worry about him."

"I don't worry about him anyway." Bianca stopped rubbing her teeth and grinned again.

"That is somewhat improved. You'll just have to live with it," said John.

"It'll eventually wear off." Bianca tossed the rag into the fire, and it flared. "I'd like to leave as soon as possible."

After putting on an extra layer of clothing for warmth, the two set out for Mayden Lane. Leaving the next morning might have been preferable, but John relented, hoping Dinmow was not as far as Meddybemps thought. Starting this late in the day, they had only a few hours of daylight by which to travel. Neither of them had ever journeyed farther than Smithfield, and stories about vagabonds preying on innocent city dwellers bothered John more than they did Bianca. While John was imbued with a healthy dose of caution from years of living behind a tavern, Bianca was cursed with the belief that her ability to skirt trouble in London would translate beyond the city gates.

After they'd banged on Odile Farendon's door until their knuckles ached, it finally cracked open and the ever-suspicious house servant peeped out at them. "Here," said John, thrusting the spaniel through the open wedge. "We'll return within a day to retrieve him."

The servant had not been quick enough to shut the door in their faces and thus avoid dog duties, but when they'd gotten a few steps away, she managed an energetic slam.

"I don't believe he is a particularly well-loved dog," said Bianca as they headed toward Aldersgate.

The city entrance was only a short walk, and the gray stone wall, being at its tallest point here along its entire circumference, was easily visible. As they neared a block of buildings abutting the gate, the air became laden with the smell of turpentine and a hint of sulfur.

"They must use it in the ink," said John, gesturing to the printworks.

The two passed through the double gate, remembering that they must save money for their return toll. More people entered London than exited. Wagons from the country filed past, following ruts worn deep with use. They passed carts loaded with pigs and packed with turnips and apples. There was a marked difference between the road within and without the wall. Perhaps the king wished to make a favorable impression upon entry from the north. Aldersgate Street had a fine surface of closely laid cobbles, but only within the confines of London. Beyond the wall the pavers grew sparse, until there were none. Soon John and Bianca were trudging along the shoulder of the road instead of in the muddy soup made worse by the churning of hooves and wagon wheels.

They passed the grounds of St. Bartholomew, where every August the buildings became crammed with merchants selling bolts of cloth or horses. Jousts and gallows were set up for entertainment. If the crowds tired of such fare, they could watch puppet shows and caged tigers. With more people came a contingent of cutpurses to work the revelers, and Bianca and John had snagged decent coin when they were younger and more fleet of foot.

The one benefit to leaving London that they were quick to notice was the smell of earth. Not the filth to which they were accustomed, this was soil dotted by the pungent odor of occasional animal manure—such a change from the stench of ditch latrines and the Fleet discharging its rubbish into the Thames.

New buildings, the fresh roof thatch perfuming the air, sprang up along the route but numbered fewer the farther they traveled. Open fields for grazing sheep and cows eventually gave way to dense forest, and as they neared the tangled wood they sensed the danger inherent in its darkness.

They had just entered the wood when a farmer approached in his dray. He did not stop and barely slowed his horse. "Night is fast upon us. These woods grow sinister at moon's rise. Turn back, travelers. Let not the sun set on you here."

John ignored the farmer's dour warning. "Is Dinmow far?" he asked.

"Not everyone sees far the same way." The farmer, now free of the woods, slowed his horse long enough to tell them over his shoulder to veer left at the cairn with an angel on top.

"An angel?" asked John.

The farmer grinned and clicked his horse on.

"Why could we have not waited until morning to start out?" John looked around, realizing that dark in the country and dark in the woods were probably darker than any dark he'd ever known. "That man could have at least told us how far Dinmow was."

"I'm not worried. The road is worn enough that we won't lose it."

"It's not losing the road that I fear. It's what's on the road that troubles me."

Bianca looked around. "Nothing seems to be on it."

John didn't say anything but quickened his pace.

"Fear you devils and goblins?"

"Don't say it! Do you want to conjure them?"

"And what shall we do if we meet a devil in the road?"

"Give him your soul."

"He'd treasure yours more."

"Have you never heard of rufflers and footpads who prey on unsuspecting travelers? They can lurk in the woods and slice us as easy as roast chicken."

"I wish you wouldn't mention food. I'm getting hungry."

"Shh!" said John, putting his hand out to stop Bianca. "What's that?"

Bianca listened to a call from deep in the woods. "An owl. There are plenty of creatures who prefer the night."

"I'm not one of them. I think we should find a spot in the woods and wait until morning."

"Don't think on that farmer's words. Besides, what if Dinmow is a short walk away? How foolish would we feel spending the night in the woods when we could have slept in a bed?"

"I tell you, there are those who lie in furtive wait for witless travelers like you."

"I shall take my chance. It is too cold to spend the night sleeping on the ground. We must keep moving to stay warm." Bianca marched ahead, leaving John to stare after her. Standing in the middle of the road, watching his love disappear into the woods, he knew he would not let her get far. He drew his knife and ran to catch up.

"Ah. So you decided to join me?"

"Someone has to have some common sense about this, and since you display a surprising lack of it, I've decided to accompany you and keep you safe."

"I am grateful for that." Bianca kissed him on the cheek, letting him believe she needed his protection. It wasn't worth arguing, and besides, she knew he was probably right. They continued on, keeping a brisk pace and their eyes wide.

"Look there," said Bianca. She pointed up the road. Moonlight reflected off a stack of stones artfully balanced into a pillar.

"It looks like a cairn."

The road began to widen slightly, and they started up a steep incline. Nearing the top, the road split, and they strained for a better look at the cairn, which was set on a jutting outcrop above them. Something perched on top of the pile of rocks.

"What is it?" asked Bianca, trying to see.

John scrambled up the jagged ledge, sending down a shower of rocks.

"Here's our angel," said John, holding up a donkey skull, then pointing it to face him. "Strange wit, farmers."

Bianca found a boulder and sat down to rest, waiting for John to climb down. She blew in her hands, warming them against the chill. As the moon rose, it took with it the warmth of day. The cold was a damp, seeping one.

She listened for John, expecting him to rejoin her, then realized he'd become suddenly quiet. Alarmed, she stood and stepped away from the boulder. She was about to call to him when something hit her head. The donkey skull bounced into the road, and she had gone to pick it up when she heard it, too. Men talking.

Bianca looked up at John, who was waving her away. She dove into the woods and flattened herself against the ground.

Two carls, countrymen, but perhaps of more rascally intent, walked into view. They stopped at the fork, crept around the precipice, clinging to its stony face, and took a gander up the road intersecting with the one they had just traveled. Listening and hearing nothing, they stepped back into the road.

"I hear no hooves or glupping mud of men," said one.

"Aye that," said the other. "I thought I heard voices."

"Just the antics of your craven mind, Horatio." The first man uncorked a flagon and pulled long on it.

Horatio took the opportunity to water a patch of earth within spitting distance of Bianca. She could see the steam rise and flattened herself as much as she was able, imagining herself part of the ground.

"Ho, what is this?" Horatio's companion touched his toe to the skull, then picked it up. "This is not where you belong," he said to the cranium. He leaned back and looked up at the cairn on the precipice. "It must have fallen." He sighed. "Alas, poor donkey! I knew him, Horatio. An ass of infinite vigor, of most excellent hocks. He hath borne me on his back a thousand times. And now how abhorred my imagination is. My gorge rises at it." He turned the skull to face his companion. "Here hung those lips that I have kissed I know not how oft."

Horatio cringed. "It is a boast better whispered."

"We should set him on his perch. He should not be stamped upon and buried in mud."

"It is too dark to climb, you doddypoll. Set it at the base; his purpose will be seen and understood."

The man sized up the climb as his friend spoke.

"See that night has fallen? It is cold and your dead donkey knows no suffering. Cuds me, it knows nothing of my numb feet or the abuse I suffer traveling with you. Put your silly skull there and let us be gone. We have far to travel."

Reluctantly, the ass kisser laid the skull at the foot of the crags and gave it a pat.

The two slogged on, muttering to each other and cursing.

Bianca got to her knees and listened until their voices faded to nothing and she could no longer see them. John scrambled down the escarpment and they met in the road.

"I'm glad you didn't miss," said Bianca, looking at the donkey skull.

"You are an easy target."

Bianca looked askance at him. "I could not tell how far they had come. They gave no clue."

"Except to confirm that our angel is an ass." John bowed to the skull in mock respect. "The farmer said to take the road veering left."

"Then left we shall go," said Bianca, rewrapping her scarf and trooping off.

"I hope these woods end soon," said John, keeping his voice low. "Their shadows and strange stirrings trouble me."

"If we should break free of the wood and find an inn, then we should rest for the night."

John stopped, took her face in his hands, and kissed her. His hope restored, he resumed a lively gait. Nothing motivated him more than the thought of an ale and some sleep. Above, patches of sky peeked through oak branches reaching over the lane on either side of the road. The limbs creaked, rubbing against one another as the wind blew. A flutter of wings lifted an owl from its perch, and the creature took to the air, receding into the deep snarl of forest.

They moved on, stubbing their toes on rocks or an occasional paver probably fallen from a cart en route from a brickyard. The road was frozen in spots and mucky in others—the indecision of earth and season. The days would warm, and sometimes they would not. Mostly, though, the sun was swallowed by winter's argument.

John spoke very little, and Bianca followed suit. They walked quickly but kept their tread light. Ears listened for movement— for the snaps of twigs, the rustle of fabric, the squeak of a leather saddle, the clopping of hooves. The incident at the cairn had primed Bianca for the possibility of danger. The forest had its own language, its own peril, different from those of the streets of London.

Another rise in the road, with slippery rocks, slowed their progress. John took hold of Bianca's hand and steadied her as they navigated the scree, which loosened and gave way, providing no sure footholds.

"How do wagons manage this?" asked Bianca.

"Maybe the other road is more forgiving."

"But probably longer."

Finally the pines thinned and the sky opened out above them. They left behind the random drape of low-lying clouds and confining woods for the expanse of pasture and field. In the distance they saw the faint winking lights from a structure they hoped would be an inn.

John brightened. "I see no one skulking between hither and yon. Granted, it is not a village, but we can get our bearings and start rested in the morn."

"I haven't any idea how long we've been walking. Have you a sense?" Bianca hustled along, trying to keep up with her husband's long legs. "There is no church clock or chimes in the country. No watch to call the hour."

"Just the bleating of sheep," said John.

"Not even that."

A brook cut a deep swathe through the pasture, and they crossed a bridge laid with wooden trestles that wobbled from their steps. The building did seem like an inn of sorts. Lanterns glowed from scattered upper windows, and the low buzz of activity carried across the field.

"Wait!" Bianca grabbed John's arm and stopped walking. "We should stash our money in case there are thieves."

John patted the dirk he kept on his belt. "There is no need to trouble with that."

Bianca shook her head. "Nay. You will sleep like the dead tonight."

"You've grown worried?"

"I've grown wary. Running into those men on the road has made me realize how far we are from London. I don't know these roads or these people. I don't know their brand of trickery."

John smiled. "I think we should take enough for a room and board and perhaps a piddly sum extra in case we feel a blade on our throat in the middle of the night. We'll leave a coin out in clear sight when we go to bed. Mayhap they will just take it and let us sleep."

John noticed a small knoll with a clump of trees and boulders a short walk away. The two tromped across the muddy field and found a memorable rock to place on top of their buried purse. Satisfied they would not be left penniless, they angled back to the road and approached the inn.

Rough-hewn oak timbers ran diagonally and vertically, giving the building a solid, resolute presence in its isolated setting. Perhaps just over a knoll or beyond a stand of woods lurked signs of humanity, its houses and stables of animals. Certainly the pigsty out back hinted at this inn's industry, if travelers or locals were not enough to keep coin in the owners' pockets.

John pushed open the door, entering a room that had been made into a cramped tavern. It ran the length of the house, narrow and jammed with trestle boards and benches. Overhead, the rafters hung low, and John stooped to avoid being knocked senseless. Their entrance drew the stares of a loud crew of patrons, who stopped midsentence, midsip, midbite, to inspect the newcomers.

"Whose inn is this?" John asked.

A ruddy-faced woman rose from a table and sauntered over. "'Tis mine and me husband's. Are you in need of a room?" Her soiled apron reeked of animal fat and manure and spoke of her many duties.

"Aye, and board."

"Board is extra," she said, resting a fist on her hip. Bianca said nothing as John dickered with the innkeeper over the cost. She gazed around the room, aware that their haggling was being watched with interest. Finally, a price was agreed upon and the woman led them up a set of stairs to a narrow hall with three doors.

"How far is Dinmow?" asked Bianca.

"It is a couple hour walk yet." The woman lit a candle on a table. "Why? Be you headed there?"

John looked at Bianca. He'd not thought they might be asked.

"I'm looking for my cousin," said Bianca.

The woman straightened. "I know lots of folks in Dinmow. What's his name?"

"Emm, *her* name. Littleton," she said. "Margaret Littleton."

"I knows Margaret." Her face brightened. "So where's ye coming from?"

"London," murmured Bianca, surprised there was an owner to the made-up name. She hoped the woman wouldn't be nosy, and she wondered if admitting they were from London might be used against them. But she knew of nowhere else to be from.

"London, ye say? Hmm. I nevers knew the Littletons to have much to do with the place."

Bianca smiled wanly.

"Well, what are ye seekin' Margaret for?"

Bianca dropped her gaze to the floor, feigning diffidence, while John's eyes grew wide.

The woman noticed Bianca's reticence. "Wells, not really me business. Just makin' talk; that's all." She set the flint on the table next to the candle. "When ye get peckish, come down and we'll give you a tankard and stew." She edged out the door. "Mutton stew. The husband made it." She poked her head in one last time. "He likes his mutton."

The door clicked shut and Bianca and John let out their breath.

"We had better get a story straight, for now and Dinmow." John threw himself across the bed and kicked off his boots. "I'm going to get a permanent crick in my neck from these low beams."

Bianca dropped onto the bed beside him. "We can just say we have some news for Margaret."

"Nay, that makes people curious. They'll start asking more questions."

"What might we say that wouldn't make them ask questions?"

They both stared at the ceiling.

"Tell them you had some questions about her uncle."

Bianca wiped her runny nose. "What if she doesn't have an uncle?"

"Who doesn't have an uncle?"

"You, for one. Me, for another."

"As far as you know."

"As far as I know. But if I had my father for a brother, I wouldn't admit it."

John rolled onto his elbow and grinned. "He doesn't like me, does he?"

"Who—my father? It matters not. I'm his only child and he doesn't like me, either."

"Well, I like you." John kissed her, felt some fluttering, then made himself sit on the edge of the bed. "Let's get some mutton stew."

"I have great expectations for this mutton stew," said Bianca.

The two sat apart from the clientele, listening to a man sitting in a corner play a recorder. They kept to themselves and didn't say much as they downed their mutton stew—hearty fare with plenty of meat. Soon the patrons lost interest in them, so much so that they were mostly ignored. Bianca kept a watchful eye out for any inquisitive folk.

Content, with rounded bellies, the two retired to their room. The hearth in the tavern below provided enough heat so they were warm and could dry their wet stockings. They hung them from the beams, and soon Bianca's kirtle, John's jerkin, and their smocks dangled from the rafters. After leaving a penny next to the candle by the door, John crawled into bed, tucking his dirk beneath his pillow.

"We have no way to lock the door," he said.

"She's given us a special room." Bianca hopped out of bed and opened the door. "Hear that?"

"I hear the voices carry from the tavern." John sat up and patted the bed beside him. Though it was dark, John delighted in the faint outline of Bianca's figure. "Come to bed, wife. I have something to show you."

"No sound." Bianca swung the door back and forth. She ran her fingers along the hinges, then sniffed them. "Wool wax." She shut the door and crawled back under the covers.

"Well, if they should take our coin, at least they won't disturb our rest."

As she predicted, John fell fast asleep. Bianca lay awake, wondering if she should wedge something against the door to alert them if someone tried to enter. But there was no chair, nothing except the table. Sleep eluded her, as she could not rest while listening to the house settle. Every creak in the floor startled her. Finally, she rolled out of bed and moved the table in front of the door.

"I work hard for my coin," she muttered. "Even if it is just a penny."

CHAPTER 21

The added assurance worked like a charm, and Bianca followed John into a sound night's rest. The next morning they woke to the murky light of a dreary day. The table had not been moved; the coin had not been taken. After a breakfast of more mutton stew, the two set out in the direction from which they had come and retrieved their purse.

"That worked well," said John as they set off for Dinmow. "I don't think they even bothered to try our door."

"Still, we should avoid the place on our return." Bianca wrapped her scarf several times around her neck, tucking the ends down her front. "Now that they are familiar with us, they might become more daring."

They had not gotten far before a horse-drawn cart loaded with hay ambled past, headed for London. Ahead, another wagon approached, laden with sacks of grain.

"Is Dinmow far?" asked John when it neared.

"A bit," came the reply.

Unsure of the length of "a bit," they plodded on. A wind came up, dispersing the low clouds and letting in rare streaks of sun.

They spent time discussing what they had learned and speculated about the men whose secrets they did not know. "Have you heard that rhyme, 'Goosey, goosey, gander'?" asked Bianca.

John recited the rhyme with an easy lilt.

"Goosey, goosey, gander, where shall I wander?
Up stairs, down stairs, and in my lady's chamber.
There I met an old man who would not say his prayers.
Take him by the left leg, throw him down the stairs."

"I know the gander month is a woman's final month of pregnancy, and I know men tend to roam about then. Up stairs, down stairs . . . wherever they might find a willing, or unwilling, partner. But there I met an old man who would not say his prayers?"

"Perhaps a person who refuses to take responsibility for their actions," John suggested.

Bianca thought on that. "Could be. Or a papist who won't say his Paternoster in English."

"What has this rhyme to do with it all?"

"That is what I am trying to understand. It may have nothing at all to do with the deaths at St. Vedast; however, the woman who fell from the roof sang it at the top of her lungs."

"She was mad, Bianca. You cannot consider the ravings of a lunatic."

"Sometimes I think a lunatic is more honest than the rest of us."

Eventually the road climbed to a crest. Below, the land flattened out, and in the distance a small village appeared, sprouting up like a thistle in a cow patch. A river ran alongside the community, marked by uncut trees and overgrowth. Fields stretched before them, previously planted in barley and wheat or left fallow for grazing sheep and cows.

With the village in their sights, the couple forgot the cold and the inconvenience of the open road. Ahead was their destination and their hope to learn more about what had happened in Dinmow. Perhaps, thought Bianca, she would find connections between that and the strange incidents at St. Vedast.

The road wound around clumps of trees, avoiding a steep in-cline that could prove disastrous for an overfull dray. Bianca and John opted for the shortest distance and abandoned the road, leaving it for the wagons. Instead, they cut across the fields. Three-quarters of the way there, the two rested next to a stone wall. John took a sip from his skin of ale and offered it to Bianca. "I hope Meddybemps hasn't gotten the name of the village wrong."

"Or the story wrong. Not that I wish ill on anyone," said Bianca, "but this is a long way to travel for naught."

John agreed and picked a stem of grass to chew.

In the distance, Bianca noticed a ridge of worrisome clouds roiling in the western sky. "Look there. Rain is moving in."

John took off his boot and rubbed his toes to warm them. "We'll be able to stay ahead of it."

Bianca studied John relaxing against the wall. His chin tipped back and wisps of golden hair blew loose from his gathered tail. The grass arched from his mouth, and his bristly face needed a blade. She looked out over the field unevenly scythed, at crows feeding on untilled stubble and sheep grazing in the distance.

Bianca had another drink of ale. "Are you hungry?" she asked, tipping her head at the stalk hanging from his bottom lip.

"I'm not eating it," said John, tossing it over his shoulder. "Shall we go? The clouds are moving faster than I thought."

They avoided entering the village by the main thoroughfare, following the bank of the river until they came to a stone bridge above a gristmill. They paused briefly to watch the waterwheel turn. Neither of them had ever seen one before; no such contrap-tion existed in London.

"It looks like there is a stem that goes into the side of the building," said John, studying its mechanics. "I'd like to see how it works."

"Perhaps later," said Bianca, squinting up at the sky. "I felt a drop of rain on my face."

The two hastened across the bridge onto the main road part-way down the street. The lane saw heavy use and was churned into a trench of mud just wide enough for two wagons to pass. Thatch-roofed timbered buildings lined either side. Beyond the structures, the remains of an abandoned monastery hid behind the village—a blight on the landscape and harsh reminder of the king's new policies.

Bianca looked up the street and down it. A few men hurried along, holding their hats against a stiff wind. The creak of a sign swinging from an iron rod caught her notice. "The Stuffed Goose of Dinmow," she read. A corpulent goose wielding a tankard of ale winked at them overhead. "We are in the right place."

The words had barely escaped her mouth before the rain began falling as if a gate had been opened. They dodged a horse and rider, angled over to the tavern, and heaved open the door.

Others had a similar idea. The door swung open and slammed, admitting a steady stream of townsmen escaping the downpour. John and Bianca found a spot next to a farrier, the smell of horse manure wafting from his boots. They wedged themselves next to him.

John waved over the serving wench and ordered up tankards of ale. "I'd rather have snow than the rain at this point," he said, making conversation.

The farrier, an amiable fellow, must have been used to seeing newcomers in the village. "Stay that. I don't agree with ye," he said. He removed his cap and set it on the table in front of him. "Snow makes for a slippery way of it. It piles up and blocks the doors. Rain needs no shovel."

Bianca pulled off her scarf and unfastened her cape at the neck. She gazed around at the crowded tables, at the steam rising from people's heads and shoulders. The combined body heat and fire snapping in the hearth created a clammy ken.

"Where are you from?" the horse coper asked.

Not seeing the sense in lying, John struck up a conversation with the man.

"There are better places than Dinmow in the winter. The days are short to travel such a distance from London. But you are young. I suppose ye can run if you had to."

"We did not have to," said John as he paid the wench for their ales.

"Ah! Then you've luck on your side. But she smiles only if she wants. More often than not, she is a capricious trug."

"We are only passing through," said Bianca. "Be this Dinmow's only tavern?"

"Why do ye ask?" The farrier took a sip of ale.

"If more arrive, they'll have to straddle the rafters. For our next meal, I prefer a less crowded ordinary." As if she had just said the devil was her father, the men seated nearby stopped talking and looked over.

The farrier set his tankard in front of him. "The monastery alehouse sits on the edge of town."

"It is less frequented?"

The farrier glanced around at their tablemates exchanging looks. "It has fallen out of favor."

One of the men snorted. "Cuds me, generously worded, Grayson."

On the other side of Grayson, a man leaned in front of the farrier. "The devil pisses in the food."

Grayson elbowed the man back. "The monastery has been dissolved. The royal commissioners stripped its lead, smashed the saints, and took the relics. They dropped the bells, shattered them, and carted off the metal. The prior is gone. Almost all of the monks are gone—pensioned or fled. When the commissioners rode out of town, the looting began."

"Did the town think so poorly of the abbey?" asked Bianca.

"Nay." The farrier shrugged and his tablemates agreed. "But why should we ignore what the king didn't want? It helps no one if it is left to rot."

John undid several buttons on his jerkin and loosened the collar of his smock. "There isn't a monastery on this island that hasn't fallen to the royal commissioners. The punishment comes by the king's hand, not the devil's water." He had grown warm from the ale and room of packed bodies. He took off his cap and fanned himself with it.

The farrier grumbled. "Maybe the king holds the devil's member and aims it where he wants." He leaned over and fixed John and Bianca with a stern look. "Ye go to that alehouse, ye is playin' with your everlastin' soul."

A man sitting separately from the others broke in. "Grayson, ye is perpetuating an untruth."

"How is it an untruth? Ye seen what happened. There is no explanation for it. Once the commissioners cleaned out the priory and church, there was nothing sacred left to protect it. They are just barren buildings, stripped of everything that made them holy. Weak and falling to ruin. Vulnerable to the devil's mischief."

Bianca spoke. "And that mischief be?"

"The grounds were plucked clean by a nobleman who owns two others and cares not what happens to the property. A handful of brothers convinced the townspeople to leave the brewery be until they spoke with the man—there being no other source for the quantity of ale to quench the thirst of Dinmow. He agreed to let them stay and keep it as their means. But the brothers raised the price of ale for the Stuffed Goose. Elgin, the owner, balked and planned to start his own brewery." Grayson took a sip of ale. "The brothers countered. They promised not to raise their price of ale for five years on condition the Stuffed would not pursue brewing. They convinced Elgin that the tavern couldn't make their own ale for less."

One of the men listening to Grayson chimed in. "The brothers couldn't raise the price of their brew, so they entered into an agreement with the parish church and started serving fare. No one says they couldn't. They did a decent business. The Stuffed wasn't happy about the competition."

Grayson laid the back of his hand on the man's chest and looked round at them. "But then they offered their fare for less than the Stuffed. Who wouldn't choose to eat cheaper if it tasted the same? No one has a penny to spare these days." His eyebrows lifted as he nodded. "The competition seemed a healthy wager between the two. One week the Stuffed would bring in more, then the next week the church alehouse. Elgin at the Stuffed settled down when he took over the house next door and added more rooms to his inn. His business balanced out. Everyone got by."

"Oh, I thinks the Stuffed took exception. Soon every bench was filled at the alehouse," one of the men commented.

"Perhaps the food tasted better," suggested Bianca. "Besides, a man with more money could buy more ale."

The man responded. "The food is the same. The farmers are the same. Neither place could make a better pie than the other. Only difference bein' the price of the fare."

"And maybe something more," said Grayson, coyly.

"Like what?" said his mate.

"Like maybe the brothers promised a couple of Paternosters for your soul every time you ate there."

The men laughed.

The man on the other side of Grayson looked around, then leaned in again to whisper. "Methinks the Stuffed may have contrived against the alehouse."

"Naw, ye can't go accusin' Elgin of mischief," said Grayson, pushing him back. "I've known him since he was a bump in his mother's tummy. His mother looked after me when I was a pup. She was a moral woman."

"Children can turn out differently from their parents," said John. "Could anyone else resent the church alehouse making a profit?"

The men grew thoughtful.

Grayson spoke. "I tell you, it is by the devil's hand." The farrier was not to be convinced otherwise. "One night nearly everyone who ate at the church alehouse got sick within a day of it. People started trembling. They lost their gorge. They soaked themselves in their own sweat." He looked round at the men. "Royson Davis squawked and ran out of the house like his arse was on fire."

"If I had to dock that wench of his, I'd run too," sniped another.

"It was as if they'd left their wits at home in a jar," continued Grayson. "But then, some of them acted like they knew the ale-house was to blame for their ailments. They gathered on the monastery cemetery and danced like their spines were made of rope. Dipping and swooping, screeching mad. They gave no mind to stepping and stumbling on the graves; we were sure a hand would reach out and give them a tug. Not one would listen to reason. There be no use in leading them home; they had none of that. They were numb to everything and everyone. So, the families called on Father Paston at the parish church. They found him hiding under the altar. They had to drag him to the cemetery."

"All they wanted was his prayers. Cowardly man of God," said one of the men.

"I think he worried he'd be blamed for their strangeness," said Grayson. "He being the last practicing cleric in the village. When they pillaged the monastery, they took something of Father Paston's faith along with it."

"Did anyone recover from the 'strangeness'?" asked Bianca.

The men shook their heads and crossed themselves.

"Not a one. Six died." Grayson finished off his ale and sat a moment in reflection. "One climbed to the top of the paddle wheel at the gristmill and thought he'd ride it around. The miller was working late that night, grinding flour to get ahead of the orders. By the time someone got to him and told him to turn the sluice gate, it was too late. Stukes rode the wheel down, all right. Got wedged beneath it and drowned before they could pull him out. Davis and another took to the river and drowned. Weston fell off the stone wall and cracked his head open. Bled to death. Fletcher danced until he died. Stomping fierce, he wore the big toe off a foot and broke his leg. The fool danced until he dropped.

"And Richard Beys was the strangest of all. Makes me think that the devil sits in the ruins. Beys started screaming that a nest of vipers was in his stomach. Said they were eating him from the inside out. He grabbed a knife and begged his brother, Tom, to slice him open and remove the snakes. Tom wouldn't do it. He wrestled the knife from Richard's grip and did his best to try to calm him. But then Richard seized the blade and sliced his own hide from navel to sternum. He reached into his belly and pulled out his entrails."

The men at the table sat still from the memory of it. The mood grew subdued. Whether the men's silence was from dismay or superstition, Bianca couldn't say. But a village such as Dinmow was small enough that neighbors were as close as family. There was a certain shame that came from talking about your crazy aunt to a new acquaintance. They had just overstepped the bounds of decency.

CHAPTER 22

From their chamber window at the inn of the Stuffed Goose of Dinmow, Bianca watched the forlorn monastery at the edge of town sulking in the relentless downpour. No one came or went from the parish church next to it or the associated buildings. The rain might have had something to do with keeping parishioners away, but certainly the alehouse was struggling with a battered reputation.

"We must go have an ale at the brewery," said Bianca. "We shall talk to them like newcomers and pretend we haven't heard what happened."

John was listening to the patter of rain, dozing in comfort on their feather-stuffed mattress. The inn or, rather, the bed had won him over, and the thought of slogging through mud to sit in an alehouse possibly cursed by the devil did not appeal to him. "We'll go when it stops raining."

"Where is your determination to free Boisvert from Newgate?"

"It's somewhere on this mattress." John flipped over and covered his head with a pillow.

Bianca pulled the shutter closed against the rain. "Then I shall see you anon."

Slipping in the mud and feeling it squish between her toes reminded Bianca that she had not saved money for a pair of pattens to lift her feet above the slop. The holes in her flimsy boots had gotten worse with their travels, and now she suffered from the disagreeable consequences. There always seemed to be goods she'd rather spend her money on—beeswax, ceramic pots, cadmium ore for her popular salve to tame the French pox. "I've no excuse," she muttered as she held her kirtle above her ankles and hopped about like a rabbit to avoid the puddles.

Only those whose necessity required them to face the elements were out mucking about. An ostler led a horse out back to a stable for a traveler, but for the most part Bianca was alone on the main thoroughfare, and the only person headed to the church alehouse.

A stone wall separated the monastery from the rest of the town, and Bianca passed through an arched opening and followed a flagstone path, the remnants of a time when the grounds were well taken care of.

The monastery was a Norman structure made of tan rubblestone. Pointed-arch openings gaped to the weather; splintered wood and metal jutted at angles where stained glass had been carelessly pried out. The roof had caved where its metal and gutters had been salvaged. In the cemetery, leaning markers were covered in green and yellow lichen, accumulated from years of marking generations of monks and clerics at their rest.

The wind blew the rain sideways, and there was no avoiding the deluge as she followed a path to a smaller building nestled behind. This building was annexed to a smaller church, left intact. The parish church sat modestly in the shadow of the greater ruin, serving the needs of the villagers. As Bianca neared the door of the annex, she stepped over the carcass of a raven, its wings spread and body flattened against the ground. Keen black eyes that had once watched mice scamper along the riverbanks were fogged in death. At the entrance, a sign tacked to the door read, "Alehouse."

Whereas the Stuffed Goose was literally stuffed with people, the alehouse had an abundance of empty tables and benches. Across the room, a torpid wisp of smoke faltered in a brazier. A lone monk dressed in a coarse-woven robe hunched over his pot of ale. He straightened at the sound of the door yawning open.

"Is this the church alehouse?" Her voice sounded puny in the empty space.

"It is," answered the monk into his drink.

Bianca ignored the lack of customers and the brother's disinterest. "I'd like an ale, if I might."

The brother swung his head around to look at her, his eyebrows knit with suspicion.

Bianca's cordial manner waned, wondering if she would be refused. The two stared uneasily at each other until a man entered from a back room, drying his hands on a towel.

"Ye say ye want ale?" he asked. His pleasant face mirrored a similar welcoming manner. He wore a jerkin of black homespun wool of the same fabric as the monk's habit.

"Aye. If it is not a trouble."

"Well, we are not one to deny ye. It is a fearsome weather. Sit a spell," he said, motioning to a table. "I shall fetch you an ale of our most fresh." Before disappearing into the kitchen, he flashed the sullen brother a look of reproach.

Bianca sat at a table behind the grizzled monk, leaving him alone to nurse his ale and foul mood. Her intent was to strike up a conversation, find out more about the alehouse, but the man had managed to erect an impenetrable wall as surely as if it were made of brick.

However, after a moment, to Bianca's surprise, the monk made an effort to engage her. He spoke over his shoulder, avoiding direct eye contact. "I don't recall your face, my child. You are not from Dinmow."

"I am from London."

"Ah." He turned back to his drink. "What brings you here?"

Bianca had come prepared to lie. Perhaps in good conscience she should have checked herself, but when faced with apathy she responded in kind. "I am only passing through. Once the weather settles, I shall move on."

He took another sip of his ale. Apparently, this was the extent of his welcome.

Soon his counterpart returned with a pewter cup and set it before her. "A traveler might be hungry. Can I offer some fare? We have a fine mutton stew."

Bianca tried not to flinch. "Nay, this will suffice." She paid him his coin and looked around at her empty surroundings. "Should I have not come? Are you closed for an occasion?"

"No occasion," he said.

She heard the sullen monk snort.

"It is a large enough alehouse. I should think people might prefer coming here instead of the crowded Stuffed Goose."

The two remained stonily silent.

Bianca took a sip. "This ale is quite fine." She meant it.

The more hospitable of the two perked up. "Aye. It is a goodly batch. I am pleased."

"I don't believe the Stuffed Goose has as fine a brew."

"Oh, they do," he said, frowning at a spot on the trestle table. "They don't serve it properly." He rubbed the spot vigorously with his towel. "They pour it in tankards with the dried remains of soup. Ye get bits of onions floating about. The taste is not a concern for them."

"Does their disregard trouble you?"

"It is our brew that they sell. I'm the brewer. Call me Felton." He gave up rubbing the spot and folded the towel. He draped it over his shoulder. "Of late, I am also the cook."

"I should like to see how you make your brew. I have a curiosity for ale well done."

The brewer glanced at the old monk, then nodded. "I haven't any patrons to tend to. I need to see after it anyway. You can pour a tap, Brother March?"

Bianca followed Felton through a kitchen that was sparsely

stocked with food in the way to cook. A lone baker kneaded dough on a dusted board and watched the brewer lead Bianca out the back door. Holding his cap to his head, the brewer suddenly dashed through the rain to a building behind the alehouse and held the door for her. Bianca followed.

The brewery was smaller than the alehouse, with a fusty smell permeating the air. She noted that the brewhouse had not lost its windows like the other monastery buildings. The brewery had avoided the widespread ransacking Grayson had told her and John about. Gray light lent the interior a melancholy feel. A large vat, taller than either of them, sat in the middle of the room, its oak staves bound by iron hoops and rivets. Felton took an empty jar from a shelf and lifted a paddle off a hook on the wall.

He climbed a ladder propped against the side and skimmed the surface. After a moment, he handed Bianca the jar of foamy liquid. "For Brother Fromme, the baker," he said. He then lowered the paddle into the vat and, with concentrated effort, swept the wood oar around the perimeter.

Bianca could see that the brewer prided himself in his work. He took great pleasure explaining the process, adding colorful asides and even laughing once. "Would you like to see how we malt grain?" He led Bianca up a set of stairs to a room and explained that in the warming days of spring, they raked the grain over the floor, then added water to encourage it to sprout. When all of Bianca's questions had been answered, she followed him back down the stairs and crossed the room to the door. The man's good cheer fell away as he looked at the alehouse before running back through the rain.

"I'm sorry the people of Dinmow don't appreciate the care you put into your brewing," said Bianca when they entered the kitchen.

"Perhaps we are being righteously punished," he said. He brushed the rain from his sleeves.

"Sir, you deserve to do a fair business like anyone else."

He handed the baker the jar. "The truth be, we are blamed for several deaths of late."

Brother Fromme, who had remained quiet, spoke. "Felton, we are unjustly accused. Why must you tell of our woe?"

"The priest hides in his room. He does not defend us."

The baker went back to his table and began scraping off the flour into a bowl. "Paston is a gutless caitiff. He can't even perform his godly duty. He should leave and let the town find another who cares for their needs."

"Perhaps he will leave on his own accord."

"He cannot leave soon enough! He will see us ruined or run out of town."

"We haven't been run out of town yet," Felton reminded Brother Fromme. "I hope, in time, we are forgiven."

"I am beginning to think this town has a long memory. And if another incident happens like before, who do you believe will be blamed?"

Bianca understood their burden, having had to prove her innocence in a friend's death. She could not remain quiet. "I know, personally, the frustration of being falsely accused. It is easier for people to cast blame than prove a man innocent. Guilty men would have run by now."

Brother Felton glanced at the baker, then lowered his voice. "About a month ago, several people took ill after eating at our alehouse. They all died."

"And was the cause for their deaths determined?"

The brewer shook his head. "It was peculiar. They all acted strangely. They had all eaten here the night before they took ill."

"So you are accused of poisoning them?"

"We have been accused, aye."

"Our food is the same as the Stuffed Goose," said the baker.

"It comes from the same farmers?" asked Bianca.

They both nodded.

"But perhaps the food is not prepared the same?"

Felton straightened and lifted his chin. "I do nothing different. Why would I taint the food? What reason would I have to do that?"

The baker spoke. "The townspeople blame the priest."

"What issue have they with him?"

"Father Paston is not respected. The townspeople think him weak. They say the deaths are proof of his inability to protect the monastery, the church, and Dinmow from evil." The baker stopped his furious scraping. "He is not our choice. When the monastery was dissolved, he was assigned to the parish church."

"Could the Stuffed Goose have wished ill for you? Would they benefit making their own ale rather than buying it from you?" Bianca wanted to hear their response.

Brother Felton spoke. "They looked into brewing their own. They haven't the means to accomplish it. We convinced them that the expense would not be worth it. Under our agreement, we make ale for the owner of the monastery property for the right to stay here." Felton tugged on his jerkin. "As you can see, our habits have been turned into ordinary garments, and we may not pursue our previous calling. Eventually we hope to buy the alehouse and brewery outright."

"If your reputation is called into question, would it not present someone with an opportunity to buy?" suggested Bianca.

Felton doubted the possibility. "I would not imagine Elgin at the Stuffed Goose to be so devious."

"You are naïve, my brother." The baker placed his bowls on a shelf. "I do not wish to think ill of him, but it is possible."

"Nay, it is not me who is naïve. You make these loaves and no one buys them. We will soon run out of money for flour."

"I will continue to bake my loaves until no one wants them."

"Our customers have abandoned us. No one wants them anymore."

"I stand by my bread over Duffy's any day. Soon people will tire of his soured dough. Besides, I plan to offer the villagers free loaves. We must show the people what they are missing."

Bianca regretted inciting the two men to argue. She wished to depart leaving them with something on which they could both agree. "Brother March still wears his habit."

The baker sighed. "He shall not abandon it." He scraped the flour off the board into his palm. "If it costs him his life, he has resigned himself."

"How will it not? I should think he must avoid notice." Bianca looked toward the open room.

"He never leaves the grounds," said Brother Felton, "and so far has avoided notice by the commissioners."

Bianca returned to an empty bedchamber at the Stuffed Goose. She stamped down the stairs and entered the back of the tavern, scanning the tables for John.

"Ye lookin' for yer old man?" asked the serving wench, sidling past with five tankards hooked through her fingers.

"Have you seen him?"

"He took off in the rain, foolish man. Said to tell you he was gone to the gristmill."

Bianca looked out the window at the rain still pouring with no sign of slowing. She was already as soaked as if she had taken a swim. What did it matter if she went out again?

This time she glupped through town in the direction from which they'd first come. Instead of taking the stone bridge across the river, she kept on and arrived at the gristmill. She found John enjoying a thorough instruction in grinding flour. Between the two of them, they would walk away with enough knowledge to start their own village.

"Bianca," said John. "Meet Daniel Littleton, the town miller."

Bianca did a double take at the man's last name, then curtsied.

"I have learned how they operate the sluice gate for the water, how the paddle wheel works. Look at this." John extended his hand beneath a chute and showed her a fistful of fine flour. "Before now I've never given any thought to how flour was ground." John smiled, then gazed in admiration at the contrivance turning the millstones.

"What grain do you mill?" asked Bianca.

"Barley mostly. Although I mill wheat and rye."

"And the flour is for Dinmow?"

"And London."

"I wonder if we eat bread baked with your flour."

"I've a merchant who distributes my goods, so I need not bother with individual bakeries anymore."

"Show her how you hoist the grain," said John. "You will enjoy this," he said to Bianca. "Mayhap I will convince Boisvert of a pulley system."

Miller Littleton went to the sacks of grain piled against a wall. He lifted a bag onto his shoulder as easily as if it were a toddler. John watched with admiration as Littleton carried it over and dropped it on the floor next to the millstones. He secured the sack with rope, then swung the wallow wheel aside and pulled on a chain that hoisted the bag through a flap door in the floor above them.

"Come see this," said John, tugging Bianca's sleeve. Though she lacked John's passion for cogs and mechanicals, his enthusiasm was contagious. She followed him up the stairs to the second floor. Realizing a young woman had arrived, the assistant shook off his boredom and cheerily untied the rope, then slit the cloth with a knife. He tipped the grain into a wood hopper, the hard kernels clattering down the shaft and spilling onto the turning millstones below.

Bianca peered into the hopper. "Is this from neighboring fields?"

"From the farmers who grow it."

Bianca wandered to the row of sacks leaning against the wall. She reached into one and withdrew a fist of grain, running her thumb over the dried husks. The golden brown kernels left a powdery residue on her fingers. "Do the kernels get burned from too much sun? They are of differing shades."

"The darker kernels are probably from the bottom of a bin. Sometimes they get wet."

After watching the grain disappear through the hopper, Bianca and John descended the stairs to the bottom floor, where the miller was bagging the ground flour.

"And who shall get these sacks?" asked Bianca. "London?"

"Nay, these will go to the bakers in town. To the Stuffed Goose and church alehouse."

They watched Littleton bag the remaining flour, then thanked him for his kindness in showing them the mill. Just as John's hand went to the door, a man with the bearing of an ox threw it open and entered. A young boy accompanied him, diminutive by comparison.

"I've come for me flour," he said. "I've completely run out. I wouldn't bother coming, but Elgin sent me to settle our account." He eyed Bianca and John, and the miller introduced them.

"They hail from London," said Littleton.

"That is a journey," said the cook, who went by the name of Duffy. "Being in London, I doubt you give much thought to farmers and millers."

"Nay," said John. "I've learned a great deal in Dinmow."

"I wonder, sir," said Bianca, "if I might help in the kitchen tonight?"

The man was neither surprised by her request nor particularly keen for her help. "Have you skills?"

"I learn quickly. I would like to see how an inn cooks for so many people. I might even learn something on how to make a proper mutton stew."

"There is no pay and the owner looks unkindly on barter."

"My compensation is to learn."

John blinked at Bianca's sudden interest in cooking. He was always hopeful that she might improve in the kitchen. He turned eagerly to the cook. He had to stop himself from begging the man.

"All right," said Duffy, noting a look of desperation on John's face. "Come when you are ready. But don't expect to stand about. I'll put you to work." He stepped back, shirking John's attempt to embrace him. "Don't think either of you will get a free meal out of this."

"What was that for?" asked Bianca when they got back to their chamber at the inn.

"Can't I kiss my wife on occasion?"

"You never kiss me when we've come in from getting soaked to the bone. I suppose I should stomp about in the rain more often."

John unbuttoned his jerkin and hung it from a rafter to dry. He couldn't contain his cheerful mood. "It gratifies me that you wish to improve your cooking."

Bianca set her boots upside down in the warmest spot of the room and peeled off her stockings. She hung them near John's coat.

John's smile collapsed. "You aren't spending time in the kitchen to learn how to be a better cook."

"Nay. It is not my first order of interest."

John took off his shirt and wrung it out. "Perhaps you might surprise yourself and find cooking food to your liking," he said.

He didn't need to add, "instead of medicinals," because Bianca sensed it was what he was thinking.

"I want to learn more about Elgin, the owner of the Stuffed Goose. I want to see what he is like."

"Bianca, we needn't try to solve another set of deaths. Boisvert is sitting in Newgate Prison awaiting his fate."

"But the peculiar manner in which these people died is similar not only to Odile's demise, but also to that of the woman who fell from St. Vedast. Even the young boy who was taken with demons might have something in common with all of this unusual behavior."

"I'm not seeing a connection to any of it," said John, crawling under a blanket to get warm.

"I don't know what all of these people had in common,"

Bianca admitted, peeling off her wet kirtle and standing on the bed to drape it over a beam. "Perhaps we will never understand."

"In which case this trip to Dinmow has been a waste of time."

"Well," said Bianca, cheering, "all is not lost. I'll go down to the kitchen and maybe I'll learn something about cooking food—after my clothes dry."

"It'll be a while before that happens," said John, smiling archly, and Bianca dropped onto the bed beside him and kissed the impish grin off his face.

CHAPTER 23

The difference between Bianca's brand of cooking and Duffy's was that his smelled undeniably better. John believed Bianca's sense of smell had been ruined by years of assisting her father in his alchemy room. In fact, Bianca had an acute olfactory sense—it was just that it was more finely attuned to cooking chemistries, not comestibles.

She could discern the difference between terebinth and hemlock, but put a rotten egg or a bowl of sour milk in front of her and she might not reject either. Instead she would snatch them up and stash them away for use in her experiments later.

That night, Duffy found he could not trust the girl to know when to pull carrots off the fire or onions off a grill. She seemed content to watch them caramelize and then blacken before she made a move to save them. He decided she was a lost cause and was about to send her away when she showed an interest in learning how to make bread. He was busy trying to remedy the ambiguous stew caused by her negligence and figured she could not possibly find a way to ruin bread, unless she burned it, but he would watch to be sure that she didn't.

He instructed her to measure the needed flour using a scale in the corner and handed her a cup of gloppy dough. "Add this to the mix," he told her. "It will make the dough light. We can't get barm from the alehouse, and we haven't time to sit and wait for God's goodness."

"Why can't you get barm from the alehouse?"

"They won't sell it to us."

She looked at him expectantly, but he declined an explanation.

Bianca took a whiff of the jar. "It is sour," she said.

Duffy shrugged. "That is how it should be." He instructed her on what to do and watched her take care adding the ingredients one by one, like she was expecting an explosion if she added them too fast. He had never seen a girl so enthralled with mixing ingredients.

With Bianca occupied, Duffy now took care of the orders the serving wench kept screeching through the open door. The woman's voice sounded like a crow cawing in his ear. Duffy wished the nag would work somewhere else, but since he had little control over the owner's hiring, he amused himself with devising ways to be rid of her. She had an ill effect on the kitchen staff, and the sniping usually built to manic proportions before it was quashed by the appearance of Elgin.

Such was the case tonight. The Stuffed was doing an unprecedented business, the rain being such that no one wanted to sit home and stare at their spouse when they could be drinking ale and staring at their neighbor's spouse instead. So the Stuffed earned its nickname and Duffy the cook grew more prickly by the minute.

He served up bowls of stew and saw that more would soon be needed. He directed more carrots to be chopped, more onions to be diced, and more mutton to be thrown in the pot. The loaves of bread disappeared off the shelves, and Duffy eyed Bianca happily kneading dough that should be set to lighten. She must have seen enough people work dough, for the girl took to it without being told how.

"Let it rest," he yelled, and tossed a wad of damp cloths at her to cover the dough.

The kitchen struggled to keep up with the requests, and tempers flared. With the prospect of a long night ahead, Duffy paced himself and tried to ignore the serving wench, who was grating on his nerves. He might have made it through the night without serious mishap if she hadn't announced that the ale had run out.

"What do you mean the ale has run out? You were to take the stable boy this morning and secure more."

"It was raining," she said.

"When doesn't it rain in this madding village? I gave you a task, and now there will be a house full of angry customers. Shall I tell them there is not ale because it is raining?" The wench turned away from Duffy's spray of spittle. He grabbed her chin and jerked her face toward him. "Fie on thee, wench!" He took hold of her shoulders and shoved her toward the door. "Tell them you did not fetch the ale!"

The wench said nothing; nor did she take a step.

"Do this, or walk," said Duffy.

The kitchen staff froze in their duties. Here was the wench and Duffy hard by. It was not just the cook who did not care for her. More than one of them wished the woman slapped.

The woman turned and faced Duffy. "Nay," she said. "I will not go for ale, and I will not tell them we have none."

Duffy reared back to deliver a meaningful blow, but his arm was caught up by the owner. Unbeknownst to Duffy, Elgin had entered the kitchen through a back door.

"Stay you, Duffy," said Elgin. "I've got five barrels in a cart to be unloaded."

"The woman is a lazy, vicious jade," said the cook in defense. "She is better suited to slop pigs than to serve our patrons. The staff likes her not. I like her not. Tasked to fetch ale this morning, she refused. Instead, what was her duty was left for you to tend. The owner should not have to waste time doing a serving wench's chores."

Elgin got between the woman and Duffy and lowered his face

to within inches of the cook. "What I may do for the Stuffed Goose concerns you not. Verily mind your kitchen."

The owner turned to the insolent bodge and cuffed her sharply. Her coif flew like a coot to the sky, sending her hair to tumble in her face. "Now shall you learn to bend, iron wench." He grabbed her arm and pulled her through the kitchen to the back room where the casks were stored.

After watching the owner haul the wench to the rear and listening for the sounds of a beating to commence, several sets of eyes returned to Duffy. It wasn't the sound of a beating that the kitchen staff was privy to.

"Well, get on with it," he said, disgusted, looking round at them.

Two of the boys whose task it was to unload the wagon shuffled up to him, hesitating. "Sir, should we wait to unload the casks?" they inquired.

"What do you think?" said Duffy. "I work with a crew of fools," he muttered.

The boys hung back next to Bianca, who had succeeded in making herself nearly invisible. They stood by as she covered the mounds of dough and set them aside to rise.

"Where you be from?" asked one of the boys. He was more genial than the other.

"London," said Bianca, taking a portion of lard and tying it in cloth.

"Ot, someday I will go there. They say the streets are lined with desirous women."

"Not quite," said Bianca.

"Well, more than here," he said. He laughed nervously, looking to his friend, who dropped his gaze to the floor.

Bianca had started scraping the flour from the board when the door from the cask room flew open. The serving wench, lifting her chin, sashayed back through the galley, tying the strings of her bodice and ignoring the stares and snide remarks from Duffy and the staff.

Elgin, the owner, appeared at the rear of the kitchen, his codpiece hastily tied so that it angled crookedly. "Get these kegs un-loaded!" he yelled at the boys. "Do I have to do everything my-self?"

Once Elgin stalked from the room, Bianca approached Duffy, asking if she might return to her husband. He had nearly forgotten she was there.

"Please do," he said, glad to be rid of one more irritation.

Bianca joined John, who was sitting with a man who turned out to be a cooper. The two of them glumly sat before empty tankards and, like the rest of the tavern's patrons, had seen the serving wench strut past, her hair in a tumble, ignoring everyone's requests on her way out the door.

"I don't suspect she'll be back tonight," said Bianca, squeezing in next to John.

"Who will serve the clientele if not her?" asked the cooper, a man twice their age with half as many teeth.

"I shall not go back in there," said Bianca, taking John's tankard and closing one eye to squint at its empty bottom.

"She looked a bit disheveled when she left," said John.

"Aye that." Bianca set the tankard down and looked at the cooper. "How long have you lived in Dinmow?"

"As long as I could walk," he said.

"Are you familiar with the recent deaths?"

"I wish I wasn't. Frightful, they were." He crossed himself.

"What do you think caused people to suddenly act out, then die?"

"If I knew, then I wouldn't live in fear of it happening again. Some blame the priest because it happened at the church ale-house. But I'm one of the few who suspects"—the man put his hand next to his mouth so no one could see—"Elgin." He nodded knowingly. "He might have had something to do with it."

"And that doesn't stop you from coming here?"

"That is expressly why I come here. I'd rather be a sheep and keep an eye on the wolf than be a dead troublemaker." The cooper smiled nervously.

"So you are not with the majority in thinking the man innocent?"

"I am not with any one man or the other. I think for myself, but foremost I am a man who knows how to survive. But I also know of what Elgin is capable. And I like him not."

"Say you, not so gently."

The cooper ran a grubby finger around the circumference of his pottage and licked it off his finger. "I have special cause," he said, setting down the bowl. "He got my sister with child and wouldn't marry her."

"Truth be, sir, she is better without him," said Bianca.

"Nay, my lady," said the cooper. "A woman shunned and her bastard child is never better off."

Across the way, Duffy entered the dining room and was immediately set upon by a table of thirsty patrons. The cook attempted to pacify the men while scanning the room—Bianca thought probably for an able female, namely, her. She turned her back toward the cook. "I am certain Duffy is desperate to find help to serve the patrons. We need to leave before he suggests I take her place."

The two acknowledged the cooper and rose from the table to scoot along the periphery toward the door. They slipped out just as Bianca thought she heard Duffy call after them. The two made for the stairs, starting at Elgin and a woman in conversation beneath the risers. The owner stopped talking and watched them pass.

"We certainly learned a bit between us, today," said Bianca when they got to their room. She removed her coif and ran her fingers through her thick hair.

"I wouldn't mind being a miller."

"There are no gristmills in London."

"But imagine if I could build one close by."

"John, you need a quick-flowing stream or river."

"Maybe there is one near Southwark."

"What? Morgan Stream? That sludgy runnel?" Bianca flopped

onto the bed. "Rats would forever be clogging your paddle wheel."

"I mean south of Southwark." John pulled off his boots. He dove onto the bed beside her.

"I miss my chemistries. Someday, in the not so distant future, I will return to making my balms and salves. And I can tell you now, after seeing a village such as this, that I would be hauled off and burned at the stake if I tried making my medicinals here. There are too few people in this place. Everyone knows about everyone's business. It is easier for me to conceal my work in London. There is safety in numbers."

"There is also danger in numbers," John reminded her.

Bianca got up on one elbow and looked down at John. "True, but I understand the dangers better in London than I do here. I do not want to be a miller's wife."

"Perhaps you do not want to be my wife."

"Perhaps I only want you to understand that I am unhappy unless I dabble with my chemistries."

John sighed. It was little use to argue the point. He wished he were her passion—solely and without concession. He understood this would never be the case. Even his near death from the sweating sickness had not dampened Bianca's desire to devote time to her concoctions.

"John, you have always known this. Why do you frustrate yourself? Why do you try to change me? Being an indulgent wife is not my inclination."

"You have always been my dream, but I shall never be the reason for you to get up in the morning."

Bianca leaned down and kissed him long on the lips. "Do not doubt your worth to me."

CHAPTER 24

"Does it ever stop raining in Dinmow?" John stared disconsolately out their window the next morning. A permanent storm cloud seemed fixed in the sky overhead. The pair had agreed to leave for London provided the rain had stopped. An intermittent rain would have sufficed, but the steady, heavy downpour held no prospects for a tolerable journey home.

They had asked the stable if any wagons might be headed to London that would be willing to share a ride. But this had proved fruitless. The weather had put a crimp in their travel plans.

To pass the time, they spent the day downstairs playing tables. Bianca had an innate sense where to move her pieces, so that she easily won every game against John. Others challenged her, and the matches became a source of entertainment for the patrons. Raucous betting and swearing filled the room and kept spirits high despite the incessant rain. Bianca blithely defeated every challenger. Her playing was so effortless that at one point John pulled her aside and told her she had better lose a few games or risk being accused of cheating—or worse, reading people's thoughts. Losing on purpose, she found, took greater concentration. After a sufficient number of defeats to keep everyone in good cheer, Bianca announced she was bored and quite done.

If the endless hours spent mindlessly moving chips around a board had any benefit, it was that Bianca was able to rehash what she had learned in Dinmow. Elgin was not the blameless man Grayson, the farrier, thought him to be. She believed the owner of the Stuffed Goose was capable of discrediting the church alehouse and brewery for his future benefit. Why should he pay for his ale when he could buy a ruined brewery on the cheap and control the production and cost in all of Dinmow? Any man capable of docking a woman within earshot of his staff did not think in terms of moral conscience.

But *was* Elgin scheming the alehouse's ruin? Or were the unfortunate deaths a result of something else? Nearly all the victims had been distraught. Only Odile had not exhibited the madness that they, the young boy, and the woman at St. Vedast had shown. Neither did Odile speak of vipers or dance until she wore herself to exhaustion.

Bianca thought back to her time at the brewery and then in the kitchen of the Stuffed Goose. Both cooks claimed to have gotten their food from the same sources. She wondered if she should pay a visit to the farms.

"John," she said, partaking of yet another bowl of mutton stew. "I think we should visit the farmers who provide food to the tavern and alehouse."

"They may live a distance from here. Must we slog through muddy fields to find them? Why not question the cooks? That would save us the misery."

Bianca poked at a turnip floating in the broth. She was beginning to think the trip to Dinmow had been a waste of time. Not only had she not found any answers to her questions, but now they were mired in a disagreeable village with only mutton stew on the menu.

"What could have caused all of these people to act so strangely?" she mused.

John shrugged. "There is no outbreak of vermin, from what I've observed."

"Nay," said Bianca. "All of the victims suffered from a disease of the mind. An inexplicable madness that consumed them. They gave no thought to the danger they put themselves in. Most often when people get sick, they feel so poorly they lie in bed. But nearly all of the victims became strong and fearless."

"Remember the man with the snakes in his stomach?" said John. "He showed plenty of fear."

"He had an imagined fear, and yet he gave no thought to the consequences of his actions."

John shuddered in disgust. "I prefer to leave tomorrow, rain or nay. Nothing is accomplished sitting here. I fear what may have become of Boisvert in Newgate."

The two fell into contemplative silence. Around them, the tables began to fill with people wanting an evening meal. The lethargy caused by the tedious damp had dulled everyone's spirits, and it seemed the villagers knew instinctively that they needed the company of others in order to stay content.

Business at the Stuffed Goose picked up, and soon the tavern rang with laughter and camaraderie. The serving wench was back, albeit more subdued, but the previous night's incident had not deterred her from returning to work.

John and Bianca had finished their last ale for the evening and rose to head back to their chamber, when a woman abruptly blocked their passage. Her face appeared pained and ashen.

Bianca recognized her as the woman in conversation with Elgin under the stairs the previous night. She touched her arm. "Good lady?"

The woman swayed unsteadily, started to speak, but then bent over, holding her sides. John helped her to sit.

"She is not well, sir," said Bianca as her husband made his way over. "She looks to be in pain."

"Meg!" said the husband. He shouted into her ear. "What ails you?" He, too, was unsteady—but from drink.

The woman pushed him away, which did not sit well with her

husband. He shook her by the shoulders. "Aw, Meg will be right in a bit," he said. "She be a little puny, that's all." He'd started to wander off when Meg threw her head back and laughed at the ceiling. Her husband turned, thinking himself to be the butt of her jest.

But her laughter was not from mirth. The entire tavern grew quiet watching her. When her amusement ended with a shriek, the silence that followed was more disquieting than her laughter.

As if she found them mesmerizing, Goodwife Meg smiled at the rafters. Her muscles tensed. Her body grew rigid. Her eyes stared without blinking.

"His evil breath blows upon us," someone said. "He has not gone."

Goodwife Meg turned her smile on the speaker, finding him instantly in the room of patrons. What was a smile twisted into a leer, reminding Bianca of Odile at her wedding.

With a sudden start, the woman got to her feet. She shouldered past Bianca, lurching for the door. When she got there, she threw it open and paused at the sight of the rain. A sour look came over her, and she doubled over, heaving her stomach's contents onto the stoop. Wiping her mouth with her hand, she glanced over her shoulder with wild eyes and stepped around her sick as she stumbled out the door.

A troop of citizens filed out of the Stuffed Goose in pursuit of Goodwife Meg. No one gave a care about getting drenched. The madness had returned. Meg stumbled and danced down the muddy lane of Dinmow, one arm drawn up against her chest, fingers curled like claws.

Meg's husband begged her to stop, to come inside, but she ignored his pleas and laughed at the rain, her head thrown back, her face to the sky. She continued a stilted parade down the street, oblivious to the town folk trailing after.

"This feels similar to the exorcism I witnessed at St. Vedast," said John under his breath. "Family members in pursuit . . . and she's headed for the monastery."

"He's returned," someone cried. "See how he leads her to the church grounds? He's back to wage another battle with Father Paston."

The couple followed the crowd filtering through the archway onto the monastery's grounds. Bianca feared the woman was going to the church alehouse. After spending time with Felton, the brewer, she thought kindly toward the man. The alehouse could ill afford another accusation.

At the steps of the monastery, Goodwife Meg stopped. She lifted her eyes to the massive structure, ignoring the rain pummeling her face. Bianca remembered the similarly stricken woman dressed in a sheer linen smock at St. Vedast. The witness had said she hadn't noticed the cold, that her feet were bare and blue.

Meg looked around, and, seeing her husband, she stiff-leggedly hobbled down the steps in the direction of the alehouse. Her husband grabbed her arm and held her fast, calling for men to help. A half dozen men came to his aid, restraining and lifting her, carrying her kicking and screaming across the monastery grounds toward the gate.

"John, follow and see where they take her."

"And you?"

"I want to speak with the brewer."

The two parted ways, Bianca taking a few steps, then watching until John disappeared through the gate. She turned and followed the path beside the monastery to the church alehouse. Finding the door locked and the shutters bolted, Bianca skirted the perimeter to the rear of the building and dashed across the yard to the brewery.

At first, the brewery seemed abandoned too. Bianca knocked on the door, and after a disagreeable minute during which she was further soaked from the roof's eaves, the door cracked open. Felton peeped out.

"Oh," he said, moving his head to see behind her. He opened the door. "Come in out of the wet."

"Sir, a woman, Goodwife Meg, has taken ill. I was at the Stuffed Goose when she suddenly began acting queer. She left the tavern and made it to the steps of the monastery before anyone could stop her."

The brewer's mouth opened, and his wide eyes swept the floor.

"I'm wondering if the owner of the Stuffed Goose may have a part in this."

"Why do you say that?"

"I spent last evening working in the kitchen at the tavern. My feeling is that Elgin is the sort of man who might intentionally stage a woman to act foolish in order to cast the monastery and your brewery in an unflattering light.

"Last night I saw him speaking with her under the stairs. They pretended nonchalance when they saw me. Then, when the goodwife became ill, she was careful to step around her sick on the way out the door. Would a person so afflicted possess that kind of wherewithal? If nonsensical and morbidly ill, they would take no care."

A sound of someone on the stairs drew Bianca's attention.

Brother Fromme, the baker, had trundled partway down from the malt room. He paused to look over the railing. Seeing Bianca, he hurried down and joined them. "You suspect Elgin of deceit?" he asked.

"I think he is capable."

"But what of the people who died a month ago? Is he to blame for their deaths?"

"Perhaps not. Their deaths may remain a question, but I think Elgin could manipulate your alehouse's struggling reputation for his future gain."

The baker brought his hand to his mouth, considering the possibility. "Who became ill?" he asked.

"Goodwife Meg."

Fromme's cheeks went as white as the flour dust in his hair. "Only she is taken ill?" he asked.

"Only Meg, as far as I know."

He nodded slightly, lost in thought.

"What troubles you?" asked Felton, alarmed.

The baker signed the cross. "Goodwife Meg came by this morning with a delivery of eggs. I spent the last funds on a bag of flour yesterday. My hope was to give away these loaves to encourage customers to come back. I had nothing with which to pay her. I gave her a loaf of bread in exchange for the eggs."

Felton shrugged. "Why should that trouble you?"

"We have not sold any bread since the first incident. Indeed, we have not sold a single meal since then. Only ale."

"But Brother March has not become ill. I have not taken ill. You have not."

"We finished yesterday's bread today. She is the only one I have given a new loaf to."

"So the new loaves are made from fresh flour? Where are they now?" asked Bianca.

"Surely it is not the bread to blame," said Felton in disbelief. "You would not taint the loaves?" He scoured the baker's face, a look of confusion on his own.

"I did nothing different. The loaves are in the alehouse kitchen."

Without a word, Bianca dashed across the grounds to the back entrance of the church alehouse.

CHAPTER 25

"You recall when the incident happened before," said the baker, out of breath. "The loaves moldered on the shelves after a day, so I threw them out to the birds and dumped the flour in our cesspit. I complained to Littleton that the flour worked up disagreeably, that it did not keep, and he gave me fresh. I kept baking, hoping the people of Dinmow would return."

Bianca felt the color drain from her already pale complexion. "My husband and I visited the mill yesterday. Littleton was bagging flour to give to you and the tavern. If there is something in the flour, then the whole town may become ill." Bianca gathered the loaves in her arms. "Where is your pit? We must see that no one eats these."

The baker gathered the remaining loaves and led Bianca out a door to an area in back of the church and brewery. Beyond a slight rise, a pit had been dug and filled with the discarded filth of monastery life. Even the rain could not drown the reek of waste. They stood at the edge and tossed in the bread.

They were about to turn away when something caught Bianca's

eye. She leaned in for a better look. She could make out the remains of ravens amid the kitchen scraps and brewery mash. Wood ash and excrement partly covered them, but the rain had washed much of it off. It was not merely a couple of birds, but more than a dozen. "Do you see that, Brother Fromme?"

The baker took Bianca by the arm. "We must return."

Bianca pulled her arm from his grasp. "This is not the first time that you've seen this."

Brother Felton arrived and saw Bianca's expression of disbelief. He looked from her to the baker, the rain falling in sheets between them. "Is something wrong?" he asked.

The baker closed his eyes and dropped his head. The rain battered his back like hundreds of arrowheads. He sighed and looked at them. "It began after our patrons took ill."

Bianca gestured for Brother Felton to look in the pit. The brewer went to the edge and stared down into it. He squinted, then suddenly realized what he was looking at. "And you did not think to tell me?" he cried, looking at Fromme in disbelief.

"I came out to dump wood ash and noticed a bird nearby. One or two dead birds is not strange. I thought it was the cold."

"Brother Fromme, there must be twenty in here! Did you not think that the bread may have killed them?"

"I did not want to think."

Bianca looked between the two men glaring at each other. "It does no one any benefit standing here in the rain." She tugged on Brother Felton's sleeve and the two somberly followed her back inside.

In the alehouse kitchen, Bianca took a small sack of the questionable flour. "You must bury the remaining flour," she said, tying the top closed. She broached the possibility of Littleton harboring ill will toward them, but they both adamantly rebuffed the suggestion. "At least there is a reason why people are getting sick. And it's not because your stripped monastery is vulnerable to evil."

Bianca returned to the Stuffed Goose wondering if Meg and Elgin had fabricated this sham in an effort to further discredit the church alehouse and lower its value. She entered the inn and discovered John sitting by himself near the hearth, nursing a tankard. The room hummed with speculation over Goodwife Meg's sudden illness. A few watched Bianca sidle past on her way to John. She ignored their elbowing and hushed whispers and sat next to her husband.

She helped herself to John's ale, waiting until the room became loud again before speaking. "What happened to the goodwife?"

"Her husband took her back to their place, and now there are a number of villagers keeping vigil outside their home."

Bianca reached under her cape and pulled out the sack from the alehouse. "I believe the flour is to blame for the sickness."

"Why so?"

"The church's cesspit is filled with dead ravens. It is where the baker threw the tainted loaves and flour from a month ago. And now it seems the alehouse has been given a second bag of fouled flour."

"Are you saying that Littleton gave them poisoned flour?"

"Possibly."

John tilted his head in disbelief. "I refuse to believe it. Why would he give them contaminated flour?"

"Perhaps a bribe from Elgin? Perhaps to settle a score? There may be some history between the miller and the monastery that we don't know about."

"Bianca, does anyone ever escape your suspicions?" said John.

"Children. Children most certainly always do."

John raised his voice, unable to stifle his exasperation. "I, for one, am finished wondering about these people. I shall not continue to speculate about their private lives."

As John's words grew more emphatic, the tavern quieted, so that the last sentence landed awkwardly, like a drunk falling face-first in his meat pie. Chagrined, he glanced around at the staring clientele.

The serving wench sallied up to the pair with a contemptuous look on her face. "What's this?" she asked, snatching the bag off the table and holding it up.

"Flour," answered Bianca.

"Flour?" said the wench. "What ye got flour for?"

"It is tainted," said Bianca.

The wench dropped the sack on the board like it had just bitten her. "What do ye mean, tainted?"

Bianca stood and addressed the patrons. "I believe the flour is to blame for Goodwife Meg's poor health. Until I can prove otherwise, do not eat any more bread."

The clientele stared with slack-jawed suspicion. Then, from across the room a voice said, "What do you mean, 'until *I* can prove otherwise'? Who are you?"

John tugged on Bianca's sleeve, trying to get her to sit, or at least measure her words.

"I am merely drawing a conclusion from my observations. I have no means to prove anyone's guilt."

"Who are you saying is guilty?" asked the serving wench. "And if this flour be tainted, why do you have it?"

A woman got to her feet. "When they carried Meg off the steps of the monastery, I saw her leave and go to the church alehouse." Perhaps the woman believed she had been summoned for testimony, and was glad to give it. Her eyes narrowed at Bianca.

"Is this flour from the church alehouse?" asked the wench.

Bianca felt the weight of a dozen stares. She felt compelled to protect Brother Fromme, as she did not think him complicit, only naïve, perhaps. Nor did she want to cast doubt on the miller without being sure. "I am saying the bread may have gone off. It is better to avoid it for now."

A man snatched the bag of flour and opened it. He removed a fistful of flour and thrust it in Bianca's face. "If this is tainted, then it should not be in your possession."

Before Bianca could utter a word, the man stalked over to the hearth and threw the bag into the fire. It momentarily doused the flames; then the cloth caught on fire, snapping and curling. Bianca did not object; to have done so would have looked suspicious.

"I ate an entire loaf today, and I don't feel any ill effects," said Grayson. Several nodded in agreement. Far from being scared off his daily staple, he asked, "If the bread from the Stuffed is fine, the only other baker in town is Brother Fromme at the church alehouse. Are you saying he gave Meg a poisoned loaf?" He paused, letting the words hang in the air like bad vapors.

John groaned, muttering under his breath, "Careful how you tread."

Before she could answer, another man stood. Bianca and John recognized him as the assistant to Littleton. "If you is thinking the flour is off," he said, "why has no one at the Stuffed Goose become sick? The stock is the same."

Bianca swallowed, thinking what to say. Why should they avoid bread from the Stuffed when they were living proof that it was fine? She wondered if Littleton or some agent had poisoned the flour before its delivery to Brother Fromme. She could not conceive that Fromme would have cause to see his own livelihood fail. But perhaps her theory was ill conceived. Perhaps the flour was not polluted. Attempting to allay their fears, she said, "I may be wrong thinking the flour is to blame for Goodwife Meg's malady. There is no reason to believe, nor do I have any proof, that the alehouse gave her tainted bread. The cause of her sickness may be something altogether different. I simply do not know." Bianca sank down on the bench, feeling defeated. She had not thoroughly thought her argument through before speaking.

John stood. He laid a hand on her shoulder. "You must forgive my wife. She is full of ideas that she cannot prove."

Bianca started to stand; however, the pressure from his hand prevented her.

John smiled down at Bianca and patted her head. "She has had a tiring journey and her heart has been burdened with a sad loss of late. At times, strange ideas swim between her ears and I cannot dissuade her belief in them." He smiled indulgently, like this was a cross he had to bear. "Please do not give her yammerings any more thought." He ignored a painful kick to his shin from under the table. "She needs rest." John took hold of Bianca's arm, pulling her up. "Come along, now; let us retire and leave these good folks to their dinner."

Bianca's jaw clenched and she pressed her lips tight to prevent herself from arguing, but she followed John's lead. She had no explanation to defend her thinking. At least, she deferred to John so he could help her out of this predicament. She followed him from the tavern, affecting a confused manner.

When they got to their chamber, John turned on her. "Have you lost your wits? What are you thinking telling these people that their flour is tainted? What proof do you have? Because it is my guess that you have none. Is this 'just a hunch'?" He walked off, pressing his fingers against his temples, then turned. "You have managed to accuse not only your monks at the church alehouse but also Littleton of wrongdoing. This, after he graciously showed us his mill."

Bianca sat on the edge of the bed. "It may not have been Littleton. Someone could have sneaked into the alehouse kitchen and poisoned the flour."

John shook his head. "Littleton kindly indulged my interest. Not only have you made us unwelcome, but you've incited the suspicions of an entire village against him—and your baker monk."

"One of Elgin's minions may have poisoned the flour."

John furiously paced the length of their bedchamber, which was not very long. "Why should they listen to you—a stranger? Let us hope that they do not." He paced another few steps. "And what if the people of Dinmow protect their own and accuse us instead? I wager you have not considered that."

"John, I did not expect the serving wench to question the sack of flour."

"You dropped it on the table like it was a sack of gold angels. Of course it stirred her curiosity."

"I only meant to tell you that we needed to warn the citizens and try to protect them from another bout of deaths."

"God save us from your good intentions." John covered his mouth with his hands, bracing his elbows against his chest. He continued to pace, thinking.

Bianca flopped back onto the bed and stared up at the rafters.

"We have to leave as soon as possible," said John.

"We should warn the church alehouse what has happened."

"Do you think they will not hear of this? I am sure someone is on their way to tell them," said John. "Or accuse them!" The floorboards creaked as he trod back and forth, from one end of the room to the other. "I fear that when they find no answers, they shall accuse us of mischief. After all, the town was finally settling back into its routine. The deaths were beginning to fade from memory. Then we show up and Goodwife Meg gets sick."

"If indeed she is sick and this is not staged."

John ignored the comment and kept ranting. "And here we are newcomers with an interest in what happened a month ago. Strange how the problem reappears once we arrive."

"John, they can't blame us for Goodwife Meg's sickness."

"You think not? Never underestimate the reasoning of a small village full of small minds. And if she dies? Ooooh, I shall not wait around to find out."

Bianca gave only half an ear to John's tirade. If the miller's assistant was telling the truth, that the same lot of flour was given to both the alehouse and the Stuffed, then why were the loaves from the alehouse making people sick—if indeed Meg was not acting—and the tavern's loaves remained harmless? John was right. Their time had run out. They could not delay while she figured out what or who was causing the outbreak.

John lit the candle on the small table. A cobweb billowed lethargically in a corner from the rising heat in the tavern below.

What was the difference between the flour at the alehouse and the flour at the Stuffed? One was deadly and the other was not. Assuming the flour was exactly the same, assuming that it had not been tampered with, and assuming Meg's behavior was not for show, what would cause the loaves from the alehouse to harm while those from the Stuffed did not?

"We must leave tonight. If we leave right now, it is as suspicious as if we had admitted our guilt."

Bianca closed her eyes and thought back to her time in the kitchen making bread for Duffy. He had given her a jar of soured dough to add. "He said we can't get barm from the alehouse."

John stopped pacing. "What? Are you even listening to me?"

"Aye. Go on." Bianca closed her eyes and recalled the details of her visit in the brewery. The brewer had skimmed the vat of ale and given her a jar for the baker. "That is it!"

"What is it?"

"The barm."

"What are you saying?"

"John, the difference between the loaves is in the method of bread making. The alehouse uses barm from their brewing, while the Stuffed adds soured dough to lighten their bread."

John stared at her.

Bianca sat up. "We need to get a measure of flour from the Stuffed. We also need some soured dough from them. And I will need a jar of barm from the alehouse. I've figured out a way to find out if that is the difference. Of course, the flour might still be tainted from the alehouse, while the tavern's flour is not. But this is a starting point."

"Let the matter of Dinmow be, Bianca. I don't see that it matters to Boisvert being in Newgate."

"John, a few days before Odile's wedding, she received several gifts while I was collecting the gown she gave me. Crates of wine were delivered, an ouche from the Gold Guild—which pricked her, I remember. Then a young boy arrived bearing pax bread from the priest. At the dinner, Boisvert finished off the wine

Odile sipped and did not suffer. The food did not poison her, because everyone partook of it. There was nothing served to her that was not served to the rest at the table."

"So you believe the pax bread was poisoned?"

"It might have been tainted. It was given to her. It was meant for her alone."

CHAPTER 26

It took some convincing, but John finally agreed to delay leaving town long enough for Bianca to raid the kitchen and brewery. Neither of them thought it wise to sit in the tavern, so they stayed in their room, waiting for nightfall. Worried that the citizens of Dinmow might be plotting against them, every so often, John crept down the stairs to listen in on the chatter from the tavern.

"I think they are waiting to see what happens to Goodwife Meg before they come after you."

"What did you hear?"

"They were mentioning the visitors from London and called you a strange girl."

Bianca humphed. "I don't think I'm strange."

"Nay, you wouldn't."

"If they are associating me with Meg's malady, then let's hope she survives until morning. By then we should have gotten some distance from here."

"I heard them say all was well until you showed up in town."

"It never fails to astonish me how quickly people blame new-comers." Bianca cracked open the shutter and gazed out at the dark street below. "But I don't suppose we can tell them that." She looked up the street in the direction of the monastery. "I don't see much activity outside."

"There are still plenty of patrons in the ken," said John. "But it's getting late. Hopefully, they will go home soon."

"We'll have to rely on our best guess when it will be safe. We'll stay awake until everyone has left, then wait extra for the kitchen to close." Bianca secured the shutter when the wind changed direction and blew rain into the room.

John chewed at his thumb. "I am anxious to be on our way."

"Then why don't you slip out and go to the brewery to get a jar of barm? I can meet you by the gristmill."

"Firstly, it is late, and do you expect them to answer when I knock? They don't know who I am. And if they *were* to answer, shall I tell them what happened here and that you inadvertently cast blame on them regarding Meg?"

"You might word it differently."

"I won't leave you alone. It isn't safe."

Eventually the sound of conversation thinned from below and the two prepared to leave Dinmow. There was no clock to chime the hour, no night watchman to announce the time. They relied on their wits and sense of human nature to tell them when it was safe to creep from their room. John sneaked down the stairs, careful to land his feet softly on the treads. Bianca waited at the top, crouching, watching him disappear into the serving room. It was not the first time in her life that she had been suspected of wrongdoing. She concentrated on calming herself. Her thudding heart never sounded as loud as she imagined.

In a moment, John appeared at the foot of the stairs and motioned her down. Bianca clutched her boots to her chest, gathering her kirtle in front. She slowly descended to his side.

They moved carefully through the vacant room. The fire had burned down; weak embers flickered in the downdraft. Pausing beside the hearth, Bianca leaned against John to pull on her boots. Cinders sizzled from an occasional drop of rain from the chimney. No light shone from the kitchen.

Bianca kept a hand on John's back, feeling his muscles tense as he navigated through the dark, past trestle tables and benches. At the entrance to the kitchen, they stopped. The only sounds of stirring were their own.

The kitchen was as dark as the water in Morgan Stream. Lifting her nose, Bianca relied on her sense of smell and memory to find the starter dough. She moved ahead and led the way to a back wall, her hands in front of her, feeling the way. Within feet of the storage shelves, Bianca paused to concentrate.

"Hurry!" John hissed. "Someone's coming!"

Her sense of smell rarely failed. John never put much faith in her keen nose, dismissing her ability as lucky guesses. But more than once, her skill had proved useful. She put her hand on a jar and took a whiff.

She had just pinched off a goodly portion of dough when John pulled her down, nearly knocking the jar out of her hand. The two stooped behind the large trestle table and held their breath.

Someone moved through the tavern, muttering, and stumbled over a bench. They heard him curse, then shove the bench irritably. Whoever it was, he knew where to find a candle. After some bumbling and additional cursing, the room became illuminated in an unwelcome glow. The visitor moved around the periphery and lit the wall sconces. The light threw intrusive shadows into the corners of the kitchen.

"We've got to go!" John breathed in Bianca's ear.

"I need flour."

"Fie the flour! I'd rather have my life!"

A second person entered the tavern from the front door. The two spoke loudly enough for them to hear every word.

"It is sad about Goodwife Meg."

"Aye that. 'Tis a sorry shame, but at least she is at peace now."

"A terrible time of it. Allen is unhappy."

"As well he should be. I have not much empathy for the man. Meg will find more cheer in purgatory than she ever did in his bed."

The front door opened and soon the inn came alive with opinions. The conversations became jumbled, a confusion of words and declarations.

John kept his voice low. "In a matter of minutes they shall come through looking for ale. We must leave!"

"I need some flour; then we shall go." Bianca swiveled on her heels, feeling along the dark back wall for the sacks. She found an opened bag and had to presume it was from the same stock given to the church alehouse. Asking John to lug a three-stone flour sack back to London wouldn't happen on the best of days, and it certainly wasn't going to happen now.

"Here!" she said, thrusting the jar of soured dough at John. "We'll take it with us." She turned her attention to finding something to put the flour in.

No empty sacks were stashed, as they were continually returned to the mill and refilled. As she felt with her hand along one of the upper shelves, she found a folded cloth used for covering the rising dough. She shook it out and laid it on the table in front of her. "You'll have to dump some flour into it," she whispered, taking back the jar and dropping it in her pocket.

"I can't see well enough to do it without making a mess!"

"You can feel, though." Bianca pulled his arm and laid his hand on the sack of flour. "This one."

"What if they—"

"Shh!" Bianca placed her finger against his lips.

The voices grew louder and their chance to steal a measure of flour was almost gone. John dragged the bag away from the wall, then hoisted it over the square of linen. He began shaking it out, missing the cloth, spilling flour on the table and floor. Exasperated, Bianca tried directing the cumbersome bag over the square. The sound of voices nearing the kitchen sent a surge of panic down both their spines.

"Stay!" Bianca put her hand up to stop his pouring and tugged John down beside her on the floor behind the table.

Light from a candle invaded the kitchen, and following close behind it was Elgin. The suspicious mound of flour on the board and the slightly quivering shadows against the back wall went unnoticed. He headed to the cask room and was soon joined by two others.

Bianca and John listened to ale being poured.

"Take those back to Grayson and Stevens, then come back for more."

Bianca wondered if Elgin was going to be trooping back and forth fetching drinks for the next hour, then dreaded the thought of the entire village of Dinmow arriving to discuss Goodwife Meg. As soon as they saw their chance, they would have to bolt for the back door.

They peered between the trestle's legs, following the human ones passing through the kitchen. The purpose was for ale, but Bianca feared it would not be long before someone lingered, scrounging for food. Perspiration trickled down her front, and it wasn't from the layered clothing and cape that she wore.

More disconcerting than worrying when a chance to escape would present itself was hearing "the couple from London" mentioned. She tried to suppress a growing sense of outrage at being blamed for this latest outbreak. There was no use in explaining her methods to the people of Dinmow. They needed an explanation for this strange affliction, and she and John were convenient to blame.

However, when Bianca heard the word "witch" being bantered about, her knees nearly gave out. John took her hand. He'd heard it, too.

"I'll be there in a minute," said Elgin, emerging from the cask room. "I have something to take care of."

The men exited the kitchen, leaving Elgin alone. Bianca and John heard him fumble about, securing the stopcocks. In a moment he returned to the kitchen and strolled toward the serving room, taking the candle and the light with him. Soon they would have the cover of darkness to their advantage.

But watching his heel disappear through the door, they were unsettled to see him return just as quickly. Elgin paused in front of the trestle where their pile of flour sat on its square of linen. The light of the candle shone on either side of the table and the back wall. They stared, wide-eyed, at Elgin's legs, his boots worn and covered in mud.

"How strange," Elgin said. Then he turned away and headed out the door.

John squeezed Bianca's hand. Without a word, they slowly stood, listening for the sounds of a surprise return visit. John stepped from behind the trestle and glanced over his shoulder, expecting Bianca to be on his heels. Instead, she was hastily gathering the corners of the linen and tying them together.

She ignored her husband's dagger stare and motioned him on.

As a matter of survival, John kept his mouth shut and quickly cat-toed through the kitchen. Bianca followed. At the rear of the building, in the cask room, they faced a door. She yanked the back of John's jerkin as he reached to open it.

Bianca pointed to the rusty hinges and shook her head. She thrust the bag of flour into his hands, then shouldered in front of him, unwrapping a cloth. Bianca dipped several fingers into a chunk of lard and smeared it on the worrisome iron. After a final check over her shoulder, she nodded for John to let them out.

John cautiously opened the door just wide enough for them to slip through. They'd moved to leave, when unexpectedly their way became perfectly lit.

"Well, well," said the candle bearer. "It is the strangers of London."

CHAPTER 27

Elgin stood in the doorway of the cask room, his face lit ghoul-ishly by the candle he held near his chin. "It is late for a walk. Rascals who avoid their debt are roundly flogged in Dinmow."

There was no time to quibble. John spun about, knocking the candle out of Elgin's hand, and punched him square in the face. The innkeeper staggered and received a second blow—this time to his stomach. As Elgin grunted and doubled over, John threw a final jab to the jaw. The man fell, sprawling backward into the kitchen.

"Come!" John grabbed Bianca's hand and pulled her out the door.

They ran down an alley, slipped between two buildings, and came out on the main thoroughfare. As they stood huffing for breath, they saw several men outside the Stuffed Goose tavern and dove back into the gap between buildings.

"When Elgin is discovered, they'll come after us," said Bianca. "We can't use the alley."

"I don't think those men in the street saw us," said John.

"At least the rain is to our advantage. They won't stand around in it for long. They'll go inside."

John cautiously peered around the corner. His head snapped back. "They're still there."

"We've got to get to the church alehouse."

"Are you mad? I imagine that is the first place they'll come looking for us."

"I've got to get a jar of barm."

"Leave it, Bianca! We'll be lucky to escape with our lives."

"We can't waste time arguing. Meet me at the gristmill bridge. I'll only be a short while. They'll be looking for the pair of us. They won't be looking for one person walking down the street."

"Do I need to remind you that at this hour, anyone out walking is cause for suspicion?"

Bianca gave John a peck on the cheek. "I won't be long." Without a second's hesitation, she skirted past and walked boldly out into the lane.

It was too late now, thought John. He peeped around the corner a second time. The last man had filed into the tavern and was pulling the door closed behind him. John leaned back against the building. Bianca was nothing if not lucky.

At first, Bianca didn't dare look behind her—to do so would have appeared suspicious. So she kept a quick pace, slogging up the muddy road toward the monastery. When she had the chance to run without anyone noticing, she did.

Dark is an advantage on a rainy night, and Bianca folded easily into it. At the monastery, she slunk along the exterior wall. So far, no one seemed to be following her. She disappeared through the arched gate and hurried toward the alehouse, a low-lying fog obscuring her path. But like an apparition rising out of the sulfurous vapors of hell, the alehouse appeared to her out of the thick brume surrounding it.

The building was closed and shuttered. Bianca tried the door, banging loud enough to be heard over the rain. Water poured off the eaves, and she stepped back, checking behind her. Still no one had followed, but she didn't believe that they wouldn't.

Deciding no one was in the alehouse, Bianca ran to the rear of the building to try the brewery. She expected that door to be locked. To her surprise, it was not. Cautiously, she stepped inside and closed the door behind her. She threw the bolt to give herself extra time if she needed to escape.

"Brother Felton? Brother Fromme?" No answer came. With hands outstretched, she felt her way to the large brewing vat and found the wood ladder leaning against it. One hand on the staves, she walked around to the back side, where jars and bowls were kept. Her toe stumped the table, rattling the containers, and Bianca grubbled around until she found an empty jar with a stopper. She circled back to the ladder and climbed.

At the top, she lowered the jar and skimmed the surface of the mash. She was tipping the jar to try to see how much barm she'd gotten, when the sudden scratch and flare of a flint startled her. She nearly dropped the sample into the ale.

"Brother March!"

The aged Benedictine lit a lantern and held it before him.

"I cannot delay," she said, descending the ladder. "I've taken some barm to test. All things being equal, the only difference between the food at the Stuffed Goose and the alehouse is in the way the bread is made. That may be the key to what is making people sick."

"You believe we are at fault." He said this flatly, a statement rather than a question.

"Nay." She shook her head adamantly. "I have given it much thought. I may have uncovered a connection between what has happened here, and a similar incident in London." Bianca stepped off the bottom rung. "I do not believe you are to blame. I believe you may be a victim, either of circumstances or of purposeful mischief."

The light from Brother March's lantern flickered. His expression remained unchanged. Neither idea seemed to be important to him.

Bianca looked around. "Where is Brother Fromme, Brother Felton?"

"They have fled. Everyone has left."

Bianca met his somber stare. In that brief moment, Brother March's face told her everything. There comes a time when one doesn't run.

"If I could stay, I might be able to determine the reason behind these peculiar deaths." She said this not as an offer, but so he would understand that she didn't think them culpable. If circumstances were different, if the villagers hadn't become suspicious, if Boisvert weren't sitting in Newgate accused of murder, if John hadn't struck Elgin . . .

The lamp illuminated Brother March's weary face—a face grizzled with age but peaceful in resolve. He met her eyes, and she felt the shame of her hollow claim. If the town of Dinmow wanted blood, Brother March was prepared to give them his. There was beauty in his acceptance. He did it for the good of his brothers—even for the good of her.

It was useless to encourage him to change his mind and flee. Nor did she suggest that he hide. Her time had run out, and, sadly, so had his. She firmly pushed the stopper into the jar of barm and dropped it in her pocket.

Brother March shone the light toward the back of the brewery. "A short set of stairs leads to the storehouse. At the far end is a door that faces the river." He signed a cross in the air in front of her. "Godspeed."

John stood in the gap between the buildings for a long minute, pondering. He could do as Bianca asked and wait for her at the gristmill bridge, but that made him uneasy. Bianca had a knack for getting into trouble. He shuddered, thinking what might have happened to her if he'd not followed his instincts and checked a certain warehouse in Romeland just nine months before.

Biding his time by the gristmill while she sought to outrun a swarm of angry villagers did not sit well with his conscience.

After all, he was the one who'd punched Elgin and put their lives at risk. Though, at the time, he had reacted on instinct; delaying their escape by talking to Elgin could have ended badly. At least now they stood a chance of escaping Dinmow without being hanged, or worse.

John peeked out from the gap in the buildings and looked toward the Stuffed Goose. The road was empty. He looked in the other direction. Bianca had disappeared into the mist near the monastery. He took off after her.

He could keep his distance and watch for the inevitable angry rabble that would try to find them. Once they discovered Elgin's body sprawled in the cask room and the back door swinging wide, it would not take them long to react. He had no plan for preventing their coming after him. But he could warn Bianca and possibly distract them off her trail.

Ducking into the monastery grounds, he could not see far enough into the fog to know in which direction she'd gone. He relied on the feel of the worn path beneath his feet, hoping it would lead him to Bianca.

To his relief, the path took him alongside the church, where he was briefly protected from the driving wind. Seeing no sign of Bianca at the alehouse, he assumed she must be inside. There was no time for polite knocking and waiting for someone to answer. He pushed against the door. It resisted, and he drove his shoulder into it. Nothing. He pounded and tried kicking—all to no avail. The shutters, he noted, were closed and secured. Sliding his fingers under a gap, he tried prying them open, but they did not budge.

In the thick of fog and night, John heard the unmistakable shouts of men entering the monastery grounds. It had not taken them long to find Elgin and decide where to go. John ran around to the back of the alehouse and saw a second building a short distance away. Surely that was the brewery, and Bianca must be in there.

To his exasperation, that door was also locked. Just as he raised his fist to knock, the voices behind him grew distressingly loud.

A glance over his shoulder confirmed the spreading glow of torches and lanterns approaching.

John abandoned the door. He skirted along the side, jogging down the structure's stone façade. Partway down, the stone turned into an attached wooden structure, which he followed to the end, then slipped behind. He waited a second, then edged forward to peer around the corner. Amber torchlight seeped into the dark at the front, where he'd been just moments before. The crowd banged on the brewery door, insisting to be let in.

He pushed his back against the rear wall. As he considered what to do, his nose caught a whiff of wet wood and river. Ahead, he heard the muffled sound of water tumbling over rock. Had Bianca managed to get the jar of barm from the brewery and leave? What if he had misjudged and she was already waiting for him by the gristmill? If that were true, then he had wasted scarce time. He concentrated on the sounds of the river, straining to hear her moving along its bank. Torn between waiting and going, John peeped around the corner again and listened to the crowd's indignant demands. His stomach roiled with indecision.

The snap of a dried limb heightened his senses. Someone was near the riverbank. Was it Bianca, or had someone crept around from the other side of the brewery? He didn't dare call out.

John drew his dagger and held it at the ready. Measuring each step and the weight he placed in it, he inched along the rear of the building, keeping his ears primed toward the river.

He had taken only a couple of steps when, without warning, a door flew open directly in front of him. Its force caught him off guard. His dagger impaled itself in the wood, wrenching the blade from his hand, and just as quickly the door slammed shut.

Like a phantom, a figure swept toward the woods, swiftly disappearing into the fog. With effort, John pulled his dagger from the door and ran after it.

Bianca's first instinct was to run toward the river. The light from torches caught her eye as she hurried away from the church grounds. She followed the river's course, climbing a berm to get her bearings. The dark ensured that she would not see the grist-mill in the distance. She would know she had gotten there by running into it. John would not have any means to signal her way.

Over her shoulder, she caught a glimpse of movement barreling in her direction. She skittered down the mound of earth and made herself slim behind an oak tree.

Her pursuer came to an abrupt halt. She heard him catch his breath and mutter a quiet curse. Bianca held completely still, not daring to breathe or look.

After a few seconds, his breath evened out and he continued on, the spongy ground swallowing the sound of his tread. Undergrowth brushed against his legs. Vines must have created a webbed obstacle and tripped him, for she heard a stumble.

As he moved past, she waited a moment, then peeped out and glimpsed a figure swallowed by fog along the riverbank. He was headed in the same direction as she.

Bianca stepped away from the tree and kept to the river side of the berm. She wondered if John would see this person coming and be able to avoid him. She was contemplating how to warn him when she heard the crowd jeer. The rain had slowed and the rushing river could not muffle their indignant shouts.

If she must deal with one pursuer, then that was better than a tribe of them. She hurried on, her eyes searching for signs of him lying in wait. Every tree, every boulder, could easily hide someone.

She had turned the curve in the river when the sound of shattering glass stopped her in her tracks. One by one, the high windows of the brewery were being smashed with casks. The inclination to destroy property puzzled her. Destruction never solved a murder, never paved the way for reconciliation. If the brewery were destroyed, she hoped the town's vengeance would be served and that Brother March would be spared. She regretted she would probably never learn his fate. She hoped he would not be held responsible for the deaths of Dinmow. Likewise, she also hoped to avoid being unjustly accused.

Ahead, Bianca made out the faint leak of light rimming a shuttered window. A house sat closer to the water than to the road.

She wondered if this might be Littleton's house next to the grist-mill. She hesitated. If she passed too close, would she alarm a dog? Were people still stirring inside, unable to sleep after the news of Goodwife Meg's death? She was studying how best to avoid the house when she heard a strange sound near the river.

Her vision still hindered by fog, Bianca crept forward, feeling her way from tree to tree. At a boulder, she strained to see through the settled murk, then crouched behind the rock and listened. The unmistakable sound of dull smacks and groaning carried to her ears. Peeking over the rock, she saw two men wrestling in the clearing next to the house. She couldn't tell if one might be John, but she couldn't ignore the possibility. She skirted the perimeter for a better view.

It was only when she got within a few feet of them that she caught a glimpse of John's ubiquitous tail of wheaten hair flailing as he struggled. Bianca moved to get a better look at his foe, then gasped to see that it was Littleton, the miller—a dagger between them.

With one hand, John pinned the miller's free arm against the ground, but it was Littleton's opposite hand that held the knife. Despite John's hold on his wrist, the man held the blade within inches of John's face.

Bianca hadn't the luxury of time. Her eyes quickly found a heavy rock, and with effort she carried it over to the wrestling men. Without a thought, she shouted, drawing John's attention. She centered the rock waist high over Littleton's surprised face and dropped it.

His arms fell limp against the ground. John released his hold on the miller and rolled off of him. He collected the knife and tucked it in his belt. "I shall refrain from asking why you are not at the bridge waiting," he said, gasping for breath. "Because you could ask the same of me."

"Neither of us listens to the other."

John got to his feet. "That could be a problem."

"This time, it is to our favor."

CHAPTER 28

Bianca and John fled across the bridge. No one lurked behind the gristmill or the hedgerow on the other side. The destruction of the brewery punctuated the quiet with shouts—the unleashed venom of men. As they distanced themselves from Dinmow, the discord of mayhem grew faint and then was gone. It wasn't until the two had reached the high road above the village that they stopped to catch their breath. They held their sides and considered Dinmow below.

The village should have been a shadow on the horizon, huddled in the dark. There should have been only a hint at its place. But Dinmow raged. It would not sleep this night. Flames streaked toward the sky in a fury of orange fire. The brewery, indeed the entire monastery, was burning.

"That's a strong reaction to a woman's death." John blew in his hands to warm them. "Why does fear incite destruction? How wasteful. How senseless."

"You've answered your own question. Fear is the absence of reason." Bianca turned back and watched the billowing cloud of flames. "And men rage against fear."

Bianca didn't mention Brother March, though he was heavy on her mind. With a final look at Dinmow, the pair moved on.

"How did you and Littleton get into a brawl?" asked Bianca after a time.

"I was looking for you. I didn't think you could get the jar of barm and leave before someone found you. So I followed you to the monastery. When there was no answer at the alehouse or brewery, I figured you had somehow made it to the bridge ahead of me. When the door of the building flew open, my dagger caught in the wood. It took a moment to free it. I didn't get a good look, though I figured—or rather, hoped—it might be you. I never caught up and I would not dare to call your name—others may have heard. As it was, Littleton dropped out of a tree and knocked me over. I never saw him."

"That house was his?"

"Nay, Goodwife Meg lived there. The miller lives next to the church."

"We're lucky no one heard the scuffle."

"Aye. There were plenty of people out in front keeping vigil earlier."

"But what cause has Littleton to attack you?"

"I imagine he heard about your flour comment in the tavern. Folks take offense at being accused of wrongdoing."

"I didn't accuse him of murder!"

"You said that the flour might be tainted. Perhaps he was hoping it would be you—not me. I just happened along first."

"His was a strong reaction to criticism." Bianca rewound her scarf several times around her neck as she looked at the deep wood ahead of them.

"I think we have another hour before the sun rises," said John, studying the horizon.

"You should have called for me. I would have answered." Bianca began to walk.

"I thought I heard someone in the woods behind the brewery before you burst out the door. Whoever it was, I didn't want to alert him to my presence."

"But to sit in a tree and wait for you or me to happen along?"

"He guessed our most likely course out of Dinmow was across that bridge. And anyone looking to cross without notice would have clung to the stand of trees to avoid the open yard. Littleton had issue with us separate from the rest of Dinmow."

John stepped up the pace. "Littleton is used to hefting bags of grain. He was not easy to subdue. I'm grateful you came along with that rock. You made a bloody mess of his nose."

"He was still breathing," said Bianca defensively.

"Aye. You just forced him to take a long nap."

Bianca and John reached Aldersgate late in the day. Their final leg of the journey was shared with a farmer they met at a crossroads. En route from the east, the farmer had no knowledge of the havoc going on in Dinmow. Bianca and John sat in the back of the wagon, huddling between crates of chickens and a pig sleeping in the straw. Although glad for the ride, John soon grew surly trying to talk over the squawking. Inhaling chicken and pig manure for several hours left him testy and tinged green.

Once they paid their toll at the city gate, he sprang off the wagon, leaving Bianca to give the farmer her last coin in thanks. She hurried to catch up.

"I should like to eat something other than mutton stew for dinner," she said.

"I should like to get a fire going and change these wet clothes."

"Should we stop at Mayden Lane and collect Nico?"

"I'll go tomorrow," said John. "I want a good night's rest after all of this, and Hobs and Nico will be up the whole night antagonizing each other—and us. Nay. The dog can stay there one more evening."

Outside Boisvert's shop, Hobs spied them from the front window and they could see his mouth working—either greeting or chastising them; they didn't know which.

"He's enough to deal with," said John, working the key in the lock. Hobs was right at their feet the moment they stepped through the door. "So help me," he said, sniffing the air, his eyes narrowing.

"I don't smell anything," said Bianca, edging past.

John ignored Hobs at his heels and scrunched his nose, snorting the air suspiciously. At last he relaxed. "If he had watered Boisvert's wall mural again, I would have killed him."

"It wouldn't have done any good." Bianca lifted Hobs off the floor to receive several smears of affection across her cheeks.

There being no difference between the temperature outside the forge and that inside, John started a fire in the hearth. The two of them changed into dry clothes for the first time in two days. Bianca set the jar of barm, the jar of sour-smelling dough, and the flour on the cleared table. She was still not used to the orderliness of their new home. Wandering over to her crates of equipment, she ran her hand over them. It was almost as if she wanted to assure herself that they were still there. Then, remembering her cages of rats, she found some food scraps and went downstairs to feed them.

"Hobs, you'll only upset them," she said, carrying him back up and handing him off to John. She returned to the rats and dropped the food into their cages, checking to be sure they were still alive. She didn't fancy going down to the wharves in the cold to trap more.

"I must visit Boisvert," said John, getting the fire to roar. "But I haven't any good news to bear."

Bianca walked over to the hearth and warmed herself. "He shall be glad for your company," she said, studying the oven built into the bricks. She stuck her head inside the arched opening to look around. "Not everyone has the means to bake bread in their own home. Did Boisvert have this built?"

"Aye. He always complained about the food here. He said it was only by God's grace that he wasn't dead from it. He is a practiced cook."

Bianca found three bowls and set about mixing dough. "This is not for dinner," she warned. "This is for my purpose. I'll test it later on the rats."

John sighed. Bianca's idea of "cooking" was always an experiment. Craving anything other than mutton stew, John left for the market in search of something edible.

Bianca divided the flour into three parts. In one, she would use a portion of soured dough from the Stuffed Goose. The second loaf would be made using the church alehouse barm. For the third loaf she would use neither barm nor soured dough.

It didn't take long before she and the table were covered in flour. John came home and grumbled over having to make dinner while Bianca appropriated the entire board to her baking project. The two sniped at each other for getting in the way, but their banter was good-natured. Bianca was in her element. She wasn't watching liquids boil in glass-bottomed retorts, but she *was* combining ingredients with a specific purpose in mind. And she took great pleasure in doing so.

Remembering the content of each, Bianca instructed John not to move or switch the bowls under any circumstances. She set them on the bench near the hearth to rise and covered them with a damp square of linen.

They had no sooner sat down when the shop door rattled from someone's insistent knocking. John looked as though he might cry. He lifted Hobs from the bench, tired of fighting him for his meal, and dropped the intrepid nuisance on the floor.

"Sit there and eat your pottage," said Bianca, getting to her feet and heading for the stairs. She returned shortly and took a candle with her, as night had now fallen and the shop was dark. "I'm coming!" she called. "Don't split the door!"

Bianca lifted the latch.

"Fisk!" She had not expected to see the ragamuffin so soon after their return. She smiled, impressed by his tidy appearance. Not only was his hair smoothed down; his face glowed from being scrubbed clean. Clearly, working as an altar server had improved him. But even this startling transformation didn't hide the agitation in his eyes.

"I didn't think you would be gone so long." Fisk stepped inside, and Bianca closed the door behind him. "Father Nelson is in custody."

"When?"

"Yesterday. A constable showed up with the churchwarden and led him away."

"For what reason?"

"People's been accusing Father Nelson of siding with the devil. Some parishioners have started acting strangely and Father Nelson hasn't been able to help them."

"Come upstairs and warm yourself," said Bianca, laying her hand on his shoulder and guiding him to the steps. "John has made cabbage soup."

John had never met Fisk. Bianca had told him how the cagey lad played an important role in discovering Ferris Stannum's murderer. John had been indisposed during all that business. Still, he welcomed the rascal at his board. He had a fondness for young ruffians, having been one himself.

Bianca ladled Fisk a generous portion and settled in across from him. "John, Father Nelson has been taken away by the constable. Accused of standing by while parishioners become ill."

"Methinks there is an epidemic amongst priests these days," said John, slurping his soup. He set down his bowl. "Father Paston in Dinmow was deemed useless and a coward."

Fisk shook his head. "Nay, Father Nelson is no coward. He faced several angry churchgoers claiming he conjured evil on their loved ones."

"When was that?"

"It was the night after you left. Some parishioners came calling, saying their loved ones were acting strange."

"Only a few parishioners came?" asked Bianca. "Did you recognize them?"

"Nay. 'Twere mostly men who complained. I'd never seen any of them before."

Bianca's eyebrows rose. "So when they said their loved ones were acting strange—what did they mean?"

"They said they were acting unnatural. One man claimed his wife sat on the side of the bed and howled at the moon. There was no getting her to stop. She set all the neighborhood cats to caterwauling at their window. He threw rocks at them and considered throwing rocks at his wife. He couldn't get her to quiet. So he beat her, thinking she needed it, but it didn't settle her. Another man said his wife and daughter writhed in agony and their eyes had a terrible look in them. He swore their bodies were warring with evil spirits for control."

John met Bianca's eyes. "Another few cases of possession?" said John.

"I don't believe demons are to blame. If my theory is proved, then we should be able to lay that fiction to rest. Be prepared, though, to see some wicked rat behavior."

John cringed. "How will you tell?" He made a face, disgusted. "Nay, don't answer me. I don't want to hear." He noticed that the boy looked uncertain. "Fisk, Bianca uses rats in her work."

"Oh," said the lad, untroubled. "Some folks keep chickens. Others keep rats." He drank down the bowl of broth and set it on the table.

"I think I need to pay Henry Lodge a visit." Bianca took a sip of ale. She lifted a floating cabbage leaf from her bowl and dropped it in her mouth. "Fisk, there is another server at St. Vedast, is there not?"

"Martyn, aye."

Bianca thought a moment. "When Odile gave me a dress to wear to her wedding, a boy showed up with a pax loaf. I wonder if that was Martyn."

Fisk shrugged. "Was he as thin as a stick and a nose most like a pig's?"

"I suppose you could describe him so."

"That was Martyn."

"Did he ever mention delivering bread to Odile at the house on Mayden Lane?"

"Nay."

"Ask him. Find out who gave him the loaf to deliver." Bianca saw Fisk to the door, reminding him not to eat anything at St. Vedast. "Stay watchful. Don't trust anyone—except me."

CHAPTER 29

Bianca knew where to find Henry Lodge, member of the Worshipful Company of Goldsmiths and churchwarden to St. Vedast. If he was not at the church or the Goldsmiths' Hall, she knew where he lived. Her luck held, for she did not have to spend half the day tracking him down. The man assumed his role as churchwarden that next morning, and Bianca found him in the cleric's office, straightening papers on Father Nelson's desk.

She had stayed awake well into the night, waiting for her bread to rise, then preparing the oven for baking. John had helped shovel coals into the oven and had fallen asleep by the time it got hot, so that Bianca was tasked with removing the ashes while he snored, content in bed. She had plenty of time to think and not so much to sleep. She had dozed for a couple of hours, deciding to test the loaves after visiting the churchwarden. The short walk to St. Vedast in the bracing cold revived her like a slap to the cheek. Her arrival went unnoticed in the echoing interior of the nave; she stood outside of Father Nelson's office for a long minute before Henry Lodge realized she was there. He startled at seeing her watching him.

"One usually announces one's arrival," he said, his tone short.

"You looked intent; I thought I should not interrupt."

Lodge neatened a stack of papers and laid a leather cover on top of them. He squared his shoulders as he stepped from behind the desk. "I have a great deal to take care of. Do you wish to speak with me?"

"I understand Father Nelson has been detained."

"You are mistaken," said Henry Lodge. "He has not been detained."

Bianca looked around. "He is not here. There is no mass this morning. Where is he, if not here?"

"Father Nelson has been taken into custody for his own protection."

"Protection?" said Bianca. "Has God forsaken him?"

One of Lodge's eyes twitched.

If the man found her distasteful to speak with, then she would match his rancor with her own simmering resentment. "So where might this 'custody' be, sir?"

"Perhaps you might inform me why it is a concern for you."

"My husband's master is in Newgate Prison, accused of a murder he did not commit. It was simple to take him into custody, especially when the constable received a bribe for doing so." Bianca noticed Lodge's eyes widen. "I saw the constable smile after consulting Oro Tand at Boisvert's wedding dinner. The constable tucked a coin into his pocket."

"Perhaps you only thought you saw this."

"I know something of crafty slights of hand, sir—I used to be a cutpurse." Bianca enjoyed telling him this. "And now a priest is sitting—perhaps in prison—to be protected, so you say. Is his 'protection' by your recommendation?"

Henry Lodge pressed his hands together lightly at his fingertips, pointing them toward the floor. He turned his ear toward her, regarding her through the corner of his eye. "My recommendation?" His mouth turned up as if he thought she should know. "I seek to mollify a precarious situation. A crowd gathered, accusing Father Nelson of conjuring evil upon their loved ones. I removed him so that nothing would happen to the man. I do not trust the decisions of an unpredictable and vulgar rabble."

"So it was not just a small number whose families were affected?"

Lodge ignored her question. "I wish to avoid trouble. St. Vedast can ill afford another death associated with it."

"And have there been any deaths resulting from this latest condemnation?"

"I do not know. However, Father Nelson is safe if that should happen."

"Where is he?"

"The ward constable guards him."

"The same man who took Boisvert to Newgate?"

Lodge hesitated. "It is the same constable. However, I do not measure his scruples based on a bribe that you . . . supposedly . . . saw. He is a thoughtful lawman, bound by principle."

"Bound by principle?" Probably those principles were malleable depending on who was setting them. Her eyes scanned Father Nelson's office while she considered the churchwarden's response. If he was telling the truth, then she could not fault his acting in the best interests of the priest and St. Vedast Church. Perhaps his motivation *was* to protect Father Nelson and the building.

But what if he sought to rid the building of Father Nelson? Bianca's gaze settled on the churchwarden, who was glaring at her with his arms now folded across his chest. Did he harbor a secret desire to be the holy cleric of his own church? Had he had the priest removed to save the man? Or was there another incentive behind the priest's removal?

She remembered Lodge's show of approval at the wedding dinner. He was an entirely different man, considering his cold exchange with Oro Tand just hours before at the ceremony. In fact, he had upset Odile's goblet in his attempt to take her hand.

"Were you surprised about Odile's death at her dinner, Master Lodge?" Bianca watched him carefully.

"It was sudden and unexpected. A cruel way to end a marriage—for anyone."

"Did you know Odile well?"

Lodge hesitated to answer. "I first met her at court. She attended Anne Boleyn." His eyes took on a faraway look. But just as quickly, his features hardened and he resisted further prodding. "Her death is an unfortunate turn of fate. But one that is not mended by simply wishing it otherwise."

Bianca got nothing more out of the churchwarden. He was a cold cuffin, to be sure.

Bothered by Henry Lodge's reasoning, Bianca paid the constable a quick visit to confirm the churchwarden's claim. The tinkling bell alerted the constable of Aldersgate to her arrival, and he interrupted his conversation with his deputy to watch her enter.

"That will be all," he said to the man, who bowed, then quit the room.

The constable, dressed in a smart fig-colored doublet, turned to face her. "How now?" he said. "Are you here to challenge my decision to gaol Boisvert? You have already expressed your opinion on the matter. I needn't hear it a second time."

"Nay, Constable. I have learned that you have taken in Father Nelson of St. Vedast Church. I understand he is under your protection."

The constable's head tilted in question. "Protection?"

"Henry Lodge informed me."

"Ah," said the constable, his chin lifting. "He has a peculiar way of stating it."

"Sir?"

"The priest is here for practicing sorcery. His parishioners claim he cavorts with Satan."

"There must be some misunderstanding," said Bianca. "Henry Lodge told me that members of the congregation have suddenly begun acting erratic. But it is through no fault of Father Nelson's.

Lodge worried the priest might come to bodily harm from rioting parishioners. He said you agreed to keep him in custody for his own protection."

"So say he? I suppose that sounds less inflammatory." The constable snorted. "Churchwarden Lodge did not ask for Father Nelson's protection. He asked for Father Nelson's removal. The priest is responsible to the members of the congregation and is blatantly remiss."

Bianca blinked. "This is not a temporary detainment?"

"Decidedly not. The practice of sorcery is a felony by order of the king's writ—*de heretico comburendo*."

"I believe there is a misunderstanding."

"There is nothing to misunderstand. The churchwarden said Father Nelson would destroy the parish and its members. His conjuring produced strange effects in people above the course of nature."

Bianca puzzled over the constable's wording. Had Henry Lodge lied to her? Or had the constable read something more into Lodge's request? She wasn't sure whom to believe. "Has anyone died since Father Nelson's arrest?"

"Two have become gravely ill."

"Meaning . . . ?"

"They act as if they are possessed with the demon's malignant magic."

"Sir, can you describe these effects?"

The constable sighed, then ticked off a number of symptoms that were similar to those that preceded the deaths she'd studied over the course of the past week. The young woman's demise at St. Vedast, Odile's sudden death at her wedding, the Dinmow deaths . . . If the bread was suspect, how did it get rationed to the victims, and was it dispersed with malicious intent?

"I have an idea how people are becoming sick," said Bianca. "It may have import for Father Nelson as well as for Boisvert. But I have some missing pieces to find." Bianca started for the door.

"You have some pieces to find?" repeated the constable, incredulous. "How sure of you." He lifted his chin. "Pride doth bloom today, but take heed, sweet maid; there always comes a killing frost."

The gravity of proving her theory spurred Bianca back to Boisvert's rent to finish her work. She had no real sense of how long it would take for the rats to react to the different breads. In fact, she wasn't certain the bread was to blame for the strange behavior. As she thought back on the victims of Dinmow, tainted flour was the strongest possibility that came to mind. If the same flour had been used by both establishments, and only the church alehouse bread made people sick, then it was possible that either someone had gotten in and contaminated the church alehouse flour and left the tavern's flour alone or there was a difference in how the two breads were made. However, the flour she'd used to bake her loaves came from the Stuffed. If none of the loaves harmed the rats, then she would know that the flour at the church alehouse had indeed been tampered with.

If she put aside the victims of Dinmow, was there a connection between the victims in London? How or why did particular people come in contact with a poisoned bread? Had it purposely been given to Odile, the maid who fell from the church, and the boy whose parents claimed he was controlled by malefic spirits? If one of the loaves made the rats sick, then the issue was in how the bread was made. And if that was the case, then Bianca would have to find bakers in London who used the same method of baking and received shipments of flour from Dinmow—a daunting task. Either that or uncover a common link in any or all of the deaths. And she hoped the common link might be a person.

Bianca went upstairs and saw that John had left a fire to burn itself out. Hobs slept curled on the floor in front of the hearth, content and happy to have his people back home to stoke the fire.

"Where is John off to?" she asked him, placing her hands on her hips.

Hobs briefly opened his eyes, then closed them. Bianca moved the three loaves of bread onto the board. For the time being, Hobs seemed more interested in sleeping than in gnawing on freshly baked bread.

In the corner of the forge, the rats stirred in their cages at the sound of her approach. She had made enough money from her balms to employ a blacksmith to create the iron pens. Though heavy, they were a small inconvenience compared to her previous cages, woven with serrated rush to discourage their chewing their way out of them.

She chose three cages, each containing a pair of rats, and set them at the bottom of the steps. It was possible to carry only one while climbing the narrow stairs. The commotion woke Hobs from his nap, and he came round to peer at the rats through the slats and hiss.

One by one, Bianca lugged the pens across the room, then hoisted them onto the board. Mindful to keep them separate, she set a cage next to each baked loaf. "There," she said, satisfied. She then pulled off portions of the three loaves and fed the rats.

Hobs wandered between the pens, sniffing and troubling the vermin until finally sitting partway between two of the cages.

Bianca nursed the fire alive and prepared a cup of infused rosemary and peppermint to drink while she sat and observed the results. She was grateful this experiment was easier than prying open the rats' mouths to feed droppers of solutions down their throats—a necessary undertaking that had proved her innocence nine months before.

She was no more than settled with her tea when the fire snapped from a sudden downdraft as the door slammed below and John stomped up the stairs.

"You missed the excitement," said Bianca as he entered.

John removed his hat and coat. He eyed the cages on the table. "You and I have different definitions of the word." He frowned at the loaves of bread, then ambled over to the cupboard to pull out a bag of oats. "Porridge again?"

"Better than bread that will make you crazed." Bianca took

the oats and dumped them in a kettle of boiling water with her leftover mint leaves. "So tell me, what have you learned?"

"I visited Boisvert at Newgate." He sat down on the bench between the cages. "Can we cover them? I don't like their beady eyes staring at me."

"I have to be able to see what happens." Bianca stuck a wooden spoon into the pot and stirred the oats. "Just ignore them."

John positioned his back toward the cages and continued his story. "Boisvert is not well. The fleas and lice are chewing him to bits. He has been pent up without proper food or warmth for too long. There is talk of a trial. You can imagine how his spirits have suffered."

"They have no evidence against him. Just an accusation. Why are they so quick to try him?"

"They want to be rid of him. He can't inherit Odile's money if he is dead." John pulled off the leather strip holding his hair in a tail and teased Hobs with it.

"So you believe this has something to do with the Gold Guild." Bianca chopped an apple and added it to the pot.

"Consider the connections between Odile, Boisvert, Oro Tand, Henry Lodge, and the Company of Goldsmiths. If Odile had not contested her husband's will, as you said, the Guild would have benefited. There is plenty of ill will between them. Someone wanted Odile and now Boisvert out of the way."

Bianca peered into the cages. "The question is—who will benefit?" She went back to the pot of porridge and stirred it. "I don't understand how the Guild can inherit the money if Boisvert is out of the way."

"Perhaps if Odile's last will and testament is reneged, Lionel Farendon's will is reinstituted."

"But what is the connection between the Goldsmiths' Company and tainted bread?"

"If, indeed, the bread *is* tainted, and if, indeed, there *is* a connection," said John.

"Boisvert said Oro Tand was sitting outside of the solicitor's of-

fice when they went to attend to her will. When I confronted him
with Boisvert's claim, he denied being there—until I pressed him.
Then he said he had business with Benjamin Cornish."

Hobs hooked a claw into John's finger, so John abandoned the
leather strip and let the cat chew on it.

"I wonder what sort of business Oro Tand had with Benjamin
Cornish," mused Bianca, returning to the porridge.

"Perhaps Cornish handles the guild's legal work. There might
be several goldsmiths who use Cornish's services. If he does well
by one, then he is recommended to others. Tand's appointment
may only have been a coincidence," said John.

"I'm a little surprised you find the Gold Guild possibly suspect."

"I am not blind to their treatment of my master. No one from the
guild has come to his aid at Newgate. My first obligation is to him."

Bianca stirred the oats, found two bowls from the previous
night's stew, and dumped the leftover cabbage bits into the oats.
"The only way to know Tand's business is to go through Cornish's office and see if we can find any relevant papers concerning him. What if it was Tand who enlisted Cornish to contest
Odile's will?"

John's stomach tightened. "Are you proposing we break into a
solicitor's office?"

"If you didn't know me so well, I could accuse you of hearing
me think." Bianca sniffed the oats and squinted.

"Tonight?" he asked, knowing full well what to expect.

"Tonight," confirmed Bianca.

John propped his chin in his hand and watched the rats. So far,
the creatures looked content. Their bellies were slightly dis-
tended from their meal. A couple of them ground their teeth, and
their eyes quivered.

"Look there, his eyes are throbbing," he said, noticing the behavior in one particular rat.

"They do that when they are happy. A little like Hobs twitch-
ing in his sleep." Bianca ladled a bowl of porridge and set it before him, then served herself. She sat down opposite John.

The oats tasted oddly minty, but Bianca didn't notice and John was too hungry to care. They had taken only a couple of spoonfuls when Hobs sprang from the table, his fur on end, his claws bared.

A rat ran up the side of the cage, clawed across the top, upside down, dropped off, and repeated its antics. Its mate cowered in a corner. This mad frolic repeated, until after a few minutes, the second rat joined in.

Bianca slid down the bench and peered into the other cages. "If these rats stay quiet," she said, nodding to the middle rats, "we'll know that the bread from the church alehouse is to blame. The Stuffed Goose used a soured dough in their recipe. The church alehouse used barm from their brewery." She beamed at John, who had taken his bowl and was eating standing up. "I was worried that neither bread would have any effect. I would not have been able to prove that the flour at the church alehouse had been tainted."

John offered a wan smile of encouragement. He went back to his porridge and was grumbling about how most men did not share their board with cages of rats when, without warning, a second cage of rats began acting out. "So you've now got more than one pen going mad."

Bianca went over to watch the rats rasp and hang by their hind legs from the top slats. "These were given bread made with only flour and water."

"So what does this prove?"

Bianca thought a minute. "So far, the rats that ate bread with soured dough are acting normal. Since the common ingredient in all of the breads is the flour, there must be something implicitly wrong with it. The soured dough must be able to negate or stop whatever is in the bread that is causing the strange behavior."

"So how do you connect this to Odile's death?"

"Someone has been distributing bread made of this flour using barm."

"It may not have been done on purpose," said John, tending the fire.

"True that, but these deaths have St. Vedast in common." Bianca pushed her porridge aside and sat studying her rats, lost in thought. "I still believe we should visit Benjamin Cornish's office tonight." She watched the back of John as he poked the fire, jabbing logs. "You haven't gotten Nico. Did you not want to pick him up from Mayden Lane? Or did it conveniently slip your mind?"

"Neither," said John. "He's dead."

"He was in fine health when we dropped him there."

"Remember that sour housemaid who answers the door? A more wretched soul I have never seen. She told me she found the dog expired in the street two days ago. It had gotten a window open from the top floor and jumped to its death."

"Is that common behavior for dogs of that breed?"

"Nay, I would not think so. Mayhap he sought to find Odile."

"Mayhap he went the way of Odile."

"Mayhap he was tossed."

CHAPTER 30

Bianca and John woke themselves out of a respectable night's sleep to don their woolens and set out across town. They had slept overlong, and when Bianca finally stirred, she sat bolt upright, realizing they hadn't time to delay. To their advantage, the air nearly cracked with cold—discouraging anyone with half a wit from being outside. Even murderers and malcontents preferred warmth to skullduggery on a night such as this.

They hurried through Newgate market, its stalls empty, the road littered with frozen waste. Lest she become complacent, John reminded Bianca that the most desperate of men would not be deterred by the cold, as they probably had no bed to go to. So the couple remained wary, hearing the watch call four in the night—confirmation that, indeed, a few men stirred. So with speed they moved through the empty lanes. They crossed the Fleet and followed the like-named street to the row of serviceable buildings connected to Middle Temple.

At New Inn, no lights shone within, no midnight oil burned, no early risers labored. John and Bianca strolled down the lane, pretending they belonged there. Onlookers glancing out a window would scarce have noticed them pause in front of a certain window. They would have seen a woman pull her cape closed and given no mind to it as they hurried back to their warm beds.

Bianca kept watch while John removed a flattened strip of metal that he'd hidden up his sleeve. He reached above his head and ran it between the closed windows until it hit upon the crossbar securing them. With an upward flick of his wrist, he released its latch and a window fell ajar.

"A heft up, m'lady?" he asked, knitting his fingers together and stooping for Bianca to gain a foothold.

She wriggled through the opening and dropped to the floor, hands first. A quick glance around confirmed she was in Benjamin Cornish's office. Bianca leaned out the window and offered her hand to John.

"A presentable office," he said, setting down one foot and then the other.

Bianca lit a candle she had brought from Boisvert's. "See that no one can walk in."

John checked the door and opened it. He poked his head into a small entry with a bench for seating and saw that the exterior door was bolted.

"What are we looking for?" he asked, seeing Bianca fingering the files on the solicitor's desk.

"Anything pertaining to someone we know." Bianca turned over a cover to a portfolio. "Ha! Like this." She read the name on a document. "Oro Tand."

"Paa! What does it say of the gold master?"

She brought the candle near and read. "This looks like a deed for the purchase of property."

"He has the right to buy property. That is not strange."

"True; however, the property is not named. It is just an opening statement of the intent to purchase." Finding nothing else of interest, Bianca closed the portfolio and picked up a sheet under it.

"This is a property appraisal from the Court of Augmentations."

"Is Master Tand planning to buy a monastery?"

"One does wonder." Bianca read on, quickly skimming to the end. "This is a statement of particulars for St. Vedast submitted by Thomas Myldmaye, auditor for the Court of Augmentations of the King's Revenue."

"You're not going to take it?" said John, challenging her.

"I don't know what this proves. It isn't in Oro Tand's folder; it is lying beneath it."

"Who requested the audit? That should tell us something."

Bianca studied the document more closely. "It gives the property boundaries, describes the church and its grounds, and lists its valuables. It doesn't appear to be requested by anyone. I know it was a matter of course that every religious house be inventoried. However, this doesn't have anything to do with Odile." Bianca laid the paper on top of the gold master's portfolio. "I wonder, though, if Tand wishes to buy Odile's residence on Mayden Lane once Boisvert is no longer a beneficiary."

John ran his hand over a row of bound books. Finding nothing but tedious tomes of legal doctrine, he dropped into the solicitor's chair to watch Bianca. As soon as his bottom hit the padding, he sprang to his feet with a yowl.

"Soft! Do you want to stir the entire building?"

John massaged his violated rear end. "No wonder you found Cornish an ill-tempered nit." He eyed the suspect furniture and leaned against the desk instead. "Are you nearly done? I thought I heard something."

Bianca picked up the next portfolio and turned over the cover, dismissing John's warning as impatience.

"This folder concerns the accounting for the Haberdashers' Company." Bianca quickly skimmed through the documents. "It seems to be a letter to the Royal Exchequer about the guild's tax accrual. Cornish must tend their accounting on the side." She hadn't the time to thoroughly study the paperwork, but she thought it was a standard record and saw nothing untoward about it. She set it aside and picked up the next portfolio.

"Hold this." Bianca handed John the candle and turned over several sheets in the file, stopping at one in particular. After a moment, her brow creased. "James LaVerdiere Croft."

"James Croft was the fellow angered by the self-murder at St. Vedast. He thought she should have chosen a different church lawn to fall on."

"Ah. The fellow who was more concerned about St. Vedast's reputation than for the loss of a mother's life."

"He's master of the Brown Bakers' Guild."

"He is also French. Another intent to purchase property. Cornish is a man of varied talents." Bianca folded the paper and stuffed it in her pocket. She read the document beneath. "God's teeth!" she said. "This is a sworn statement from Henry Lodge asserting that James Croft is a papist."

"Such accusations are dangerous for a man."

"And could be dangerous for the accuser." Bianca thought a moment. "Didn't you overhear a conversation with Lodge and Croft?"

"I did, but I could not tell what it was about. Odile's name was mentioned, though."

"I'm taking this." She rolled the parchment and stuffed it in her pocket.

"What if Oro Tand wants to buy St. Vedast?" said John. "A property assessment would go with a planned property deed, I would think."

"Mayhap," said Bianca, thinking. "The Crown owns all religious property. One must go through the king for permission to purchase. But I am wondering if there is a connection between the Brown Bakers, the Gold Guild, Odile's death, and St. Vedast. This is becoming tangled, indeed."

John suddenly put his hand to Bianca's mouth. He turned his eyes toward the door. They heard the distinct sound of steps in the hall. Bianca pinched the wick of the candle. Someone stopped outside of Benjamin Cornish's office.

CHAPTER 31

Fisk found the chancel unsettling without Father Nelson wandering in to correct him. He'd grown fond of the priest despite the man's obvious preoccupation. Father Nelson was a man prone to worrying. Fisk had never seen a person react to hardship in so calm and measured a manner. His mother never bothered to hide her irritations—the welts on his bottom were proof of that. When she became worried, it was better to spend as much time out on the stoop, or away from home, as possible.

He wondered if he should mention to his mother that maybe she should pray. Perhaps talking to heaven would help her. He'd never seen anyone pray as much as Father Nelson. Fisk supposed a quiet demeanor and hours spent on one's knees was what God expected of his servants. It obviously calmed the priest. Even when accused of cavorting with the devil, Father Nelson had remained unruffled.

Becoming an altar server had taught Fisk to be respectful. He did not go so far as to genuflect and balance on his knees for any length of time, no; that was dull and too much to ask of any nine-year-old. But Fisk knew that by being courteous and fading into the background, he might learn more about the goings-on at St. Vedast.

Martyn, the other altar server, came from circumstances no better than his. Yet Martyn's hours spent under Father Nelson's tutelage had little effect on the boy. It could have been because he was always hungry, and when one's stomach incessantly growled, one couldn't concentrate on anything but food. He'd even seen Martyn become fuddled off the dregs in Father Nelson's wine chalice.

Now that Father Nelson was gone, Fisk wandered through the empty nave, with nothing to do. Bianca had asked him to absorb what he could of the everyday routine of St. Vedast—who came and went, who the regular parishioners were—and to notice any disruptions or irregularities to that routine. The church was uncharacteristically silent with no mass to prepare for. So Fisk sought Henry Lodge, the churchwarden, for direction.

He found the man in Father Nelson's office.

"Master Lodge," said Fisk, "have you any chores for me?"

The goldsmith startled from the papers he was reading and nearly scattered them. "Ah, Fisk." He returned the documents to the desk, then straightened. "Have you tended the candles on the altar?"

"Nay, sir."

"Then perhaps see to those."

"There will be a mass to prepare for?"

Lodge loosened the doublet at his neck. "Not today," he answered shortly. Fisk started to wander out but was called back. "Is Martyn here?"

"I have not seen him, sir." Fisk had turned to leave when a sour-looking woman stopped outside the office door and peered in at them.

"Father Nelson is gone?" she asked.

"He is," responded Lodge.

"Who are you?" she asked acidly.

"My name is Henry Lodge, the churchwarden."

"Oh." She ran her eyes around the office uncertainly.

"Have you a concern I might help with?"

The woman took a tenuous step inside. She held up a folded cloth. "I'm returning this. It was in Madame Farendon's possession. It isn't honorable to keep a sacred cloth." She offered it to Henry Lodge. "Madame Farendon was fond of St. Vedast. Sad what has happened, if sad is what you call it."

Henry Lodge accepted the ecclesiastical cloth, and the woman crossed herself and stepped back.

"What with Father Nelson standing accused," she continued, "I didn't want to have anything from St. Vedast about." She looked uneasy admitting this.

Fisk hung by the door, listening. Lodge tipped his head at him. "Fisk, take this and put it with the others."

Fisk took the folded cloth and strolled to the door, stretching his time in case the woman had something more to say. His boredom had been interrupted by her visit, and he was slow to return to the uninteresting task assigned to him. He lingered just outside the door, within earshot.

"I've been with me lady for near fifteen years," said the woman. "She was a kind mistress; had her quirks, grant you." She laughed a little in an effort to sound pleasant. "But then, so do most of the French."

Fisk heard her walk toward the door, then stop. "You look familiar to me, Henry Lodge. I hope you don't mind me saying so."

"I doubt our paths have crossed."

There was a hesitation, and the woman asked, "Are you a goldsmith?"

If the churchwarden answered, then his voice was so soft that Fisk did not hear it.

"There aren't many men so tall as you," she said. "Forgive me for saying it, but you look like a gentleman who used to call on the mistress."

"You have me confused with someone else."

"Nay. The more I look at you, the more I am certain."

"If I had visited Odile Farendon, my purpose would have been strictly business."

The woman cackled—a more true and less polite laugh than before. "God's blood! Well, if that is what you want to call it. I'll not argue a man's pleasure *is* his business."

Fisk's eyes grew round. He walked by the door, pretending to pass by, but in reality he wanted to see the churchwarden's lengthy neck turn a vigorous shade of cherry. He was not disappointed.

The woman exited, wearing a smug grin on her face. She tittered with satisfaction as she passed Fisk and sauntered down the hall.

Aware that Lodge might find him eavesdropping, Fisk hurried to the sacristy to store the returned cloth. This last exchange between Lodge and this woman would be of interest to Bianca.

Fisk opened the drawer where the altar cloths and purificators for chalices were stored. He laid the cloth on top of the others and straightened the folded linens, running his fingers over the smooth silk. The bright colors of the altar runners were a feast to his eyes. Wouldn't his mother love to wrap baby Anna in one? He glanced over his shoulder and had started removing one near the bottom, when out of the corner of his eye he saw a foot.

Bianca did not sleep well following their near escape at New Inn. While Hobs and John slumbered peacefully entwined on the bed, Bianca cocooned herself in a blanket before the fire. She read through Lodge's claim against James Croft and dozed, waking when the logs settled. She then fed the fire and returned to her thoughts. All monasteries and churches were property of the Crown. The king could do with them as he pleased, unencumbered by need for the pope's permission.

She puzzled over why Benjamin Cornish had an audit of St. Vedast in his office. The mere fact that he possessed the Court of Augmentations report seemed unusual. Were there plans to sell St. Vedast? But why would information on a church in Aldersgate Ward be in Benjamin Cornish's office near Middle Temple? For that matter, why was it among portfolios belonging to the masters of the Goldsmiths' Company, the Brown Bakers' Guild, and the Haberdashers' Company?

Bianca stared into the fire. To secure ecclesiastical buildings, one must seek permission from the king. A log shifted, and fractured embers spilled near her feet. She lifted the blanket until the embers snuffed themselves out. Did someone have a connection to King Henry? A favor they could ask of him? But then, Bianca suspected, all guild masters had dealings with the Crown.

Bianca remembered the pregnant woman's death the first day they arrived on Foster Lane. That woman's demented nature fit with the behavior of the victims of Dinmow, perhaps with Odile's symptoms before her death. Was all of this a conspiracy instigated by the three guilds to remove Odile from Mayden Lane? Was it set in play to murder her? To ruin her last wishes? Or was it a conspiracy to ruin Father Nelson? To remove him from St. Vedast?

The quarrels between the guilds were serpentine and likely fraught with intrigue and histories that she knew nothing about. Nor would she ever understand the extent of the deceptions these men could wage against one another. These men who vied for power and money and, no doubt, the king's favor.

What assurance, what secret, would remain silenced by Lodge's statement against Croft sitting threateningly in Benjamin Cornish's office? Was Lodge acting in his own self-interest—as a churchwarden, or as a Gold Guild member?

As the bells of St. Paul's tolled in the distance, Bianca's thoughts were interrupted by an urgent pounding on the door. Hobs woke and followed her down the stairs, chasing after the wool blanket trailing behind her.

"Fisk!" said Bianca, surprised to see him so early. "Come in." She looked out into the lane and saw that it was later than she'd thought. "Come up and get warm." She had turned to lead him up the stairs when he blurted, "Martyn! It's Martyn! He's dead!"

Bianca blinked, still bleary from the night before and lack of sleep. "Martyn?"

"The altar server. Remember Father Nelson didn't want me because he already had an acolyte?"

Bianca's mind was slow to stir. "I remember. How did this happen?"

"I don't know. I found his body in the vestry. The churchwarden is waiting for the constable to arrive."

Bianca snapped awake. "I must get over there." She ran up the stairs. "Tell me what happened while I get dressed."

Fisk followed Bianca and stood next to the hearth while she threw off her blanket and snatched her wool kirtle from the end of the bed. John woke and propped himself on his elbows.

"There has been another death at St. Vedast," said Bianca, dropping the dress over her head. "Tell me everything, Fisk!"

"This morning a servant from Madame Farendon's came by to return a cloth that belonged to St. Vedast. She said she didn't feel right keeping it. I was putting it away in the vestry when I noticed a foot sticking out from under a table in the alcove. The alcove is not lit very well. I had a sick feeling in my stomach before I even saw him. Martyn sometimes naps, but he always wakes up if someone comes in. There he was, stretched out, his eyes staring at a crucifix on the wall. I almost screamed." Fisk lifted his chin. "But I didn't. Instead, I bent down and shook him."

"So he was definitely dead."

"Definitely."

Bianca tightened the strings of her bodice and tied them. "So, you left him there. Who did you tell?"

"The churchwarden."

"Henry Lodge?"

Fisk nodded.

Bianca bit her lip. "Did you see anything unusual? Had he been strangled—could you tell? Mayhap stabbed?"

"Nay, neither of those."

"We'll have to hurry to get there before the constable and coroner. If it isn't obvious how he died, they'll cart off his body to the family since there is no priest to direct his burial."

"I did keep my eyes open," said Fisk.

Bianca threw her cape over her shoulders, then froze, seeing Fisk's earnest expression. She tipped her chin. "What else did you see?"

Fisk produced a sack and held it up.

"What is this?" Bianca took the bag and looked inside.

"Wafers," said Fisk.

Removing a flattened host, Bianca held it up to study it.

"They were lying next to him. Half of them are gone. Martyn was always hungry. Without Father Nelson to stop him and with no mass to perform, I'm certain he ate them."

A smile spread across Bianca's face. She threw off her cape and dumped the hosts on the table. "You've saved me the bother."

CHAPTER 32

Bianca headed down to the forge and retrieved a cage containing a single rat. She had dragged the cumbersome pen halfway up the stairs when John arrived, dressed only in his smock, to carry it the rest of the way.

"On the table?" he asked.

"Aye," she said, following him. "I can guess the outcome, but I need to be certain." Hobs jumped on the table to observe the excitement, and Bianca pushed him off. "So Martyn never showed yesterday," said Bianca, addressing Fisk. "You never spoke to him about the pax loaf?"

"Martyn often comes up against his father. When I didn't see him, I thought that might be why."

"'Tis a shame the boy died," said John.

"Fisk, you said a servant from Mayden Lane returned a cloth belonging to St. Vedast?"

"Aye. She had a mean look about her, like she'd been chewed by bedbugs and was tired of it."

"An older lady?" Bianca cleared the table around the cage.

"As old as God, I'd say."

"The sour servant," said John. He found his hose and pulled them on.

"The pax loaf Odile received came wrapped in an ecclesiastical cloth," said Bianca.

"Then the loaf must have come from the priest," said John.

"Or from someone who had access to the cloths—or perhaps someone who could bribe a young boy to filch one."

Fisk watched Bianca feed a wafer to the rat. "Are you going to see if it kills him?"

"Aye. Also, it will be interesting to see how the specimen acts before it dies."

While Bianca and Fisk watched the rat, John finished dressing.

"The woman recognized Master Lodge," said Fisk. "She seemed to think he had an interest in Odile Farendon some years back and visited her on Mayden Lane."

"What was Master Lodge's response?"

"He told her she was mistaken. That if he had visited, it was only for business." Fisk launched into a shaky-voiced imitation of Odile's servant. " 'Well, if that is what you want to call it. I'll not argue a man's pleasure *is* his business.' "

"Well," said Bianca. "I don't believe she would have reason to lie. That is quite helpful, Fisk."

Bianca sat a moment, remembering Lodge avoiding the question when she had asked how long he had known Odile. Obviously he'd had dealings with her and did not want it known. Bianca twisted a lock of hair around a finger while she thought. She wondered about Lodge's accusation against James Croft, filed in the lawyer's office. Was it a move made in defense? What did Croft know that Lodge didn't want him to tell?

"He ain't moving much," said Fisk, stirring Bianca out of her thoughts. The rat lay supine on the floor of the cage, its heart beating so rapidly they could see its chest quiver. Bianca turned the cage for a better look. The rat's eyes throbbed, enlarging, then returning to normal—the behavior seen when rats are content, but disturbingly exaggerated. Other than that, the creature appeared incapable of moving.

"Is that what happened to Martyn?"

"It is hard to say how the wafers affected him, since we were not there."

In a moment the rat lay perfectly quiet. Its rapidly beating heart stopped. Its thrumming eyes stilled.

"Is he dead?" asked Fisk, peering into the cage.

Bianca nudged the rat with a stirring rod. "He's dead." She looked up at John. "It appears someone wanted to kill off a few more parishioners. I need to find out where these hosts came from."

"I can tell you that," said Fisk. "I can tell you where the priest's wine came from, too."

Bianca smiled. "It was a good day when I met you."

The sanctioned bakery where St. Vedast's sacramental bread was made was tucked beside a fripperer. The clothes seller had hung a coney-collared partlet of gozelinge velvet next to the window to entice buyers inside. The gown reminded Bianca of the gown Odile had given her, of the feel of soft rabbit fur against her neck. She also remembered Odile and Boisvert's love for her and felt spurred to see the master silversmith freed.

"This is the bakery," said Fisk. "I followed the delivery cart and this is where it ended." A sign read "Foley's" in faded lettering.

Bianca pushed open the door. No one was in the outer shop selling bread, nor were there any customers. Loaves cooled in a rack, and the warmth from the ovens welcomed them in from the cold. They could hear activity in the back room, and Bianca called out.

"Are you here to purchase?" asked a man appearing from the back.

"Are you Foley?" asked Bianca.

The man glanced at Fisk. "I am."

"Do you bake holy wafers for St. Vedast?"

"We sent them several days ago."

"Then you are not aware that Father Nelson has been removed from his appointment?"

Foley scowled. "Pray tell, for what reason?"

"Members of the parish have taken ill. He is accused of cavorting with the devil."

"A priest's business is not mine. Are you here to tell me St. Vedast will no longer need wafers?"

"Sir, an altar server has died and it is believed the hosts might be tainted."

"It is believed by whom? *You?*"

"I have been to the village Dinmow and have seen a similar sickness happen there."

"Dinmow? I have no acquaintance in Dinmow."

"I wonder if perhaps your flour came from there."

"It is the guild's duty to oversee the quality of stock received into London. I buy what is offered to all bakers. Surely I am not the only one to be questioned."

"The only reports of strangeness have been associated with St. Vedast. Perchance were you asked to bake a pax loaf for Father Nelson?"

"Nay, I was not." His eyes went between Bianca and Fisk. "Are you accusing me of poisoning St. Vedast's hosts?"

"It is not my intention to accuse you, sir. I am only trying to find answers to my questions. What ingredients are used to make the wafers? Do you add anything to the batter?"

Foley folded his thick arms across his chest. "Why should I tell you if you plan to disparage my process?"

"I am only trying to sort out what I know. There may be a problem inherent in the flour. If that is true, then combined with a certain method of baking, the flour may result in a harmful product. You are not at fault. It is the method that could be to blame."

The baker's hard look did not fade as he disappeared into the oven area, then reappeared at the door. "Are you coming, or do I need the queen to invite you?"

Bianca and Fisk hurried after him and entered a sizable space with high, arching windows. The oven was a hulking sculpture of brick and mortar. Its radiant heat brought beads of perspiration to Bianca's upper lip.

Foley went to a shelf and found a large iron mold, which he handed to Bianca. "That is the mold we use to create the wafers."

"It is quite heavy," said Bianca, opening the iron cast and running her fingers over the impressions inside. The baker proceeded to describe the manner in which the hosts were made.

"Does the mix sit for any time?"

The baker snorted. "We use it fresh. Just flour and water."

"Might you show me the flour that was used?"

Foley led Bianca to a bin of flour and opened the lid. Bianca scooped out a handful and examined it. "It is quite fine in texture," she said, running a finger over it.

"Pents at the White Bakers' Guild gave the boulted flour to me at no cost."

"But I see maslin on your shelves. Are you not a brown bread baker?"

Foley grumbled, "Aye. However, it is no secret that there is more demand for manchets and the finer-floured loaves."

"So the White Bakers' Guild has given you white flour so that you may come to prefer it. Have you considered that what is given gratis now may only be to entice you from your routine?"

"White bread shall replace brown. It is only a matter of time."

"But there shall always be more who will want it than can reasonably afford it."

Foley huffed in irritation. "Why would Pents give me fouled flour if he hopes to have me as a client?"

"Perhaps it was not Pents who ruined the flour. Someone else may have polluted the sample before you received it. But, as I said, it may have been defiled at its source."

"What scoundrel would seek my ruin? The brotherhood adheres to strict standards to ensure the safety of our loaves."

"I have seen men's reputations suffer at the dastardly hands of another. Do not suppose you have no enemies. One cannot exist without collecting at least a few." Bianca brushed the flour back into the bin. "Have you sold any loaves containing the white flour?"

"Of course. My soured-dough manchets are finding some demand."

"You do not use barm in your baking?"

"Nay, I do not. It is easier to feed my dough."

"Sir, when did you last get a delivery of boulted flour?"

"I do not recall the date," said the baker, frustrated. "Days run into weeks, run into years." He stalked over to a shelf and hefted down a logbook, irritably flipping through the pages. Bianca stood beside him as he ran a thick finger down the row of dates and deliveries.

An accounting of flour, eggs, and other ingredients was taken at the end of each day. The weights and numbers were given, along with deliveries and from where they had come. The purchase price was also duly noted.

"Here," said Foley, pointing to a delivery made just over a week before. He looked down at Bianca, who was peering over his arm at the page, glanced at Fisk, then made to shut the book.

Bianca stuck her hand in the page before it closed. "Wait! I saw something." She caught Foley up in her intense blue stare. "What I saw may help you."

The baker opened the book, and Bianca ran her finger down the entries, finding a day where a discrepancy had caught her eye. "Sir, you take inventory and record the weight of your flour stock at the end of each day. Here it shows an increase in the weight of white flour by nine ounces. However, there is no record of a delivery. Could you have forgotten to write it in?"

The baker leaned over the writing and studied the irregularity. He straightened. "Last Thursday?" He thought a minute. "I remember I thought I might have recorded the weight incorrectly from the day before." He massaged the back of his neck, then suddenly stopped. His eyes widened. "The third warden and Master Croft inspected me. They went through my stores and weighed my loaves." Foley recalled the scene. "Croft aggrieved me for accepting Pents's white flour."

"You do not remember a delivery that day?"

"I meticulously record when I receive my flour and how much I pay. Even if I am gifted flour, I will record that. It is a requirement of my license, and I never forget to account for my stock."

"And was your shop secured that night? Have you noticed any signs that someone could have tampered with your bakery while you were closed?"

"I sleep above; I would know if my bakery had been meddled with." The baker shrugged off the suggestion like a pesky fly on a horse's withers. "Except..." His eyebrows shot up. "Croft asked to see my records, and when I returned with the books, he was peering into my bin of boulted flour!" He stalked over to the bin and threw off the cover. As he stared at the suspect stock, Foley's face grew as red as the bricks of his oven. "By God's sacred blood—what did he do?" He slammed down the lid. "And now a boy is dead. I shall be accused of murder!"

"Nay. I don't believe it is you who will be accused."

CHAPTER 33

With a sack of Foley's white flour in hand, Bianca hurried back to Boisvert's to make her version of holy wafers. Foley had told her his process, and she reduced the recipe to a manageable proportion. As the wafers baked in the oven, Bianca remembered the rhyme recited by the woman who had fallen from St. Vedast's steeple on the morning they'd first arrived in Foster Lane. She had pondered why the woman had recited that particular verse and had entertained the possibility that it was nonsensical—the rantings of delirium or madness. But as Bianca repeated its final phrases, a few ideas began to dawn on her.

"'Up stairs, down stairs, and in my lady's chamber.'" Bianca galloped down the stairs of Boisvert's to retrieve another rat. "That part has no special meaning," she said aloud. Hobs trooped after her, curious to see what his lady had in mind.

"'There I met an old man who would not say his prayers. . . .'" Bianca dragged a cage across the room and started pulling it up the stairs. "Well," she said, remembering her discussion with John about a priest who would not change his ways for the king's reforms. "I am going to generalize and say it is a person opposed to change."

Bianca rested a minute while Hobs attempted to squeeze past. "Hobs, why must you try the impossible?" Still, the feline had his way, crawling over the top of the iron pen and clawing her skirt until she stood aside.

With a burst of strength, she hauled the cage to the second-floor landing. She straightened and pushed the hair from her face. "So, perhaps the woman was telling us she was pregnant and her husband, or perhaps her lover, was unfaithful." She inched the cage toward the table with her foot. "Was she telling us her lover was a priest?" Bianca gave the cage a few more shoves forward. "A papist?" She bent over and pushed the cage to the table. "Or simply a person opposed to change?"

The smell of burning bread drew her back to the oven, and she removed the large wafer to cool. Hobs leapt to the table and squinted, trying to smell the steaming dough.

"Did Father Nelson have something to do with the woman's death?" Bianca dropped onto the bench and stared across the room. Why did Martyn, the altar boy, die from eating the hosts, and not the priest? Did Father Nelson know the hosts were tainted? Had he sent polluted pax bread to Odile, days before her wedding? Could Father Nelson have consulted with Croft of the bread company and the two conspired against Odile in an effort to get her endowment?

"What if the churchwarden knew of their scheme and decided the priest needed to be removed in order to protect others from a similar fate?" Bianca hefted the cage onto the table. "Or what if all three of them schemed to kill Odile and the churchwarden got rid of the priest in order to accept the endowment money unhindered?"

" 'Take him by the left leg, throw him down the stairs.' " Bianca tapped the rat's cage with a metal stirring rod. "Left leg . . . left foot . . . left footer," she mused. "A left footer is someone with a different stance . . . perhaps a Catholic who won't accept Henry as the supreme head of the church. Well, almost certainly Father

Nelson is of the old way. What priest isn't secretly pining for the days before Queen Anne and Thomas Cromwell?"

Bianca broke off a corner of the wafer and pushed it through the cage's slats. The rat sniffed, then devoured the entire piece. "But a left footer could also be a foreigner." She thought for a moment, her mind going back to the information she had learned at Benjamin Cornish's office near Middle Temple. "Boisvert and Odile were both outlanders. 'Throw him down the stairs'—get rid of him—punish him. Kill him." Bianca sat down. "James Croft was of French descent too. James LaVerdiere Croft."

As Bianca sat pondering the peculiarities of Odile Farendon's death and that of the unknown woman at St. Vedast, John returned and called up to her from below.

"Are you here?" John called as he mounted the stairs.

Bianca met him on the landing.

"I went to Newgate to visit Boisvert. His case has been delayed. Two priests have been accused of heresy."

"I hope Father Nelson has not been accused."

"As a matter of fact, he was."

"Who is the other priest?"

"A priest from Dowgate Ward of St. John's parish. The two incidents are unrelated," said John, going by the fire to warm himself. "But I do have news about Father Nelson."

Bianca removed Hobs from where he was batting at the leftover wafer. She scratched behind his ears, then set him down.

"Father Nelson has taken ill. He is vomiting and his hand has seized. He cannot open or use it. He may not live."

"Those were Odile's symptoms before she died."

"That is what I was thinking."

"Then Father Nelson may not have purposely conspired to give Odile polluted pax bread or his parishioners ruined hosts."

"Unless he knew they were poisoned and he wants to die," said John.

"But going the way of Odile and the others is not pleasant. And a priest committing self-murder?"

"Then perhaps someone else hoped for his death."

If Father Nelson had hoped for Odile's demise in order to save the church with her endowment, why would he kill himself? Had his plan gone awry? Did he prefer self-murder to the public humiliation of being found out? Bianca shook her head. She couldn't imagine any priest willingly damning his own soul for eternity.

As expected, it wasn't long before the rat went through a spurt of strange behavior. Its rear leg contracted, becoming rigid and useless. It fell onto its back, exposing its chest. In a matter of moments, its life was over.

"So, what did you just prove?" asked John.

"The sanctioned bakery that made hosts for St. Vedast used contaminated flour. I paid Foley's bakery a visit and found a discrepancy in their records. They had an increase in flour one day that coincided with an inspection from the Brown Bakers' Guild."

"That is interesting," said John, dropping onto the bench and picking up Hobs to sit in his lap.

Bianca raised an eyebrow, watching John amicably pet him. "It is even more interesting that the inspector was James Croft."

"The master of the Brown Bakers' Guild?"

"It makes me wonder about finding the property assessment for St. Vedast. I am wondering if he was hoping to ruin baker Foley or Father Nelson."

"Perhaps both," said John.

"Aye. Perhaps both."

After actively avoiding Constable Patch and wishing to have nothing to do with the unreliable custodian of public order, it was unusual, admitted Bianca, to hope she would find him. Outside his ward quarters, she paused a moment to organize her thoughts before talking with him. Once ready, she heaved open the door and found Constable Patch donning a woolen cap before he ventured into the cold.

"Wells, now, I should say this is an incidence. I was just going to visit you at Boisvert's." Patch ushered her to a chair and bid her to sit. "That is where you are living now, is it not?"

Bianca glanced around the room, looking for a reason for his geniality . . . or a possible ruse. Seeing neither, she eased herself into the chair and waited for him to continue.

Unable to contain his excitement, he launched into an explanation. "Do you recall that I told you the body at St. Vedast had a disarming mark of the devil on her womb?" He sat behind a table to subtly remind her of his position of authority.

"I remember." Bianca had disregarded the significance of what was likely a birthmark. She had witnessed those born with blotches suffer from being stigmatized. Rather than the evil changelings their unfortunate blemishes foretold, these people, more often than not, were of gentle and retiring natures, suffering from an undeserved "branding" from both nature and society.

Constable Patch was unfazed by her reluctance to agree with him. "Being in the northernmost corner of our city has been an advantage. Travelers from away often stop at my office to inquire about the ways of London. Such was the occasion earlier this morning." Patch's weaselly eyes shone with delight.

"A woman from Dinmow chanced into my office and sat down, imploding me with a most earnest plea."

Bianca closed an eye. "Imploring?" she said.

Patch folded his hands upon his desk, momentarily irritated by her interruption. He continued. "She was seeking her sister. The family had not seen or heard from her in nearly eight months."

Bianca sat up and leaned forward. "Pray continue, Constable."

"Her sister left Dinmow suddenly. There were no good-byes, and the family was deeply hurt by this, but the sister knew the girl dreamed of leaving the village for the city of London. Unfortunately, they did not notice her missing until late the next day."

"Why does the woman believe her sister came to London?"

"The maid had warmed to a man visiting from London."

"And they say she left with the visitor?"

"That is what is thought. Apparently she was a bit odd upstairs." Patch tapped his head. "They never heard from or saw either of them again."

"Do we know his name or his business in Dinmow?"

"He was dispatched from the Worshipful Company of Bakers. A man sent to inspect grain—Austin Jones."

Bianca sat as still as a cat. The name was not familiar to her, but the constable had piqued her interest. She waited for him to continue.

"About a month ago, several villagers took strangely ill and died. No one wanted to speak of it for fear it would happen again. All was peaceable until a young couple arrived and started asking questions." Constable Patch eyed her sharply as he said this. He tugged his chin hair, pausing, then continued. "There was another outbreak, and a woman died."

Not wishing to put ideas into his head, Bianca avoided asking if the young couple were thought to be to blame. "No one from Dinmow bothered to inquire about the missing girl until now?"

"The sister preferred waiting until spring, when the traveling would be easier, but the latest outbreak prompted her."

Bianca and Constable Patch locked eyes. A second passed before Bianca spoke. "And have you questioned the guilds about the man?" she asked.

"Two men. The man who inspected the mill eight months ago was Austin Jones. He is the man whom the sister is believed to have left with. He is third warden of the Brown Bakers' Guild and a man entirely devoted to his young wife and five children. There is record at the company of his duties in London at that time. He has never been to Dinmow. Someone filched his name."

"And the second man?"

"After the outbreak a month ago, a new representative from London arrived to inspect the mill as a matter of course. I have been to both the Brown and the White Bakers' Guilds. There is no member in the registers by the name of J. LaVerdiere."

The bits of information floating in Bianca's mind settled. She refrained from telling Patch why, but she felt the elation of satisfaction that comes with finally understanding. "I hope you asked for the missing woman's name and whether she had any peculiarities that might distinguish her."

Constable Patch's mouth turned up in a sneaky smile. "That I did."

"And . . ." prompted Bianca, growing impatient.

"The woman's name was Ellen Forbish. She had a mark on her belly like that of a claw."

Bianca sat back in the chair. The woman's name meant nothing to her; however, a slow smile spread across her face. The other name, J. LaVerdiere, did.

CHAPTER 34

Directed there by a fellow at the Bakers' Hall, Bianca expected to find Master Croft in silent contemplation at St. Vedast. "He felt the need for some quiet prayer," the man told her. But instead of meditative reflection, James Croft stood shoulder height to Henry Lodge as the churchwarden towered over him, venting his discontent and waving a holy wafer in the man's face.

Bianca ducked behind a column and listened to Lodge's rant echoing about the expansive nave. "I have it on good word that you seek to ruin Foley by contaminating his stock," he said.

"The guild has asked him to stop selling products made of boulted flour. The man takes objection to our request. But his persistence is a serious betrayal of the Brown Bakers' statutes. He is lashing out against his brothers and is loyal to neither guild. Surely you don't take his word on the matter."

"Is it my imagination that a young boy is dead because of your folly?"

"You have no cause to accuse me, sir. Baker Foley is skirting his responsibility."

"I found several wafers near Martyn's body. The lad was always hungry. Without Father Nelson to guide him, there was no preventing him from accepting a delivery and making a meal of it."

"Well, I didn't tell him to eat the wafers!"

"That is not the issue, Master Croft, and you well know it. Foley believes you conducted false inspection for the purpose of dumping contaminated flour into his store of boulted stock."

"Such an accusation is slanderous, sir. I urge you to measure your tongue. Denigrating a man's reputation is not so light an offense."

Bianca considered stepping forward and supporting Lodge's claim. However, the surprisingly discreet arrival of Patch and the constable of Aldersgate Ward caught her notice. With a finger to his lips, Patch and the constable slipped behind columns in an effort to listen to any incriminating morsels inadvertently spilled.

"It is not just a boy who has died. Father Nelson may soon follow. He suffers from the strange malady that afflicted Odile Farendon."

"Ah," said Croft. "And do I also stand accused of eliciting *their* poor health?" He tilted his head doubtfully. "Where *do* your incriminations end, Henry Lodge?" His tone with the churchwarden took on a cynical air. "Can you not admit that Father Nelson's absence is to your liking? After all, it was you who instigated his removal."

"His removal is for his own protection."

"Is that how you define 'protection'? Having him removed for sorcery? Your skewed definitions are frightening. Why not admit you found some relief in having the man gone? You found Father Nelson ineffectual, did you not? And with him gone, now you might oversee a sizable endowment left to St. Vedast. The benefice left by Odile Farendon—the lover who once spurned you for another."

"Your speculations are unfounded!"

"Are they, Lodge? I saw you eavesdropping on her confession. She spilled her heart to Father Nelson and he appealed to her guilty conscience, her fear of purgatory, for his own personal gain."

"Nay, that was *you* who eavesdropped!"

"I won't deny that I overheard. But why should you deny it? Come, now. We are alone in each other's company. Let us be honest with one another."

Just then a horrid creak boomed in the upper vault of the church. It drew everyone's attention to the belfry, where the bells sounded morning terce.

Lodge shouted up to Buxton to stop, but the resonant tolling of St. Vedast's voice drowned his useless plea. When the chiming finally died, Croft chuckled at the churchwarden's frustration.

"Ten years ago this was a beautiful church," said James Croft. "The walls were a canvas for the coronation of the Virgin and the good works of our patron saint, St. Vedast." He looked up at the rood screen. "But now those stories are gone. The walls have been whitewashed, along with our parishioners' memory of the respect St. Vedast once garnered. This sacred space has been sullied by Henry's lust to reign supreme over our land and now our faith. It is corrupted by his arrogance to bend our beliefs to his will. God gave him England to rule, but God did not give Henry control over heaven, too." Croft shook his head in disgust. "Such conceit. No mortal has the power to change God's will."

"Speak light, Master Croft. Your words are dangerous."

The baker smiled ruefully. "Lodge, have you forgotten our patron saint's story? St. Vedast restored our religion to the infidels so that they would know its greatness. Through patience and prayers he triumphed."

"And for what, Croft, do you pray?"

"Redemption, sir."

Signing to Patch and the constable not to interfere, Bianca stepped away from the column. "I do not believe, Master Croft, that redemption shall be forthcoming."

Croft turned to look at her. His look of surprise changed to one of derision. "Ah, the wife of a silversmith's apprentice. You are not a member of this parish." He took a step toward her. "I believe you have only arrived of late. How could you understand the wonder this cathedral once was?" Croft glanced back at Lodge. "It is a sin to watch this holy place fall into disrepair and do nothing."

Bianca spoke. "Do you believe God will absolve your sins if you rescue St. Vedast from those who do not appreciate it?"

"By your measure, you must think it evil to respect the past."

"It is not respect if there is no humility in it. You want St. Vedast for your own. You sought Benjamin Cornish to obtain the audit of St. Vedast from the Court of Augmentations. But when you learned the property was still too rich for your purse, you embarked on a plan to ruin her. Who would worship in a church where a woman with child and an altar server died under peculiar circumstances? Who would worship in a church where members of the parish go mad after receiving the Eucharist from the priest? And now with Father Nelson removed and accused of evil intent, who would argue against closing St. Vedast and your taking the property as your own?"

"What a fantastic tale. You have nothing to substantiate your claims."

"Sir, but I do." Bianca held up the statement from the solicitor's office naming him a papist. "Master Lodge claims you are a papist. And your argument, just now, confirms it."

He looked at her, then Lodge, and shook his head. "England is too quick to dismiss tradition. Our religious beliefs are replaced with the contrived arguments of a privy council and king who wish obedience from every man on this isle. The king is not content ruling just his terrestrial claim. He seeks complete control over God's heavenly realm.

"And we, the men and women of Britain, follow our king's dictates to keep favor with him and save our mortal lives. No one argues to preserve the past because to do so gets one hanged. We are a country full of cowards."

"But you curry favor with the king. You cannot own St. Vedast without his consent." Bianca stepped closer to better read his face. "I wondered how a master baker could afford a parish property. The building is crumbling and neglected, its valuables stripped. All that remains is a tenuous congregation held together by an overwhelmed priest. And now with Father Nelson removed, his flock runs elsewhere. This church is a shell. What value is there in a decrepit, maligned building? Why should the Crown keep a ruined property for anything but a final sale to someone willing to take it?"

"You have no proof of my intent."

"Your middle name is LaVerdiere, is it not? You are of French heritage in a country of heretics. It must feel lonely. Where can such a man find solace? Either he comes to accept his adopted country's ways or he finds a way to survive in them."

"This is a fabrication of a fantastic degree."

Bianca pulled the second paper out of her pocket and unfolded it. She turned and nodded to Patch and the constable of Aldersgate. "Your name is James LaVerdiere Croft," she said, pointing to the line on the purchase document from Benjamin Cornish's office. She handed the paper to the constable of Aldersgate. "It is also the name of a man who conducted an inspection in Dinmow within days of a strange and deadly outbreak there—J. LaVerdiere."

Bianca took advantage of the silence as the constable quietly read the paper, and then she continued. "You could not return to Dinmow as the man who inspected the mill eight months prior. To do so would have stirred questions about Ellen Forbish's disappearance. People would have recognized you. So you disguised yourself and signed your middle name to your work in Dinmow. You returned from the inspection just before your appointment to the worshipful company's highest post. And you brought flour back with you.

"But it would be scandalous if news got out that the newly elected master of the Worshipful Company of Bakers kept a woman confined in his house—especially if she were with child." Bianca took a step closer. "Your problem could have been solved if you had married the woman, but you found her odd. And her pregnancy only worsened her conduct."

"Your talents are wasted. There is a theater across the river that would enjoy your stories," said Croft.

Constable Patch could not resist imparting his own opinion on the matter. "Sir, she speaks true. A woman happened into my ward office searching for her sister, Ellen Forbish, who had left the village near eight months earlier."

"This is conjecture. How dare you question my honor!"

Bianca continued, "You made bread with the flour you got in Dinmow. Whether you purposely gave it to Ellen Forbish to eat, I do not know. But your dog was the first to suffer its strange effect."

"I have no dog."

"Nay, because it is dead." Bianca saw Croft's eyes widen, and a vein jumped at his clenched jaw. "The witness to Ellen Forbish's tumble from the steeple of St. Vedast saw you bury it." Bianca was not finished making connections. "And you just admitted you overheard Odile Farendon's confession to Father Nelson. She planned to leave an endowment to benefit St. Vedast. But because you wished to have the church for your own, you needed Odile to die before she signed her last will and testament.

"You baked a loaf of pax bread and sent Martyn, the altar server, to deliver it to Madame Farendon with instructions from Father Nelson to partake of it every day and to pray. However, Odile signed her will, then died *after* her wedding. You had your lawyer, Benjamin Cornish, contest the will, stating she was of unsound mind. My question is, did Oro Tand on behalf of the Worshipful Company of Goldsmiths support you in contesting the will?"

Bianca watched his expression for the answer. Seeing nothing to indicate she'd touched a sensitive topic, she continued, this time targeting the constable of Aldersgate. "I remember Oro Tand slipped you a coin at the dinner, and suddenly, the next day, Boisvert was taken into custody."

The constable of Aldersgate took exception. "Tand was simply paying me for services rendered. You are mistaken if you believe it was of shady purpose."

Bianca shrugged, unconcerned. She turned back to the bread master, who remained stonily silent. "I ask, because if Odile's will is thrown out, would the Gold Guild have been able to bring Lionel Farendon's last wishes forward again? With no Anne Boleyn to influence King Henry anymore, and Boisvert neatly sitting in Newgate, that will's chance of passing probate might be favorable."

The constable of Aldersgate had heard enough. Not only was this commoner—this woman dressed in stained and moth-chewed homespun—intruding on his territory, but she was conducting the matter as if she were a barrister from Middle Temple. She was an impostor dressing as a merchant's wife for Odile's wedding, interfering with the coroner's examination of the body, then poking about in affairs that were not her business. "Enough of these wild conjectures," he said. "I can conduct my own interview. Patch, will you escort this impertinent meddler to the street?"

For as much as Constable Patch had issue with Bianca, daughter of Albern Goddard, the infamous alchemist once accused of having tried to poison the king, he could not willingly discredit her. After all, he had benefited from her keen observations, which had led to his current position in a ward far from Southwark. He had to admit, her points made sense in a convoluted and unconventional way. "Wells, now, Constable," he said with a supercilious lift of his chin. He tugged on the hem of his important popingay doublet with its shiny brass buttons, and he squared his narrow shoulders. "I thinks ye should give credence to some of what she says. There is some truth in't."

The constable of Aldersgate fervidly wanted to rid himself of Patch and his unlikely associate. "Leave the intricate entanglements to me—hmm, Patch? Go back to your quaint ward of candlemakers and broderers, have yourself a nap by your brazier, and let me decide who is culpable and who is not."

"I sees no need to be coarse with me," said Patch. "Methinks I've saved ye a certain amount of bother."

Just then, another loud rumble issued from the belfry. The question of guilt was waylaid by the churchwarden's shouts to the sexton. "Buxton, you fool. Can you not help yourself from trifling with the bells? You'll bring down the whole lot of it." His warning had no sooner left his lips than a thunderous crack split the axle holding the heaviest bell in place. The two constables, James Croft, and Bianca turned their faces up to see the casing shift and wood splinter.

"God's blood!" shouted Constable Patch. The bottom of the bell tipped crookedly, and he ran from the center of the nave to dive behind a column. Bianca followed suit, as did Lodge. The clapper struck the tilted bell, muffling its clang. Shards of wood rained down, littering the floor below.

"Away, away, you dunderheads!" shouted Patch, waving his arms as the wood gave way with a deafening squeal.

There was nothing to be done as part of the floor in the belfry broke from the bells' collective weight and came crashing down. James LaVerdiere Croft ran for safety, the constable of Aldersgate quick on his heels, but with the falling wood and bell came blinding dust. Bianca heard their shouts and turned away, covering her eyes, waiting for the dissonant sounds and debris to settle.

CHAPTER 35

At first, there was nothing to see but a heap of wood crowned by a massive bell. Timbers jutted in every direction; frayed ropes snaked through the pile. A gaping cavity in the roof let in feeble sunlight that filtered through a cloud of four-hundred-year-old dust. Bianca coughed from the thick air, unable to see through it, and brushed herself off.

Henry Lodge stared in disbelief at the fallen bell and rubble. His warnings to Father Nelson had gone unheeded. He had feared the worst, and now it sat before him, like a strumpet with her legs spread. So stunned was he that if Constable Patch hadn't directed his wheezy voice into his ear, he might have gone on gawping for another several minutes.

"I do not see my counterpart and the murderer. I fear they are buried," said Patch, looking around and touching the churchwarden's arm. "It will not be so pleasant to uncover their bodies." He looked at Lodge and Bianca, then removed his flat cap and shook off the plaster and dust. "We'll need help."

Just then they heard a desperate cry from the battered belfry overhead. Through the drifting dust, they saw a slanting floorboard wrenched from its support beam and Buxton, the sexton, clinging to it. He held on by his fingers, dangling from the angled slat, his legs wheeling the air.

"Oh, God," said Bianca, crossing herself. She was not so immune that she didn't make the sign on occasion.

The churchwarden ran toward the side of the church, where lengthy stone stairs led to the belfry.

"I know not what Lodge thinks he can do," said Patch, watching the churchwarden disappear. Patch then yelled up to the sexton, cupping his hand to his mouth. "Strength, man! Help is coming!" He looked at Bianca and shook his head.

"I think he shall not get there in time," said Bianca. "He is too far out for Lodge to reach."

"I'd say the man is in his last moments," replied Patch. He looked at the debris in front of them. "He shall land on a not-so-kind cushion."

Buxton valiantly struggled to inch his hands up the plank, but with each shift in weight, the board creaked in loud objection. Indeed, the plank bowed precariously toward the floor. Bianca could feel the man's panic nearly a hundred feet below him. She and Constable Patch could only stare.

"If Lodge reaches the belfry, I do not trust that the damaged floor will hold his weight," said Bianca.

In a matter of moments, the nave began filling with concerned neighbors. The destruction had been heard throughout Foster Lane and its environs. Most stopped shy of the rubble and fallen bell, stunned by the devastation. It didn't take long for them to notice the sexton. When met with the spectacle overhead, people ignored the disaster in the middle of the church and became taken instead with watching Buxton's frantic struggle.

The sexton tried saving himself as best he could. There was no surviving a fall from such a height. He kept working his hands up the plank, but finally, the brittle wood could take no more stress. The board snapped, and with a ghastly scream, Buxton fell.

The sexton's body cartwheeled through the air. Some watched

in horror, some turned away and covered their ears to his screams. He hit the fieldstone floor next to the bell, landing on his side, the impact crushing his ribs. People recoiled from the sight and the sound of cracked bones, but Bianca ran to him and Patch followed. She knelt to support his head as the man gasped for air in vain. Blood streamed from his mouth, soundlessly trickling down his neck. There was nothing to do for the man but watch him breathe his last.

After a stunned moment, Patch looked round at the crowd. "Someone find a priest." He clucked his tongue. "He dies in a church and there's no one to give him his last rites. A sorry end, that."

Across the nave, Henry Lodge appeared, his weighty tread drawing attention to the somber churchwarden. When he got to the sexton's body, he bent over him. "Poor fool."

"He is." Patch picked up a board and tossed it aside. "Let us not forget the constable of Aldersgate and James Croft. They are buried under this."

"We'll need several men to help haul the bell off the pile," said Lodge, straightening. "It might require a horse."

As men organized, Bianca spied John entering the nave and went to him.

"I am thankful to see you," he said, embracing her. "I heard a great noise, and Boisvert's rent shook. I thought we were under siege." He looked past Bianca toward the gathered crowd. "I fear to ask what happened."

"A support gave way," said Bianca. "The bell broke through the floor and the sexton got caught up in it. He tried to save himself."

"He fell from the belfry?"

"Aye." The two walked back toward the rubble. John spied Constable Patch directing men to help dig through the wreckage.

"What is Patch doing here?"

"I enlisted his help. He collected the constable from Aldersgate to meet me at the Bakers' Hall. We ended here. It appears James Croft contrived to possess St. Vedast and dispense with anyone who might interfere. I'm afraid, though, that he, along with the constable of Aldersgate, is buried beneath the bell."

John shook his head. "Nay, you are mistaken. I passed the bread master on the street."

Bianca stared in disbelief. "Say you again?"

"People were running toward St. Vedast, but James Croft was making haste to be away."

Bianca looked back at Patch, who was delighting in ordering men about, ignoring and superseding Lodge's efforts to do the same. "Shall I tell him, or you?" They had no alternative but to recruit Patch to their aid. With no authority to stop Croft, Bianca could only try to find and follow him.

"I shall tell Patch. You know better than I where to find Croft. I'll urge him to follow."

With a final kiss of relief pressed against her forehead, John went to speak with the constable, and Bianca hurried toward the door, then pushed past the growing numbers of curious onlookers cramming themselves into the church. Once on Foster Lane, she studied the street in both directions. Would Croft have gone to his house or to the Bakers' Hall? Could he have sought Benjamin Cornish or gone into hiding? Taking a practical view, Bianca circled back to the Bakers' Hall, hoping he had not left town. At least she could warn the bakers of their master's dealings.

CHAPTER 36

For the second time that day, Bianca mounted the steps to the Bakers' Hall. When she had inquired after Master Croft earlier, she had been met by a lone guild member just inside the door. This time, as she hauled open the hall's great walnut door, she was met by a pack of raucous liverymen, pouring out of their famed Court of Halimote, where impugned bakers were subjected to the disciplinary rigors of the bread standard.

The men gave her scant notice as they moved like a multi-headed beast toward the entrance where she stood. They pushed, their voices loud in protest, and raised their fists in anger. She dared not stand in the way, but backed out the door as they spread toward it like spilled wine. In the center of the mob appeared the subject on which their venom was focused—James LaVerdiere Croft.

The men shoved their master down the steps toward a horse and waiting hurdle, taunting his every move. Croft's fine gown was gone, and the stuffing from one sleeve of his black velvet doublet hung down where it had been ripped. His wrists were bound, his ankles tethered. Two brawny bakers gripped his arms, and around his waist a rope was tied. At the end of that rope was the baker Foley, pulling him along in not so gentle a manner.

Missing from Croft's neck was his chain of office, and in its place hung an iron mold used to make holy wafers. Croft's exposed head bowed from the weight, but Bianca thought a measure of shame contributed to his humble stance. He did not see her observing his disgrace, but Foley did.

Foley nodded to Bianca, and she glanced away, wishing not to be publicly acknowledged for her work uncovering the bread master's deceit. Foley kept mum, sensing her reticence, and gave the denigrated master a particularly sharp tug, which sent Croft stumbling forward.

At the horse, they shoved Croft onto the hurdle, pushed him back to sitting, then lashed his feet to the woven slats. His resistance was met with more jeering and several cuffs to the head.

Holding his hand up for silence, Third Warden Austin Jones spoke. "Dismal mewling geck." There followed a round of agreement. "Ye shall learn well what it is to face the consequences of your foul deeds. First shall you know our court's laws and punishments—the same punishments you so liberally bestowed on others." More boisterous agreement, followed by a lone curse. "Then upon our finish," continued Jones, "you shall be cast to Newgate, where murderers wallow in the squalor and excrement of their sorry consciences."

A chorus of assent sealed Croft's fate, and a final indignity was hung around his neck over the iron mold. "Here roosts James LaVerdiere Croft," read the sign, "counterfeit purveyor of bread, better served dead."

With a spirited send-off from the rumbustious liverymen, Foley urged the horse on, enjoying the honor of leading it through all the streets of London.

James Croft despised bakers who loudly objected to their punishment, and so with conscious restraint, the master refrained from cursing his accusers or resisting his being lashed to the wattle. He did try to dissuade the wardens from inflicting so degrading a penalty on him—after all, he was the master of the guild and had risen through its ranks with hard work and sacrifice. To his dismay, they had rejected his pleas. They heaped all of their frustrations, all of their complaints, real or imagined, extreme or minuscule, upon him. While he did not understand their compulsion or agree with it, there seemed little he could do to prevent their poor treatment of him. So, with iron resolve and his chin lifted, he accepted his fate. He would await his day in court (not Halimote), where he could present his argument in a civilized forum, confident he would be vindicated. But for now, he would remain as dignified as he could. He would show by example how men of the Worshipful Company of Bakers should behave.

Never did it occur to James Croft that his crime was so deplorable. In his mind, by his reasoning, he was cultivating favor with the king—not with the fickle and petulant Henry, but with the one who mattered—the almighty one. Above all others, he served his Father. Life was short, and what mattered most was to glory Him. Croft believed his good works should honor and please only Him. Let the heathens do their worst, Croft thought. In the end he would be rewarded for his loyalty to papal supremacy, to the true religion of the land—not this contrived abomination conceived of by a blacksmith's son and sustained by a grotesque and despised king.

Bianca followed the crowd of bakers through the streets of London: first down Foster Lane, past the guildhalls of the Worshipful Companies of Goldsmiths and Haberdashers, where the jarring from the ruts in the road bounced Croft as harshly as if he'd been beaten. On to Cheapside they went, through the market, where people snickered and lobbed turnips. Then Foley circled back to Bread Street and traveled its entire length, past its bakery shops, so that all bakers would see Master Croft's discredit.

All the while, James Croft endured stones and rotten cabbage being hurled at his head. Someone from a second story dumped the contents of a jordan, which landed squarely in his lap, and he could do nothing but sit in its rank smell. If that weren't insult enough, the horse relieved itself upon his exposed pate. Croft dripped with shit; he stank of it; his face was brown. It was only in the whites of his eyes that he looked human and not a man cast from dung.

So angered were the brown bakers and Foley that a caravan through London was not punishment enough for their fallen master. He was only beginning to show signs of remorse. They would not be finished until he begged them to stop. As they approached London Bridge, a steady rain began to fall. Croft's hurdle plowed through the mud and slop of the roads, and Foley led the horse through the bridge gate to cross it. In Southwark, they would be met with even rowdier crowds, who might finally break the man's spirit so they could be finished dispensing their brand of punishment and deposit him at Newgate, a humbled, stinking cullion.

They trundled across the narrow span, and as they neared the iron grating of the drawbridge, Foley and the troupe of bakers came to an abrupt halt. Opposite, leaving the sordid pleasures of cheap boozing kens in Southwark, were a bevy of white bakers, besotted and loud. The white bakers took issue with having their way blocked, and then when they realized that their brown bread brothers were the source of their delay and that Master James Croft was the object of their brothers' blistering commentary, they could not leave the matter be. An exchange of verbal gibes commenced, each volley more searing than the one before. Old grievances were plumbed, new gripes were born, and before long, James Croft was forgotten as the two groups of liverymen met in the middle and proceeded to pummel one another.

Bianca had trailed the brown bakers, hoping for Croft's ultimate deposit at the steps of Newgate, but she did not expect a row to impede his arrival there. She stood to the rear of the brawl, tucked in a safe alcove out of the rain. Before her was a mob of fifty men, beating the snots out of each other in an attempt to settle the pent-up rage between two guilds that, while having bread and ovens in common, had little else on which to agree.

She looked about for Constable Patch or a guard on the bridge who might restore order. Seeing neither, she opted to make herself unobtrusive and waited for the men to wear themselves out. Surely some semblance of order would be forthcoming; the rain was coming down in earnest and soaked everyone to the skin.

Bianca crouched but caught only glimpses of the bread master through men's rustling legs. He was still bound to the hurdle, though slumped and leaning over, near senseless from his battering ride. The rain had washed the mud and manure from his face, and he looked barely conscious, which perhaps was just as well given his circumstances. But as the clash continued, the horse and wattle shuffled, moving to the side of the bridge next to the scant railing. Foley had abandoned the bridle and was sitting on a white baker, driving his fist into the man's face. It appeared to Bianca that no one held the horse.

Alarmed that the horse would back into the railing, Bianca ran forward, shouting. Next to the rails, the hurdle tilted, threatening to flip over. No one noticed until she grabbed hold of the bridle and the horse began to rear. With hooves lashing, the horse struck a man and knocked him cold. A baker pushed Bianca away and grabbed the reins to gentle the creature, but it sidestepped, still nervous and looking to be away from the riot. To Bianca's horror, one shaft arm wrenched free of the hurdle, which tipped so that the bread master was thoroughly raked over the grating.

Despite the interceding baker's effort, the horse could not be moved from the edge, and the hurdle slid under the railing. It hung by one shaft arm, upside down. The men stopped fighting and turned their focus to saving Croft, despised as he was. But the lashings did not hold, and from all the bumping and dragging through the streets of London, the ties had become loose.

It was then that Constable Patch arrived. Seeing his murderer suspended over the Thames, about to be lost to the frigid waters below, filled him with panic. He ran forward, shoving men out of the way. With Patch, it was not about saving the man's life—only prolonging it long enough so that he could be commended for solving yet another crime.

"Fie, what is this?" he shouted, purple with cold and outrage. "The man must be got on charge of murder—not *be* murdered!" He looked round at the liverymen and spat in disgust. Seeing James Croft attached to the hurdle, dangling by a leg, Patch grabbed on to the shaft. "On count of three, we haul him up."

Being hung upside down off London Bridge had gotten the master's attention. He came to, a look of wild panic in his eyes. Croft managed to twist himself to sitting, but his bound hands were of little use. The signage and wafer mold still hung about his neck, the weight tiring him. Indeed, he fought against their drag toward the water. But the rope holding his one leg held him, just barely. It continued to fray—the strands stretching, then breaking one by one.

With a concerted effort, Patch and the bakers heaved on the hurdle. They got hold of one end and, hand over hand, slowly worked to land it on the deck of the bridge. James Croft attempted to hold himself up, gritting his teeth and grunting with struggle. The constable and bakers had gotten within inches of his proffered hands. Foley had knelt beside the railing and leaned out to grab his master's hand and haul the hurdle onto the deck, when the final strand of rope holding Croft's ankle snapped.

James Croft slipped, and his eyes widened with realization. His deliberate reticence disappeared. He screamed, his hands grappling as he became free and fell, tumbling toward the water. Like his company's patron, St. Clements, who bore the weight of an anchor and was cast into the sea, the master baker hit the water and was pulled by the iron wafer mold down and under, never to be seen again.

CHAPTER 37

Two weeks later—

Bianca peered out the window at John and Meddybemps, who were covering the bed of the dray with blankets against a light, fluffy snow. She turned to Boisvert, who was sitting near the hearth with a bottle of cherished wine next to him. "John does not look pleased. I suppose you and I are more content," she said.

"*Oui.* I should have been happier dead than spend another day in the filth of Newgate Prison. I think I shall never be free of the itch. *Mais non*, John must learn to accept that this rise to the brotherhood, it is not so quick." Boisvert raised his goblet and tipped it toward Bianca. "He has his love—*non?* That should be reason enough for a man's content." His face clouded with sadness as he took a sip, then set the goblet down. "Life is short and love even shorter."

Bianca could think of nothing to say to comfort Boisvert for his loss. It didn't matter to the silversmith that his time with Odile had been so brief. What mattered to him was the breadth of that love—that his heart had been permanently etched and changed by it. And in the end, thought Bianca, isn't that one of life's greatest desires?

"Well," said Boisvert. "I am sorry to send you back to Southwark."

"Oh, I am not sorry." Bianca crossed the room and sat on the bench. "I know John would rather live anywhere else, but I shall be glad to get back to my chemistries."

One corner of Boisvert's mouth turned up. "I suppose that is the passion—eh?" A dark eyebrow lifted as he considered her. "John must come to realize that he would be happier if the Bianca were happy." He shrugged. "Well, I shall not move again. I suspect probate will settle in favor of the Crown." He poured himself more wine. "It is just as well. What would I do with Odile's wealth? *Non*." He shook his head. "For you and I, life must return to calm."

"Do you expect trouble from the Worshipful Company of Goldsmiths if the will does not benefit them?"

"*Non*. What more can they do to me? I have lost Odile. Let them ruin me, but I shall always have France."

Downstairs, the door creaked open, then slammed. Meddybemps and John stomped the snow from their boots and started up the stairs. Hobs arrived first, running across the room and leaping onto the table. He butted heads with Bianca and tried the same with Boisvert but was met with an indifferent stare.

"We are packed," said Meddybemps, coming to stand by the fire. "Milbourne expects his dray and nag returned by nightfall." He took off his red cap and stuck it on the end of a poke, roasting it close to the fire, as if it were a chicken thigh.

"It speaks well of him to lend us his wagon a second time. And well of you to take us back to Southwark," said Bianca.

Meddybemps turned his hat, warming it thoroughly. "So you think, and I ask that you leave it alone. But it is not kindness that convinced Milbourne."

John helped himself to a sip of Boisvert's wine. The silversmith did not object to sharing his bottle; he knew his apprentice was aggrieved at the thought of returning to their vacated quarters in Gull Hole. Such was the sacrifice of love, thought he.

Bianca did not press Meddybemps; she knew better than to ask for details of his "arrangements." She was only thankful he could rescue them from Foster Lane and move them back across the river—the sooner done, the better. She found it auspicious that tenants had not moved into her former room of Medicinals and Physickes. Probably, no one would have the place. Of course, Hobs would be kept busy clearing away any uninvited guests, but Bianca was gladdened to be going "home." Her mind whirred with thoughts of herbal combinations and concocted vapors.

Boisvert scratched his scalp. "Now that I am free, I shall plan a proper funeral procession for Odile," he said. "That is my first order of affairs. Odile would have wanted a service at St. Vedast . . . *mais . . .*"

"I don't know when it shall reopen," said Bianca. "Mayhap plan the procession to stop outside and have prayers said."

"*Oui,*" Boisvert tutted. "St. Vedast did not deserve this misery—this curse of infamy. People will remember what happened there."

"I agree," said John. "Its stones would be of greater use buried in the walls of new construction elsewhere. But it shall be a while before we know what the Crown has planned for the church."

Meddybemps removed his cap from the end of the fire poke and plopped it on his head, the warmth turning his ears pink. "My dove, you did a formidable task ordering the strange events and making sense of them."

"When I was talking to Patch, I remembered Ellen Forbish's nonsense rhyme—'Goosey, goosey, gander.' One of the lines is 'Met an old man who would not say his prayers. Took him by his left foot . . .'" Bianca looked round at them. "A man of French birth harboring resentment for the king's religious supremacy fits the description of a left footer. A man resistant to saying his prayers in English instead of Latin." She helped herself to a sip of wine from Boisvert's bottle. "I wasn't for cert, but I proceeded on logic. When faced with the unembellished truth, a man with a mote of conscience panics."

"You have the gift of reason," said Meddybemps like a proud father.

"I believe it to be my weapon, of sorts." Bianca waggled her eyebrows.

"Take heed that it does not rob you of life's greatest joys," reminded Boisvert pointedly.

"What I do not know," said Bianca, "and what I may never learn, is whether Oro Tand and the Gold Guild encouraged James Croft. A contested will might well have benefited them. Nor have I puzzled out whether Henry Lodge had Father Nelson removed for his protection or whether there was another reason."

"Mayhap Lodge conspired with the Gold Guild to clear the way for contesting Odile's will," said Meddybemps.

"For cert, that rascally lawyer Benjamin Cornish knows," said John.

Bianca agreed. "Well, a man's future is built on his past intentions. I shall keep watching these men; more may later be revealed."

John rose from the table. "We must go. Night will fall while we drumble on, bantering about other men's thinking."

With a final farewell to Boisvert, they headed down the stairs to the waiting dray. Bianca whisked Hobs from the downstairs windowsill and draped him over her shoulder, ready for the return to Southwark, where the smells were to a cat's liking and the mice were plentiful.

They rode down Foster Lane, past shops, bouncing and being rattled by the still-unfixed ruts in the road. A few of the worst had been filled with dirt hauled in from Smithfield. Meddybemps did his best to steer clear of the chasms, taking them by St. Leonard, past St. Vedast—its door chained and padlocked. Bianca looked up at the great belfry and steeple, both intact, with no indication of missing bells, except for a conspicuous silence in the chorus of neighborhood chimes.

The bloodstains in the side yard where Ellen Forbish had met her end had been washed clean by the snow and wet. As they rode past, Bianca considered the woman's circumstances. Forbish was a mere country maid—an obliging young woman from a village where travelers sat at trestles and told stories over tankards of ale. Who could dislike her? Perhaps it was the maid's unfortunate state to wish for more. Those baubles and fascinations of London had enticed her away from the simple beauty of a village on a winding river of moderate breadth. Was it curiosity or boredom that lured her? Or was it the promise from a man whose deceit she never imagined?

Meddybemps turned the corner onto Cheapside and was met by the forward guard of the king's progress, passing Eleanor Cross. The streetseller sighed. "I have no desire to be kept here while the king parades past. I'm turning around, and we shall skirt St. Paul's."

"I should like to see him," said Bianca.

"Meddybemps must return the horse," said John. "It is always a slow ride over the bridge. We cannot linger."

"Then let me walk. Hobs and I shall meet you soon enough." She looked at her husband's annoyed face. "I know where to find you." She smiled, and with a sigh, John relented.

"Mind that you remember your manners," said Meddybemps, halting the horse and seeing Bianca down.

Despite the cold, dreary day, people stopped to watch the entourage and glimpse their king. Bianca remembered to curtsy and kept her head down as the king carrier passed, suspended between a horse before and aft and balanced by men who tended the chair to assure the king a comfortable ride. Scarlet drapes hung down to keep him warm, allowing Bianca only a glimpse when he pulled one aside and peeped out. She did not see his face for very long. When later asked to describe their sovereign, she could speak only of the lavish rings squeezing his fat fingers.

Bianca watched the progress turn onto Foster Lane, and she thought perhaps Henry might arrive at the Haberdashers' Hall without mishap, despite the pitted road. She would never learn the outcome of that, but neither did it give her pause. The men in their guilds could have their position, their exclusive membership, their squabbles. She was content to have none of it. A chance to wear a fine gown for one night had brought little joy, but it had given her useful insight into the lives of merchants. She wished John did not aspire to join their ranks and wondered how she might manage the change once he did. If she had discovered one truth from this hiatus in experimenting, it was that she could not bear for an interruption to be permanent.

With Hobs still clinging to her shoulder, Bianca hurried toward the bridge, to Southwark, and to her room of Medicinals and Physickes.

There was one other who reveled in her return. He smelled the wagon's approach, the flasks and alembics stained with chemistries, and his memories were taken back to a time when he, too, dabbled in the noble art. His experiments had corrupted his body horribly and had made him the receptacle of anguished souls, but with Bianca his hope was sparked. A chance for redemption, a chance for an end to *his* purgatory, rested in her ability. He knew it; he smelled it; he smelled her as she passed over the trestles of the bridge.

A book with the recipe for immortality lay in his skiff, next to the pile of dead vermin that sustained his grip on reality—or, rather, *his* reality. If he did not repay humanity in kind by dispatching the plague vectors when possible, he would lose his tenuous connection to life and be cast into hell's steaming crypt. So he watched the rat population, the evil minions of the dark world, and killed them when he could.

Like James Croft, he believed his redemption was at hand. The wraith of the Thames, the Rat Man, would wait.

As Bianca hurried to catch up to Meddybemps and John, she thought of James Croft. How odd that he believed he would find forgiveness and protection from damnation by securing a church and restoring it to glory God. Apparently, he did not suffer from the pain of guilt in the manner of most people. His self-centered belief that his life had more value than Ellen Forbish's and Odile Farendon's had led to his misery. But had Croft sought salvation knowing he was to blame for Ellen Forbish's death? Or had his desire for absolution started before that—with his single desire to save St. Vedast from the king's reformed religion? Perhaps, she thought, morality is a personal matter and she would never understand the shades of evil in some men's minds.

Bianca hailed John and Meddybemps just as they neared the grates of the drawbridge. Holding onto Hobs she ran to their waiting dray, and John held out his hand to help her up.

"I was beginning to think I'd have to spend the night alone in Gull Hole," he said as Bianca settled next to him.

"Nay," said Bianca. "I wouldn't abandon you to enjoy that pleasure alone."

GLOSSARY

Barm—foam formed on fermenting liquor

Bodge—bungler

Broderer—embroiderer

Caitiff—cowardly person

Citizen—urban elite; successful person of the middle class, merchant or professional

Clumperton—clown

Cobnuts—hazelnuts

Codso—spicy oath, perhaps "God's own"

Coney—rabbit

Cozen—cheat

The crank—epilepsy

Cuds me—an oath

Cuffin—fellow

Cullion—base fellow

Doddypoll—idiot

Drumble—dawdle, waste time

French pox—syphilis

Fripperer—one who offers clothing for resale

Fustilarian—scoundrel

Gozelinge—pale yellow-green color

Groking—begging

Horse coper—farrier

Jackanape—bestial insult

Jade—worthless person

Jordan—chamber pot

Ken—tavern

Madding—provoking madness

Murrey—brownish purple color

Ordinary—eating establishment

Partlet—woman's garment covering the neck and shoulders

Pattens—wood lifts for the bottom of shoes

Pompion—pumpkin

Quat—small boil

Spiffled—made-up word for "drunk"

Starlings—bridge supports

Swigman—peddler

Stranger brother—member of a guild who is foreign-born

Terce—third hour after dawn, a set time of prayer

Tosspot—drunkard

Trug—whore

Author's Note

It is always a challenge shaping a story to fit perfectly within the bounds of historical accuracy. Necessities of plot and logistics don't always play nicely with one another. For those who are troubled by my solecism, I hope that by admitting my guilt, I will be given a stay of execution.

The Bakers' Hall was never in the vicinity of Foster Lane. It was located closer to the Thames, on Harp Lane. The Worshipful Companies of Haberdashers and Goldsmiths were indeed on or near Foster Lane. I had previously established that my character Boisvert kept his shop on Foster Lane, and for purposes of the story line, I moved the bakers up to Aldersgate Ward.

The bakers were at odds with one another during 1543, when this novel is set. By then, the Brown Bakers had dwindled in number and were more at the mercy of the White Bakers. The Master of the Worshipful Company of Bakers would have been a White Baker, not a Brown as I have written. For a thorough examination of the history of the Bakers' Company, please refer to *1666 and All That* by Gordon Phillips.

I wish to apologize to anyone offended by my parody of Hamlet's speech. Of course Shakespeare wrote this during Elizabeth's reign, and its inclusion is a blatant anachronism. However, I enjoyed creating this scene and I ask the reader to remember that there is a fair amount of whimsy in this series.

I took liberties representing the "citizens" (the merchant and professional class). I simplified legal matters, guild politics, and positions of authority in both the guilds and the church. Do not doubt that I read or consulted references. Working under a deadline required me to make choices. Details stymied me on more than one occasion. In the hopes of completing the work and having the parts come together to create a satisfying mystery, I had to cut and carve, then accept that I did the best I could.

A few more words about general topics: Suicide, or self-murder, during Tudor times was considered a mortal sin, and the church penalized suicides by denying them burial in consecrated ground. It was considered a sin of despair and was the one sin that automatically denied a person God's grace. It was also thought that the devil drove people to kill themselves. In *Death at St. Vedast*, the priest allows the young woman who had possibly committed suicide to be buried in the church's graveyard. This might not be historically accurate, but I wanted to present the priest as being compassionate at that juncture.

Yeast as we know it was a mystery in the sixteenth century. The average person knew that if one set out a bowl of flour and water, eventually the mixture would start to bubble. They called this occurrence "God's goodness" or "Godisgoode," believing that "it cometh of the grete grace of God." They also realized that barm, the foam created in brewing ale, leavened dough in a similar fashion.

For symptoms of ergotism, I read *The Day of St. Anthony's Fire* by John G. Fuller. The account of the small French village of Pont-Saint-Esprit was helpful and disturbing. The mycotoxins produced from the fungus ergot can cause a range of effects, among them hallucinations, convulsions, and gangrene. A side note: LSD is derived from ergot, and there is speculation that some of the women accused of being witches in Salem may have been victims of the disease.

I referred to the priest as Father Nelson to avoid confusion for the modern reader. Perhaps more appropriately, he would have been referred to as "Sir Nelson." Also, in Tudor England around that time, parishioners may have taken communion only once a year or on special occasions.

There is the question of whether a citizen could have purchased a parish church in London. Principally, monasteries and associated property were stripped and dissolved. In the beginning of the sixteenth century there were more than one hundred churches in London. Henry's Act of Supremacy and the ensuing religious upheaval certainly had an effect on these properties. Some were annexed or demolished; some were closed. Ultimately, Henry had the final say as to which properties were sold.

The concept of purgatory dates back centuries and is found in other religions, not just Catholicism. In pre-Reformation England, people took particular interest in their afterlives and feared a prolonged stay in purgatory—viewed then as a grim place more closely associated with hell than it is today. It was believed that through almsgiving and intercession their torment would be shortened. As a result, wills during this period are loaded with instructions to give generously to the church through several vehicles, which proved the deceased's charity. However, with Henry and Cromwell's campaign to denigrate purgatory, the amount of money that parish churches depended on began to disappear.

Finally, there may be some confusion for readers who have picked up *Death at St. Vedast* without having read the previous books in the series. They might question the relevance of the Rat Man character and wonder why he is mentioned. I assure them that his purpose echoes the idea of redemption, which is an overarching theme of the series. His resolution is forthcoming.

ACKNOWLEDGMENTS

Several people contributed their expertise and opinion in the writing of this book. I'd like to thank Carolyn Rosen, PhD, Tracey Stewart, Fred Tribuzzo, Andrea Jones, William Smythe, Esq., Rita Cassidy, Gail Sjostrom, Manon Glassford, and Father Steven Concannon. Thank you to everyone at Kensington who contributes their expertise and helps to make the Bianca Goddard Mysteries happen. Thanks also to the support of my family and friends, who continue to spur me on. And finally, thank you to the readers who send a kind word my way; it is very much appreciated.